GATOR MOON

MAX RAY

Cover art by David Gagne

Published by Cabbage Palm Press

ISBN-10: 1475181728
EAN-13: 9781475181722

Gator Moon

Preface

I penned <u>Gator Moon</u> over 20 years ago and tried for three years, unsuccessfully, to have it published. I discover, painfully, that a lot of book publishers use the same form letter and manuscript critique.

My motive for writing was to author an action-adventure fiction novel aimed at male readers ages 15 to 55. This literary bent dates to my childhood interest in reading and a memorable grade school education in English literature and related subjects.

In the process that led to <u>Gator Moon,</u> my evolving ideas concerning the writing of fiction seemed in conflict with accepted methodology. Over the early months of writing, I developed certain concepts concerning fiction writing and slowly established a guideline to aid in this unique experience.

To me, fiction writing is an art form of the stature of the artist stroking oils on canvas. Writing textbooks, documenting history, writing how-to manuals or composing any factual commentary is as different from writing fiction as a photograph is from a pencil sketch.

I am an artist. Words are my oils and book pages my canvas. The interplay of words represents a singular artistic endeavor, and like a painter's choice and placement of colors, is meant to convey a certain picture in the viewer's mind; therefore, I wish the work to be mine and not diluted by others' input. Did Picasso have an editor?

Words carry power, but their placement adds more power; syntax triumphs over word choice and humbles rhetoric. Wordsmith and rhetorician no more describe a writer of fiction than monkey and lizard describe King Kong and Godzilla. A writer of fiction is a storyteller, and if I may use what brittle literary license I possess, a syntactician. I use this word to describe a writer of fiction. Every word is in <u>Gator Moon</u> because I want it to enhance and sharpen the picture I wish readers to see. There are no orphaned words in <u>Gator Moon.</u>

High-tech publishing and the unbelievable computer have made this singular endeavor possible. It also makes me the owner of whatever acceptance this fiction novel receives from its readers. It has to stand on its own straggly legs and I am content with that.

Writing this novel was a private and rewarding undertaking, but trying to get it published became a group effort of gargantuan complexity that diluted, and eventually killed, my aspirations.

It is here that I wish to acknowledge the effort and faith shown by special friends that revived this tome after 20 years in the cobwebs, and through determination and technical skills I can only dream about, turned <u>Gator Moon</u> into a published EBook and my dream into reality.

Thank you, Duffy Smith. Without your encouragement and professional expertise my work is anecdotal. Thank you, Dan Ray, my son, a technical guru who guides me through this wonderland of mouse, icon and click-on. Thank you, Marie Ray, my wife and biggest booster-inspiration. And…thank you, David St. John at Elderberry Press for my first publishing contract. You are wonderful friends and you have made this old man very happy. Enjoy.

The moon was bright with dark, wispy clouds dancing erratically across its troubled face, creating an eerie effect of shadow upon shadow. The surrounding marshes were alive as if energized by some powerful, irritable force causing its denizens to become restless.

Young Joe Billie shuddered and hunched his shoulders slightly. ' Gator moon,' he thought. He remembered his Grandfather telling him of this; that when the moon was full, the swamp creatures became restless and irritable, especially the bull gators.

"This was not the time to hunt the big creatures," Grandfather had said. "The gator moon make them want to fight and kill. If you hunt them then, you will become the hunted. Even brave men fear the gator moon."

Chapter ONE

The circular overhead lights resembled stars, or halos, or headlights. He really didn't know and dreamily, didn't care. The gurney carrying him to surgery seemed jet propelled and the attendant robotic. In any event, where in hell was he and why was he here. The effort to sit up caused him to feel the restraining straps around his torso and instantly rendered him nauseous. Struggling to keep down the bile tasting vomit, he managed to turn his head as the vile material ran out of what was once his mouth and nose.

"Lie still chief and you won't do that," came a distant voice. "You won't feel a thing in a few minutes anyway."

Oh God, he thought, the robot could talk!

George Martinez, M.D., Ph.D., was a surgeon's surgeon. A slim intense man, Martinez carried his 54 years and professional expertise as lightly as an ant carries a bread crumb. He neither smoked nor drank, an occasional scotch being the exception; believed in the value of diet to health and considered Pritikin a prophet. George's eyes narrowed and his mouth formed a thin line as he reread the medical chart in his right hand; the fingers of his left nonchalantly scratching his ample shock of once black, now graying hair.

CENTRA COUNTY HOSPITAL
DATE OF ADMITTANCE: June 6, 1986
PATIENT NUMBER: 64
ADDRESS: Not available
SEX: Male   AGE: Not available   RACE: Caucasian
HEIGHT: 6"1"
WEIGHT: 195
HAIR: Black   EYES: Green
IDENTIFYING MARKS: Y-shaped scar at the base of left thumb; linear scar at base of left ring finger; multiple scars around right eye and brow; both ears moderately cauliflowered.

ANAMNESIS: Found in ditch along state road 60, 10 miles west of the Cooter fish camp on Lake Kissimmee. Semiconscious and incoherent with severe cuts and contusions on head, neck and upper body. Most likely cause—blunt trauma.

RADIOGRAMS: Multiple skull fractures with minimal displacements; fractured nose and sinus with nasal fragments depressed and turbinates rearranged. Greenstick fracture of the left humerus. General body condition—excellent.

NEUROLOGICAL EVALUATION: Numbness of fingers of right hand; lateral nystagmus. Visual and hearing acuity not able to be evaluated. Patient unable to talk but seems to hear and understand.

Something about this case bothered and puzzled George Martinez. He had spent nearly two hours at lunch with Barry Simon, a neurologist from Orlando, who had evaluated the man shortly after admittance. He agreed that this was a surgical case. Barry's opinion was that the patient had a slowly expanding sub-dural hematoma and if not operated may face life as a total vegetable, if he survived. But why, George pondered, had the severe brain contusion not killed this man? True, he was some physical specimen, a true mesomorph, but whoever worked him over didn't do it as a warning; they really dusted his rug. They meant to kill him.

2

Who is this man, and what am I going to do if there is more to this than a sub-dural hematoma?

The scrub nurse broke his concentration as she informed him that patient #64 was prepped. Tiny beads of sweat formed on the doctor's brow and smooth shaven upper lip. Self-doubts filled his mind as always. No one who knew Dr. George Martinez would ever believe that this surgical machine could have doubts about his abilities. This man hung the moon.

The brisk, slapping sound of surgical gloves forced over meticulously scrubbed hands caused an immediate change in the surgeon. His eyes sparkling, his mouth relaxed and smiling, brow dry as a sun baked bone, he stepped to the surgical table and accepted the scalpel. Six hours later, a tired, slightly satisfied surgeon emerged from the small operating cubicle. His shoulders and back muscles were rebellious. George was getting too old for these surgical marathons. The silent demeanor of the surgical team and support staff belied their inward admiration at the impossible task performed to perfection by a master of his craft. Patient #64 was finally snug, if not yet safe, in recovery.

Dr. Martinez strode into the waiting area and was immediately confronted by a well-dressed, well-built man with what looked to be a permanent smile affixed to his face.

"Dr. Martinez, Dr. George Martinez?"

"Yes, what can I do for you?" replied the surgeon.

"My name is Kirby, Charles Kirby, and I'm here on behalf of the man you just operated."

"Are you family?"

"No." came the reply.

"Relative?" asked the somewhat irritated surgeon.

"No."

Well, are any family members here?" queried Martinez.

"I don't think so. I don't believe they've been told."

"Why?" asked the surgeon. "He does have family, doesn't he?"

"Yes," Kirby replied, "let me explain…"

Really torqued, Martinez shot back. "Yeah, explain first who the hell this guy is." He was getting edgy. Two days of trying to dig up information on a John Doe had proved fruitless. No person professing

knowledge of the victim could be located. Surgery had been performed without consent. That fact alone would cause most surgeons
to schedule a golf game instead of an unauthorized attempt at fixing a cracked eggshell containing a slightly scrambled egg.

"Here Doc, take a peek." said the smiling man, holding an
open wallet to Martinez' face. An official looking plastic card identified one Charles S. Kirby, Jr. as a Central Intelligence Agency
Operative. His home address was Miami, Florida.

"Well, Mr. Kirby," replied the surgeon, "What's your interest in
this man?"

"His name is Sam Duff and I work with him, or rather he works
for me. He is a specially trained CIA agent and it is imperative
that his condition and whereabouts be kept secret. I've taken the
liberty to inform your staff and I trust that we can do this in a cooperative manner, Doctor."

Not once did the smile leave Skeets Kirby's face. George noticed
the muscle definition in the man's face and neck; eyes narrow and
piercing. Suddenly Martinez was overcome by a feeling of fear so
thick he felt he could dig holes in it. Oh my God, he thought, why
did I do an experimental procedure on this guy? Why didn't I wait
for a real throwaway? How in hell was I to know who he was—or is?
Outwardly he remained calm and agreed to cooperate; inwardly
he wanted to get away from this smiling operative or whatever he
was. Turning to leave, he noticed a man standing by the recovery
room door. He had not seen him before.

● ● ●

"For Christ's sake, George, what's bugging you? You're as jumpy as
a worm on a hot plate." With these words Dr. Larry Kochak set his
lunch tray down and slid his 6'5" frame into the straight-backed
chair designed for an average human.

Larry was a young internist in endocrinology and a close friend
of George Martinez. The good surgeon was not known as being

particularly gregarious and his friends were not legion. His friendship with Larry came from mutual need and respect. George's work sometimes needed endocrine expertise—ergo Dr. Kochak.

A very talented doctor, George could cut out any organ, almost, and throw the remains to Larry who miraculously kept the surgical derelict functioning—much to the surgeon's amazement. No less amazed was Larry Kochak. "How in hell did you get that pituitary gland out of old lady Smith without killing her?" he once asked George.

"Hell if I know." replied the surgeon. "The knife is like my dick, has a mind all its own."

"Listen Larry, I've got to tell you something." His voice was raspy, almost hoarse. Rapidly, theatrically, Martinez told the young internist about patient #64. His voice dropping, George revealed how he transplanted a section of donor brain into a defect left after suctioning out a hematoma and most of the olfactory bulbs of the patient's brain. How he used donor ethmoid turbinates and nasal bone to bridge a serious defect in the man's nasal passage. All the while he reminded Larry of his extensive unpublished work on tissue transplantation.

Work that had caused him to be ostracized by his peers and removed as Chief of Staff at the prestigious General Hospital in Tampa. It seemed that the hospital human experimentation committee didn't see eye to eye with the good doctor and came down hard when he tried to rebuild the ruined nose of a Tampa Bay Buccaneer linebacker with cartilage taken from a Beagle!

"Good God Larry," the anxious man continued, "he had a defect the size of two golf balls and I know if filled with brain cells there's a good chance they will act as a matrix in which the normal cells can redistribute and regain some normal function. You know that some of my experimental work with this technique was successful, plus the brain has such poor circulation that it may not reject the transplanted tissue. Without it Larry, he was a loser—a dead man. I feel certain the bone graft will take but we have to sweat out the brain part."

Again George thought of his work at Tampa. The many hours and experiments to develop a solution that would disguise cell surface antigens and render foreign cells immune to body reactions that resulted in the death of grafted tissues. No toxic or expensive anti-rejection drugs were needed. Just soak the tissues in George's solution and transplant away!

"What do you mean 'we'," came the reply from a suspicious Larry Kochak.

"Come on compadre, you have to figure out how to keep this guy's endocrine system in gear and what mischief a few million foreign brain cells can cause until the normal ones get going." The 'get going' part of the conversation was rapidly tailing off as the surgeon walked away from the shocked endocrinologist—nee accomplice.

Wow, George thought, if Larry knew what really happened, that I replaced the damaged olfactory lobes with those of a dog and used dog ethmoid turbinates to repair the damage in the nasal passage and sinus. Hell, Sam Duff has a right to be able to breathe through his nose. Anyway, he was certain that the large nerve trunk he encountered in the mess of #64's brain was the olfactory nerve and he did get it repaired and connected into the newly replaced tissues.

• • •

Intentionally ignoring the man guarding the recovery room door, Martinez entered and stood silently as the nurse suctioned the mouth and nose of Sam Duff. It was 48 hours post surgery and the patient had shown little sign of recovery. True, his vital signs were good; strong, steady pulse and rhythmic breathing with no mucus plugs in the upper respiratory system. His reflexes were adequate but there was no response to noise.

The surgeon's voice stabbed the silence like a stiletto, as if sacrilegious to make sound in this quiet air of desperation. "Any response yet, Ms. Jones?"

"Not really doctor. He is mumbling, something like 'jay why' or 'why' or maybe like the letters 'J' and 'Y'. But when I ask him what he is saying, I get no response."

As if on cue the man in the bed started to mumble. Leaning to the patient's mouth, Martinez thought he too heard a faint mumble—"JY, JY."

"Well, decrease the phenobarbital drip and let's see if we can get more response as the sedation lessens. I don't think the brain edema will be a problem even at a lowered dose. I'll be back in the morning." Martinez turned towards the door.

"Oh, by the way Doctor, Dr. Kochak was by earlier."

George's eyes quickly turned to nurse Jones as her words trailed off. Elise Jones was one of those females who could rouse a dead man with her looks and the surgeon admired since her arrival at Centra County Hospital two years ago. She was a package—slim, dark-haired and beautiful.

• • •

George stared at the calendar pinned to his textured office wall. June 10, 1986, four days since his surgery on Sam Duff. The intercom ended his interlude.

"Yes, Phyllis?"

"Dr. Martinez, there's a Mr. Charles Kirby to see you. I told him you were busy but he doesn't seem to take no for an answer. Should I try to schedule an appointment for him?"

"It's okay Phil, send him in."

"How are you Doctor?" Skeets Kirby asked as he simultaneously completed his half of the handshake.

"Fine, maybe a tad weary. The years seem to be catching up, you know."

"So, Doctor, what about Sam? It's been four days since you operated on him and I feel the need for some discussion."

Taking the offensive, the surgeon shot back; "I think you are dead right, so let's start with a history of this mysterious patient under the guise of doctor-patient confidentiality and you fill me in on just who, or what, is Sam Duff."

Kirby's jaw tightened and Martinez thought he might have overplayed his hand; however the agent's face relaxed as he began to talk.

"Samson Hercules Duff is his full name. He's 32 years old and the only son of Willem and Martha Duff. He was raised in central Florida, just north of Tampa and spent most of his life in the state. His father was a physical fitness and wrestling nut and insisted that Sam be the ultimate physical specimen. That's how he came by his name—from the two strongest men in the history of the earth, even if mythological. Sam was a natural athlete, so with the training he received at home he was the most outstanding kid in school, or the entire state for that matter. Every coach in the South wanted the Duff kid!

When he was 14 years old, he met the man who really changed his life. Willem Duff was from Germany and one of his boyhood friends was Carlos Otto, who became the most accomplished and feared wrestler in the world. Carlos was a huge, powerful man who not only mastered but perfected, to a science, the art of submissive wrestling. He is awesome! He mastered the various forms of hand-to-hand combat and martial arts. Carlos defeated martial arts masters the world over. Like most exceptional people he was very intelligent, appreciating most of the finer things of life. He was a student of history and of human nature. By luck, Carlos moved into the same county where the Duff family lived and Willem talked-ed the big man into taking Sam as a student.

As was his wont, Carlos ridiculed Sam because he said the boy's fantastic body was 'hollow,'—no guts or brains. Sam was crushed but something in him persisted and soon he was taking the merciless training and all the wisecracks the German could hand out. Carlos saw that this kid was something special and was soon teaching him things lesser men could never learn. Sam and the German were inseparable for more than four years until Sam left for college. Even then he spent every vacation with his mentor.

The result of this is Sam Duff, a human wreaking machine and a singular physical specimen.

That's when I first met him, at the University of Florida.

We were on the wrestling team but their program was very limited. A big time wrestler from Tampa had donated to the sport so that the Gators could field a first class team but for some reason it fizzled. Anyway, Sam could whip anyone there including the coaches. Even though I was high school all American in wrestling, Sam pinned me so fast I thought I was paralyzed. During our junior year the wrestling program was dropped so I transferred to Oklahoma. Sam stayed. He changed a lot, became more introspective and quit wrestling, at least in college. He was very reserved but heaven help the guy who didn't leave Sam Duff alone!

After graduation we ended up in the FBI academy. Due to our special skills we were sent to a school and taught every conceivable method of disabling or killing a person. We also underwent extensive psychological training in brainwashing and other counterintelligence methods. After five years with the FBI we were sent to the CIA for a special mission and we ended up staying…" Kirby's voice trailed off as his thoughts slowly slipped into reminiscence.

"We don't know what happened to Sam," he continued, "but you can bet we'll find out. That's why I have to insist on absolute secrecy and that anything relating to Sam be forwarded to me immediately. Meanwhile Doctor, how's old Sam doing?"

George's concentration was interrupted by the intercom.

"Yes Phil?"

"Dr. Martinez, the surgical resident at Centra County Hospital is on the phone. He needs to ask you about an alligator victim."

"Okay, put him on," replied the surgeon, irritated at the interruption.

"Dr.Martinez, this is Bob Bush at Centra. A white male was just presented with severe and extensive lacerations of his lower extremities. His friend says he was attacked by an alligator. The nurses tell me that this type of trauma is not uncommon but since I've only been here two weeks I thought you could give me some advice. This guy's legs are a mess. I think his ankle is fractured. He's in radiology now."

"Okay Bob, get all the bleeding points stopped and scrub hell out of the wounds—get the nurses busy. I'll be through in a few minutes and I'll whiz over and lend a hand. Just don't do any suturing until I get there." George let the phone drop, slowly, into its cradle.

"Sorry about the interruption Mr. Kirby but you know how it is. Now, about your friend." George paused to sort out his thoughts and continued. "You read the hospital records so you know how severe his wounds were. I found the damage to be messy but there is a chance that it looks worse than it is.

Most of the brain damage, in fact all that I could see in the area of the hematoma, was to the olfactory lobes. I pretty much cleaned the area and replaced the brain tissue that seemed viable. The skull fractures were not displaced to any extent so the head repairs should be good. In fact, Mr. Duff will have few visible scars unless you look in his hair when it grows back. The nose was just a matter of piecing the fragments back together. Given time he should have no externally visible signs of the trauma. The fractured arm will heal with no more treatment than the cast."

"As to his mental state, I can only wait and see. Hopefully, he will have a short period of confusion and possibly temporary amnesia. Barry Simon, the neurologist from Orlando, is very sharp and can give us a much better idea of his neurological status when Duff regains consciousness. So," continued Martinez, "we'll just have to do a little toe tapping and wait. Oh, by the way Kirby, Duff keeps mumbling about JY or something that sounds like that. Does that mean anything or have any significance?"

Kirby's eyes fixed the surgeon and the ever-present smile turned to a grin. "Yes, Doctor, it does. JY stands for Junk Yard, Sam's dog. He and that mutt are inseparable. I found him two days after Sam was hospitalized. I had scoured the area where Sam was found and left my name and phone number at several places. JY finally showed up at the Cooter fish camp and the owner penned him and called me, which was a good thing because that dog does not like to be confined unless it's with Sam. He looked as if he had been in a fight but I took him to a Veterinarian and he told me he will be good as new in a week to ten days."

"So," interrupted the surgeon, "JY is just a dog. I guess that solves that mystery. Now, if you will excuse me, I have to go see a man about a gator."

Outwardly calm, the surgeon's guts were stewing. What if this guy Kirby finds out what really happened in surgery. What if he questions some of the support staff and becomes suspicious? Even though they thought the tissues used in the surgery came from a human donor bank, they are not certain and they may not be able to convince Skeets Kirby. Also, wasn't this man highly trained and skilled in interrogation techniques? Surely, George thought, he has already checked my background and must know of my past work with allografts and transplants. He probably knows why and how I ended up in this God forsaken first aid station. Guilt welled up in George Martinez' throat like the incoming tide. Damn it, he thought, why do I always have to feel this way. I've done the best I can and I just couldn't let this guy go down the tubes because some straight-laced hospital committee doesn't like dog tissue. Oh well, as he guided his Mercedes-Benz 560SL into the flow of traffic, it's too late now.

Chapter TWO

The moon was full and bright and the large gator was restless. It took a lot of food to satisfy the energy demands placed on his ten foot plus, 450 pound body by the long summer days spent courting and fighting, mostly fighting. The sudden commotion on the far bank caused him to move in that direction; movement all but impossible to detect. Only the stubby nose and craggy eyes were visible above the water as he effortlessly eased towards the shore.

The large pond connected to the Kissimmee River by a man made canal and the gator often came to prey on the big water birds and wild hogs and cattle that frequented its shores. Tonight, however, the commotion sensed was not caused by any of those animals. He was hoping that some human had his dog playing in the water, teaching it to retrieve. Maybe he was in for another easy meal.

"You no good half-breed son of a bitch," the wiry little man was shouting. "This gator is mine. It's in my territory and I'm gonna catch him tonight. I'm gonna put a hole in that dog eatin' lizard big enough to park your truck in."

The man to whom he addressed this verbal onslaught turned slightly and the shimmering ray of moonlight caught on a gold neck chain from which hung a sparkling, whitish, finger shaped object. The man was huge and in a split second jumped on the smaller man and deftly crushed his skull with one blow from the 2 foot section of pipe grasped in his right hand. The sickening 'thunk' drifted across the pond and quietly evaporated in the murky silence. Effortlessly, the large man grabbed the dead one by the ankles and spinning like a macabre hammer thrower, threw the body clear of the bank into deeper water. Washing his hands, he turned towards the pond, shined a flashlight around in a small arc seeking the two red orbs slowly approaching. Okay big boy, eat up. I get you ass later. This one on me.

• • •

Sheriff Lonnie McCall eased his large frame into a chair and scooted forward to get closer to the desk. The pair of pearl-handled, customized .44's strapped to his ample waist prevented him from getting too close. The admittance nurse at Centra County Hospital greeted the sheriff. "Hi Lonnie, you here about the gator bite?"

"Yeah Sally, damn if it ain't getting to be a habit," sighed the sleepy-eyed lawman. "I guess these yankees won't ever learn that gators don't come from petshops and do have teeth. What's the drift on this guy?"

Lon Lewis McCall started filling in the blanks as the nurse called out the facts. He wrote methodically—programmed. So far this year he had written up seven alligator attacks. The last five years had seen a steady increase in man-gator confrontations. The sheriff's thoughts drifted back to when the alligator was hunted without mercy. His dad and he had caught, killed and sold the skins from many a gator. He had been practically raised on gator tail, fish and swamp cabbage. Now, gators were sacred and it was 'agin' the law' to cut a cabbage palm.

Inwardly he chuckled since he was still eating gator tail and swamp cabbage though he had to buy them illegally from old Lafayette Luther. More, he was wearing genuine alligator boots at $600.00—per boot. Pop Luther was a blasphemous, non-law and non-God fearing crusty old man who was a professional fishing guide at Boca Grande during the tarpon season, repairing marine motors the rest of the year. At both he was genius.

After his wife died he drank too much and moved to Centra County to be near the Kissimmee River and the expansive Kissimmee prairie. It didn't take long for him to start poaching and netting fish illegally but he never flaunted it and kept to himself. He peddled his ill-gotten goods in the four county area of central Florida. When laws were passed that stopped gator poaching, Pop applied for and got a permit to catch nuisance alligators for the Florida Fresh Water Fish and Game Commission. Whenever a gator became a pest by killing dogs, ducks or just scaring hell out of little old ladies trying to feed them marshmallows, the game commission called the designated hunter for that area to capture and relocate the misguided creature….or kill it.

For this service he was allowed to skin and process the beasts, selling the hide for upwards of $35.00 per foot and the meat for over $5.00 per pound. Since most of these nuisance gators were large, handling eight or ten a month could turn a tidy profit for the hunter.

"Did you get that, Lonnie?"

Sally's voice seemed to come from the ceiling, abruptly bringing the daydreaming lawman back to matters at hand.

"Yeah gal, I got it. That all?"

"I think so. See you later." With that, the amused nurse got up and walked into the admitting cubicle.

On the way out McCall remembered that he was to pick up meat from Pop Luther. Pop had told the sheriff that he was going after a nuisance gator that night but didn't say where. It was funny that Pop hadn't called with a blow-by-blow description of the gator catching. The crusty old fellow was getting eccentric. Lonnie yawned and decided to go home—he would call Pop first thing in the morning. He also remembered a ranchers' meeting tomorrow—more cattle rustling he guessed. Between this increase in ornery gators and rustling, not to mention the increasing theft of large equipment, McCall just knew he was getting an ulcer.

• • •

Nurse Elise Jones sighed as she adjusted the nasal tube carrying oxygen to the strange man lying helpless in the bed. She had been caring for him since his surgery 10 days ago. She was, like most of the hospital personnel, intrigued by the man and the mystery. She was intrigued by the man himself. No question that he was the most perfect male body she had ever seen; long, well defined muscles with smooth unblemished skin. His incisions had healed and the tiny punctate stitch scars were fading. She wondered what his voice was like and how coherent he would be when he awakened. Well, she thought, she would soon find out. Dr. Martinez had told her to stop the I. V. phenobarbital this morning, so Sam Duff would soon be out of his drug-induced sleep.

George said that ten days on the barbiturate drip should take the patient through the brain edema stage and so far there had been no sign of complications. George was probably right—he seemed to always be right. Elise thought back to the time over two years ago when Dr. George Martinez showed up at Centra County Hospital as the new Chief of Surgery. He was the most self-assured individual that she had ever met. His surgical skills were other-worldly and his medical knowledge endless, even in areas other than surgery. She was attracted to him.

Elise would never forget the evening he first kissed her.

They went to a few happy hours and after a few months George and Elise paired off. One evening he walked her to her car and seemed very preoccupied. She, too, was quiet. Their pent up emotion was having its effect. At the car George nervously sorted out her keys and after some difficulty opened the car door. As he did, he caught her by the shoulders and slowly turned her. Elise felt her body go limp and in one motion he pulled her to him and they kissed as if in a dream. Elise felt lightheaded as they locked in a passionate embrace. Prior restraints forgotten. Their attraction was overpowering.

Two weeks later they escaped for a weekend and in the most passionate fervor imaginable consummated their infatuation. Elise' eyes were moist as she remembered the past events. George was separated from his second wife and her own marriage to a local cowboy had been sour for five years.

Their passion grew and they saw each other almost every day. Elise marveled at how George could do so many things so well. He always found time for her so they made love frequently, under every kind of circumstance. When George proposed marriage she had not hesitated to file for divorce. Even though Elmer Jones was totally taken by the events, her divorce was final three months after she filed and she was, as of two months ago, a divorced woman.

A sharp coughing sound broke the nurse's concentration. The man in the bed was shaking and trying to pull the tubes from his nose. Quickly, she reached the bedside and grasped his wrist. The instant she touched him his other hand shot around her arm and she was thrown back by an invisible force. Unhurt but frightened, Elise ran from the room.

•   •   •

George Martinez was tired this morning. He hadn't talked to Skeets Kirby in several days so the voice on the phone didn't particularly irritate him.

"Kirby, this is George Martinez. Your boy Sam is awake. I'm going to the hospital in an hour and I'd like you to be there."

"Great Doctor, I'll see you there."

The surgeon let the phone hang in his hand for a few seconds. He had been thinking all morning how he was going to tell Elise— he wasn't going to divorce his wife.

• • •

The men gathered in the sheriff's office were all dressed the same—jeans, snap front shirts and cowboy boots topped by a wide brimmed western hat. Passed on the street, none would garner a second look; however, they represented most of the real estate in four counties including Centra. They were all ranchers, most of them third or fourth generation and were hard working, God fearing, down to earth people. For a friend they would do anything; if not a friend, forget it.

Can Martin was talking. Can owned one of the bigger spreads, 48,000 acres bordering Centra and Polk counties mostly devoted to a cow-calf operation with some tree farming and various small sidelines such as sod farming and watermelons.

Can was really Charles Jonathan Martin but was nicknamed Can after his great Grandfather Charles Jonathan Martin. Great Grandad Martin had traded cattle with the Cubans and Spaniards for gold, driving his herds to Punta Gorda for shipment to Cuba.

Since there was a shortage of banks and great Grandpa Can didn't trust them anyway, he put his gold coins into tin cans and buried them around his house. Can remembers his dad telling him about his dad playing with the cans containing the gold coins. It was his first toy—a homemade noisemaker!

"Dammit, Lonnie," Can was saying, "I lost two more steers last week. I can't keep up with it. It don't do no good to file a report with you. You know as well as me who's responsible for this. When you going to let us stop this problem?"

Several other ranchers grunted in agreement. "Y'all know I have to uphold the law," Lonnie shot back.

"You boys don't have no proof. Get me proof and I'll take care of the problem, pronto. 'Sides Can, I heard tell you boys had gotten some outside help to correct your little problem." The sheriff's voice had a tinge of sarcasm, "So why you need the long arm of the law?"

This last comment touched a nerve and Can started to say something, but stopped. Turning to the group, he said, "Come on boys, let's go to Tiny's and I'll buy y'all a beer. See you later McCall."

As the men filed out, Lonnie chuckled to himself. So the rumor he heard was true. The ranchers had hired on some outside group to stop the cattle rustling. Well screw'um, he thought. Whoever was involved had better not break the law in his county!

Still smiling, the sheriff picked up the phone and dialed Pop Luther's number. No answer. The old fart must be drunk or shacked up with that old Smith woman. For some reason old Hilda Smith had a king-sized crush on Pop and wouldn't leave him alone. They made out like mink with Hilda's wino husband watching TV on the small screened porch while they romped in the sack. Still holding the phone, Lonnie looked up as Roscoe James came busting through the door. Roscoe was one of the two Fish and Game Commission officers, game wardens, in the area. The sheriff had grown up with Roscoe and the two hunted and fished together.

"What's up Roscoe? Got a love bug up your fanny?"

"No Man, worse. I got a little bad news. A shiner fisherman found old Pop Luther this morning in 'at big pond in the public park down by Oak Point. He were dead—gator caught by the looks. The fisherman happened to see a big gator in shallow water a tryin' to twist off a leg—he thought from a cow. Turned out to be Pop's leg. Called the office 'n they got me on the radio. By the time I got out there some cowboys had helped get Pop's body 'way from the gator and man, were he pissed! Anyway, what's left are on the way to the hospital. Poor guy, what a way to go."

Lonnie McCall slowly sank into his chair as Roscoe's story unfolded. His face blanched and a lump slipped up in his throat.

Oh God, he thought—this can't be true. Getting up and reaching for his hat he motioned to Roscoe, mumbling, "I'm going to the hospital. You know good as me that no gator could catch that old fart. Something ain't right and I'm going to find out what. You coming?"

Lonnie was already out the door as the game warden replied that he had to get a gator hunter.

Roscoe sat at Lonnie's desk and picked up the phone. He might as well make his call, since the only authorized gator hunter left in the area was Joe Billie Bloodtooth. There had been four but three had either quit or moved and now with Pop dead, only Joe Billie remained. God, how Roscoe disliked the big Miccosukee half-breed. How he ever got approval to be an authorized gator hunter was beyond Roscoe. Anyway, he did—he was—he had to be called.

The phone rang for almost two minutes in the quiet tavern on state road 17. Gypsy Jack Pappadoupoulis looked up from the pool table, carefully laid the cue stick on the green playing surface and shuffled to the phone.

"Hello—yeah this is Jack."

Roscoe didn't like Gypsy Jack any more than he did Joe Billie but the only way to contact the half-breed was to leave a message at the tavern.

"Jack, this is Roscoe James of Fish and Game 'n I need to get in touch with Joe Billie. Got a man-eatin' gator. Would you tell'um to call me or the main office in Lakeland?"

Methodically Roscoe repeated the phone numbers and just as methodically came Jack's "OK" as he dropped the phone back its cradle.

Chapter THREE

With eating to be done, he eats; with mating to be done, he mates; with fighting to be done, he fights and with killing to be done, he kills.

Thus did the old Miccosukee describe the bull alligator to young Joe Billie Bloodtooth. Joe Billie's mother, Mary Cornflower, had taken the youngster far back in the Everglades to escape the brutal affection of the drunken Breed who was the boy's father. They lived with her relatives and since Joe Billie was the only youngster he was doted on. His Grandfather undertook to show the young man the ways of the animals and the beauty and benefit of the vast marshes and hammocks which form the magnificent River of Grass.

Joe Billie's people were the Miccosukee Indians, supposedly a part of the Seminole Nation but formally recognized as a separate tribe in the early 60's. They speak a different language and subsist as their forefathers on fish, wild pig, turkey, alligator and deer. Disdaining modern conveniences unlike their

Seminole cousins, the Miccosukee still cook over an open fire and live in thatched huts called chickees. The tribal elders adhere to centuries old customs and believe in the tribal legends handed down from generation to generation. The original Miccosukee, as legend has it, fell from heaven into a lake and swam ashore to build a home. They are tough, self-reliant and relatively obscure people.

The young half-breed was a fast learner. He was soon familiar with the plants and animals of the glades and as he matured he lost his youth related fear of snakes, alligators and other inhabitants of the vast swampland. His Grandfather taught him the art of tracking as well as how to avoid being tracked. As he grew, the older man was amazed at his strength. When wrestling, though unskilled, young Joe Billie was impossible to hold down and would not admit defeat or quit. Though only half grown he was as big as his mentor.

He would go into the deeper reaches of the Everglades and stay for days, emerging in good condition as if the time spent had been at summer camp. At 12 years of age, Joe Billie was independent. To him, the wild swampland was a summer camp. Joe Billie's mother insisted that he go to school, so since age eight the youth had been attending the Indian school 10 miles from the home chickees. The Indian students were classed more by educational status or needs than by age so Joe Billie frequently found himself the oldest student in the small, informal classes. Possessed of a keen mind he soon tired of the monotony the school offered, preferring to be in the glades. He liked physical education and excelled in all sports, especially baseball.

Shortly after his 14th birthday his father, James Bloodtooth, whom the youth had never seen, came to live with them—uninvited. James was a half-breed, his mother being a Miccosukee and his father an escaped convict, reputedly a murderer. It was common for convicts escaping prison in the South to head for the Everglades. Once there the authorities were helpless. The escapees either died in the glades or as James Bloodtooth's father, live with the Indians and stay forever in the swampy wildness.

Drinking heavily, he was given to violent rages when he would beat Mary Cornflower into unconsciousness. When the youth intervened the drunken half-breed would beat him unmercifully. The other members of the family were too intimidated by this behavior to interfere so the young Indian's life underwent drastic change. Joe Billie was soon spending more time in the glades and less time in school or the family compound. It was during one of these excursions that tragedy struck.

James Bloodtooth had drunk heavily for most of the afternoon and by dusk was bleary eyed and staggering. Mary had been avoiding him since his arrival, especially when he drank. Tonight was to be different. James decided that his woman was not refusing him again and he was going to be like the bull gator when he wanted to mate. Catching her unaware James dragged her to the ground, tearing her clothes as they fell. Sensing his animal determination, Mary grasped the small knife carried in her belt and began stabbing the raging man in his side and thigh. She was determined to not be beaten and raped again.

James Bloodtooth didn't realize he was being stabbed and continued to tear at Mary's garments, suddenly seeing blood and feeling the pain. The enraged man brutally pinned the woman's arms to the ground, wrenched the knife from her and slit her throat. Rolling off, he tried to stand but stumbled as the injured thigh gave way. Crawling towards the campfire to see how severe his wounds were, he was suddenly aware of movement. Looking back he saw the old Miccosukee, Mary's father, stealthily approaching with a ceremonial tribal war club raised to his shoulder. Soundlessly the old warrior was stalking the half-breed.

Like a wounded animal, James was oblivious to danger or death. Spinning like a human log he rolled against the old man's legs causing him to swing down and hit the ground with the club.

Simultaneously he put the knife behind the old man's legs and with one desperate cut severed both hamstrings. The valiant old warrior fell as if pole-axed and in an instant was rendered dead; a gurgling red slash where his throat had been.

Exhausted and bleeding, the weakened man crawled to the grotesque remains of Mary Cornflower and using his knife and teeth tore strips from the dead woman's clothes, binding his wounds as best he could. Quickly he gathered his few belongings including his whiskey. He had to have time to think and he had a friend in the Ten Thousand Islands area if he could make it. Soaking his bandages with the liquor he turned South. He knew the other family members wouldn't return until the next afternoon. Where the kid was, he didn't know or give a shit.

• • •

Joe Billie finished his meal of roasted turtle, raw swamp cabbage and young cattail roots. He was lonesome for his mother and Grandfather. In his world they were the only people he cared about. He could count on them and the old man was the smartest person in Joe Billie's limited world. He couldn't understand his father's behavior, less so why his mother tolerated the drunken half-breed—but—so be it. He was going to sleep a few hours until the moonrise and then head home. Rubbing his body with the crushed leaves given him by his Grandfather to repel mosquitoes and the ferocious deer flies, Joe Billie slept.

He was up with the moon, restless and for unknown reasons, apprehensive. The moon was bright with dark, wispy clouds dancing erratically across its troubled face creating the eerie effect of shadow on shadow. The surrounding marshes seemed alive as if energized by some irritable force causing its denizens to be restless. Joe Billie shuddered and hunched his shoulders. Gator moon, he thought. He remembered his Grandfather telling him of this moon; when the moon was full the swamp animals became restless and irritable, especially the bull gators. "This was not the time to hunt the big creatures," Grandfather had said. "The gator moon make them want to fight and kill. If you hunt them then, you will become the hunted. Even brave men fear on the gator moon."

The youth shivered as he remembered these words. Quickening his pace he headed home.

Joe Billie knew instantly something was wrong. The ever-burning fire was only glowing embers. Breaking into a trot he became aware of the blood smell—the unforgettable odor resulting from the slaughter and butchering of animals. Maybe Grandfather had butchered one of the small pigs kept in wire pens behind the chickee.

Entering the main compound the boy saw the grotesque scene. He knew about death. He knew instantly that the two main people in his life were gone forever. What he didn't know about was grief. Strange unintelligible sounds came from his throat as he went from body to body. Tears streaked his face. Finally he collapsed in the sand next to his mother's body and gave in completely to his grief.

• • •

James Bloodtooth's side and leg were on fire. He cut a limb to use as a crutch but the going was slow. The moon had been up several hours now and the wounded man had not stopped since he left the camp. Damn it, he thought. Why did that dumb bitch have to cut me? He knew this area only slightly but if he maintained a southerly course he would soon be on more familiar ground.

Wounded and disdainful of pursuit he made no attempt to conceal his passage.

• • •

Joe Billie got up from his mother's corpse and rebuilt the fire. His tears had dried and his disheveled face belied the steely look in his eye. Inside he was cold and of one resolve.

The sign was easy to read, much easier than the books at school. Picking up the war club, the young half-breed set out at a trot. The moon was still up and the trail was as easy to follow as if in daylight.

It was now midday and James was weakening. He had crossed a vast palmetto flat and was entering a large oak hammock. Feeling safe from pursuit, he decided to rest a few hours. Painfully cutting cabbage palm fronds to rest on, he sank to the ground and fishing the whiskey bottle from his pack, put it to his lips. He never felt the club. The first blow crushed the back of his head as if a quail egg. An involuntary groan escaped his lips as he sank to the bright green palm leaves. His eyes, unseeing, protruded from his head as if on stalks. Joe Billie raised the club again and again, until he was exhausted. The green bed was splattered with blood and gore. James Bloodtooth was unrecognizable as a man and this time there would be no grief.

• • •

It was a typical late August evening in South central Florida, hot and humid. The rainy season was in full swing and the daily afternoon shower had just stopped. The dusty infield was wet and the outfield sparkled from the raindrops clinging to crewcut bahia grass. Nine young men ran onto the field and began yelling and throwing baseballs. They were outfitted in pinstripe shirts and pants, spiked leather shoes and big league gloves. A large paunchy man wearing a face protector stepped to the plate and bellowed "play ball!"

A lone player sitting quietly on a crude wooden bench stood up, picked up a bat and strode to the plate. The wooden bleachers held a motley crowd; Indians, some cowboys and a smattering of better-dressed men and women. The air around the Big Cypress ball field swelled with the assorted cheers. The pitcher struck out the leadoff batter on four pitches. The next batter, wearing a brightly colored long sleeved shirt and barefoot, singled. The third youth, similarly garbed, was thrown out on a bunt. Suddenly the crowd noise stopped and all eyes turned to the Indian bench. To a stranger the cleanup batter seemed a man among boys. Joe Billie Bloodtooth hefted the four bats claimed by the reservation team, settled on one and casually walked to home plate. Not the oldest team member, he was certainly the biggest. Now 17 years old, he had the physique and bearing of a mature man. The pitcher, relaxed, began kicking the mound with his toe. The eight others—frozen in position.

Buddy Cochran, the Fort Myers High School baseball coach got up and walked rapidly to the mound. "Steve, it's only the first inning so if you want to walk him I don't care, but with the scouts in the bleachers you probably should give him a try." Steve Miller was probably the best pitcher Ft. Myers ever produced, certainly one of the best in the state of Florida.

"No problem coach, I'll take him." The first pitch was low and the big half-breed relaxed his grip on the bat and backed from the box. Even at 90 feet, Miller could feel his piercing stare - making the sweat on his face feel like ice water. The second pitch—a fast ball—never made the catcher's mitt. With a catlike step toward center field Joe Billie hit the ball in a towering arc that cleared the backpedaling centerfielder's head by 30 feet.

Buddy Cochran lowered his head and voiced a barely audible whistle. He felt sorry for his big hurler. He knew that the two baseball scouts sitting in the splintering old bleachers didn't drive to the Big Cypress Indian Reservation in south Florida just to see Steve Miller pitch. They could and had seen him in much more comfortable and accessible surroundings. If they were here because of the young Ft. Myers hurler, it was only to see if the big Indian kid could hit decent pitching.

Ft. Myers did win the game but Joe Billie went 4 for 4, hitting two home runs, a single and a triple.

Buddy walked to the opposite bench and singled out the Indian coach he knew only as Sammy. "Good game, Sammy. If I hadn't pitched Stevie I think you guys would have taken this one."

"Aw shit, Buddy, you know good as me if it weren't for Joe Billie you guys wouldn't even play us. You think you gonna get him to transfer to Ft. Myers his senior year but I'm telling you man he ain't leavin' the reservation."

"I know Sammy, but how about him going to Miami when he graduates. They have a damn good baseball program and I know

I can get him a full scholarship." Buddy Cochran was a Miami alumnus and an avid recruiter, especially when it concerned baseball.

"Well, you'll just have to get in line 'cause I get a call a day 'bout that half-breed. In case you didn't notice, those scouts didn't risk splinters in they asses just to see you boy throw... They already talking to Joe Billie's aunt 'bout big bucks to skip college and go pro."

"Aunt? Where are his parents?"

"Don't know for sure. Joe Billie showed up here 3-4 years ago and moved in with the aunt. No one ever told me where he come from. I know he a strange dude. You sure don't wanna mess with him, tough as cooter shell and mean as a bull gator needin' nookey."

"Well anyway Sammy, I'd appreciate your help and you know I'd make it worth your while." With that the Ft. Myers coach trotted towards the waiting bus.

The game had been over for several hours and Joe Billie and two of his teammates were sitting behind the wooden shack that served as a refreshment stand. The red and white Coca Cola sign nailed to the east wall shimmered in the moonlight reflecting on the green Coke bottles being topped off with moonshine. Soon all three would be drunk for the second time this week.

●　●　●

Joe Billie had been in the army for almost a year. He joined up after flunking his junior year at Miami University. The first two years at the university had been easy as he was the baseball star and the zealous alumni made sure that Joe Billie Bloodtooth made passing grades. In fact he had the best grades money could buy. They also covered up for his many fights and drunken encounters with the law. Early in his junior year the hard-hitting half-breed got seriously stoned and decided he could whip every man in a local bar. Before he was stopped, Joe Billie had almost killed two local business men and had to be restrained in a straight jacket.

It was these same two men who prevailed mightily and financially upon the army recruiters to take the unrepentant half-breed into their ranks, his burgeoning alcohol problem not withstanding.

• • •

Joe Billie was finishing special services training. The Korean conflict was history and the armed services were relatively inactive. It had been difficult for the big Miccosukee to get booze during this period of intensive training but he really didn't care. He was so caught up in the training, especially hand-to-hand combat, that he didn't miss old John Barleycorn. In fact no one in his training group wanted to go one on one with Joe Billie Bloodtooth. Always the victor, he would inflict extra punishment on his adversary, a trait that didn't go unnoticed by his instructors.

His drinking prior to the special services school had not gone unnoticed and was responsible for him almost not getting into the program.

• • •

"Rack'um up Joe Billie and I'll clean your clock again."

James Richard was a career soldier having reached the rank of Master Sergeant and content to live in the army as long as they let him. He had been in two wars, distinguished himself and was now a high ranking, non-commissioned black officer and small weapons instructor.

He and the Miccosukee had become friends after a fashion and were celebrating now the special training was over.

"Shit man, you lucky tonight." Joe Billie methodically stuffed the bright colored balls into the wooden triangle. "Let's go for that there 9 ball 'stead of the 8."

"OK Indian, for a beer."

The pool hall was downtown, large and populated by soldiers, sailors from the naval training base and civilians mostly from the nearby docks. The Sergeant and Joe Billie had been playing and drinking most of the evening and were the only uniformed men in the place. Three civilians were playing at the next table and once in a while one would comment about a shot that James or Joe Billie made. The Sergeant, experienced and cool, would grunt and ignore the remarks all the while eyeing the half-breed. Joe Billie Bloodtooth had a very volatile flashpoint!

The evening eroded and the beer flowed. One civilian asked the Sergeant if he wanted to play 8 ball for $50.00.

"Don't believe, friend. We just playin' for a few beers and fun." The big Negro had seen the amount of beer consumed by the three and was uneasy.

"That's not friendly Sarge." This time the second civilian did the talking. "Just wanna little friendly game, break the 'notony. 'Sides, we'll let you play old Mack here first," pointing his cue stick at the third man.

Mack was huge, built like a wrestler and a solid 250 pounds. The second civilian began to chuckle. "You guys can beat Mack— leastways at pool."

All three of the men began to chuckle.

Joe Billie's eyes narrowed as he missed an easy corner shot. James Richard's palms were wet.

The Sergeant's voice was flat, almost a command; "Hey Joe Billie, I've had enough of this place - let's split."

The reply, "Not just yet," caused James' palms to sweat more. "Joe Billie? Joe Billie?" The first civilian picked up where he left off. "What kind o'handle is that… Sarge?"

Mack turned and looked straight at the Indian.

"What's yore full name boy, or is Joe Billie yore whole name."

"Haw," interjected the first man. "His 'hole name is ass."

Their laughter caused the players at the other tables to stare.

The Sergeant's eyes were riveted on Joe Billie. He could see the half-breed's jaw tighten and noticed the calmness displayed by the man as he deftly sank a bank shot and straightening up stared straight into the eyes of the huge Mack. Slowly, deliberately, Joe Billie chalked the end of his cue stick, its butt on the floor. "Yea guys, my name is asshole and you what comes thru that there asshole every day—shit, white trash shit."

The pool hall became silent. Players not wanting to get involved began to move away from the group of five men. The one called Mack turned the pool cue in his hands ever so

slow, getting a baseball grip on its tapered end. His face was flushed and his neck muscles began to bulge as the blood rose like mercury in a hot thermometer. His two cohorts, ever so slowly, moved to his flanks.

None of these movements escaped Joe Billie, but he didn't move, his body still as a blue heron eyeing a minnow. The sergeant had frozen at his buddy's words and perspiration was visible on his forehead.

"Shithead!" Simultaneously raising his cue stick as he spat out the word, Mack lunged at the rigid Indian. Everything seemed to Joe Billie as if slow motion. His animal instinct had predicted his adversary's movement and his response was pure reflex and so sudden the large man didn't see or feel the half-breed's cue stick transfix his chest just below his left nipple.

His swing halted as by an invisible hand as his eyes focused on the quivering piece of polished wood protruding some 18 inches out of his chest. Joe Billie's folding knife was already in his hand as the stricken man sagged against a table. Joe Billie no longer saw Mack, he saw James Bloodtooth and they were alone—he intended to kill him.

Even though the sergeant saw it coming, the few seconds the incident consumed seemed like hours. He knew too well the outcome and he also knew there was no stopping the enraged Indian. He jumped between the stunned civilians and deftly clubbed the half-breed behind his ear dropping him just as the knife had begun its short journey from one of Mack's ears to the other.

The man, Mack, lived. The civilian court found Joe Billie Bloodtooth guilty of assault with a deadly weapon, attempted manslaughter and sentenced him to 5 years probation.

The month following the trial the army discharged Joe Billie Bloodtooth dishonorably.

Chapter FOUR

The man turned slowly in the hospital bed, his wrists and ankles painful from the restraining straps only recently removed. He had no conception of time or space. His face and head ached with a dull throbbing sensation as if a metronome were somewhere in his skull dutifully keeping cadence. He had remembered nothing until this morning when the slender nurse with the dark hair asked him who JY was. Slowly, painfully, memories started to return like sand forced through a fine mesh.

JY? Of course he thought. JY is my dog. Instantly on guard he wondered how she knew about his dog. Suddenly the thoughts came flooding back causing him to sit up and for the first time in over a month look around the room. He was alone. The room was spare with no furniture save a bedside table and he noticed no mirrors. Forgetting his wrists he slowly raised his hand and carefully, as if reading Braille, ran his fingers across his face, head and neck. Everything seemed to be in order except for stubby hair. He felt some raised areas on his head—probably scars. He took a deep breath, inhaling slowly through his nose and exhaling rapidly through his mouth. Feeling no pain he slid his legs over the side of the bed and holding to the fixed table stood up. He gasped as his legs struggled to support the unaccustomed weight. Steadying with his arms, he felt his face flush as sweat formed on his upper lip and his legs began to tingle as his circulation adjusted to the upright position.

The door opened without warning and Elise Jones stopped as she saw the struggling patient.

"Mr. Duff, what are you trying to do? You shouldn't be out of bed." Her gaze lingered on the handsome body now weak and atrophied but still the handsomest she had ever seen.

Samson Duff opened his mouth to answer but much to his surprise no intelligible sound came out. He stopped and tried again, his face flushing, as much from embarrassment as effort and succeeded in gurgling a resemblance to "who are you?" He realized he couldn't remember when he had last spoken. He also recalled nothing but bright lights and voices without bodies, but he didn't know how long ago.

Nurse Jones smiled as she went to the confused man and gently put her hands on his shoulder and elbow to assist him back to bed. Remembering her last attempt at touching him caused her to grip him cautiously but he offered no resistance.

"Here Mr. Duff," she said gently, "let me help you back to bed and maybe we can talk some."

Touching him caused her to flush like a schoolgirl, a feeling that really surprised her.

Duff, she called me, thought the helpless man. Of course, I'm Sam Duff, Samson Hercules Duff. With this a flood of memories poured from his confused brain. Places, events, people came tumbling back. It was obvious that something bad had happened and he sure needed to find out what. Back in bed, Sam fixed his gaze on the nurse. Still struggling he managed a fairly understandable "Where am I?"

Straightening the bed sheets, Elise replied. "You're in Centra County Hospital. You've been here over a month and this is the first time you've spoken."

"What happened to me." He stammered.

"Does anyone know I'm here?"

"Yes to 'does anyone know you're here' and no as 'to what happened'. No one here knows. And since you're officially awake I have to notify your doctor. Relax and I'll be back in a few minutes." She turned and walked quickly to the door. Sam's eyes followed her, approving of her sleek body and appealing way of walking.

Elise went to a nearby phone and punched in George Martinez' unlisted number.

George Martinez, MD, was in his office going over the autopsy report on one Lafayette Luther. It was apparent from the report that the old man had been dispatched by a severe blow to the head with the alligator damage occurring post mortem. There had been no water in his lungs and though not absolutely ruling out drowning, did lend credence to the theory that Pop had been murdered and not killed by the huge gator. Sheriff McCall had pressed this opinion on the surgeon and asked him to review the circumstances and put in his report that murder was a possibility. So far he agreed.

The unlisted phone rang and the surgeon hesitated, thinking it may be Elise but he wasn't ready to talk to her. Its persistence caused him to give in.

"George?" Elise Jones' voice was like silk on silk. God how he wished he were a stronger person. "George this is Elise and I hate to bother you but Mr. Duff is awake and talking. You told me to call as soon as he was able to talk, so I am."

How humble she sounds, he thought. I guess she senses something different in our relationship. Women sure are funny.

"Thanks babe, I'll be over inside the hour." Wanting to say he loved her but choking on the words he let his voice trail off.... "Thank's again, see you soon." The click of Elise' hang up seemed to echo around the room—along with George's guilt.

George wheeled his Mercedes-Benz into the hospital parking area and saw Skeets Kirby's car. Good. I won't have to see Elise alone. One thing about Kirby—he was prompt. Pushing through the waiting room doors the anxious Doctor saw the nurse and Skeets engaged in animated conversation.

"Hope I'm not interrupting anything." At his words conversation stopped and they turned to greet him.

"Nope," Skeets replied, "Nurse Jones was just filling me in on Sam's apparent resurrection."

"Well then, let's not wait." With that Martinez led the way to the patient's room.

Sam Duff heard the door open and was looking that way when the trio entered. Seeing Skeets caused him to gasp—he didn't recognize the surgeon but Kirby's face sure rang a big bell.

Skeets exhaled relief at the sight of his friend sitting up and apparently out of danger. He didn't quite know what to say.

Martinez interrupted. "Well Mr. Duff, how do you feel?"

Sam had been practicing his speech and with little hesitation responded. "Fine. Are you the doctor who did all this to me?" simultaneously pointing to his face and head.

"That's me. Someday I'll tell you all the gory details but now we need to talk some and see how much you remember. I see your speech is returning and likely will be normal within a few weeks. How 'bout that head of yours? Any headaches or stuffiness in your nose?"

"My head feels okay except for a mild throbbing and my nose does feel stuffy but I can breathe alright. It doesn't seem to be stopped up. In fact, if anything, I am more sensitive to odors. This hospital is driving me up the wall with all of its different smells."

Finishing the examination Martinez nodded to Kirby and quietly replied to Sam, "You're doing great. Just try and relax and let things fall into place on their own. Don't force yourself and you'll be out of here in no time."

Inwardly he was smiling. Sam Duff stood a good chance for a complete recovery, memory and all. He felt better about the surgery. Motioning to Elise to follow, George went through the door and left Skeets and Sam alone. It was up to Kirby now.

● ● ●

Twenty miles from the hospital two pickup trucks, headlights out, eased up a dirt road and stopped about a half mile from the hard road. The two men in the lead truck got out and quietly walked back to the second truck. Behind the wheel sat a large man, alone, with a .356 cal. Marlin in the gun rack adorning the rear window; a large merle colored hound sat quietly in the back. As the two approached, the hound offered a low guttural growl, exposing serious fangs glistening with saliva. At the growl both men stopped. The smallest of the pair, Jake White Raven, spoke quietly to his partner Bill Two Bucks.

"Damn hound. Why do Joe Billie haf to bring that mutt everywhere he go? That deaf son a bitch bite anybody even Joe Billie if the wind ain't right."

"Shut up Jake," countered Two Bucks, "Joe Billie hear you an he sic Stump on you ass and you be standing a month."

He's right, thought Jake, Stump would sic and Joe Billie Bloodtooth needed little reason to put his dog on man or beast.

Stump was birthed by a purebred leopard hound bitch Joe Billie won in a poker game at Gypsy Jack's four years before. The bitch had 7 pups, all female save one. The sire was said to be a huge blue brindle pit bull with a bad reputation.

Like most Indian dogs, the bitch and pups were on their own.

She was a good mother, feeding and caring for the litter while scrounging food scraps and whatever small animals she could kill for herself. In the process of digging out an armadillo, she was struck and killed by a rattlesnake with the pups only 6 weeks old. Joe Billie found the dead bitch and promptly killed all the pups except the male. This he gave to Lily Turtle, the waitress at Gypsy Jack's. He had been seeing her for over two years and unlike his father seemed kindly disposed to women. The pup proved to be a survivor and by six months was whipping the dogs that hung around the bar and Lily's house.

Teased, as Joe Billie often did, the pup would fly into a rage, not stopping until exhausted or held at arm's length by the half-breed until his anger cooled. It was during one of these temper fits that Lily told Joe Billie she thought the pup couldn't hear.

"You crazy Turtle woman, that there shit-eater hear good as you or me."

What really changed his attitude occurred when the pup was almost 10 months old. Joe Billie pulled up in front of Lily's small frame house at 4 am, having been coon hunting and not being sleepy, decided to pay Lily a visit as she usually left the bar between 3 and 4 am. His dog box was still in the truck holding two coon hounds. A third, large male redbone hound paced the free space around the dog box alternately growling and pissing on the box and its occupants. Old Red was Joe Billie's catch dog—always on the muscle. His scarred face and ears spoke eloquently to his myriad encounters with boar, coon and lesser dogs.

The house was dark with only a dim porch light straining to lighten the quiet darkness. The pup, now almost 60 pounds, was curled up on a doormat on the small porch sound asleep. The Indian got out of the truck and walked to the porch letting out a low whistle as he approached the sleeping dog. Getting no response he spoke to the pup. "Get up you mangy turd."

No response. By now the man was at the porch and instead of using the two crude steps, bounded onto it and had just steadied himself when 60 pounds of blue gray meanness was on him. The surprised man tried to kick the pup but could not shake him loose. Shouting, Joe Billie held to the 4x4 supporting the roof and half-heartedly tried to climb it. Hearing the snarling and shouting, Old Red bounded from the pickup and in a flash was on the porch and caught the pup by the hind leg.

The blue merle pup turned back like a snake and caught the red bone by the cheek and ear. Relieved of his burden Joe Billie leaped from the porch with the idea of getting a stick but changed his mind and turned to watch his red dog dispatch the crazy leopard pup.

What the hell, he thought, that there young son a bitch should know better than attack him.

Hurting from the vicious face hold, the older dog let go the leg and started to roll under the big pup hoping to break him loose from his face. Off the porch went the two combatants. Shouting encouragement to his hound, Joe Billie didn't hear the car drive up or see Lily Turtle until she ran screaming to the two dogs.

"Stop him, stop him," she pleaded, trying to get a hand on her pup.

"Back off, back off. You get them there hands chewed up 'n I can't stop them now if'n I was a mind too. Old Red ain't gonna quit and I don't give a dam about that there glass-eyed pup o' your'n "

By now the dogs had stopped rolling and the redbone was still caught by the face making it difficult to bite anything but air. He couldn't understand this adversary. Usually the rolling would break even an old boar coon loose just long enough for him to get a good neck hold. Suddenly, Old Red felt a little tired.

The big half-breed couldn't believe his eyes. Old Red should have killed this pup minutes ago; he outweighed him by some 15 pounds and had never lost a fight. Missing Lily, he looked up just as she swooped down on the fighting canines holding a length of 2x4, mortally cursing Joe Billie and his hound as she came on. Before he could stop her Lily swung and hit the red dog a glancing blow, also hitting the young dog. This and seeing Lily caused the pup to loosen his grip, sensed immediately by his adversary who instantly pulled free.

Joe Billie was on Lily in a flash and pinning her arms, lifted the cursing, screaming woman off the ground. Leaving the hound, the merle pup went for the big Indian, causing him to fall backwards while still holding Lily. The wily old hound sensed the advantage and went for the pup's throat, a maneuver he had performed dozens of times before—with great success.

This time was to be different. Through some extra sensory mechanism coupled with an innate ferociousness, the pup sensed the maneuver even with the added confusion and deftly rolled to his back catching the charging hound with his head and neck extended and unprotected from below. Instantly he caught the older dog by the throat and went deep into his hold, his neck and back muscles rigid as a corner post.

The red bone had been dead a full five minutes before Joe Billie got Lily calm enough to turn loose. He was totally shocked by the outcome. Lily was quiet and only the primitive deep guttural sounds coming from the pup as he worried the dead hound broke the stillness of the night. Looking up, Joe Billie saw that the moon had risen full and shining with wispy clouds flitting eerily across its face. He shivered.

Joe Billie took the pup and for the first time since childhood developed an attachment to a living thing. He soon realized that Lily was right and the pup was deaf. It had been the big man's weight on the porch that aroused the sleeping dog; the wind was wrong for him to pick up the man's scent. He gave his upset woman a young birddog pup and since the merle pup couldn't hear, named him Stump—deaf as a stump the Indian would say.

In time the two became inseparable.

• • •

Opening the pickup door, Joe Billie Bloodtooth stepped out and stretched his legs, the heavy gold neck chain supporting the gator tooth amulet shimmering in the moonlight. The amulet was bone white and large as a man's middle finger. Touching the complaining Stump on his nose to quiet him, the big man motioned to the pair to follow. He carried a rifle and a half full feed sack. Stopping at the formidable looking non-climb fence, he quickly found the opening he had cut in it a week before. Carefully unwiring the gap, the three Indians passed through, followed by a four-legged shadow.

As he had done the past five nights, Joe Billie opened the sack and began scattering large range pellets on the ground. Within minutes a dozen or more large shadows materialized from the semi-dark woods and began eating them. As if choreographed, the three men produced rifles chambered for .22 caliber shorts and walked among the feeding cows, methodically shooting them between the eyes, killing them as if by touch alone. One stricken cow stumbled and turned to run, blood streaming from her nostrils, only to be caught by the 80 pounds of shadowy fury. A second shot ended the escape and Stump begrudgingly loosed his hold on the cow's bloody nose.

Jake and Bill Two Bucks were butchering as Joe Billie dispatched the wounded cow. Two hours later both pickups were loaded with fresh prime beef and headed for Gypsy Jack's.

Chapter FIVE

Tiny's cafe sat in the middle of Centra and had been in operation for the past forty years. Can Martin's Grandfather and father had frequented it and Can had breakfasted there most mornings unless out of town or working cattle. He was sitting in his 4x4 pickup nervously thumping the steering wheel to the beat of a country western song when the cafe opened. It was 5:30 am and he had been up most of the night since the slaughtered cows had been discovered. The signs had been clear and Can was as pissed over the sheer audacity of the butchering as he was over losing the animals. That damn half-breed didn't even try to hide his sign.

Can was still fuming as he crossed the street to the cafe.

He didn't see the man emerge from the shadows and quietly walk toward the cafe door.

"Hi Martin." Skeets Kirby's quiet greeting startled the rancher.

"Oh, there you are. I was wondering if you was here yet.

Let's go to the back where we can talk."

The two walked slowly to the far end of the cafe and seated themselves in a small booth. Can knew that Glory would be right over with coffee so he continued the small talk. "How's your friend doing, Kirby?"

"Good so far. The doctor says that he should make a complete recovery, even his memory. In fact I'm to visit him this morning to test his memory and bring him up to date on what's happening."

"Well I'm glad," Can replied as the waitress poured two cups of coffee. "Morning Glory." Can's eyes narrowed and his mouth displayed a wide grin as he threw his one liner at Gloria Waters—he had done this for as long as she could remember.

"Morning Can, want breakfast?"

"Nope." Can looked inquiringly as Skeets replied. "Me either, only coffee."

As the waitress retreated to the kitchen, Martin's tone turned serious. "I lost six fat cows last night," he began. "And that thievin' son of a bitch didn't even try to cover his tracks. He may as well have come in my front yard in broad ass daylight. I had a notion you guys couldn't handle this!"

"Wait just a damn minute," Skeets interrupted, "let's not jump to conclusions. You hired us to do a job and we'll do it. What happened to Sam was a monumental screw up, even stupid, but it's not a detour. It's only a speed bump and it won't happen again… Guaranteed. We'll do the job."

Cattle rustling had been a fact of life for these ranchers as long as anyone could remember—an occasional thing with sporadic loss of a few cows. Once in a while someone would be caught with his hand in the cow and turned over to the authorities, causing the offended rancher to throw a barbeque and celebrate the modern version of frontier justice. The hapless perpetrator usually turned out to be an ex-hired hand and his sentence would be suspended; a rumor has it that one such rustler even made the barbeque.

The past five years had been different. The rustling was now big time. Fences would be cut and dozens of beeves herded into stock trailers pulled by 4 wheel drive pickups. Fat steers shot and butchered where they lay with only the choicest cuts taken. None of the ranches were exempt. The local cattlemen had petitioned the State Cattleman's Association for help but were told the usual;

get more posted signs up and alert local law enforcement people. Big deal.B.F.D!

The local gendarmes, including Lon McCall, were only too glad to help—just catch one of those rustlin' sons' a bitches and we'll put his ass away for good. That is if you catch him in the act, red handed, and everyone knew that just wasn't going to happen.

Can and his fellow ranchers had been working on the problem and had made little progress until one of them, while playing pool at Gypsy Jack's, overheard a drunk Indian tell Jack about what had to be a cattle rustling. He mentioned Joe Billie Bloodtooth, the Indian stores on Indian land and acted as if Gypsy Jack was his long lost cousin. Two of the more militant ranchers waylaid the guy and tried to make him talk. He laughed at them and said he'd rather be dead than snitch on Joe Billie Bloodtooth. The next week, a mile of fence was down on each ranch.

It was then that Can and the ranchers connected the big half-breed to their problem. They hired a private investigator to check him out and the reports, up until he disappeared, showed beyond a doubt that Joe Billie was the main force behind the rustling. The reports showed that the Indian had appeared in the area about six months before the rustling started and that he had contact with Gypsy Jack Pappadoupoulis and the Indian stores. Since the Indian stores were on tribal property, they were not subject to state or federal taxes and the goods were seldom inspected. Rustled beef would never be found there. As an aside, the investigator reported that the half-breed handled a lot of alligator skins and meat through Gypsy Jack or the Indian stores—or both. His last report was that he intended to check out Joe Billie's home place. He was never seen again.

The ranchers finally decided to get serious and go for big time help. They decided to fund it anonymously with Can the go between. Whoever they picked would be unknown to them and would be strictly on their own. If they worked outside the law, no one would help them and their only job was to stop the rustling.

Enter Samson Hercules Duff and Charles Skeets Kirby. Can continued. "So what have you found out now?"

"For starters I have proof of Gypsy Jack's involvement with poached gator hides and meat. He also deals in beef, uninspected and no bill of sale. He is very wealthy even though his lifestyle doesn't show it. Apparently he's buying off the Fish and Game people, but Joe Billie must have something else going. I just don't see how he could do so much poaching and get away with it unless it ties in with his designated gator hunter status. Anyway, the key to your problem is the half-breed. Joe Billie Bloodtooth."

"Well," Can interrupted, "you have half the money and if you want the rest you know what to do." Ignoring the sarcasm Skeets looked at his watch and stood. "Well, I guess that's enough for today. Hopefully we'll be back in business shortly if Sam's OK. I'll let you know."

More than a little pissed, Skeets threaded his way through the tables and exited, leaving Can Martin sitting, his chin in his hands.

Skeets climbed into his car and reflected on the conversation he just had with Can Martin and on events leading to Sam's beating. They had been approached by the rancher two weeks before the incident and were more than a little skeptical about his story. They had no problem working outside the law and certainly no problem with the money offered. Their concern was that the situation wasn't serious enough for them. It seemed to be a straightforward law enforcement case. They were wrong. Dead wrong!

Their preliminary investigation supported what Can Martin had told them—and more. Joe Billie Bloodtooth was, indeed, terrorizing the cattlemen and local law seemed helpless. Also it didn't appear to be connected with the Dixie mafia, just a local operation involving a few Indians and some higher placed go betweens. However small, the ones involved were stealing and getting away with it.

The day of the beating, Sam told Skeets that he was going to Gypsy Jacks, play a little pool and nose around. With a 30-30 Marlin lever action hung in his pickup and a pit bulldog riding shotgun, he figured to fit right in. That was about 3 pm and they were to meet at 8 pm. Sam didn't make the meeting and the rest, Skeets thought, is history.

Starting the engine, Skeets revved the motor and the sound brought him back to the present. He headed for the hospital.

• • •

Elise watched as Sam finished his sweeping pushups, sweat pouring off his forehead and upper body. That body, invalid a few weeks ago showed remarkable change. His speech was almost normal and the nurse knew he wouldn't be in the hospital much longer. He had been exercising vigorously for the past 10 days and even George Martinez couldn't dissuade him.

Elise had worked with him daily to regain his speech and memory. The neurologist had seen him once a week since he regained his senses and had marveled at his recovery, physical and mental.

He is, Elise thought, one hell of a man. Skeets Kirby walked in as Sam was toweling off, nodded to the sweating patient and greeted the nurse. "Hi Elise, how's the big guy today. Looks like he may be about ready to go." Kirby had made it a point to get to know the pretty nurse the past few weeks and found her resourceful as well as attractive. In fact, the more he saw of her the more attractive she became.

"He's doing fine Skeets. As you can see, he's fast regaining his strength, not to mention his physique." Even this reference caused her to blush. "He sure does crazy exercises but they seem to work. Anyway he's all yours. I'll be at the nurse's station if you need me." Touching Skeets on the arm as she walked by Elise whispered, "Go easy on the big guy, okay?"

Pulling a straight-backed chair to the middle of the room, Skeets sat quietly while Sam finished his warm down and dropped into the one easy chair in the Spartan room.

The sweating man sighed, "Well, Skeets old buddy, what in hell do we talk about today? I'm tired of weather reports and the daily news and all the other trivial shit things you've come up with these past two weeks."

"Cool down Samson. Take your time and tell me what you remember about the night you were beaten." Skeets then reviewed the past events as he knew them and took the confused man back to the first contact with Can Martin. Several times Skeets caught a glimmer in his partner's eye, signs of recognition. Encouraged, they spent the next four hours reliving Sam Duff's life. By evening Skeets was convinced that Samson was ready to go and that his memory was returning.

"Samson, I'm going to arrange your discharge for tomorrow morning." Skeets measured the words carefully. "We have a job to do and the boss is getting antsy. We're going back to work."

As Skeets put the chair against the wall Sam let out another sigh. "I'll be damn glad to leave this place. For one thing the smells drive me up the wall. About the only thing I'll miss is that pretty nurse. What a package!"

Skeets paused as he went through the door. "Pretty, huh?

Well I guess you are getting back to normal. See you tomorrow." On the way out Kirby thought of Samson's parting words. I don't smell anything different or especially bad. I wonder what the hell he means? I better mention this to Martinez tomorrow.

• • •

It was a cool, dark October night and the two men had been in and out of the water several times. The smaller one, Jake White Raven, was pulling a rope, the end of which was noosed around the tail of a large and very agitated alligator. "Dam Joe Billie," he complained, "I can't hold this sum bitch by myself."

The leopard hound, Stump, was pacing the edge of the pond emitting a low, throaty growl. Occasionally he would pin his ears and charge the water's edge. He hated alligators.

"Yeah," the harried Jake kept on, "and get that pig eatin' dog o' your'n out the way. You know them gators don't like that sum bitch."

Ignoring both, Joe Billie was waist deep in the water holding a pole attached to a wire noose. Deftly evading the thrashing beast he looped the noose over the gator's mouth and with an explosive grunt struggled out of the water and tied the pole to the front of his pickup truck. Moving quickly to help Jake he tied the tail rope to a stout post a few feet from the water's edge.

"Okay Injun," the half-breed said, "don't let me kill this un'." With that he slid behind the wheel of his 4x4 and backed up, tightening the cable looped around the creature's snout stretching him out like a team roped steer. As soon as the gator was stretched, Jake White Raven waved frantically at Joe Billie to stop, as the last one they did lost its snout and had to be shot. Jumping from the truck the bigger man, with Jake's help, trussed the possum playing gator with sash cord and taped its mouth. Easing the truck forward to slacken the line, he produced two cans of beer, threw one to the smaller man and silently viewed the gift-wrapped alligator as he gulped the other.

Stump had watched the struggle and was now sniffing the gator, occasionally nipping the harried beast when he thought no one was watching.

"You dum' ass turd-roller," Joe Billie thought. "That there bullgator make short work o'you, he get loose. You sure got more guts then smarts."

Stump was four years old and had shown no fear of any creature, including man. Many times the deaf dog had met a mouth popping wild boar head on to save his master from being cut or having to climb a tree—rapidly! At Lily Turtle's suggestion, Joe Billie purchased a high-pitched whistle and found the dog could hear it. He taught the hound to respond to one whistle by attacking and two by releasing. With this control Joe Billie Bloodtooth and Stump became a legend among the locals.

Not a popular one.

The pond that produced the captured gator was one of four on Joe Billie's home place. Each pond was fenced by stout non-climb wire and homed alligators of various sizes. A rundown aluminum shed sat behind the shack he called home, and slightly beyond were two larger buildings bordering the first pond. In it were buckets of fish and rustled beef in varying stages of decomposition used to feed the gators. This was Indian land and invited no visitors—curious or official. Joe Billie knew that a hungry gator wasn't real choosy about what it ate.

Jake broke the silence. "Where you gonna put this 'un, Joe Billie?"

Crushing the beer can in one hand Joe Billie appeared to be thinking. "Well, I thought bout that there little lake behind that there new subdivision to the north side of Centra. They's plenty dogs and old farts there, shouldn't take too long to get a call. That there big sucker is shore hungry cause I ain't fed him in two weeks. Too, I got five more fat ones we can sneak in with that'un when we catch him again." A big grin crossed the half-breed's face. He was thinking the white man wasn't all that smart after all.

Throwing down the crumpled beer can he motioned to the smaller man to get the winch cable. He wanted to load the trussed gator and move him to his new, albeit temporary, home.

• • •

Dr. George Martinez finished his examination of Samson Duff and noisily shuffled papers while the patient finished dressing. He was amazed at his recovery. No significant scars were visible, his hair had regrown and his senses seemed normal. Or were they? Sam had asked the surgeon several times about his sinuses and about his sensitivity to odors, a phenomenon he was not previously aware of. George recalled Sam's remarks when he entered the exam room. "Damn George did you use formaldehyde for aftershave?"

"What do you mean?" shot back the puzzled surgeon. "Well, you smell just like formaldehyde. What kind of martini did you have at lunch?" Sam sniffed the air and crinkled his nose.

"Hell man," came the reply, "you must be sniffing the stuff yourself or else glue." George quickly dropped the subject but his mind was spinning. He had been in the lab examining formalin preserved cadavers that morning but had meticulously washed his hands after removing his gloves and had left his lab coat there. Could Sam actually be smelling a trace of the formalin? My God, he thought, it would take a Bloodhound to do that.

"Well guy," George continued, "you seem good as new. I guess your buddy Skeets will be happy. As far as I'm concerned you can get back to normal, whatever that is. My only advice is to stay away from baseball bats."

The happy patient stood up, smiled at the surgeon and headed for the door. "Don't worry Doc, the next trauma case you work on won't be me, I promise."

Sam drove to the house he and Skeets had rented upon arrival in Centra some three months ago, where he anxiously reunited with his canine companion, JY. He had him since a pup, an American Pit Bulldog and had trained him. JY stood for Junk Yard and there were few, if any, dogs that could stand up to him.

He was four years old, a deep red color with jet-black nose, muzzle and rear half of his tail. He weighed 75 pounds and one could strike matches on his muscular body. His prime purpose in life was to protect his master and woe to the person or thing who didn't fully understand this.

Hearing the car drive into the garage the lithe animal pricked his ears, his emotionless eyes narrowing to slits as he recognized the car's occupant. Tail wagging, head swinging, he stood at the door Sam would enter and his mind went back to the night he had been separated from his master. He had been in the back of the pickup the fateful night Samson visited Gypsy Jack's bar. As his master went in he was commanded to stay, even though he would liked to have gone with Sam. He seldom questioned his master as he had done when a pup.

JY remembered the expensive 4x4 pickup with the funny look-ing hound in the back. It turned in and parked about 30 minutes after Sam entered the bar. He still didn't understand why the big dog hadn't snarled back when he throatily challenged him. He didn't like being ignored but since Sam wanted him to stay he would. Trying to ignore the deaf hound, JY focused on the door his master had entered. Suddenly it exploded off its hinges and a man's body tumbled into the parking yard. It was quickly followed by three struggling men—one being Samson Hercules Duff!

Quick as a heartbeat JY was out of the truck and caught the nearest man by the upper thigh. Squealing like a stuck pig, Bill Two Bucks screamed at the large man swinging at Sam Duff with a small bat, "get this thing off'n me, Joe Billie, get'em loose."

JY had his hold and his back muscles were jerking in a spasmodic rhythm as he shook the Indian like a macabre rag doll. The one called Joe Billie fished an object from his shirt pocket and blew it one time. The high-pitched sound had hardly thinned before 90 pounds of blue merle fury hit the Junk Yard hard on his right shoulder. Accepting the new adversary, JY turned and rolled as Stump tried to establish a neck hold. Regaining his feet he ducked low under the hound's persistent charge and caught his rear leg. Biting once he let go and as Stump turned to protect his leg JY caught him by the shoulder. The sheer size and strength of the big hound prevented the pit from getting a good hold and Stump twisted in half trying to catch JY's off leg. The feisty pit was now excited. Here was a worthy opponent—he had to give up his hold to protect his foot and leg. This hound dog was tough!

Suddenly a fat man came through the open doorway holding a shotgun. He fired once in the air causing the struggling men to stop. JY blinked at the sound of the shot allowing the deaf hound to catch his neck and the front of his shoulder. He knew then he was in trouble and shot a sideways glance towards Sam. The fat man had Samson backed up to the fancy pickup and the larger of the two men crumpled him with a vicious blow to the head. Quickly they dragged the semiconscious man to the truck, still beating him.

Emitting an unearthly snarl, JY tore loose from the surprised hound. Ignoring the resultant wounds to his neck and shoulder the crazed pit bulldog charged the pickup as it pulled away from the parking yard. With the vehicle rapidly gaining speed the half-breed saw the pit bull charge and marveled at the dog's quick-ness and strength. No dog had ever gotten away from Stump once he had a hold. Well, so what, he thought, he'll never catch the truck and he better find a new boss cause his current one was soon to be made dead, if not already.

JY remembered the frustration that grabbed him as he chased the escaping truck so when Sam opened the door the big dog could not control himself, exploding into a wriggling, licking, whimpering pile of dog meat. This affection put Samson on his knees and save for extraordinary balance, would have put him flat on his back. Warming to the playful nature, the obliging man grabbed him by the neck and rolled across the floor, liking noth-ing better than to roughhouse with the muscular canine. Across the room went the struggling pair with Sam trying to turn the dog to his back and the pit resisting with every ounce of strength in his considerable body. It had always puzzled Sam as to how a 75 pound animal could be so tough and determined that a trained athlete weighing more than two and one-half times as much could not force him to his back.

Determined, yet only playing, Samson ducked under JY's front leg and grabbed the off forelimb and heaved the surprised canine onto his side. Sam saw the change in the pit bull's eye as soon as he heard the throaty snarl. Playtime was over. Tightening his grip on the dog's down leg he tried to shift his knee onto the animal's chest and use his weight to hold the dog down. JY had other ideas. The growl became a snarl, the squinting eyes turned to blood-shot orbs and thick saliva appeared at the corners of his mouth. Turning his head and body even while in Sam's viselike grip, JY grabbed his master just under the left arm on the side of his chest. The suddenness and ferocity of this maneuver brought the man back to reality and he quickly let go of the dog. He was caught!

"Dam you JY," he cursed, "you started this shit now let go." As he spoke he sat down so the pit's feet could rest on the floor there-by relieving the tortured hunk of flesh held viselike in the dog's jaws from the added burden of his weight.

Just as fast as it started it stopped. As JY's feet touched the floor he loosened his grip and dropped to his chest and began licking his master's hands as if nothing had happened. He truly loved Samson Hercules Duff!

Sam rolled his eyes at the affectionate dog and removed his shredded jacket and shirt to survey his bruised and punctured flesh which was beginning to bleed. Oh well, he thought, after what I've been through this is only a hangnail. A little peroxide and iodine and I'll be good as new. Turning to JY, Sam crinkled his nose. "Dam you dog, you stink worse than a dead skunk. I don't remember you being so stinky and soon as I tend to myself I'm going to bath you, maybe in lysol."

• • •

Gypsy Jack picked up the ringing phone. "Yeah," a pause.

"This is Jack, who'd you want? Joe Billie?" A longer pause. "Yeah, I'll give him a message. When I see him." Dropping the phone into its cradle, Gypsy Jack Pappadoupoulis moved his bulk through the narrow archway from the bar into a small room off the larger barroom. He was a huge man even though less than six feet tall, with coarse, coal black hair and prominent black bushy eyebrows framing dark, marble like eyes. He had the hands and forearms of a German butcher not to mention their legendary capacity for beer. Gypsy Jack drank a case of beer a day. His banana like fingers were adorned with rings, his swarthy neck encircled by uncountable strands of gold chain. At 45 years of age, 320 pounds, he was the master of intimidation and of himself. Even the big Indian sitting at the table waiting his return experienced twinges of insecurity in the Greek's presence, but it was only transient as Joe Billie Bloodtooth respected no man.

Easing into the beefed up chair, his deep, raspy voice growled. "Roscoe wants you to call 'em. Gotta gator call at that new subdivision north of town. Must be a mean one," he drawled, slowly fixing his eyes on the Indian and with a crooked smile, winked, causing his eyebrows to bounce.

"Well," Joe Billie chuckled, "That there didn't take long.

Guess that there gator kinda upset them lil' old ladies in white tennis shoes. Shore wouldn't wanna hand feed him any marshmallows. That there sucker was pissed after his little midnight ride in that there truck." Pausing, Joe Billie raised the beer to his mouth and inhaled its contents, waiting for the fat man to speak. He knew Jack had more on his mind than alligators.

Shifting in the chair the swarthy man began.

"Indian, I'm getting a little antsy 'bout what's been happening, 'specially 'bout that jerk we dusted a few months back. I hear he's alive and was hired by that group of cowboys to do vigilante work to stop the rustlin' going on 'round here. He got a friend and they supposed to be bad asses. What've you heard?"

Picking his teeth, Joe Billie allowed as how he hadn't heard much except some talk about the disappearance of a private investigator and how it was said that the man was at Joe Billie's place the night he vanished—which he knew to be true. Many a man had visited the Indian's home place on the last night of his life.

Changing the subject Joe Billie continued. "I know I gotta get them gator hides to the buyer. I sure got a pile of 'em and if you count that there other big 'un, I might just have too many…"

Jack interrupted. "Don't worry about too many, what we pay that guy he's gonna only report legitimate skins. All the rest go under the table. Those Europeans' buy every gator hide in Florida if they could."

"Well then Jack I ain't gonna worry 'bout no bad ass investigators then cause if they show up at my place they might just stay there permanent like." Narrowing his heavy eyelids the man's voice cut like a piece of glass. "Gators don't give a shit what they eats."

Gypsy Jack eyed the half-breed as he talked, wondering how he came to be so cold blooded. Even he didn't know Joe Billie's past and the taciturn Indian never talked of himself, period. They had an arrangement that seemed made in heaven, or hell, since their chance meeting some six years earlier. The cattle rustling came first then the gator deal followed by stealing heavy equipment and selling the hot machines in the north and west. Gypsy Jack's meat distributors sold custom cut meat to half the restaurants and hotels in south Florida at a whopping profit not to mention the gator meat and scads of hides sold to the European buyers compliments of Joe Billie's legitimate license as a gator hunter.

Joe Billie headed up the complaint department so complaints were rare—or short.

With their heavy cash flow more than a few people in high places were tempted, making the operation very difficult to control, a fact all too evident to the cattlemen led by Can Martin.

The fat man's ample girth shook with laughter as these thoughts ran through his head. "Yes sir, Joe Billie, we're gonna be a tough act to break up."

Chapter SIX

Dr. George Martinez quietly nursed the bar scotch swirling in the small water glass, his buzzing mind trying to sort out thoughts of Elise Jones, wife Jan, patient Duff and his career. His outward calm was patina and cheap scotch—cheap veneer. The isolated table overlooked the back parking yard and Elise had met the hassled surgeon here on many occasions. It was not the kind of place that attracted their peer group and they were, as far as they knew, not an item.

Glancing at his watch he began to drum his fingers on the table wondering how late Elise would be. She had always been punctual, appearing only minutes after his arrival. Dreading this particular rendezvous he had palpitations from the anticipation of her arrival but didn't know how to broach the subject of ending the affair. He had decided not to leave Jan about the time Sam Duff appeared at the hospital and it was partially due to his intense involvement with the battered man that he had delayed the Dear Jane missive.

George knew he would have to give up everything to be with Elise and he wasn't sure he could pay that price. He was tired after long days at the hospital and had precious little extra energy to fuel the fires of passion; he felt inadequate to continue the torrid pace their intimacy commanded. He truly reveled in the affair yet worried that it might consume him and everything he had accomplished these past years. On the other hand, the thought of not seeing the slim beauty caused him to wince and close his eyes. He imagined her sculpted face with the tiny cleft on the tip of her nose and a matching shadow of a cleft on her chin being so distinctive as to make her unforgettable. The surgeon had never seen a woman as singularly attractive as Elise and beads of sweat were showing on his forehead. God. He wished to be somewhere else.

A solid tap on his shoulder interrupted his catharsis. Startled, he slopped the scotch as he jerked his head around.

Gypsy Jack's dark eyes crinkled with mirth. "Take it easy, Doc, I'm not gonna bite ya. I just wanna give you a message. That sassy little piece you waitin' for ain't comin'. She just phoned and told me to tell you she can't make it today." The fat man chuckled. "Guess you don't get none today, huh Doc?"

George turned, slowly, until he was looking straight into the black marble eyes of the fat man. Though he knew who Jack was he had assiduously avoided contact with the man so to remain anonymous. A thin smile spread across his face as he realized the futility of that effort. He was aware of the man's reputation and knew he had to be careful playing this hand.

The surgeon formed his words carefully. "Who are you 'fella' and whom do you think I am?"

"Cut the crap Doc, uh, George. Dr. George Martinez I presume. And that was Elise on the phone. Elise Jones—remember? Read my lips 'cause she ain't comin'." George started to reply but was cut short. "And I know lots 'bout you two. Never know when something like that will come in handy. Who knows, Doc, I may need a vasectomy some day—free." Laughing, Gypsy Jack turned and walked to the door, ignoring the sweating surgeon.

Goddam it, George thought, what in hell do I do now. No telling what that fat ass wants.

He guessed Elise picked up on his mood and somehow divined his intentions. Now he really was in an awkward situation; he would have to see her at the hospital tomorrow.

Does she know? Who else, he wondered, has that Gypsy asshole told?

George downed the scotch in a single gulp as he pushed the chair back and hurried out. The hair on his flushed neck was standing but the Indian and the proprietor didn't seem to notice as they stared, knowingly, at the departing surgeon.

• • •

Samson and Skeets were sitting in Skeets' car in front of the cafe having finished a redneck country dinner called supper by the locals of pork chops, grits, red eye gravy, collard greens and homemade sour dough biscuits topped off by the best deep dish peach cobbler either had ever eaten.

"Damn Sam," Skeets volunteered, "few more meals like that and you'll be back to normal with some to spare."

Patting his stomach, he replied, "I can handle it old horse but I'll have to work more… speaking of which, what are your plans about this Gypsy Jack fellow?"

Concern skewed Skeets face. "Well, for one thing, Can Martin is pissed at us and I'm afraid he's going to do something on his own. I just hope we can put this deal to bed before a war breaks out. While you were on trauma duty I had Gypsy Jack and the Indian checked out and for sure they're unredeemable. Jack Pappadoupoulis has an interesting history but not near as sanguine as Bloodtooth. If they are in this together then we'll have to get both because stopping one won't stop the other plus Martin will need some proof and I'm not sure we can get what we need if we go by the book."

Samson chuckled. "Sure Skeets, we always go by the book. Hell… who's book? If you think the Greek is behind this shit then let's do it. Our way."

"We will, Horse, but carefully. I'm not sure who is involved but you can bet some high placed hombres are on payola and we for sure need to know who they are before we stir those coals."

Sam nodded in agreement.

Skeets went on. "So let's do some Sherlock Holmes-ing and I'll simmer Can Martin down and we can avoid a high noon. In the meantime I'll dig up the Greek's rap sheet and you sniff out the Indian's digs."

Sam interrupted abruptly. "Speaking of sniffing, Skeets, I've really got a problem with this nose of mine. Silly as it sounds I can smell food from the cafe as if I were sitting at the table eating. Hell, I can smell things I never knew had a smell! What the hell do you think really happened to me at that hospital? Tell you what, man, when this caper is over I'm going to have a long talk with one Dr. Martinez." Stopping abruptly Samson turned toward Tiny's café as he felt the faint breeze drift through the partially opened car window.

"There goes the nurse from the hospital." His voice dropping to a whisper. "See her? She's going into Tiny's."

Turning his head towards the cafe Skeets whispered, "Hey man, I see a nice looking brunette but I can't tell who it is. What makes you so sure it's Elise?"

A far away look clouded Sam's eyes. "I smell her."

• • •

Can Martin cursed silently as he sat in his 4x4 pickup staring into the darkness. His right hand opened and closed repeatedly on the stock of the semiautomatic shotgun leaning on the seat next to him. The luminous dial on his watch showed 11:30 and the moon wasn't due to rise until 1 am. He didn't want any slip-ups. He was fed up with losing cattle, repairing fences and having to be around some of the men he knew to be responsible, knowing they were laughing at him; indeed, at the entire Florida Cattleman's Association.

The fire of self-righteous independence burned brightly in Can Martin. His forebears were beholden to no one and if faced with his current problem, Can thought, would do as he was doing now. Eliminate the problem.

The army of mosquitoes trying to get through the windshield was a momentary distraction as he glanced at his watch and resumed his vigilance.

Can didn't expect to see headlights until the moon rose but he didn't want to chance missing the men should they decide to come early. His mind slipped back in time and as the seconds ticked away his thoughts skipped back to the meeting with Skeets Kirby shortly after Sam had been so brutally beaten. It was only due to the insistence of the other ranchers that Can had called in professionals to handle the rustling. He had wanted to summarily shoot every rustler, proven or suspected. In his mind they were all Indians anyway and that approach would stop the cattle thieving even if the guilty ones weren't caught. A few shot up putative Indian rustlers would be a powerful deterrent to others of the same persuasion.

Can Martin really didn't want to spend the money the two pros required. His holdings, though extensive, did not provide a predictable cash flow and his expenses had been considerable. He had bought new motorized equipment to facilitate his farming and ranching operation and damn if several pieces hadn't been stolen, leaving him embroiled in a stalemated hassle with his insurance company and the bank. Fortunately, he was chairman of the bank board but even he couldn't hold Federal bank examiners at bay forever—especially old Bob what's-his-name from Tampa. He hoped that zeros and decimals couldn't talk!

A sudden movement caused him to stiffen, his hand tightening on the gunstock. Barely moving, he rolled his eyes slightly and exhaled as a deer crossed the clearing heading toward the lake-like lagoon to his left. The lagoon was really the confluence of two creeks draining into a large swamp stretching for miles beyond the flatwoods lying north of the rancher's truck- an area of abundant wildlife.

The rancher's thoughts immediately returned to his dilemma.

He wasn't impressed with Kirby and Duff but had to admit they seemed capable and came highly recommended. Whether they could produce remained to be seen. Can chuckled as he thought about ending this matter without their help. It wasn't his fault one of them was beaten half to death and took months to recover. He wanted to fire them and demand their retainer back but the rest of the association disagreed. Oh well, he thought, he would take care of this and then he could wiggle out of paying the balance. On the other hand he could sure use the money. Maybe he could keep it and somehow bluff it out with them; after all, none of the other members knew anything about the principal players in this deal and didn't seem to care.

Can Martin's brain was kicking into overdrive and all sorts of possibilities began to formulate. First he had to get rid of one Joe Billie Bloodtooth. He had been told by one of his day hands that the big half-breed with the deaf hound was at the bottom of his problems and he was determined to control this destiny.

The luminous watch face glowed 12:45 and the rancher strained to see. If things went according to plan a truck carrying two men should be coming down the dirt ruts in about 20 or 30 minutes. Can bribed a day hand to tell Joe Billie about a huge gator and how it could be seen on the full moon. He had the man promise to meet the half-breed at moonrise this night and guide him to the beast. Martin knew that Joe Billie would probably have Jake White Raven with him but no matter because he, Can Martin, instead of the hand was going to meet the unsuspecting pair.

There was a large reptile in the lagoon although not an alligator. The property the rancher was on was protected parkland but most of the lagoon and swamp was on his property and was extremely isolated. If his mission was successful, human remains would never be found.

The native alligator was not the only reptile to increase in population since gator poaching had been curtailed some years before. The forgotten reptile, the Florida crocodile, also benefitted from this protection and had slowly, insidiously, increased in numbers without the fanfare accorded the alligator. Can had been aware of strange happenings at the lagoon and when his hands told him of missing cattle, drowned cattle, funny looking gators and such, he finally took time to check out the situation. With the aid of a zoologist friend, Can discovered a family of crocodiles living in the lagoon. Three mature individuals were identified along with one confirmed nest. Of the three, one was quite large, around 9 to 10 feet long and was thought to be a male. The zoologist surmised that the south end of the lagoon and the swamp contained more of the secretive creatures so his parting remark to the rancher was, "don't go near the water."

The rancher's thoughts vanished as faint bouncing lights appeared in the darkness. Like twin fireflies they flitted through the trees and bushes, noiselessly announcing the expected arrival. Can's hands trembled as he opened the truck door and slid out dragging the shotgun. The cooling night breeze made him realize he had been sweating and he wiped his forehead with the back of his hand. Bringing the hand to his mouth he tasted the bitter mosquito repellant he had applied earlier and wondered if the Indian would be able to smell him. He had heard old-timers talk of the Indians' ability to smell as if kin to a hound dog.

He crossed the small opening and quietly started down the trail leading to the big clearing about 50 yards from the lagoon— the appointed place. His grip of the shotgun caused his knuckles to blanch and a thought to flash through his mind. Why in mother hell was he, Can Martin, respected rancher, father, businessman, bedrock citizen, out in the middle of the night stalking one, maybe two, human beings with the premeditated intent to kill? Can Martin was not a man killer.

Not able to give up these thoughts, he replayed his step-by-step descent into this hellish situation. Was he displaying the same single-mindedness and toughness that characterized his noted forebears or was he a self-serving shadow of these time-magnified ancestors? What would his namesake, great Granddad Can Martin say? What's the difference, the sweating rancher rationalized, no one would know what he did tonight much less his illustrious ancestors. Can Martin stalked through the underbrush—to his destiny.

Joe Billie was always suspicious when approached by friends, of which he had precious few. He really trusted only Stump and then only when not within smelling distance of a bitch in heat.

Even though this deal seemed straightforward he couldn't help feel something was wrong. True, a lot of gators caught were the results of tips or comments by some pool player or local pulling on a longneck at Gypsy Jack's. Mostly, he was given directions but he couldn't recall ever having anyone guide him to a gator. Also true was the fact that this place was unfamiliar to the Indian, was on Federal parkland and may be a continuing source of alligators. Justified or not, Joe Billie Bloodtooth was uptight as he steered the truck through the woods, his eyes searching the enveloping darkness but seeing nothing. Since Jake White Raven was unusually quiet and since the big half-breed wasn't feeling garrulous, the pickup interior was silent as the surrounding woods.

The full moon was trying to do its thing but Joe Billie noticed the clouds flitting across its face creating eerie shadows on the sugar sand and surrounding foliage. He left the truck door open as he slid out and started toward the rear of the pickup to urinate. Jake had his back to Joe Billie and was, from the sound, already producing a healthy stream. The nervous half-breed glanced toward the sky. Gator moon, he thought, sending shivers through his muscular body. The ever-present flood of memories spilled from his shallow subconscious simultaneous with Stump's low warning growl. Instantly he dropped to the ground, barely avoiding the rapid twin blasts from Can's shotgun that cut the smaller Indian in half as he was zipping his pants. Scrambling around the truck, Joe Billie couldn't hear the merle hound's enraged snarl nor see him bound from the pickup into the teeth of the fiery display that had somehow threatened his master. With the intuition of a wild animal Joe Billie sensed the fate of his companion and knew it was meant for him. Reaching the front of the vehicle he regained his footing and sprinted towards the dense underbrush at the south side of the clearing. Can had cursed out loud as he saw the bigger man duck as he fired but saw that it wasn't wasted as Jake White Raven collapsed. Still cursing loudly, the rancher started to the truck now visible as the clouds uncovered the face of the moon.

The surprise and ferocity of Stump's attack spun the cattleman around, almost knocking him down. He felt a searing pain in his right thigh as the powerful jaws tightened. Realizing what was happening the dog-caught man tried to beat the beast with the gun barrel but only succeeded in making him tighten his hold. Unable to run with this appendage, Can pointed the shotgun barrel at what he thought was the dog and pulled the trigger. He wasn't quite prepared for the ungodly pain that accompanies a shotgun blast of 00 buckshot into one's lower leg. The rancher crumpled, loud moans replacing the cursing. Stump, oblivious to the gun blast, felt surrender and in a flash was off to find his master.

Running through the trees and bushes posed no significant problem to Joe Billie. It only took seconds for him to reach the edge of the lagoon and scant seconds more to wade out and silently breaststroke towards the shadowy center of the confluence. He could see vegetation about 50 yards out and knew no one could find him if he made it that far. He couldn't know that he was already found—not by human eyes. Hearing the third shot caused the swimming man to face in the direction of the commotion. Keeping his head barely above water he strained to see through the cloudy night, simultaneously removing his water filled boots. Faintly, then more clearly, he heard something running, instinctively knowing it was too rapid to be a man. The slow, deliberate movement in the lily pads behind him escaped his notice as a large spear-shaped head slowly aimed at the waterlogged Indian. But Joe Billie was no ordinary man and as the crocodile cleared the edge of the pads, the hair on his neck stood up causing him to turn and face off with this new menace. Joe Billie's first impression was one of just another day at the woodpile until the lagoon suddenly lit up. The full moon was shining in all its glory as it dawned on the man that the huge reptile facing him wasn't a gator but, by God, a crocodile. He had to act fast as even Bloodtooth wasn't a match for that model eating machine. Quickly deciding to take his chances on land he turned and headed for shore. A glance confirmed that the running noise had been Stump who was pacing back and forth at the water's edge, snarling, always eyeing his master.

Joe Billie lengthened his stroke trying to remain calm yet wanted desperately to break into a freestyle and get the hell out of the water. He resisted this as he knew the croc would try to slip quietly up to him before grabbing, but if he panicked, the beast would abandon stealth and attack full throttle. A sideways glance told him he was losing, but it was a look shoreward that turned his blood to ice water. Stump had seen the crocodile and though hating the big reptiles, feared nothing and sensed a threat to his master. A piercing growl left his throat as he plunged into the water. Instantly the croc changed direction, the tapered snout locked on the swimming dog. Stump, loyal Stump, was flat out in the water with his powerful shoulders pumping like an oversized otter, blood smeared lips raised in a malevolent grin and ears flat to his head.

The bottom fell out of Joe Billie's stomach. "Stop," he screamed, "Stop! Go back! Go back! Stop!" Useless words. Jabber.

Desperately the stricken man groped for his whistle, the only way to stop the deaf hound. Unable to force his big hand into the pocket of wet wranglers he rolled and thrashed in the water, uncaring seconds ticking away. Stump and the croc were locked in and Bloodtooth was powerless. They came together within 20 feet of the half-breed, the dog not slackening. The croc lunged and snapped in one motion, causing the water to explode into grotesque froth. The awestruck Indian seemed unable to comprehend the simple majesty of this happening—watching as if hypnotized. Suddenly the surface was quiet—the combatants gone—the fading ripples breaking past the man's body just to taunt him. Then, suddenly, the water roiled and Stump shot to the surface not 30 feet from the engaged Indian. Behind came the terrible snout of the croc. In all his years Joe Billie had never seen a gator give up a hold on anything caught in the water... no less the crocodile. His brief surprise quickly drowned as the beast grabbed the dog. He could not comprehend the effort it took for the valiant hound to free himself from the croc's grip while underwater. Damn me! Damn me! Joe Billie screamed and started to the dog as fast as wet clothes permitted. Stump swam a small circle and in a flash was back on the croc. The realization hit the struggling man like a thunderclap—Stump wasn't trying to escape. He was out to kill. Kill the croc! The crocodile lunged out of the water, fell back on top of the snapping hound and caught him by the chest. The water quieted and the unfeeling beast sank beneath the bloody surface. Joe Billie saw his indomitable Stump locked in the croc's deadly maw, still tearing at its face. Tears flowed from Indian eyes. The surface of the lagoon was returned mirror-like with only a thread-line of bubbles marring its polished surface. Slowly. Inexorably. Toward the lily pads.

Crying freely, Joe Billie crawled through the grass and mud onto the bank of the lagoon, previous danger forgotten. His shallow subconscious flashed to his childhood and graphically displayed, over and over, the grotesque scene of his slaughtered loved ones.

So, slowly, the shivering man rose to full height. The copious tears streaming down his face stopped as if by command. Tearing into his wet pocket he extracted the brass whistle, turned to the lagoon and with a terrible, primitive scream threw the tiny object as far as he could. Silently he watched until he saw the splash and the tiny, almost perfect ripples form and try valiantly to reach the bank knowing they would fade long before that goal was reached.

The water would prevail and its surface deny the existence of man, of crocodile, of whistle, of ripples—of dog.

Joe Billie Bloodtooth turned and started to his pickup—again, once and forever, the hunter.

Chapter **SEVEN**

It was 2:30 am and the red Mercedes-Benz 560 SL was parked two blocks from Centra County Hospital under a huge live oak overlooking a pond. Faint sounds of classical music emanated from the vehicle, occasionally giving way to muffled sounds of conversation. Inside the car the soft background music belied the tension building between the two occupants.

"Why didn't you meet me last night?" George Martinez choked the steering wheel as he posed the question. "The least you could have done would have been to ask to speak to me. Not have that fat ass barkeep give me the message."

"Darling, I told you earlier I didn't tell him to give you any message. When I asked to speak to you he said okay and was gone for a few minutes, came back on the phone and said you were talking to a patient and for me to give him any message. I swear, George, I never intended to not talk to you. Please believe me." Elise's face was turned away from the surgeon's gaze but he saw the quiver start in her lower lip and chin. When upset, her chin quivered giving her face a pouty look. Irresistible.

"Whatever, babe. Now Gypsy Jack and God knows who else knows about us. You know damn well we can't afford publicity. It would ruin me and there's no way I could leave Jan under those circumstances. I can't chance losing everything I have."

"George," Elise interrupted, "I don't care what you have. I just want to be with you, to love you and be your wife."

George put his hand under her chin and gently turned the sculpted face. "I've told you many times that if I lose what I have I don't intend to start over. I just don't have the drive anymore. I wouldn't feel worthy of you. Listen babe, you're a package, a total package and if I lose everything in a messy divorce I'm bye- bye, adios, gone… Alone."

The quiver of her chin gave way to soft choking sobs as tears moistened her uplifted face. Instead of a reply George cleared his throat and tightened his grip on the steering wheel. He wanted to take her slim body in his arms more than ever but knew he shouldn't.

"Wh-what will I do?" Elise was sobbing openly. "I love you George. I've given up everything for you. I've never loved a man like I love you." Her voice tailed into tiny sputtering sobs.

The surgeon knew he was in trouble and if something didn't happen he would throw his arms around her and that would be that. He couldn't resist her. Her femininity and surrender to him was an aphrodisiac too powerful to resist. Dear God, he thought, if I were younger, or not so deep in debt, or, or, or… The sudden beep of the cellular phone reoriented the Doctor.

"Dr. Martinez here." His monotone belied his emotional catharsis. "Repeat? Can Martin's in emergency? Gunshot? I'll be there in a jiffy."

Silent now, he backed the Mercedes onto the hard road and gunned the racy machine toward the hospital. Elise's quiet sobbing stopped as she sat next to the man she loved—in abject surrender—the hard fact of George's intent bearing down on her psyche like a runaway truck..

When George examined the rancher's leg he could only whistle. He knew Martin well enough but had never developed a liking for him. Can Martin seemed detached, holier than thou and always condescending in his attitude and conversations with the surgeon. But, dislikes aside, his leg was a fully funded mess and George Martinez was a surgeon.

A deputy sheriff, around 2:00 am, had found Martin slumped over the steering wheel of his truck which was stopped in the middle of the main road into Centra. He was still unconscious when wheeled into the operating room. Four hours later, a tired George Martinez walked into the waiting room. The sun was just up and to his surprise Elise was there standing next to his patient, Sam Duff, with Skeets Kirby behind them talking in quiet tones to the deputy who found the wounded rancher.

"Hi Doc," came the cheerful greeting as Sam Duff stepped toward the surgeon. "How'd it go? You think he'll be okay?"

As Sam fired the questions, Elise turned away, avoiding George's inquisitive glance as she moved slowly toward the other men.

"Slow down big guy. Let's get me a cup of coffee before this third degree." Inwardly he was curious as to why Elise was here since she headed for her car as soon as he stopped in front of the emergency room. Also, he thought, how did Sam and his partner find out and why were they here? A twinge of resentment crept over him as he thought of the pretty nurse and Samson Duff. Was he why she was here? He was, after all, a virile, attractive man. "Okay, shoot, but I know my rights and I don't have to answer any questions without my attorney present, but I waive that right and swear to tell the truth, the whole truth and nothing but the truth."

George's feeble attempt at humor caused a momentary blank look in Duff's eyes but he quickly recovered. "Hey Doc, nothing official. We just happen to know this fella' and are concerned about him, that's all." The big man lied.

Skeets appeared and continued the fabrication. "Yeah Doc, Can Martin has been our best friend since we came here. I knew him from before. What happened?"

"How would I know?" shot back the agitated surgeon. "All I know is that he has a horrible wound to his left calf and foot and I'll be lucky to save it provided he survives the blood loss and shock. You should know what happened. You were the one talking to the deputy." Directing his gaze at Kirby, he continued. "You tell me what happened."

"Well, I did talk to the deputy." Skeets' reply was slow and deliberate. "He told me that he found Martin slumped over the wheel of his pickup, out of his head and mumbling something about dogs or a dog."

Martinez interrupted. "That's interesting, because he has deep puncture wounds on his right thigh and they sure looked like bite wounds. Possibly dog bites....but they were nothing compared to his calf muscle"

"Excuse me Doctor." The O.R. nurse had been waiting to speak and seeing no entry into the conversation, interrupted. "But we still can't reach Ms. Martin. Apparently she and the kids are out of town. We don't want to call his mother because she is old and not well. What shall we do?"

"Nothing," snapped the surgeon. "Call the sheriff and let him get in touch with Martin's wife. He'll know where to reach her and it's his job anyway." With that he visually dismissed the woman and turned back to the two men. Casually glancing around the room he noticed that Elise was gone.

"Anyway," Skeets was still talking, "Can's shotgun was in the truck covered with sand and blood and had recently been fired—according to the deputy. But we really can't be sure. Anyway, the authorities are doing blood tests to see if all the blood belongs to Martin."

"Is that it?" The doctor's query had a hollow ring. 'Fraid so," interjected Sam, "until Martin himself can fill us in on what happened."

"How long Doc?" countered Skeets.

"I really have no idea." The words carried a certain heaviness reminding the two interrogators that George Martinez was a tired man. "If he lives, maybe a day or two."

"Okay Doc, we'll stop," Sam volunteered. "And by the way, I need to talk to you about my nose ..." But the surgeon was almost to the door.

• • •

Joe Billie Bloodtooth studied the moonlit clearing through the eye of the predator. He heard the truck leave seconds before reaching the edge of the ominous patch of sugar sand and sensing no danger, glided to his truck, removed the .356 Marlin and jacked a shell into the chamber – the metallic sound a soothing balm to his raging mind.

Jake White Raven was dead, never knowing what hit him.

Reading sign as if in bold type, the big Indian followed Can's blood trail to where his truck had been parked. Only one man, he thought, as he carefully studied the sign. Rubbing the gator tooth amulet, the muscular man squeezed his eyelids—one man took form in his obsessed mind.

Back at his truck he dragged Jake's stiffening body to the lagoon and left it in the shallow water. Returning, he quickly erased all signs of the incident including Can Martin's bloody trail. Slowly driving out he was overcome by his burgeoning grief for Stump… the last expression of emotion from Joe Billie Bloodtooth.

• • •

Can Martin's eyes scrunched with pain as he tried to shift his body. His heavily bandaged leg hung grotesquely from the Rube Goldberg arrangement of cables and pulleys. This was the third day since his accident and the infusions of pain killing narcotics were only now being changed to a PRN basis. Wanting a clear mind, the anxious rancher had purposefully not asked for a fix so to clearly lab-test his predicament. This assessment caused sweat to form on his face as his mind, with deafening impact told him he had screwed up. Royally! The bloody scenario flashed through his mind on a circular tape with each replay reinforcing Can's deduction that his only connection to the incident was Wishy Wishart, the day hand bribed to tell Joe Billie about the gator. His flashbacks also assured him that the Indian he shot was a dead one. He could still see the man's body illuminated by the muzzle blast explode. Also, the sheriff had his shotgun so that would be no problem. That left only the day hand.

Wishy was from Ocala and Can knew he was heading there after his work at Martin's ranch. Hopefully he had left the day of the incident, or worse case, the next day. In any event the rancher knew he had to find out and not attract attention; it wasn't going to be easy. He shuddered as he thought of Joe Billie Bloodtooth finding out who bushwhacked him.

● ● ●

Samson Duff downshifted the four-speed 4x4 to second gear as the narrow, potholed blacktop rudely turned into two dirt ruts. He figured he had 2-3 miles to reach Joe Billie's home-place. He wasn't totally sure of his destination but had to chance it. He chuckled as he recalled the trouble they had getting information on the big guy's domicile. They just couldn't ask anyone in Centra for fear of a leak to either Gypsy Jack or Joe Billie himself. There was no telling how many of Centra's citizens were involved in the suspect activities. What a stroke that Skeets had a friend in the postal service enabling him to obtain a list of mailing addresses for all Indians in south Centra county including the general area of Joe Billie's home-place. He also got a description and license number for the half-breed's pickup truck.

Glancing at the silent man sitting next to the window, Sam spoke as if his thoughts had been heard. "Well pal, with a little more luck the big bad Indian will be off hunting or stealing and I can get my work done without a hassle."

At his master's voice, the lithe, muscular dog sitting between the two men turned.

"Yea, old sport," continued Sam, "maybe we can get this little caper put to bed without either one of us breaking wind."

It was a moonless night and Samson knew he couldn't see well enough to drive without lights. Thinking traffic on this road to be minimal he decided to chance it, use the headlights and hope that nobody was out and about. The map showed the half-breed's property to be on Indian land, adjacent to a large ranch owned by one Gypsy Jack Pappadoupoulis.

Sneaking up on a sharp turn Sam stopped the vehicle, turned off the lights and got out. He guessed the place he was seeking was within a mile and didn't want to drive closer. Turning to Skeets he spoke in low tones. "Give me 4 hours and meet me here. If anything goes wrong, I'll walk out so don't take any chances, especially if you think you've been made or if there is traffic when you come back. JY and I will be okay even if we have to hoof it. If he's home, we'll wait. If he stays home, we'll just meet you here and come back later....take care."

Darkness ate man and dog as the pickup's taillights faded. In full camo outfit and face paint, Samson Duff was all but invisible as he silently picked his way through the weeds paralleling the dirt ruts; JY—a shadow.

The damp night air provided little comfort and Sam had only covered a few hundred yards before his perspiration soaked clothes stuck to him like hot grits . Though dark, the quiet man had little trouble staying parallel to the ruts, occasionally detouring around a ditch or pond. About a mile from the drop off Sam saw a dim light to his left and felt a slight breeze as he turned towards it. The main ruts turned north along a fence line so the light must be the end of the road going south and had to be Joe Billie's place. As the breeze danced around the cautious man he sensed a strange, new, sensation. His sense of smell told him there were dogs plus something different—putrid—ominous. Though all the vapors had been more noticeable and confusing, these peculiar ones caused the hair on the back of his neck to stand.

Glancing at the Junk Yard dog, Sam took note of his stilted walk. His trimmed ears were drawn straight over his head causing large creases in his forehead, narrowing the demon like eyes... possessed by no other animal. JY was wound tight as a spring and God help whatever set him off. Sam fingered the handle of the knife belted to his left hip. Custom made by a Japanese master, its multilayered 6-inch blade could quarter a bowling ball and still shave a man's arm. Planning no confrontation, he carried no firearm. Stealth and secrecy were the essential ingredients of this operation and carrying a weapon was a temptation even the disciplined Samson Hercules Duff had to avoid.

Scenting that the yard dogs hadn't moved he approached a rusty wire fence enclosing a small yard, a dilapidated frame house sitting almost in the middle of the enclosure. A porch light, naked, glimmered bravely from the open front of the shack illuminating several rusted out truck bodies in its dim circle of light. There were no vehicles and no light in the shack. Sam could see the outline of several more structures behind the frame house and all were dark. Deliberately sniffing the still night air, he sensed no smells save the ones the earlier breezes had tattled on.

Still cautious but somewhat relieved the silent man eased up to the porch, JY at his heels. The tattered screen door was slightly ajar and a quick search uncovered no security devices; in fact, the demeanor of the place was totally intimidating as if no one would dare trespass—or the owner just didn't give a shit. Slowly opening the screen door, Sam became aware of danger. Simultaneously, a low growl came from behind the shack. Letting go the door Sam turned toward the side of the porch but JY was already there, tail rigid, tensed body reflecting the light rays as if from polished marble.

The huge, rawboned hound never knew what hit him. As he rounded the shack and started to climb the porch the pit bull grabbed him by the throat and the only evidence of a struggle was a subdued gurgling noise as the hound was quickly suffocated; his thrashing body rigidly anchored by the muscular JY, the sand effectively muffling the sounds of the twitching carcass. Sam smelled the second dog as it rounded the front of the porch totally ignoring the man, intent only on the two animals locked in the death struggle with a quizzical, menacing growl the only announcement of his arrival. Magically Sam produced a thin plastic cord with a one-way slipknot. As the hound turned the corner of the porch the agile man deftly slipped the noose over the creature's head, simultaneously pulling the slack and looping the free end around the porch support post. Pulling the noosed head tight to the post he avoided the splashing urine and thrashing body as the hung dog unwillingly expired.

Smelling no more dogs Sam cut the cord and turned to get JY off the other hound. It had taken years of training to get the big pit to give up a hold. It didn't matter to him that his adversary was dead and even with this training it was still difficult and even iffy getting him to let go.

Inside the shack Sam quickly moved through the rooms, not looking for anything in particular. The main room was sparsely furnished with a color TV and a large couch. Animal skins were scattered over the floor and on chair backs. An ancient metal wood burning stove stood patiently against the wall waiting for cold weather so it could devour the stack of wood piled next to it. In front of the couch spread the largest alligator hide Samson Duff had ever seen. Even JY paused to sniff its seemingly endless length. A few snapshots, some in frames, some not, were scattered around the room. Some were on shelves and some on a table along with several empty or partially filled booze bottles. One picture looked fairly recent and was a pretty Indian girl holding a merle colored bulldog-looking pup. Probably a girlfriend, thought the curious man as he rapidly viewed the other pictures. No papers or officious looking journals were seen as he entered the only bedroom. To his surprise he found a neat antique glass fronted bookcase filled with books. Titles like; KENDO, MUSASHI, JAPANESE MARTIAL ARTS, BOOK OF FIVE RINGS. All jumped out at him. Bad boy Billie was apparently a well read Indian, especially along certain lines. Sam wondered what kind of man this dangerous half-breed really was?

The bed was unmade and large. Hung over the headboard was a large portrait of two Indians. One an old white-haired man, the other a youngish attractive woman. The frame was ornate and obviously expensive with old-fashioned bubble glass facing. Of all the objects in the room this picture was not dusty, the glass facing was clean and no cobwebs adorned its frame. This picture apparently meant a lot to Joe Billie. No hiding places were evident and the Spartan bathroom yielded no information to the silent inquisitor.

Leaving the shack Sam and the pit bull slipped towards the closer of the two outbuildings. Shining the flashlight around the back perimeter he illuminated a chain link enclosure with all visible gates padlocked and nothing in the yards. Probably for hunting dogs, Sam mused and empty, so he's probably in the woods. The thought of being caught on the Indian's home place sent a sliver of concern through him and he quickened his pace, clucking to JY. Unlike the fence around the shack this one was formidable; 4 feet of non-climb wire topped by 3 strands of razor wire and locked. It only took a few minutes for Sam to pick the heavy padlock and only seconds to reach the door to the building.

The solid door was unlocked and Sam felt a pang of urgency as he slipped through the doorway into a large room. Shining the flashlight around he found himself in a single room with a half wall partition. One side had a varied selection of barbells and benches, various loose weights and assorted strength devices. So the Bad Buck was into training. This was more impressive than the bedroom. The other half was some sort of workroom with large tables and water hoses scattered around. A floor drain was obvious, as were various and sundry knives scattered on the tables. Dark stains covered most of the cement floor and some parts of the tables. Fastened to a beam across one wall was a selection of hooks—meat hooks, Sam surmised. Bloodtooth apparently used this room for his alligator butchering and from the looks it was a busy place. Glancing at his watch he let go a low whistle. "Come on dog breath, only 90 minutes left and we sure as hell don't want to miss the bus."

Cocking his head at the words, JY trotted after his man. Quickly skirting the first building the pair headed for the second structure about 100 yards away. The putrid odor was getting stronger, in fact, overpowering to the sweating man. Stopping, he tied his handkerchief around his face and nose hoping to deter the penetrating stink. As the masked man started to the building, JY voiced a warning growl causing Sam to instantly stop and squint into the inky blackness to locate the unsettled dog. Knowing time was limited, Sam switched on the flashlight and froze as the beam picked up JY standing face to face with the biggest live alligator Sam Duff had ever seen! Beyond was a dark pond, its surface resplendent with red orbs shining like Christmas decorations in the beam's reflection. Sweat poured into the kerchief. Giving a low command to the fired up canine Sam backed slowly away from the huge reptile. He gave the command again and reluctantly the feisty dog turned in retreat. Once out of danger Sam slipped the plastic cord through the pit's collar, not quite ready for another such surprise.

Shaking, Sam stood to his full height and shined the light in a big circle. The entire area was nothing but ponds and alligators. No place to be tripping the light fantastic—in the dark and with a dog.

The sobering experience reminded the man of the dead dogs at the shack and he sure didn't want Joe Billie finding those beauties. Trotting back to the big gate he tied JY to the fence, gave the stay command and hurriedly retrieved the carcasses. Dragging them to the first gator pond he quickly pushed them to the water's edge, hearing movement in the water even as he did. Turning rapidly to get away he stumbled but landed on his hands and knees. In his hurry to back away from the dead dogs he touched a soft, tube like object. Redirecting the flashlight he gasped as the beam displayed a human arm, entire from shoulder to fingertips. Duff's heart was beating so hard he could hear it. An experienced glance told him that the grisly find had only recently been relocated. Traumatically! Hearing JY whimper, Sam looked up and the paired lights bouncing across the pasture to the south deepened his sense of urgency. Whipping out his knife he deftly severed the hand at the wrist, threw the remains into the pond, wrapped it in his face kerchief and stuffed the gory bundle into one of the large pockets on the leg of his camo pants.

Rapidly retracing his steps, he loosened the complaining JY and locked the gate. Silently the pair moved through to the north and melted into the trees. Sam watched as the truck neared the area. Since it was coming through a pasture he figured it to be the Indian back from hunting, tired, maybe a little in the bottle and with luck wouldn't notice anything until morning. A glance at his watch told him he had 10 minutes to get to the pickup place. Time to get it in gear.

● ● ●

Tiny's cafe was not crowded and the usual tasty food had relaxed Skeets Kirby and Samson Duff almost to the point of nirvana.

"How's about more coffee, Skeeter?" Sam was poking at his partner.

"Either that or a jump start, Samson. I'm about half asleep."

The evening meal had been the culmination of a serious discussion concerning the increasing complexity of the case. It had been two weeks since Can Martin's accident and four days since Samson's surveillance of Bloodtooth's place. Can was recovering rapidly but wouldn't talk. His story was always the same and just didn't add up—he was leaving something out.

Aware of these concerns, Skeets recalled their earlier conversation to make sure nothing was being overlooked. "Sam, looks like we're going to have to take a look at the Greek's digs, 'though it won't be easy."

"You're right about that," Sam interrupted "and if the badass Injun found any trace of my doings from the other night I'm sure the fat man will be on guard. I tried to be neat and tidy but he's sure to question why the two hounds suddenly decided to pick the lock on that gate and go for a dip in the gator pond. Also, pardner, he'll be able to read the sign Junk Yard and I left whilst tiptoeing thru his tulips in the pitch ass dark. Plus, we really don't know just how sharp this guy is but I guess a 9 or 10. I know for sure I don't want to underestimate him."

Skeets dittoed. "True and on top of it all I just don't trust the rancher. Even though he hired us, his actions since you were banged up just don't add up to trust. By the way old horse, I ran into your doctor friend, Martinez, this morning and he seemed a mite upset. We started on some small talk and guess what? Can Martin went home, insisted on it and hired your Florence Nightingale for his private duty, live in nurse. Seems as how Mr. and Ms. at the ranch aren't exactly lovey-dovey and he apparently pays good. Anyhow, the good Dr. M. wasn't very happy about it…"

"You know why, don't you?" interjected his partner. "The hospital grapevine had it that the Doc and the nurse had something going. He may just be jealous."

"Well Sam, we need to see Can again anyway so maybe next week when he can't play hurt as much we can get down to some sure enough serious Q and A. I feel he has a lot more to tell us."

"Also," Sam added, "we should have a rundown on the prints from the finger I found. Find out what he did for a living and what he was doing that pissed Joe Billie off. What was his name again?"

"Wishart, Charles Zachary Wishart, a.k.a. Wishy."

• • •

Chapter EIGHT

The Martin ranch was 20 miles southeast of Tiny's cafe as the crow flies. Can Martin's great grandparents had been among the first settlers in what is now Centra County and the ranch had changed little in the intervening years. The contemporary ranch house stood within yards of the original cabin and sported most of the modern conveniences. Can's wife, Marti, was not local bred, making her acceptance by the cracker blue bloods impossible. Coupled with the love and passion of a fledgling union, this meant little to the aggressively amorous Can but as time passed and the marital privilege became too familiar, as passions aged and grayed, the rift between Marti and the locals widened to a chasm and became a millstone necklace to the rancher.

Marti's propensity for lubricity gradually gave way to spiteful maliciousness and Can was left seeking female favors elsewhere; there was no sweet talking the domineering Marti Alice Martin, so Can's tomcatting was soon of legendary excess and Marti's presence at home a convenience effecting the appearance of a solid rural American marriage. Their children, two girls, were totally devoted to Marti and the rancher's paternal instincts had long since been blunted by the total female presence. He paid the bills, asked no questions and would sooner submit to castration than leave a toilet seat in the upright position; he frequently caught himself lowering the seats in the men's restrooms, a realization that left him mumbling and red faced.

It was no surprise to him that Marti and the girls split after his accident with the excuse of an extended visit to her home state of New Jersey; Can knew the union was history.

He had tried to contact Wishy Wishart. His apprehension continued to grow but with each passing day the ranch hand's absence became a favorable rationalization and Can Martin gradually relaxed. His attempts to find out about Joe Billie Bloodtooth were also unsuccessful. None of his contacts could remember even seeing the big Indian lately. Again, rationalization came to the injured man's rescue; maybe Bloodtooth was dead. Maybe he drowned that night as Can knew he had to use the lagoon in any escape effort. What about the crocodiles? Can smiled. Hell, maybe everything had worked out in spite of the screw up. He felt better.

He also felt good about his new nurse. What a dish! He remembered when he told George Martinez he wanted to go home and that he would have excellent care so the good Doctor needn't worry. When told who was to provide this excellent care, Martinez suddenly seemed reluctant to sign him out but Can was insistent so he was going home today with Elise Jones as full time nurse.

The rancher's leg was healing without complications, another testament to the consummate skill of George Martinez, MD, PhD. He could manage on crutches and he believed he would regain full use of the leg.

Thinking of Elise caused him to remember his last conversation with Kirby and Duff, in her presence. He thought he noticed tension between Duff and the beauteous nurse. Could they have something going? A twinge of envy shot through his body but quickly passed as he recalled their discussion. He had made it clear he was disappointed in their lack of progress and he was going to do his best to get the cattlemen to abort the mission and give a refund. Also, what happened to him was strictly an accident caused by a dog and no more, thank you! From the way the two took it, Can figured he had overestimated them. All the better, he thought. I shouldn't have any trouble getting the money from those two candy asses. He also didn't think it would be too difficult getting the cattlemen to agree and since they didn't know Kirby and Duff, there was a good chance they could be blamed if any thing surfaced about Joe Billie Bloodtooth or Jake White Raven.

Indeed, things were looking up for Can Martin.

• • •

Gypsy Jack squinted into the sun as he turned the Lincoln town car into the yard at Bloodtooth's shack. Even with the air conditioner on 'Eskimo,' rivulets of greasy sweat trickled down his furrowed face. His jet black hair glistened as the droplets worked their way through thick bushy eyebrows into his eyes triggering a wipe with the back of his banana fingered hand. Avoiding the sandier places he guided the low slung vehicle into the only shaded area and began to extract his bulk from the car.

He seldom visited the moody Miccosukee but it was more than two weeks since he had seen him and he knew the guy wasn't on a trip. Joe Billie never left town without the Greek's knowledge. Also, he had not seen Jake White Raven and usually where Bloodtooth was the small, feisty Indian wasn't far away. Jack and Joe Billie had business that needed attention and if something was wrong Gypsy Jack needed to know, pronto.

Trudging through the sand to the porch he noticed the Indian's pickup but no dogs. Usually there were two yard dogs and since Joe Billie was home Stump should be burrowed in the sand under the porch savoring the coolness. The fat man stopped and looked carefully for the merle colored hound as he for sure didn't want to stumble over the deaf Stump and risk some serious dog doings. It had happened before.

Something was wrong. Jack didn't know what but he felt it and the feeling wasn't good.

The screen door was partially open and Jack knocked sharply on the thin wall.

"Who you want?" came a languid reply. "You, Indian," echoed the Greek. "That you Gypsy man?"

"Yea."

"Come on in." Joe Billie appeared at the door with the words, indicating with a sweep of his arm for the sweaty man to enter. His appearance was of a board certified wino; clothes disheveled, unshaven, long hair plastered to his head and slightly unsteady on his feet.

Pappadoupoulis' narrowed his obsidian eyes and looked around the room. He had seen the half-breed drunk many times and knew the man's propensity for John Barlycorn but this episode had a different echo. Something was wrong—big time.

"Wanna drink?" Joe Billie gestured with the bottle of Jack Daniels as he chewed on the slurred words.

"Naw—I wanna know where you 'bin."

"No where. Here and there, mostly roun' here." Pulling a swig the tipsy half-breed lurched to the couch and sat.

The perturbed Greek followed, lowering his bulk into the over-sized chair next to the couch. "Where your dogs?"

"Dead."

"Dead? What the hell you mean dead? Where's Stump?" The fat man's eyes were now slits searching the room. The place was a mess.

Slowly taking it all in, his eyes stopped at the table.

There laid a costume, or garment, displaying colors such as the Greek had never seen. They appeared to be neatly arranged and clean. Jack could make out patterns of delicate beadwork and braiding. The main garment appeared to be a multi-colored knee length dress. Next to it were knee length buckskin moccasins textured as soft as fine suede. Stretched across the dress lay a similar buckskin belt, a colorful sash and a turban adorned by 5 magnificent bird plumes. The Gypsy Man had never seen anything like this. Also on the table were two pictures; Lily Turtle holding a puppy and a portrait of an old white-haired Indian with a young, handsome Indian woman beside him.

"Stump's dead." Quietly uttered, the besotted man's proclamation echoed around the room causing Jack's head to snap forward.

"Whadda you mean?"

"Stump dead, Goddamit, you deaf? I didn't know you deaf." Jack's face puffed up. "I'm not deaf 'n you know it. Now quit this bullshit and tell me what happened." He knew he shouldn't push the tipsy man too far but he was upset and needed to know the problem. "If Stump's dead then I wanna know what happened and by God you're gonna tell me....now!"

A malevolent look flashed the Indian's eyes but faded to a stare of infinite emptiness. The Greek's mouth was dry as his hand sought the .22 cal. magnum derringer in his hip pocket. He knew too well Bloodtooth's reputation of unpredictable volatility and his impersonal application of it.

Slowly Joe Billie lowered the Jack bottle and the antsy Greek relaxed a notch as he saw shoulders sag and his face relax. The Gypsy man had not seen this attitude before, increasing his curiosity.

"You wanna know about that there shit-eater..." Dead. The grieving, liquored up Miccosukee told his partner the entire story, including finding and questioning Wishy Wishart.

Though Bloodtooth's attachment to his dead hound had been real, the stoic Greek couldn't help feel that his partner's melancholy was overplayed or the product of something even more tragic yet unspoken. Rancher Martin's involvement really bothered the fat man. It was one thing to kill an itinerant ranch hand, but quite a different matter to knock off a man of Martin's stature.

"So what're you gonna do?" Gypsy Jack squeezed the words through clenched teeth. This drunk bastard seemed intent on bringing down the temple and wanted Jack Pappadoupoulis to position his hands on the pillars.

The Indian's reply sent shivers through the fat man.

"I'm goin' a kill that there son a bitch—slow like. He'll be mostly well soon and then he has one last appointment... With me, Stump an' hell!" His sagging face seemed chipped from old concrete, its taut mouth no longer slurping words. Joe Billie

Bloodtooth appeared stone cold sober and Can Martin a marked man.

"Listen Indian, we need to talk. You don't need to do that. You'll ruin everything if you take out that rancher. Let's talk." Outwardly the Greek was low key but his guts were churning. Some of the high placed people on the fat man's payola were close friends of Martin and would not take kindly to his other than natural demise. Bloodtooth didn't know because it was better business to keep him out of that kettle of fish; after all, Joe Billie did his thing more for spite or fun than financial gain—so the Greek thought. He just couldn't comprehend why the son of a bitch would blow everything over a Goddam dog. A deaf one at that!

"Talk all ya' want Gypsy man, but that there turd-rancher is dead." At Joe Billie's words the shivers started again.

Pappadoupoulis' mind was spinning. What to do now, he thought, change the subject, leave, or kill him. All three were probably indicated but Jack knew he couldn't kill the man without undue risk to himself. He needed time. Time to think and maybe talk Bloodtooth out of his plan.

"What's that on the table, Indian?" Jack's voice was lower, almost a hoarse whisper as he pointed to the table supporting the clothes. Maybe a change of pace would be helpful.

The Miccosukee's eyes darted to the questioner. "Come... Look."

Jack followed the unsteady man to the table and watched as he held the dress-like part to his shoulders. Even though it looked a tad too small it appeared as if it would fit the broad shouldered half-breed.

"Beautiful." exclaimed the fat man. "What is it?"

"Warrior dress of my grandfather. He was a great Miccosukee war chief. I got this here after he was killed by my father, no good son a' bitch." Bloodtooth's voice faltered at the mention of his grandfather but did not break. The Indian's face was dry but Jack could feel the intense emotion radiating from his stoic features. "This too," he went on, producing an ornate war club from under the table.

Goddam, Jack thought, this guy's losing it. He fingered the derringer.

The war club was covered with dark stains. "Look Indian, I'm going back to the place so why don't you sleep this off, clean up a little and let's talk tomorrow ..."

"Come outside." Joe Billie's interjection stopped the fat man in mid sentence. "Come on." This time, a command, Bloodtooth headed for the door motioning his agitated partner to follow. Shuffling through the hot sand the plodding Greek marveled at the balanced step of the inebriated Indian. How could he do it? Jack knew that even though drunk the half-breed Miccosukee was aware of everything and could react in a heartbeat, if necessary. Pappadoupoulis decided he wasn't going to make it necessary.

The unseemly couple went into the big building behind the shack and Joe Billie, still carrying the war club, pointed it at a table. "Look Gypsy man, what got to hell early thanks to Stump."

Fat Jack rubbed his eyes to displace the horde of gnats fighting over his excess tears. He didn't understand Joe Billie because the only thing on the table was a huge stinking gator hide with the head still intact, or so he thought. He posed the obvious question very carefully, not wanting even his voice to disturb the uncountable flies lounging on the reptile's misshapen head. "So what's special about that gator?"

"Not a gator, Gypsy man." As he spoke, the amused Indian pounded on the rotting head with the war club." It's a God'am crocodile. Ate my dog. He didn't die easy but he in hell now and waitin' for the turd-rancher." Flies went everywhere.

Pappadoupoulis shook his head and turned for the door. He had serious thinking to do. His half-breed partner was headed for hell and he didn't want a ticket. Jack had relatives in Tarpon Springs and was long overdue for a vacation or sabbatical. The gulf coast ethnic community of Tarpon Springs was a fetching place, especially this time of the year and Jack always liked fishing and boating. What was the old story about the cabin boy on a Greek sponge boat? A lecherous leer flitted across his face, stayed for an instant then gave way to an abstract stare. Gypsy Jack Pappadoupoulis didn't think he could handle the situation if his vengeful partner killed Can Martin.

• • •

It had been a dry spring and the big cottonmouth's stomach was not as full as he would like. There was still plenty of water but the spring rains always meant young, innocent food. Now he had to actually work to get his meals and with mating season just around the cattails he felt the need for more victuals. He was four years old and in his prime. He had long maintained his territory and due to his extraordinary size had little trouble convincing pretenders of the error of their ways. The watershed of his abode was in an isolated area of the Everglades and only visited by a few Indians or an occasional hunter in an airboat or half-track. The remnants of abandoned chickees were the only reminder of putative encroachment by man and were abandoned long before the cottonmouth was born. Just south of the confluence was a tremendous stand of *melaleuca* trees, newer to the area than the rotting chickees.

Commonly called punk tree, *Melaleuca* is the bane of south Florida, growing everywhere and displacing native vegetation with a vengeance. This particular stand of trees covered over two hundred acres with trunks as close as a picket fence making it virtually impenetrable. The animal trails crisscrossing this foliate desert had grown with the grove and were as permanent as Alligator Alley. For a human to step inside this raging verdure was to be lost.

It was noon and the resting moccasin was sprawled on a fallen tree savoring the warm sunlight filtering through a tall bay tree overhanging the bank. The fish digesting in his innards was testimony to his bountiful kingdom and hypnotic to his senses. It was with great effort that he turned his fist sized head toward the opposite bank at the sound of lapping water.

The gaunt coonhound was lost and backtracking. He had missed the spoor a few miles back and was circling to straighten out his innate homing instinct prior to returning where the truck parked at the start of the hunt. He had done this before and knew there would be food there for him, so while not worried, he was ravenous. He never seemed to get enough to eat during hunting season as the dry dog food just didn't stick to his ribs. He needed meat. He had never encountered a cottonmouth moccasin.

The dirty brown snake slipped fluidly into the water. He didn't know what this creature was but didn't want him in his territory, period. As the hound waded into deeper water and started to roll and splash, the territorial serpent rose to the surface and extended his full six and one half foot body to warn the errant canine away. The curious dog cocked his head, followed the snake's progress for a few feet and then returned to his refreshing diversion. Feeling threatened, the cottonmouth closed the valves in his throat and rapidly filled with air, bloating his body to three times its normal size and turning into a dirty brown, freakish, water monster. This tactic never failed to scare lesser snakes, predator birds, big turtles and small alligators. The tired coonhound wasn't impressed.

The moccasin is by nature ill tempered and the dog's attitude wasn't helping the situation. Darting through the water the angry cottonmouth attacked. Striking the surprised animal's ear the huge snake whipped his body in violent serpentine waves while the muscle encompassing his venom glands contracted, injecting a stream of deadly poison into the shocked coonhound. The stench of the cottonmouth filled the dog's nostrils adding extra incentive to the tremendous effort it took to shake the creature loose. But the cottonmouth wasn't finished. They are born with an ill temper and this particular one suffered a relapse shortly after birth. He had no intention of letting this strange beast go. As the hurting dog turned to run the cottonmouth struck again, hitting the right side of its throat. Again the powerful undulations pumped venom into the poor hound's body. This time the stricken dog could not shake the heavy snake loose.

The cottonmouth moccasin is a street fighter; no finesse, just slugging, hitting below the belt, gouging or whatever it takes. No pinpoint precision injections like his more deadly cousin the great eastern diamondback rattlesnake. The only way the coonhound was going to get away alive was to kill the moccasin or rip out of his fangs. Desperately the hound rolled and snapped at his adversary, trying to drag the stinking reptile to the bank. In getting to shallow water the force of the struggle pulled the snake's fangs through the dog's skin resulting in a savage lacerations but freeing the hound.

The whimpering coonhound had enough and with a singular effort jumped clear of the coiling reptile and disappeared into the bushes lining the bank. His face and ear were bleeding freely and swelling was evident across his muzzle. He was running with no destination, his breath reduced to agonized gasps with his tongue protruding, swelling, blacker with each step. Thirty minutes later the hound crawled under a cabbage palm, blood oozing from his mouth, eyes, nose and anus; his throat the size of his body.

He died there.

• • •

Elise Jones was upset. She couldn't sleep and had no appetite. Her svelte figure was losing its trim, athletic look and appeared gaunt. Though still gorgeous, her drawn appearance cast an aura of consumptive radiance and if anything, more seductive.

Can Martin was crazy about her.

She had very little contact with George Martinez since coming to the Martin ranch. In fact, the reason she took the job was to get away from her ex-lover and think things out. She was totally devastated by his rejection but the strong feelings lingered. She knew if he came she would seek his arms though her mind was telling her to forget it. She was at sea about these feelings. On one hand she wanted to be free, independent and in charge of her own destiny, yet the comfort of being wanted and adored by one such as George overpowered these more practical emotions.

What to do? What about her interest in the strange Samson Duff? These feelings, unwarranted, were not to be denied. His presence caused her to blush and tingle – a new experience. She thought about him a lot; who was he, where from, married, engaged, have a girl friend? Stupid questions but irrepressible. Definitely not the concerns of a self sufficient career oriented woman.

The injured rancher had been a problem at first, constantly questioning about her personal life. His attitude was condescending and it took almost a week of gentle rebuffs and subject changes for the covetous Martin to finally understand that he hadn't hired a piece of ass. With this realization, Can started paying court to the dark haired nurse and if not in love with her, was blindly infatuated.

His leg was doing fine and he was taking physical therapy every day, thanks to nurse Jones. He could walk much better than he let on. With proper bandaging he could manage without a crutch and the pain had all but abated but not wanting to lose the nurse, he became a pretender.

Elise had been present at Sam's last visit and though not privy to the conversation heard enough to know that all was not right between the two newcomers and Can Martin. This served to stimulate her interest in the handsome Sam Duff and a twinge of red appeared in her cheeks as she thought of the virile man. Was he really the mystery those piercing eyes reflected? George had dark, expressive eyes full of questions and answers but no mystery. Sam Duff's green eyes would pierce you to the soul. To the smitten woman they held no answers, only mysterious, devilish magnetism.

The introspective nurse turned her thoughts to her ex-lover. Her feelings for George had been genuine but not spontaneous as they were for the newcomer. Elise, her singular attractiveness notwithstanding, married young as the thing to do. Her sexuality was learned and not the result of glorious awakening so she bestowed her sexual favors as a means to an end, not the end itself. Truly she was attracted to the doctor, but in a way that bespoke comfort and security. She wanted George Martinez to take care of her the rest of her life and if intercourse was necessary, so be it.

Elise thought she knew about love.

The wine with dinner tried to relax her but the lonely woman did not allow it. Lying on the bed and closing her eyes brought visions of her former patient and remembrances of his handsome body glistening with sweat as he struggled to regain strength. She wondered what it would be like to be in those powerful arms.

Finally appeasing the wine, her trim body relaxed and tiny beads of perspiration appeared on her upper lip as nectar materializes on the petal of a rose. Her mind convinced her body that it was embracing Samson Duff. Half asleep, she wasn't fully aware of the slight undulating movements of her lower body in concert with her panting. She was aware only of her ethereal lover and her desire to be with him, take care of him—touch him. She wanted him, totally. The thought of him caring for her never intruded her reverie. The thrusting undulations increased and soon released the sweating woman from her sensuous torpor. Sitting dreamily on the bed Elise became aware of her sweaty body and her moist undergarments. Suddenly self-conscious, she quickly removed them and pulled on a dry cotton running suit. She wasn't quite ready as the door to her room metamorphosed into a huge, garish specter crowned by a plumed turban carrying a gore splattered club and leading a slobbering Can Martin by a wire noose.

● ● ●

The two men threaded their way through the maze of tables to the small booth at the rear of the cafe. It was 11:30 pm and Kirby and Duff were tired and in need of coffee. Dropping in at Tiny's had become ritual and they were recognized by appearance, if not profession.

Glory Waters appeared as soon as the duo slid into the vinyl covered bench seats. "What'll it be guys?"

"Usual." Sam spoke first.

"OK, coffee-black, sweet and low, no cream… right?"

"Ditto, gal." This time Skeets chimed in.

Turning to go the garrulous waitress did a 360 and asked why the two weren't at the Martin place.

Samson's face was resting on his hands as the waitress spoke. "Why, he having a party?" The reply was a lisp.

"You mean you haven't heard? I thought you guys were friends or something, way you been acting and meetin' and all that. Milo Suarez came screaming in 'bout 30 minutes ago 'cause he seen Lon's, Sheriff McCall's, car out front. I dunno, maybe I shouldn't say anything ..."

Kirby's eyes narrowed and the timbre of his voice raised goose bumps on the startled waitress. "Tell us what happened. Now! Everything!"

Duff jerked his face up. "Elise must still be there. Come on... tell us what happened!"

"Give me a chance, guys. Anyway, Milo comes running in hollering for the sheriff. I hear him say that everybody's dead!

The startled waitress's words tailed off as she watched the two men sprint from the cafe.

Fifteen minutes after leaving Tiny's the straining pickup slid into the yard at the ranch house. Blue lights flashed everywhere creating an eerie, disco like panorama of EMS vehicles and uniformed men. Running to the front door Sam nudged his partner, "you do the politics and I'll get inside, pronto." With that he angled for the side of the house away from the nagging blue lights.

Skeets slowed to a fast walk and sought out Lonnie McCall.

The haggard sheriff was talking to EMS personnel and barely looked up as Kirby approached. Just beyond the men lay two German Shepherd dogs, their arabesque positions a mockery of their death. Lon's voice was barely audible as he spoke to the driver. "How many so far?"

"Four. All dead."

"You're certain Martin or the girl wasn't one of them?" The sheriff's question sent shivers through the stoic Kirby.

"Sure as I can be." The driver's voice broke as he continued. "No one fitting their description was removed by any of my people. Maybe they'll turn up later. Still have places to look."

Lon looked up and eyed the intruder. "What the hell you doing here? I thought I had this place roped off. Who let you by?"

"No one. I just heard about this and wanted to offer our services." The measured tones of Kirby's voice agitated the troubled sheriff.

"Look, fella, we don't need any help and you got no business here. I've got enough trouble without having to fool with you. Who the hell you think you are, anyway?"

Skeets restrained the urge to slap the piss out of the sassy lawman. He was after time. Samson needed all Skeets could buy or beg and for that the steely eyed ex-government trained killer had to be nice. He had scanned the immediate area as he waited on the conversing lawman and nothing other than the two dead Shepherds was evident. He gathered from the bits of conversation overheard that Can Martin and Elise Jones had not been found and may still be alive. Skeets could feel the blush creeping into his neck, expanding his collar. His prominent jaw muscles were in spasms, his icy stare fixed the sheriff's eyes. Patience, he thought, patience.

Lon ran on. "I know you said you were CIA but even so you don't have any jurisdiction here. I haven't had a chance to check you and your partner out but you can bet I will soon as this shit cools down. You big time guys aren't here in glorious Centra county for a vacation, are you? What's so important that would bring the CIA to central Florida?"

Self controlled, Skeets voice droned. "I might as well level with you. We're here to investigate the increase in cattle rustling and ..."

"And bullshit! Don't feed me that line of manure. The United States government don't give a crap if every cow in Centra county gets stolen. Give me a break, fella."

The irate sheriff's words cut Skeets to the bone. He knew his face was red now because his forehead was throbbing like a sandpapered dick. Goddam he hated to get caught in a stupid explanation. His tight jaw muscles cranked down another notch as he gritted his teeth in embarrassed frustration. I know better, I know better, he thought. Why do I do things like this. That goddam sheriff's no dummy and I know it.

Sensing the man's frustration McCall went for the throat.

"I bet you two assholes are the ones working for Martin and his group to clean up the rustling. Ha-ha-ha, big frigging deal. More like the blind leading the blind, I'd say."

Kirby's fists were clenching and unclenching as the righteous lawman piled it on.

"… and on second thought maybe you know something 'bout what went on here tonight. Hell, you and you partner may even be involved. How 'bout it? You know anything about this? Where's that friend of your'n? He off snooping?" A devilish look slipped into the haggard expression on Lon McCall's face. Like a good fisherman he was fixing to set the hook.

"Kirby, is it? I want you and your pal in my office at 9:00 in the morning and if no show, I'll have an APB on your asses by 9:30."

Skeets Kirby was really pissed.

• • •

Samson slipped along the outside wall of the Martin home. As he went he carefully sensed the air. He was in awe of his strange power but had come to accept it and was exploring its boundaries. He had not reached them. He was not bothered by mundane smells anymore and was cataloging new ones fast as he could. He had already cut the spoor of the enigmatic Miccosukee half-breed Joe Billie Bloodtooth and the tingling sensation accompanying piloerection bore witness to his dread. Sam wanted to get inside the house. He had not crossed Elise's scent; the Indian's trail was to the house and he was alone.

Samson remembered the last time he asked George Martinez to explain what happened during the surgery and how he came to possess this ungodly ability to smell. He acknowledged the surgeon's brilliant, frustrated talent but why he refused to explain was beyond Sam's ken. Maybe he was hiding. Stranger things have happened. The best Sam could get was a 'someday soon' utterance but no date. Since he truly liked the flippant surgeon, Duff was hesitant to be more insistent since recovery from his surgery was a miracle and Martinez, in spite of shortcomings was a Godsend to this community. But—Sam was tempted.

Coming to a side door the silent man stopped and studied the small porch at the doorway. The area was taped off and Sam detected the odor of a strange man and death. Blood, splotches of tissue and hair were evident on the stained tile. Stooping for a closer look he became aware of a sinuous movement across the edge of the tile stoop. A closer look proved the movement to be a line of ever-present ants, each tiny behemoth loaded with the gory remnants of Bloodtooth's visit. Like a macabre conga line the industrious insects were taking full advantage of Joe Billie's largess. In the overall scheme of nature, tragedy was, indeed, relative. Samson shuddered as his nose and eyes told him whoever was killed here had his head horribly bashed. Sensing a presence Sam rose, turned slowly and was confronted by a uniformed man.

"Hi. Haven't seen you before. You with the Highlands county sheriff?" The man's look was friendly but a twinge of suspicion edged his query.

Sam noticed he could read people more accurately and that their posture and attitudes were more meaningful than before; the look in a person's eye, position of their hands, arms, tilt of their head, color and smell of their skin, especially smell. He could detect fear, aggression, intimidation, friendliness—every emotion. These mannerisms were a window to their soul.

"Naw, with the EMS from Centra. Name's Sammy." Samson kept his head down as he answered. "Gotta take measurements." Seeing that the man wanted to talk, Sam turned abruptly. "Forgot my tape measure. Back in a second." Slipping through the doorway he turned up a hallway and started looking for bedrooms.

Entering the kitchen he saw another taped off area and smelled the gore of the female Negro cook. Her head had been bashed.

Though air conditioning compromised smelling, a picture of the murderous half-breed skulking through the house was taking shape. Sam whistled quietly as he pondered. What a way to depart life!

Moving into the hallway he came to a splintered door dangling from one hinge like a satanic omen. Her bedroom. No doubt. His heart was racing as he slipped into the scent filled boudoir. He was overpowered by the residual fragrance of her body, instantly homing in on the recently discarded undergarments. A lump welled up in the big man's throat as he gently lifted the delicate, silky reminder of what men were all about. Gloriously aware of his mood, Sam felt his face redden as he stuffed the pheromone drenched scanties into his pocket and seeing no signs of death went quickly to the kitchen and sealed the sensuous items in a plastic bag. Avoiding contact with the officious people, Sam finished his appointed rounds and magically appeared in the pickup next to his stone-faced partner.

• • •

Chapter NINE

Two miles from the Martin ranch Skeets Kirby pulled the pickup off the road. "Look old hoss, I've been thinking. We may be in a heap of shit if we're not careful."

'Old hoss' laughed as his introspective partner's veneer peeled back to reveal the grammar of his youth. Sam knew the polished Kirby was deadly serious.

"I mean it Samson. We may end up being the fall guys in this deal if we don't get busy."

"Well, spell it out stone face and let's see where we sit ... Sam knew his buddy's concerns were well founded. He and Skeets were like brothers and so attuned that ones attitude mirrored the other's. Skeets had been raised middle class and early on developed a respect for life, especially human life. He also developed a tough body and a strict set of personal values. His mental discipline had been legendary at the FBI and CIA schools and his physical prowess second only to Samson. Skeets Kirby was probably the only man Sam ever met who would be invulnerable to brainwashing. As much as his pal respected life he held no such respect for some humans, specifically the smart ass, macho male loud mouth. Sam remembered the expertise shown by Skeets in the kill classes during their training. No one demonstrated more aptitude at killing than Skeeter Kirby. Sam knew that one of Skeets' biggest problems concerned the moral dilemma of his respect for life but dislike for certain men that forced him to deprive them of life to settle this dislike. It was this hypocritical dichotomy that caused Skeets to be detached. Sam knew this to be the reason no one liked his partner. He also knew this moral Gordian knot could not be solved by the whack of a sword. Samson Duff believed that if given reason Skeets Kirby would kill him—and hate himself the rest of his life! Maybe this represented a form of insecurity or some weird personality disconnect but whatever, Samson Duff knew there was no better man in the world to have as a friend; no worse as an enemy—even the German.

"First, fill me in on the party. I didn't learn much from that Goddam smart ass sheriff and he wants to see us at nine this morning—that can wait…" Skeets forced the words.

Skeets knew of Sam's expanded sense of smell but not the true scope of it. He had tried to get George Martinez to discuss it but no luck so he kept quiet and only touched on the subject when talking with his muscular partner. Sam's recovery had been so complete that Skeets could hardly tell the guy had been beaten half to death. He was glad. His mind seemed more acute and for that he was especially glad.

"Here's the way I see it." Sam turned and relaxed his shoulders. "First, it was done by that crazy Indian, Bloodtooth, that we've been checking out. Why he has a thing for Martin I'll never know but he did it and I'm sure, alone. He must have parked a good ways off 'cause I couldn't find his tire marks but I didn't follow his trail much past those big oaks on the south side of the house. He slipped up to the house from the north and tied a small bitch in heat…"

"How do you know that?" Skeets voice carried a hint of doubt.

"Shit, Skeeter, how'd you think I know. I found his diary under a tree—no, I smelled it. Believe it pal, I could tell plain as day where he tied the little Jezebel. Anyway, when the two macho guard dogs came to play he scattered their brains over the acorns. The guy is smart…"

"You think he was alone?" Skeets seemed skeptical.

"Bet on it pal. I'll give you money back on that." Sam shifted slightly and glanced out the window. "Once the two mutts were deactivated, he slipped up on the two guys Can had on yard patrol. Apparently they never heard the two dogs being sent to the big kennel in the sky. That Indian is a smooth operator—his military record told us that."

"Why did Martin have guards?" Skeets turned and looked at Sam. "You think he suspected something? You think maybe this is something personal and not to do with the cattle rustling? Why didn't he just kill the jerk and get it over with?"

"Whoa, Skeeter, one thing at a time." Some of these same questions were running through Sam's mind like why the crazed half-breed didn't just kill Elise if his feud was with Martin. Certainly he was cold-blooded enough and surely didn't want witnesses. He didn't seem able to spell mercy. "Anyway, he bashed the cook and the old man with her and according to the sign took Martin first and the girl next. I couldn't find any sign of struggle so however he did it Martin and Elise went quietly. I can't figure that out unless this guy is better than we think."

"True pal and if we don't get it in gear we'll be a lot worse than we think." Skeets closed his eyes for a minute and rested his forehead on the steering wheel. Sam's description of the massacre was incredible. Even if only half true, his new ability was unbelievable, giving Skeets no reason to doubt.

"You know Skeets." Sam's voice was barely audible. "None of this ties in with the Greek. How come? He's got to be the brains behind this whole shebang. That goddam bloodthirsty Indian for sure isn't. I'll bet your sweet ass that he knows about this deal and he may be our only source."

"Right on hoss and that's got to be our next stop. We don't have time to play with the sheriff if Martin and the nurse are still alive. He wants us at nine this morning and it's two now. That gives us plenty of time to "talk Greek." Skeets eyes brightened.

• • •

It was 4 am when sheriff Lon McCall leaned back in the desk chair nervously tapping a pencil on the stack of officious looking papers piled in front of him. He had left the grisly scene in charge of his deputy and had been in his office less than 30 minutes. Lonnie was tired and totally frustrated. His fiefdom was erupting and he felt powerless to stop or even understand it. He needed to talk to the Greek. Roscoe James's quiet, unannounced entry did nothing to alter this mood even though Roscoe was the sheriff's best friend.

James, though a Fresh Water Fish and Game Commission officer, had been called to the Martin place by the sheriff as the State of Florida mandated full police authority and power to these game wardens.

"Whadda you think, Lonnie." Roscoe's tone was querulous.

"What in hell happened out there? Where you think Can and the nurse are?"

"Easy Roscoe. We'll get the answers." Lonnie's proclaimed bravado belied his doubts. In truth he didn't know who, other than the FBI, to notify in order to start the investigation since nothing like this had happened since his swearing in. Like his pal, McCall also wondered what happened to Can Martin and Elise Jones and who did it. The sheriff still hadn't put the questionable drowning of his longtime friend, Pop Luther, to bed. He was more convinced of foul play than before. His perplexed mind automatically thought of a connection between Pop's death and this truculent Martin party.

"I'll haf' to get the FBI in on this since the evidence screams kidnapping. I think Martin and the girl are probably alive—least ways we've had no calls about their bodies—no notes either." Lonnie was not happy about calling the FBI. They knew what to do but he knew they could be nosey. Maybe he could check on Kirby and Duff at the same time—kill two birds with one stone. He was feeling better.

"Roscoe, you think old Pop's death could be connected to this?" Lonnie's mind was relaxing. Putting the pencil down he kicked back and put his feet on the corner of the desk as the hypnotic look of introspection eased into his perplexed stare.

Lonnie remembered the first time he met the old reprobate.

It was about ten years ago that Pop lived in the little subdivision on Long Acre Road. Pop hated cats so everything at his house was cat proof, even the fence. The little guy, five and one half feet tall and 140 pounds, had Bougainvillea growing in his chain-link fence so nothing could get through or over it. The gorgeous flowers may attract but God help anything that tested the heinous thorns hiding in the rich green interior. Cats included. The gate was slightly less formidable, consisting of tightly woven wire topped off by ornate flat iron scrollwork about five feet high.

This was when the old man had his fling with the Smith woman, Hilda. It seemed they were always making out; his place, her place, no matter. Pop was a widower. Hilda, married. The wizened little man pictured himself as quite the stud, so to uphold this ideal he conned a doctor friend into providing the hormone, human chorionic gonadotropin, plus instructions and paraphernalia for its use. He quizzed all his physician buddies and their consensus was that gonadotropin was the best remedy for a genetically substandard, overworked 74-year-old male sexual organ. One injection a week and he was off and running—with his dick pipe-hard. He made Hilda happy. Her husband preferred vino to pussy so he didn't care.

Pop and lady friend had a spat one night and the ornery old cuss ordered her off the property. Not wanting to go she resisted and in a fit of frustrated passion Pop threw her ass out the gate and locked it. Shortly after midnight Hilda decided to kiss and makeup so off she goes to Pop's house. The gate is still locked and no one is going to climb the fence. The gate? Now that was another matter—no Bougainvillae. For reasons rightfully arcane Hilda decided to challenge the gate, scrollwork and all; a totally injudicious decision.

The smiling sheriff remembered it was a neighbor's call that alerted his office. Something about a woman dying in front of a house on Long Acre Road. Anyway, when Lonnie arrived old Pop was standing behind the locked gate cursing a blue streak and Hilda was straddling the gate squalling like a banshee with a toothache. Seems as if in scaling the formidable gate she overestimated her athletic prowess and settled onto the topmost curlicue of the iron scroll adorning the gate top; which unexpectedly penetrated her unrepentant genitalia. Hilda was hooked. No big game fish ever caught was hooked more securely. As in most accidents involving the genitals the unfortunate resists attempts to help; violently if such attempts or attempters don't cease and desist! Of course such resistance had to be vocal since the poor soul couldn't release her hand holds for a second for fear of embracing her unfeeling lover ever more passionately.

Reasoning with Hilda became difficult.

The grinning sheriff shook his head as he remembered the rescue. The EMS crew had to get two muscular neighbors to support the wailing banshee while they cut the iron bar. It was left to the emergency room physicians to relieve Hilda of her curlicue dildo. Pop laughed and joked during the rescue—that old codger was something else; the only person Lonnie knew who could get a fight started in an empty room. He loved that old man.

"… phone, Lonnie. Telephone for you. Whatsa matter with you? You day-dreaming or something? It's that surgeon from Centra Hospital—what's his face? Martinez?"

Roscoe's voice sounded like it was down a well as the maudlin lawman surfaced from his thoughts and reached for the phone. "McCall here."

"Sheriff, this is Doctor Martinez. I'm at the Centra county hospital emergency room. Where is Elise Jones? What's happened at the Martin place?"

"We really don't know yet, Doctor, but we're working on it."

"Working on it hell. The EMS boys just hauled in four dead ones and you're working on it…"

"Okay Doc, calm down." Lonnie was trying to be reassuring but he knew it was a useless gesture. "We didn't find Martin or the nurse. We think they've been kidnapped and the FBI has been alerted. Sit tight Doc and I'll have you notified if anything breaks— you can bet on it—bye." Holding the phone in his hand Lonnie turned to his boyhood pal. "Well Roscoe, it starts and it sucks.

Everybody and their brother will be calling asking about this one or that one. You know, come to think of it, that Martinez fellow is supposed to have something going with that pretty nurse…

according to what I hear. Think I'll have to ask him a few questions in the morning. Along with those two yahoos we saw at the Martin place.

Whadda you think, Roscoe?"

The game warden really didn't think anything as thinking was not one of Roscoe James' strong suits. He and Lonnie McCall had been pals through high school in Centra county. Lon was Mr. everything—the James boy nothing. Lonnie was a top athlete and scholar. Roscoe was passed just to make room. Lonnie was voted most likely to succeed—Roscoe never made the ticket. But Lonnie McCall was Roscoe James' hero. He worshiped the ground Lonnie walked on and knew that Lonnie would end up the most famous man ever from Centra county if not the entire State of Florida. Lonnie never left Centra county and like most people intelligent beyond their education never realized his potential and settled into the sheriff's job as the path of least resistance. He viewed himself a failure to which sarcasm and temper bore witness. Lonnie McCall dreamed of pretty women and muscle cars all through high school and a sheriff's salary just didn't cut it, nor the county cruiser a substitute for a Corvette. Roscoe. on the other hand, thought Lonnie a genius and looked at his election as sheriff as the high point in Lonnie's career and an achievement second only to being Governor. Since Roscoe's education greatly exceeded his intelligence he never wavered in his feelings and this adulation become a balm, if not a crutch, for the sheriff's bent psyche. Lon McCall needed Roscoe James.

• ✖ •

George let the phone slip into its cradle. He had been called to the emergency room without any idea of what transpired, and the four DOA's meant nothing until he overheard the EMS guy talking to the admitting nurse. The words "Martin ranch" got his attention but none of them knew anything about Can Martin or Elise. They just knew there were no more dead ones and his phone call to the sheriff didn't ease his apprehension. His mind started spinning. What if she were dead? What if alive, but a kidnap victim? Who would do such a thing? What if he was questioned? The worried surgeon knew if drawn into this mess there would be no way to cover his affair with the beauteous woman. He wondered if the fateful evening at Gypsy Jack's was connected to this. Could he be the target of the kidnapping and expected to pay a ransom for her release? Why not blackmail? It didn't make sense, yet the harried man knew the situation explosive and not to be swept under the rug of presumed innocence.

Maybe he should pack up and leave, but go where? How could he explain that to Jan and his friends? The confusion edging its nakedness into his mind seemed to take control when this intro-spection suddenly turned to thoughts of the kidnapped nurse.

What an ass I am, he thought. Elise is probably scared out of her wits, if even alive and here I sit worrying about my own tush.

I've got to get hold of myself and play this hand. I didn't deal but I can't cut and run. Like it or not, George Martinez was go-ing to face reality. The fiery guilt eased up his neck as he remem-bered the innocence of Elise's surrender to him and his cavalier attitude when the sanctity of his selfishness was threatened. Well, he rationalized, she was 21 and he didn't take her to raise. He also rationalized that he should not be vocal or inquisitive about the putative abduction; he didn't want to draw attention to himself.

Slowly he leaned back in his chair. George had a problem.

• • •

The 4x4 pickup eased off the dirt road a half-mile west of Gypsy Jack's bar and sightless picked its way through the cab high dog fennels until well off the road. Two men clad in black with their faces covered in black grease paint and accompanied by a vaporous dog sat silently as the grinding vehicle pushed down the green wall of weeds. Satisfied they were far enough from the road, Skeets Kirby stopped the truck and opened the door. A silent Sam Duff slid across the seat and exited through the same door, whispering the guard command to the dog-meat beast now the sole occupant. To enter this vehicle would entail killing the dog.

The two were clad in custom made, dull black, long sleeved jumpsuits with deep, flap-covered pockets on the front of the trousers. Each belt supported a sheath knife and a fanny pack containing items of their profession. One such item was a plastic cord one-quarter inch thick and serrated its entire length. The special plastic was flame proof, very resistant to cutting or abrasion and stretch resistant. One end was a specially designed locking device that could not be loosened once the other end was threaded and tightened. Sam developed this plastic loop restraint while in the FBI and for want of a name was called Sam's loop. The fledgling agent endured a constant barrage of ridicule, especially from the older guys, as he developed his brainchild and the device quickly became known as Samsloop, then Samloop and finally, zamloop. This zamloop quickly proved to be a versatile and effective physical restraint aid.

The only way to remove the tightened plastic noose was to cut it and that was next to impossible. The length was sufficient to allow it to slip over a man's head, wrists, or ankles. The noose was pre-threaded through the lock end and a small fat toggle handle allowing rapid closure was attached to the free end. A person could be immobilized in seconds by zamlooping the wrists and ankles.

Zamlooping the head with the loop bitted through the mouth and brutally tight rendered the person incapable of speech. When looped over a person's head to their neck and jerked tight the device became deadly, depriving the victim of air with soundless collapse all but instantaneous. No human could effect a release even with a knife, as the force of closure resulted in the plastic biting deeply into the neck resulting in severe but futile self inflicted lacerations to the dying unfortunate. It was a deadly device.

Like shadows the two made their way to the back of the bar.

They didn't communicate as this was their element, their actions second nature and predictable. It was 3:30 in the morning and they knew the Gypsy man closed at four. They knew he had hired extra guards and was extremely cautious. After leaving the Martin place, Sam checked out Joe Billie's home place while his partner went to the Greek's digs to see what he could find. Both drew blanks and knew the fat man to be their only chance at getting the answers they needed. They also knew he held the key to their survival since Can Martin was the only person who knew of their mission in Centra county. If he was murdered, then the two erstwhile investigators had no alibi and would be suspect. For sure the sheriff didn't like them and their unobtrusive style only enhanced their mystery to the locals. The cattlemans' committee knew nothing. They had to get a confession from Pappadoupoulis, the rampant Miccosukee, or disappear—pronto. They suspected the sheriff to be good as his word and by 9:30 this morning they would be wanted men. If they allowed that to happen before they were finished, Joe Billie Bloodtooth would in no way release the two alive and the Greek would simply carry on as usual. A check into their background would reveal two outstanding operatives, highly trained, considered dangerous and released from government service under mysterious circumstances. No past records or information would be available—ever. Under these circumstances sheriff Lon McCall would have cornered and caught two desperate kidnappers, nee murderers and end up a local hero. No parochial jury would absolve them of guilt, fancy lawyers or no.

Both men had the same thoughts as they watched the lights go off until only two rooms showed light. The last patron staggered wearily to his junker truck and weaved out of the parking yard. Two men remained on the steps smoking as the moon lifted above the dense clouds. Both were armed.

It was a gorgeous night.

"He doesn't have any dogs." Samson whispered. "I wonder why?"

"Dam, that nose of yours is a trip! How the hell should I know why he doesn't have dogs. Maybe one pissed on 'em while his mother was carrying him." Skeets' voice was subdued but sharp as he motioned for Sam to move back.

Away from the yard Skeets sidled next to the all but invisible Duff. His low tones were barely audible. "Go 'round the place and see what you can sniff out. I don't want to take these guys out if it isn't necessary plus we need to know how many extras are on the set. If you have to chill one, okay, but try not to. Fifteen minutes... Back here."

Sam glanced at his watch and evaporated. Working into the wind he approached the back of the building and cautiously started around it. He had detected no suspicious scents save the two men on the porch. Moving under the first lighted window Sam cautiously raised to peek into the room. This was the poolroom and two different men were shooting pool, occasionally pulling on a longneck and engaging in what appeared to be serious conversation. Two lever action carbines rested against the cue stick rack. Smelling the two guards still outside, Samson backtracked and went to the other side of the building. The other lighted window was in back, an apartment or office. Suddenly his senses warned of an approaching man. Falling to his knees he scooted to the nearest clump of bushes and flattened out. One of the men from the porch walked by, pausing now and again to look into the darkness. Remembering his partner's words, Sam remained still until the man had passed. Back under the window the cautious operative rose up and looked in. The curtains were partially drawn but he could see under the bottom. His breath was air escaping a punctured tire as he viewed the incredulous scene.

Fat Jack Pappadoupoulis was spread-eagled on a massive bed, wrists and ankles tied to the corner bedposts—on his back and stark naked! Two Thai women, also nude, were working vigorously on the huge body. Sam stared in amazement as the women massaged the writhing, groaning mountain of flesh. The table adjoining the bed was covered with various tubes and plastic squeeze bottles; balms, oils and assorted massage media, the peeping man surmised. What looked to be a dildo and a vibrator lay on the edge of the bed.

Samson Duff had never witnessed anything like this and a feeling of voyeurism-induced guilt came over him. He experienced a twinge of embarrassment for the fat man. Sam wouldn't want anyone peeking at him! As he watched, one of the women began massaging the fat man's flaccid penis while the other picked up the vibrator. Even though the window was shut Sam could hear muffled groans and low pitched words as the two women spoke to each other in their native Thai. Sam was fascinated. His sexual experiences had so far been conventional and his upbringing precluded his delving into anything erotic. The groans grew louder as the woman began with the vibrator. The one massaging was now sitting astride the writhing man simulating intercourse but Sam could see his penis was still flaccid. That the Greek was caught in the throes of an orgasm was evident—but how, Sam wondered, if he didn't have an erection? A sudden movement at the corner of the house brought the engrossed voyeur back to reality. Dropping to the ground he was aware of fullness in his groin as if his pants were too tight. It was apparent that Samson Duff's sexuality had not yet plumbed its depths as thoughts of Elise Jones and her scent welled into his consciousness, stimulated by the swinish saturnalia just witnessed.

Sensing time was short he eased back, keeping to the shadows and headed for the rendezvous with Skeets.

"You won't believe this Skeets." Sam's tone was controlled—though still stimulated.

"Try me."

"Fats is stretched out between the bedposts hogtied with two Thai women working his ass over. Never seen anything like it. That guy is one piece of blubber. Those gals are sticking things up his ass and…" Sam's voice started to intensify as his partner cut him off.

"Quiet down and tell me what the hell you mean." Skeets voice had an edge. "How many and what kind—come on man—cut the bullshit and let's get on with it. Draw me a goddam picture." There was little room for levity when Skeets Kirby went to work and Sam's report didn't qualify as serious.

"Four men, armed. Two females inside with the Greek and he's tied to the bed." Sam's reddening face couldn't be seen in the dark or even in light due to the face paint but his embarrassment was self-evident. "If we hustle we can get him without a struggle. I imagine he's pretty much peckered out by now."

"Whatever. You take the two inside… I'll handle the outside pair. Knock on the door to the outside when you're ready and we'll check out this bedroom scene together." Skeets opened his fanny pack and fastened several zamloops to his belt. Before Samson could reply his psyched up buddy had vanished.

Approaching the corner of the building Skeets melted into the wall. He had watched the two men while Sam was gone and observed one walking around the structure every 15 or 20 minutes. He knew it was close to that time and was why he had left Sam in such a hurry. The sound of muffled footsteps effected a dramatic change in the preying man. Sweat appeared on his face as his jaw muscles clenched and unclenched. His body became rigid and coiled tight as a Swiss watch spring. As the unsuspecting guard turned the corner Skeets stepped in behind him and followed, footstep for footstep, until halfway along the building's length. Striking like a cobra the agent applied a carotid chokehold, feeling the man go limp almost instantly. There was no sound as he lowered the guard and zamlooped his feet, wrists and mouth. Pushing the immobilized guard under the edge of the tavern Skeets eased back to the corner. He never ceased to be amazed at the awesome effect of a properly applied carotid chokehold. He had heard about it most of his life but it wasn't until he met Samson Duff that he learned its proper application. Sam had been taught by the German, Carlos Otto, and had mastered it at an early age. Like a loaded gun, the chokehold had to be used with great caution or instant death could result. With death the desired effect the hold had no equal, especially in hand to hand combat.

Skeets had met the big German on many occasions but he didn't know the man. At first he felt Carlos didn't like him but as they became acquainted he realized the big guy was very reserved and non-committal. He never praised anything relating to conditioning or combat. He figured if you had it you had it and praise was unnecessary since skill spoke eloquently. Praise was redundant, embarrassing, patronizing and belittling. Until he met someone who could defeat him there was no one to praise. It was unlikely that big Carlos would ever bestow praise unless to the Grim Reaper—from his deathbed. He did praise artists and professionals in other fields but they had to be truly outstanding. Carlos Otto could spot tinplate a mile away. Skeets had mastered the chokehold through his workouts with Samson but was unable to master all of the techniques imparted to his buddy by the German. As good as Skeets was he didn't approach Samson and as good as Samson was the German was better. It was a consensus among combat masters the world over that the big German was the best martial arts and combat master alive. Skeets had seen him in action many times and shared that opinion. Carlos was simply the best.

The other guard sat smoking his cigarette marking the time he knew it to take his cohort to circle the structure. His stare fixed the opposite corner where his man should appear. With audacity born of unyielding discipline, Kirby walked up boldly behind the intent guard and struck again.

Securely trussed, he was disposed of in the same manner. Stepping onto the porch he awaited the knock.

Reaching the far side of the tavern Sam peered in the window and saw the two men playing cards. The rifles were as before and the faint scent of Cannabis was evident around the window. One man got up and went to the restroom. Marking the location, Sam waited until the dark complexioned man returned. His appearance or walk or something kindled a spark. He looked strangely familiar but Samson couldn't put a handle on him and hair standing on his neck told him the guy wasn't one of his favorites. He wondered where he could have run into the guy or if he was just imagining a putative acquaintance. Anyway, he didn't like him and he needed to get busy because one didn't keep Skeets Kirby waiting.

Reaching the window to the restroom he produced a flat prybar and deftly pried the window. Inside he lifted the back off a toilet and removed the valve from the bottom of the tank. As the water drained from the reservoir he went to a sink and plugged it, turned the water on, went to the door and eased it ajar.

"Left the john running." The smaller man, Bunny, didn't raise his eyes at his utterance. "I hear the dam thing running an' if one 'a your blue ribbon turds is choking it ta' death we'll be up ta' our balls in water here directly an' fatso'll be a mite putout. Best take 'at peashooter 'o your'n case hit ain't drown' yet."

"Fun-nee, fun-nee. You just jealous 'cause you has to hang on the sides so your gimlet ass don't fall in." Mick, the big swarthy one chuckled as he turned toward the restroom door. "Hey, you right. Thay's water comin' out th' door. Damn, that john oughtn't be stopped up to where hit's spillin' over. Maybe a valve broke…" Sliding his chair back Mick sauntered over to the restroom. Pushing the door he stepped through trying to avoid the thin sheet of water on the floor and looking down never saw the thin wire-like plastic loop encircle his neck, adorning him with a necklace of death. His face turned black and his eyes, unseeing, unable to comprehend the event, bulged like quail eggs. No sound came with the copious saliva drooling from his bulbous lips since swallowing was not possible. Urine soaked his Wranglers. Terminal spasms convulsed his body as if induced by strychnine as he slid across the wet floor.

"God dam Mick, you al-rite?" Bunny heard the fall and lowered his cards. "Valve shot? Answer for Christ's sake, doan wanna have us a flood." As he spoke, he turned toward the restroom and cocked his head.

"Get yore ass in here 'n hep. Hurry!" Sam hoped his disguised voice was convincing.

Bunny came through the door and saw the body. His reflexes reacted as Samson applied the chokehold rendering the little man's efforts comically futile. His unconscious form had barely reached the floor before it was gift-wrapped. Sam ran to the outside door and tapped lightly. It was 4:30 am. Wednesday.

• • •

Chapter TEN

4:30 Wednesday morning. The red 4x4 pickup turned south off Alligator alley just past a "Watch For Panthers" sign and with headlights off slowly moved away from the road. It was 50 miles west to Naples and almost 35 miles due north to the south end of Lake Okeechobee. The truck was pointed south and there was nothing between it and Florida Bay but 70 miles of swamp, hammocks and saw-grass; the dark, brooding, river-of-grass called Pay-Hay-Okee by the indigenous native Americans—the unique, fabled, Everglades. The bruised truck's weather beaten homemade topper appeared awkward and out of place. The mumbling driver also seemed out of place and as the truck picked its way through the unique vegetation, it, too, seemed out of place. Though the land was flat the vehicle was all but invisible once it had gone a hundred yards, naively inching its way through the navel into the very bowels of this magnificent, uncaring, Grassy River.

The driver squinted as he eased along looking for landmarks while trying to avoid the steel hard lighter knots and stumps. Abruptly hitting one, Joe Billie Bloodtooth grinned impishly as the sudden stop was punctuated by a loud thumping followed by the sound of muffled voices.

"Don't worry turd-guy, this here ride the easy part."

Speaking to no one in particular, the costumed half-breed's grin widened. In full ceremonial war-dress, the bedeviled Miccosukee was extracting his revenge in the manner directed by the spirits. He first heard the voices several weeks before, telling him what to do and in only a few days he was conversing regularly with the spirits of his grandfather and mother. Belief in spirits and in talking to the dead was ingrained in Miccosukee folklore and Joe Billie accepted his visions never thinking anything wrong. It wasn't long before he could call them up at will and it was only since the kidnapping that they had directed him to the old home ground. Joe Billie's intent at the Martin home was to kill everyone, Can included. It was his grandfather speaking to him on the way there that caused him to take the two hostages. Grandfather said to take Can Martin on the journey of torment in the manner of ancient Miccosukee warriors, allowing the pain to cleanse his black heart and truly atone for his crimes against Joe Billie. He was to start the journey at the place of his greatest torment, the old home place. He didn't bash Elise due to his belief that she was Can's mistress and her pain would be his pain. At times the possessed man could see these guiding spirits, causing him to slowly lose the fact of their death.

Inside the beat-up topper a man and woman lay on their sides facing each other. They were trussed with annealed wire at the wrists, ankles and neck. The slightest movement resulted in excruciating pain and each had devised a method of avoiding painful motion resulting in minimal conversation. Because of this face-to-face position their words could be better understood since even moving the lips caused pain. No effort had been made to gag them nor had their abductor spoken to them. Martin's cursing and the nurse's tears had long since stopped and they knew they were in the possession of a madman; escape was either impossible or meant death.

The truck inched its way into a large oak hammock with headlights only now turned on. Picking its way through the lush silver myrtle bushes edging the hammock the headlights recorded the surprised stares of two raccoons climbing down a huge water oak. The rhythmic drone of the diesel engine blotted out their chattering while the lights' shadows bouncing beneath the ancient oak evidenced the myriad life found in its gnarled branches. A great horned owl glided silently from the interior limbs as its reticent mate voiced a low call. The ground sheltered by the tree's near hundred-foot drip circle was carpeted by leaves and as well groomed as a state park. Stopping the truck, Joe Billie Bloodtooth stepped out, club in hand and walked to the back of the truck.

● ● ●

4:30 Wednesday morning. The FBI had been in Sheriff Lon McCall's office less than five minutes and he was already exasperated. There were two agents and their coolness and efficiency was a source of painful frustration to McCall. They introduced themselves as Bob Long and Ralph Woodham, with Long being senior agent and doing most of the talking. Bob Long had been with the Bureau going on 20 years and had developed a theatrical monotone when asking questions that rubbed the sheriff's nerves like a wet bathing suit on a sunburned ass—and he couldn't hide it. The two agents had arrived unannounced, identified themselves and were questioning the sheriff before he could say anything but name, rank and serial number. Bob Long seemed imperturbable and appeared to view Lon McCall's intransigence as just part of the job—nothing personal.

"… no ransom notes." Long had asked the same question at least four times and the sheriff was having a difficult time handling it.

"I've told you a dozen times there was nothing at the scene and no one has turned up anything written, or by telephone. Jesus, you'd think you guys would learn new questions after a while. Why would I hide a ransom note? Maybe you think I wouldn't recognize one—is that it?" Lonnie's face was flushed and his voice was rising. Turning to Roscoe, the wound-up sheriff didn't let up. "Hear that Roscoe? They think we ain't got enough sense to come in out of the rain. Did you see any notes? Go on, tell 'um."

"You know good'n well I din't see no papers or notes, Lonnie. If there had been any you wood'a found them and you know it." Roscoe's faith in his lifelong pal was rock solid.

"Take it easy McCall, we're just…" Agent Long was having difficulty suppressing the grin inching its way across his face. "…trying to do your job. I know all that crap, fellas. I use those same lines—'specially when I wanna' snooker someone. Say, now that I think of it, just who in hell called you guys? And how'd you get here so fast?" The agitated look on Lonnie's face was fast turning into one of incredulity and the wheels in his head were spinning. "You call the FBI, Roscoe?"

"Aw, you know damn good and well I din't call nobody, Lonnie…" The game warden's mouth stayed open as the sheriff went on.

"Well now, ain't that interesting! Maybe they're connected with those two drugstore cowboys Can Martin and his group hired to stop the cattle rustling." McCall's eyes narrowed as they met those of the senior agent. He knew the closest FBI office was in Tampa but had no plans to notify them.

"What drugstore cowboys? Got some cattle rustling going on?" Agent Long's store-bought facial expression didn't change. "Tell me about it."

"Nothing you'd be interested in. Just a few locals needin' some groceries—to feed the kids." Lon's voice dropped to normal. Goddammit, he thought, why in shit did I hafta' go and say that? He didn't want the FBI nosing around in his county for any reason. "Nothing serious… usually Indians anyway and the tribal council takes care of them."

"Tell us anyway." Bob Long's monotone seemed somewhat clipped as he pursued the subject. "Maybe we can be of help…"

"Naw, guys, you boys are too busy to worry 'bout a few hungry half-breeds." Lonnie wiped his lips as he tried to downplay the cattle-rustling thing. A surge of body heat caused his face to flush, leaving his mind stuck in neutral as he tried to change the subject—in a logical, unsuspicious manner.

What the piqued Lawman wanted was to be on his air-conditioned house boat on Lake Kissimmee, kicked back sipping a cool one while five Missouri minnows connected to five cane poles frantically avoided the hors d'oeuvre-ish overtures of speckled perch. He had paid cash for the plush craft six years ago and spent as much time on it as he could, usually on the Q.T., even to his office—unless an emergency. Then he left the number of the Live Oaks fish camp—instead of the boat's unlisted phone.

"I'm really glad you guys are here." Lonnie's voice jumped an octave as his face displayed a forced appearance. "I've been wanting to get a couple of men checked out by your office, so maybe you fellas' can help and save me the trouble of calling allover. These yahoos claim to be CIA or FBI or some such shit as but I think they just a couple of private eyes trying to con this dumb cattlemens' group out of some cash."

"Who are these men?" These were the first words by the junior agent. His voice had none of the controlled qualities of his partner and his rapid-fire delivery irritated the Lawman. "How long have these persons been in this area?

"Oh, they've been nosin' around several months now. 'Course they don't have much to do with me and they haven't broken any laws—yet."

"Do you know their names...?" Agent Woodham's tone was dripping intimidation and his heightened interest all too evident.

"Yes, McCall, we would like to know their names." The senior agent's interruption of fellow agent Woodham's question didn't escape the sheriff. His nervousness returned—in spades. It was going to take a theatrical effort for the edgy McCall to maintain his composure.

"Let's see, I think their names were Kirby and Duff ..."

"Charles Kirby and Sam, uh, Samson Duff?" Again the junior agent seemed unable to restrain himself.

"Yeah, that's them. At least I think so. That may not be their real names but that's what they told me and Can Martin... right,

Roscoe?" Lonnie turned to his quiet friend for support as his control of the situation showed signs of erosion.

"If you say so Lonnie. I think that's what they said…" There was no question that the game warden was intimidated by the FBI.

"That may not be their real names… who knows?" Lonnie had been fidgeting with the safety strap on one of his pearl handled .44's when he realized the agents' gaze covertly trying to see what he was fiddling with. The sheriff lowered his eyes for a split second and realized the visual impact the two pearl handled, customized revolvers, not to mention the custom alligator boots may have on FBI personnel. Wanting to get up and pace, the culpable lawman scrunched his chair further under the desk. Sheriff McCall was oozing serious perspiration.

"That's their real names. Charles S. Kirby, Jr. and Samson Hercules Duff." Bob Long made the rapid reply just as his partner's mouth was forming a word and directed it straight at the reddening face of junior agent Ralph Woodham.

Lonnie came back with. "You know 'em? How'd you know their names if you don't know'em? They workin' for you? What the hell's going on?"

"That's all I can tell you, sheriff. That their names are, in fact, Kirby and Duff. If you want to know more I suggest you call the CIA—not the FBI." Senior agent Long was back at the helm and agent Woodham stood silently as his superior continued the questioning.

"Whatta' ya' mean that's all you gonna' tell me. Hell man, if you know something lets hear it. These yo-yo's may be up to their little pink ears in this kidnapping—murder shit. Just who the hell are they?" Lonnie saw his chance to be righteously indignant.

"That's all I can say." Long's pursed lips bespoke limited patience and a slight break in his monotone caused the sheriff to lower his head and fumble with loose papers on the desk.

The two agents moved away from the desk. Roscoe sprawled out in the overstuffed chair and closed his eyes.

He was totally snookered by the FBI and wondered why his buddy was so testy.

The few minutes of silence seemed eternal, giving the law-man a chance to gather his wits. Sensing an exposed nerve McCall backed up a notch and went up a different road. "Well, I guess I'll just have to pick those boogers up and do a little serious Q and A. I feel sure we'll get straight answers by acting real nice to them. How about it Roscoe?" The tone of Lonnie's voice was ominous and no way was Mrs. James oldest boy, Roscoe, going to answer.

"A little free advice sheriff." The senior agent's monotonous drone was back but this time his face displayed a mirthful grin. "Unless you have substantive cause and a dam good SWAT unit you'd best leave Mr. Kirby and Mr. Duff alone. I get the impression that your luck is pretty bad now and not likely to change—but I'll tell you one you can bank—if you try to arrest those two, you're luck will change. It will get worse by a factor of ten and you will find things out about them you don't want to know. They are not, repeat, not involved in the Martin case. Now sheriff, we've had about enough of this bullshit so let's finish our chat about the Martin kidnapping so we can get something going."

Thirty minutes later, the county lawman breathed a sigh of re-lief as the two agents finished their questioning. He had displayed meekness that seemed out of character yet definitely speeded up the meeting. Lonnie hoped this would be the end of his FBI experi-ence and having played the mouse would be worth it. Deliberately he pushed back from the desk, got up and stretching his arms overhead, proceeded to pace the room. Roscoe was asleep.

Agents Long and Woodham paused at the door. Turning to face the pacing sheriff, Bob Long, hand on the doorknob, voiced a parting remark. "By the way McCall, we'll be back at two o'clock to discuss the rash of heavy equipment thefts in central Florida and your possible relationship with one Jack Pappadoupoulis." His fi-nal, "be available," sent chills down the lawman's spine. His paired revolvers and gator skin boots suddenly weighed a ton.

Sheriff Lonnie McCall had a problem.

• • •

4:30 Wednesday morning. Like a shadow Skeets slipped through the partially opened doorway and whispered to the anxious Samson. "What's the score? I've got two wrapped up outside."

"One wrapped, one zapped and let's hit the door." As Sam spoke, Skeets could see the muscles contracting across the big guy's shoulders and arms as he prepared to launch himself at the door to the Greek's bedroom. Samson Duff was ready. He had thought of Elise since leaving the Martin house and knew that the fat man tied to the bed held the key to her rescue. Every time he closed his eyes her erotic scent filled his being—body and mind—and the thought of her in the possession of the Miccosukee madman was more than he could take.

Timing their approach, the two men delivered well-placed kicks to the door just lateral to the knob. The unannounced splintering of the wooden barrier produced temporary catatonia in the busy Thai masseuses. The fat one had his feet untied and was being toweled off when the door exploded. In a single motion the intruders pounced on the frozen women and in seconds had them trussed. The full realization of the intrusion finally got through to the satiated man and his strenuous effort to free his arms shook the bed as if an earthquake. Samson went to the foot of the bed and began to retie the thrashing, cursing man's feet. Skeets checked the remainder of the rooms and returned just as the hefty Greek planted his flailing foot solidly to the side of Sam's head.

"You miserable bastards! You don't know who you're fuckin' with! I'll show you assholes... Mick—Bunny—get your ass in here!" Gypsy Jack's face was bloated and beet-red and the venom coated words could blister elephant hide. "Mick... Mick ... for God's sake get in here!"

Dodging another kick, Samson, with Skeets' help, retied the cursing man's feet to the bed.

"Calm down, you big gorgeous stud, you." Sam's voice rose to a falsetto, infuriating the helpless Greek.

"You assholes'll pay for this!" The mountain of flesh slowly relaxed as the futility of struggle became apparent. "I've got four guns here and anyone of them'll blow your ass straight to hell!

"Correction darling." Sam's falsetto was perfect. "You have no gunnies and the big, bad boys will have their way with your magnificent body. Oh, big daddy, will we ever make you forget those silly little dildos!" As he spoke Samson walked to the front of the bed and gently pinched the fuming man's cheek—precipitating another, although much shorter, struggle. This show of affection by his partner caused a .50 caliber smile to cross the face of the morbidly taciturn Skeets Kirby's.

The smell of fat man sweat was overpowering the sweet-scented oils previously applied by the talented masseuses.

Still in high pitch, Sam went on. "Lie still gorgeous so you won't perspire so much—you stink. Skeets, you want to go up the dirt road of a stinking Greek? For sure I'm not going to bath him..." Laughing, Sam picked up the vibrator and began to rub the apoplectic Greek's navel. "How you turn this robot dick thing on?"

"Okay pal, playtime's over. Time to get serious." The smile evaporated from Skeet's face and Samson knew the words were meant as much for him as for the spread-eagled Gypsy man.

Sam didn't care what his partner thought about his sense of humor—Skeets being devoid of such. To Samson, humor was an outlet, an escape from the deadly serious burden of their activities. When Samson Hercules Duff got mad he laughed and the madder he got the harder he laughed. This had gotten him into trouble as a youth since the threat of punishment, while taken seriously by the young Samson, never failed to provoke the mad-laughter response resulting in more punishment since dad Duff wanted his punitive efforts to be taken seriously—Sam just couldn't help laughing when provoked—even if he wanted.

"Pappadoupoulis, we're going to ask a few questions... we want straight answers... we don't want a lot of bullshit and we won't like asking a question more than once. Your men are totally disabled and unable to help or go for help. You are totally alone." When Skeets Kirby got serious, his words, though aimed at the stunned mound of flesh, caused goose bumps on Sam. The man was a total master at intimidation.

"Fuck you and the horse you rode in on!" shot back the recharging Greek. "I'll see you in hell before I tell you assholes a goddam thing!" Aiming his gaze at Sam he spit but succeeded only in covering his chin with ropey saliva. "You amateur cocksucker, we should have killed you when we had the chance. I told Mick and Joe Billie to blow your goddam brains out but no, not them. They said nobody could live through the beatin' they put on you."

"Mick, huh? He one of the boys that whipped up on me?" Sam's voice was suddenly very low and very deliberate. "So that's who used my head for a rug, eh? Good. I knew I didn't like old Mick and now I know why. So you, the ding-bat Indian and your recently gone-to-hell gunnie, Mick, are the ones l owe the favor to. Well… well… well… one down, two to go. I guarantee Mick won't be around looking for work—ever—and the party's over; it's talky-doodle time!"

The deliberate change in the men's demeanor did not escape the bombastic captive nor did the silence that followed his refusal of their request. Now slits, his ripe olive eyes darted from one face to the other intuitively knowing their silence to be a form of communication between the two. The gypsy man's mouth was dry and any attempt to generate saliva, futile; his bluff had not only been called by the intruders but by his own physiology as well. He truly thought them to be bluffing and only hoped that friends would arrive and end this embarrassment. The audacity in trussing him like a pig and tormenting him rankled the pompous fat man much more than any fatuous threats. Also, the fact that his guards screwed up wouldn't be forgotten. He was going to chew them a new one, by God! It was all Joe Billie's fault. He should have killed that crazy son of a bitch when he had the chance. Him and his stupid idea to revenge that shit eatin' deaf mutt and all that costume Indian warrior crap. Well, Jack Pappadoupoulis would show 'em. When he got this shit cleared up he was definitely going to subtract a few complications from his business equation—permanent like.

"Alright guys, I've seen enough. Name your price. I'm startin' to get a little bored with this game." The Greek's eyes settled on Samson and his tensed bulk relaxed like a giant balloon losing air. Gypsy Jack's vainglory was alive and well. "I know you men have a price—every body does…"

The continuing silence became an anachronism to his bravado and his words trailed off as he studied the movements of the silent pair. Skeets Kirby took a small recorder and a rubber band from his fanny pack and with a nod to Sam positioned himself behind the Greek's left arm. Samson stepped to the front of the same arm and in one motion locked the gaping man's wrist and elbow against the bed.

"Wh-wh-what the hell you doin'? Leggo my arm..." Audacity was rapidly departing the Greek's demeanor.

With the speed and precision of a medical technician, Kirby wrapped the rubber band around the sausage-like ring finger of the dumbfounded captive, pulled his hand against the wooden bedpost and without so much as the blink of his eye severed the digit with a knife that seemed to materialize in his hand.

"Arggg... ahhh... ahhh..." The maimed man's gurgled cries seemed to ooze from his body as if by excretion instead of vocalization. His heavy head lolled uncontrollably and the dark, piercing eyes rolled upwards seeking escape or solace behind their pendulous eyelids. Strings of saliva appeared at the corners of the man's mouth, pushed there by a useless tongue as his arrogant brain refused to believe this happening and rebelled. All the air exited the balloon-like body; Gypsy Jack Pappadoupoulis was in shock.

"I'll be dam, old hoss, you're gonna' have to go back to manicure school or at least take a refresher course—think you got the quick on this one. How're we gonna keep any payin' customers?" Samson released the flaccid arm and watched the blackish teardrops of blood force their way from the glistening stump, against the constrictive effort of the rubber band. "Better wake 'em up or we'll be here all night."

As his jocular partner was talking, Skeets produced several ampules, picking a green and white one while setting aside a black and red one.

"Green and white see the light; black and red make you dead!—or was that about a snake?" Sam's jocosity had no effect on his taciturn buddy as Skeets Kirby bore the same facial expression as when he burst into the room. "For sure don't mix that cyanide ampule with those ammonia jobbies. We don't have a license for a seance." Sam's voice lost its playful tone.

Breaking open the ammonia ampule, Skeets waved it under the fat man's nose. "Get that fan and let's get his blubber ass in gear."

Sam turned the electric fan on full and pointed it at the nodding head. The man's stench threatened to overpower Sam's fine tuned sense of smell. He reeked of fear and submission as if his masseuse had rubbed him down with it. Instead of evoking pity these odors birthed a contemptuousness that took him by surprise; for the first time in his memory Samson Hercules Duff was devoid of empathy. A low, bovine groan was evidence of the ammonia's effect and in a few seconds the heavy eyelids stirred and like the curtain on opening night, slowly but surely lifted. The black orbs peering between the lids, unable to focus, silently surveyed the room. Their stare touched on everything but gave no hint of recognition—the eyes of a zombie. The severed finger, gaudy rings in situ, lying on the table next to the small recorder evoked no response. If the obsidian searchlights were seeking help, they found none; if reason, they found none; and if pity, they certainly found none. The gypsy man was ready to cooperate.

Skeets spoke in a clipped but deliberate tone. "Okay fat one, the preliminaries are over and the main event is about to start. As part of the introduction I'm going to read you your rights: You have the right to remain silent, because anything you say can and will be used against you. You have the right to call an attorney and you have the right to one phone call. The only right I have is this knife." As he spoke, Kirby blatantly tested the blade's razor edge with his thumb, the reptilian slit of his eye belying his mammalian birthright. "If you insist on using your rights then I will use mine and in a few sessions your hands will make a seal's flippers look like the hands of a concert pianist. Do we understand each other?"

"Yu-yu-yes, I understand. Whatever you wu-want, just don't hurt me, please...please..." The man's subdued tone was total submission... Skeets turned on the recorder.

Charles Sylvester Kirby, Jr., viewed the slobbering mound of flesh as less than human. Unlike his counterpart, Kirby had no empathy—never had—never would. The flinty eyed agent was a sociopath; intelligent, educated, controlled. Nonetheless, a sociopath. That he could function at all was due to the happenstance of finding Sam Duff, the only man he truly respected, and being accepted by the FBI after law school. Skeets was born into poverty and it wasn't long before he realized the difference between having it—and not. The have-nots scrounged daily to exist while the haves never let them forget it. To the fledgling sociopath this was an invite to confiscate or destroy; except for Josephine Kirby.

Jo Kirby was the kind of mother that caused kids to leave home. Tough, wiry, self disciplined to a fault and disinclined to take any shit from her kids, genetic influences notwithstanding. She was clean and neat, shopping at bargain basements and dressing above her means. Ditto for her two children. Skeets and his sister, 'Chita, lived in a low water boot camp operated by a motherly martinet but they were always clean and neatly garbed. Their father had been killed when caught raping a neighbor's wife, a fact never revealed to his offspring. This upbringing, while unable to change the young man's mentality did alter his perception of society to the extent he became something of an idealist and less of an unfeeling user of people. He learned and understood that society has a conscience and he had to act a certain way if he was to survive—and Charles Kirby was a survivor—not self-destructive.

Meeting Sam Duff and fighting his way to a college education and a law degree further honed his skills in coercion and lying. Many times the young law student lost the relationship between truth and lies. Results were all that mattered and other peoples' suffering was their problem, not his. He learned early that people will tolerate a lie if it's something they want to hear and most people want to hear only what they want to hear. As his relationship with Samson and fellow Bureau agents ripened, Skeets found himself developing a strong sense of justice. Not as spelled out in the law books and statutes but as found in the justice of simple folk—almost biblical. An eye for an eye, a tooth for a tooth and as long as it wasn't Skeets Kirby's eye or tooth, screw you. He would steadfastly stand up for another's rights and defend both to the death but if said fellow happened to piss him off, he had no compunction about doing him in; means and methods of little importance, only results.

Samson Hercules Duff came into his life during his freshman year at the University of Florida. Sam was the most physically fit man Skeets Kirby had ever seen; the most open and straightforward. But underneath this veneer of naivete coursed a stream of insight and perception that was incomprehensible to Jo Kirby's mendacious son. The two opposites hit it off immediately and once Skeets decided that Sam was physically invincible, his demeanor mellowed and Sam became Skeets Kirby's only true friend.

Sam Duff accepted his new friend as he did everyone—for what he was. It did Skeets no good to coerce or lie to young Duff; he simply didn't believe anything anybody told him unless he had first hand knowledge of it and this included Skeets. Sam didn't want pity or patronage so Kirby's lack of empathy had little effect on him. As time passed the two developed a sixth sense that bordered on mind reading. Skeets matured and his sociopathic tendencies focused on his work, neutralizing him as a public threat. In time Samson would know intuitively every time his cohort lied; and in time Skeets discerned this and quit lying to him. Even though tiny sparks of resentment occasionally flew from the flint rocks of competition, they were closer than brothers.

"What is your full name." Skeets voice was monotone and deliberate.

"Ja-Ja-Jacquelis Skouris Pappadoupoulis." The deflated Greek had stopped sweating and his skin had an ashen hue that reminded Samson of death. He hoped the fat guy didn't expire before they were through with him.

"Repeat that you are giving this information of your own free will, totally voluntarily." His interrogator turned the recorder off as he spoke, flipping it back on as Jack repeated the phrase letter perfect. As soon as he finished the statement, Sam stuck the ammonia ampule under the flaring, meaty nose, causing a gasp that awoke dormant vibrations in the rolls of fat as if the skin knew something and wanted to crawl away from the body. The ammonia shock brought light to the hassled man's dark eyes as Skeets continued. "Tell us about the cattle rustling. Name names and give facts—don't make me ask twice." Again the little recorder was turned on.

The compliant captive was only too happy to talk, believing his only chance at salvation lay in satisfying these maniacs or delaying long enough for a miracle rescue to occur—which was unlikely at this hour of the morning. The tavern didn't open until 11 am and none of his help ever showed up before 10:30. He detailed the meat operation, how he started about ten years ago when a friend who picked up dead farm animals and processed the carcasses into dog food got into financial trouble and came to Jack. Most of the dead animals were horses, since the ranchers and dairy-men hauled their dead cows to the back forty and let the buzzards have a go at them. One of the Greek's regulars was an emigrant Belgium who had been raised on horsemeat and hearing of Jack's new business, asked to buy some as he swore it made the best chili in the world. Word got around and the tavern became the place for foreign nationals to get horsemeat; a staple in many European countries. A German suggested that Jack try the equine tenderloin in place of filet mignon—that they were indistinguishable from their bovine counterpart—and they were! It wasn't long before the enterprising Greek was selling prime "filet mignon" to most of the swank eateries on Florida's lower east coast. "But," he said, "I couldn't keep up with the demand." With only a limited num-ber of horses available and veterinarians' preference to destroy their equine patients with a lethal injection rendering them unfit for consumption, unlike the time honored bullet-in-the-brain, the gypsy man was soon bribing these horse doctors to shoot their pa-tients with a gun instead of a syringe and needle. That wasn't too effective since most horse owners abhorred the idea of ending old Dobbin's misery with a coup de grace and these owners would be served, Jack's needs notwithstanding.

"Get on with it, fatso. What about the Indian?" Skeets' impa-tience was gnawing at the edges as he signaled his silent cohort to do the ammonia thing again.

"I'm okay, I'm okay." The Greek's attempt to avoid the acrid ampule was futile as Sam gestured to insert it up his nose if he didn't cooperate. "I met Joe Billie 'bout six years ago, when I really needed some meat, and he told me to get cattle and quit foolin' with the ponies. Anyway, we worked out a deal and he supplied me with all the beef I could use—anytime I needed it….didn't matter to him." A scowl ran across Jack's face as he mentioned the half-breed. "If it wasn't for that crazy son of a bitch, I wouldn't be here like this, you can bet on that." The scowl was quickly replaced by a grimace. "My hand hurts…"

"You want me to cut the band off? Keep talking." Skeets voice held no mercy but it was evident the submissive man was regaining his composure.

"Joe Billie connected me up to the tribe 'n we started letting them have some meat—the law never bothered them—then Joe Billie got his gator thing going and first thing I know we got people from all over the world wantin' gator hide. With his gator catcher permit he could legally sell whatever he caught for the state but he poached ten times that amount and nobody asked any questions when they bought 'um."

"Who's on your payroll. You couldn't do this without help,"

Samson interjected. He was getting nervous about time. He wanted to know where the big Miccosukee was and if Jack thought the captives were alive, or what. He couldn't rid his mind of Elise Jones.

The Greek's voice was barely audible as he answered.

"The sheriff…"

"McCall?"

"Yea, him." Jack continued and named people the two had never heard of.

"Why do you need the sheriff if the Indian does all the rustling?" Samson's query was as much quest as question.

"I needed him for the machinery."

"What machinery?"

"I got into moving heavy equipment up north and out west and needed the sheriff for that." The round man seemed relaxed as he detailed his operation involving stealing earth moving equipment and trucking it out of Florida for resale at enormous profit. He had enlisted the help of a colony of Thai people and found them to be piratical as hell when properly motivated; to the extent of furnishing him young women to satisfy his exotic sexual preferences while the men stole bulldozers, draglines, lowboys and any other equipment that the Greek had an order for. "Then they screwed up 'n took some new stuff belonged to Can…"

"Can Martin, the rancher?"

"Yea. He knew about me. I lent him big money 'cause he was always needin' some and he liked these young Thai gals 'cause they do anything you want. Not like these American gals. Can never took anything… just knew. Then the Thai's got his stuff. He was royally pissed but couldn't say anything and we couldn't get the junk back. He was going to stick it to the insurance people but they gave him a hard time and he had to come to me for more green."

Samson was curious about this new can of worms. "How does the Indian fit in?"

"He don't… in this. That shit-ass don't know anything about the equipment deal and don't give a dam anyway. All he want to do is show off his deaf dog, hunt and bash gator heads. If'n he had left the rancher alone I wouldn't be in this shit—it's his goddam fault—him and his goddam deaf mutt." Gypsy Jack was starting to breath heavy and his tongue seemed too big for his mouth. His gravelly voice was becoming unintelligible so the two men had to strain to hear. Sam left, returning with a glass of water. With his discomfort eased, the temporarily revived Gypsy man told the two about Joe Billie and Stump, how the dog got killed, Can wounded and how the fretful half-breed swore eternal vengeance.

Samson turned to Skeets after hearing about Joe Billie's dog. "Well, old Hoss, that explains Martin's case of nerves after his accident. Poor Wishy, whoever he was. You might want to discuss interrogation methods with that Indian—he may be on to something—with those gators." The display of questionable humor didn't ease his apprehension about Elise. Suppose that crazy son of a bitch had fed her to the gators. Sam felt blood rise to his face and throb the foreboding pulsations of frustration.

"Did Can Martin know about your meat dealings?" Skeets had a problem believing that the conniving rancher wasn't in on the entire operation.

"Naw... not really. He knew I had somethin' going with ga-tor hides and meat but he thought it was small time and mainly tied to the Tribe. Can didn't give a rip 'long's he had that young Thai pussy and money." The fat man's voice was stronger and his heavy lidded eyes began fixing those of his captors, a sign the two had been looking for. They could tell by his tone that contemp-tuousness was creeping back into his mien and though fat, slop-py and securely trussed, Jack Pappadoupoulis wasn't to be taken lightly. "Joe Billie didn't wanna do anything that was complicated or forced him to deal with people. Somethin' pissed him off with Martin. I don't know what it was because everybody knows Can hated Indians. I think Joe Billie rustled his cows just for the heck of it—'till he caused Stump to cash it in. This whole thing's his fault, think he just has a hard on for all white people now."

Jack's hand was throbbing like mad but the initial shock had worn off and intimidation turned to anger. So these two yahoos think they're mean, huh. Well the Gypsy man has a few tricks yet and that finger ain't gonna be cheap. As he thought, he remem-bered The old Webley .455 cal revolver loaded and under the mat-tress at the head of his bed. The venerable piece was tucked in a pocket out of the way so not to be lain on. If he could get his right arm free he could have it in a heartbeat and these two could be on their way to hell in a hurry. The Greek prided himself on his smarts and felt the equal of any man in the game of wits. Admittedly a challenge, Jack's honest opinion was that he overmatched these guys by daylight; they never once looked under the mattress or bed. Too bad—dumb—he thought.

"What do you know about the killings and kidnapping at the Martin ranch? Where is that crazy asshole Indian—you think they're alive?" Samson could contain himself no longer. These questions had been branding his brain since his first look through the tavern window.

The Greek's returning composure was evident as he answered Sam. "He did it alright. I tried to talk him out of it but he's losing it and nobody'll stop him 'less with a dose of lead." The throaty, growl-like voice was back with each word weighed and measured before being forced out by the padded tongue. "He don't want no ransom, he just wants to bash Martin. I don't know why he took the nurse 'n I don't know where they are or if they're still 'live." The Greek's replies were more deliberate, more thought out and his surrender to intimidation no longer evident. The Gypsy man was coasting.

Sam sensed the changes in attitude and worried that he would start lying. He knew it would take longer before his partner could discern this but the Greek's recovery was real and would soon be apparent. He also knew Skeets' reaction if he thought the man was fooling with them—no more Greek....period. Casually sliding his knife from its sheath, Samson began to clean his fingernails as casually as a dog sniffing a turd. Bending over the bound man's face, Sam exhibited the razor-edged tool as he dropped his voice to an eerie whisper. "Where is the Indian? You know his territory... where do you think he's gone with those two? I think you're in on this..."

"No... No... I'm not in that..." Sam's display put the Greek back on the defensive and he pressed harder.

"Tell me where he's gone..."

"All I know is what he's told me 'bout where he grew up. He raised in the 'Glades south of the alley and one time he showed me where he went in off the road to get to the old place. It's 'bout 30 -35 miles from Naples. Just past a roadside stop and right past a panther sign. That's all I know....swear to God!" Samson knew about Alligator Alley and the Everglades but had never actually set foot in what was fast becoming a compelling, fascinating, piece of real estate. Though native, Sam's boyhood meanderings in west central Florida did nothing to insure knowledge of the brooding Pa-hay-okee; nor did his extensive survival training. Unless in the Everglades, no survival training area dared duplicate its unique and foreboding environment. It was a different world. Samson knew that the volcanic Miccosukee and his captives were in that vast, trackless domain and would not be found by conventional means unless Joe Billie so ordained. Time became a monstrous burden to the perturbed Samson Hercules Duff; time that would work against the lithesome nurse given the uncaring attitude of Joe Billie Bloodtooth and the Pay-Hay-Okee.

Skeets remained silent but was aware of his buddy's anxiety. He knew the futility of following anyone into the Everglades and wanted to finish with the fat man, get the recording to the cattlemen, explain their position and collect the rest of the money; screw Can Martin. He was truly sorry about Elise Jones but Skeets Kirby wasn't one to lose sleep over something beyond his control—the Florida Everglades was certainly that. He knew no one would ever see those two, possibly three, again. He also had enough from the Greek to fulfill their obligation to the cattlemen and was going to make sure the Pappadoupoulis organization was history. To Charles S. Kirby, the case was closed.

Laying the recorder down Kirby shifted his blinkless stare to Sam. "Heard enough? It's daylight out there and we've got a lot to do. Too bad about the girl. Let's cut this lard ass loose and hit the boards." Skeets flinty tone held the faintest promise of sympathy. Sam accepted it, not caring if it was a true expression or Kirby's deference to societal conscience; however, the Greek absorbed it like a dry sponge. It was time for his move and he could barely calm his spirit.

"I can't breathe… can't breath…" The bulbous head was lolling as if connected to the main blob by a rubber cord. "…chest hurts,…need water." The two captors looked at the histrionic heap, then at each other. No words were exchanged but their response was as if choreographed. Sam held the glass of water to the anguished man's lips while Skeets deftly cut his feet loose, then the maimed hand. Gliding to the far side, the efficient operative severed the cords binding the Greek's good hand. Jack struggled to sit up but kept his coal-lump eyes closed for fear of telegraphing the rapture of his impending retribution. Revenge would, indeed, be sweet. "More water, please." As he begged to buy more time, Jack tried to move the fingers on his good hand and found it next to impossible. Even though he had tried to relax them after regaining his composure, he wasn't able to move them enough to negate the compromised circulation. "Help, I need help, can't feel my fingers…"

Skeets eyebrows arched but he didn't look up. "Okay, lard ass, I'll massage your hand, then it's up to you."

Skeets help the Greek? Samson thought he was hearing things—couldn't be—but, it was. "Here," Skeets went on, "hold this ammonia to your nose and it'll improve your circulation, pronto." As he spoke, he massaged the fat man's bloated fingers before placing the tiny ampule between Jack's tingling thumb and index finger. The Gypsy man could feel mobility surging into his hand and fingers, his bulky body coming alive. His slitted eyes were aglow with morbid anticipation as his erstwhile tormentor pushed his hand under his nose and with the admonition, "Squeeze," pressed against the two fingers fracturing the ampule with a tiny tinkling sound that would have been a thunderclap to Gypsy Jack Pappadoupoulis—had he known.

Skeets instantly turned away and motioned to the bemused Samson to follow. The bloated being on the bed took a deep breath and as Sam watched, the man's eyes suddenly opened wide and his immense bulk began to quiver as it fought to finish its breath so to take another—but couldn't. The bulbous eyes displayed confusion as the huge body tried to take another breath.

His hue was darkening and his protruding tongue showing black as his eyes reflected confusion, now mixed with a little hope. The bulging obsidian orbs were silently pleading with its hypoxic brain; BREATHE, BREATHE—but nothing happened. As if to try for a miracle, the dying man's hand frantically pushed the ampule closer to his flared nostrils desperately seeking the breath of life. But none was there. The violated eyes were now unseeing, pupils terminally dilated, confusion gone, hope gone, yet fixed forever in their final stare—the curious look of total disbelief. Gypsy Jack Pappadoupoulis was on his way to hell.

Skeets paused at the door, turned slightly and saluted the Greek as the last of his life gasped away. The blubbery carcass relaxed and a tiny, crushed, red and black ampule fell from the limp fingers and rolled innocently to the floor. The rotund body, sitting upright in the bed bore marked resemblance to Buddha—before he had his head shaved. The cherubic Buddha grin of righteous immortality was replaced by a slack-jawed rictus of shock; thick lips formed a cupid's bow around a discolored tongue, now much too large, as if to blow a kiss. Skeets snapped his hand to his side and paid his final respects to the frustrated carcass of Jacquelis Skouris Pappadoupoulis. "So long grouper lips....you're a good interview. Should have told you I was colorblind."

• • •

Chapter ELEVEN

The sun was cracking the horizon and the dew-wet saw palmettos appeared silver-black in the transitional dimness. The palmetto flat bordered a large oak hammock that stretched south into the bowels of the Florida Everglades. This was Federal parkland, many miles south of the Indian reservation and seldom blessed by human intrusion, either Indian, park ranger or lost soul; hunting, though prohibited, was done on occasion by a few adventurers in half-tracks. Dense willow and myrtle supported by thick sedges, cabbage palm and wicked blackberry fringed the hammock like verdant spit curls parted by the myriad game trails; pathways used as freeways by panther, bear, deer, bobcat, raccoon, wild hogs and wild cattle—especially wild hogs.

Florida wild hogs are totally feral, descended from stray domestic hogs. None are related to the savage European wild boar of medieval classics; though these had been loosed and permitted to take root in a few locations.

Any comparison of the Florida wild hog to its domestic counterpart would be semantic and easily resolved by face to face confrontation with the wild variety.

The dewfall started about 2:00 that morning and was heavy since the summer rainy season was yet a month away. The scattered afternoon showers were infrequent during these spring days and the cool nights and mornings often gave way to intense heat as the inexorable sun journeyed through the heavens. The huge shadow finished rooting the moist, peaty soil at the edge of the palmetto flat and vapidly headed back to the cool depths of the hammock to lie up during the intense heat of the day. Food, not plentiful, was adequate but the big boar found it took longer and longer to satisfy the demands placed on his stomach by his 400 plus pound body. It seemed as if he did nothing but root for edibles; suffering hunger during the mating season and losing weight while his normal ill temper worsened. Usually herbivorous, mature boars like Big'un would eat meat when found and many developed a taste for it, much to the detriment of neighborly creatures; rattlesnakes being a favorite since they were frequently rooted up and never learned that these boars were impervious to their deadly bite. In truth, though, old Big'un didn't cull his groceries—if he could catch it he would eat it.

It was the beginning of the breeding time and Big'un was near his prime: 38 inches at the shoulder and six months past his fourth birthday, his bristly, wire-haired body virtually fat free. His shoulders, face and snout were armored, unyielding to tooth or claw, root or rock. The considerable strength in his neck and shoulders was never fully tested nor the stolid glint in his eyes—small, round and perennially bloodshot. The ivory-like tusks protruding from his lower jaw cleared the lip by a good four inches, their posterior edge honed razor sharp by years of competition with the upper pair. The black beast ambled through the thinning palmettos to the thick fringe and found the trail he wanted, passing between two fallen bay trees covered by a dense growth of vines and thorns. There was plenty of headroom but the trail was narrow for 50 or 60 feet before opening into the more spacious hammock. Fifty yards to the east was an ancient cabbage palm close by a thick trunked

Magnolia tree, nailed to which was a human skull, its ghostly white pate bearing the marks of severe disruption. This emblem had been placed many years before by hog trappers after finding the scattered remains of a man around the old cabbage palm. To them and the few that followed, this place, from then on, was known as Skull Hammock. Their hog trap was usually within sight of the skull, making it easier to find.

Fifteen feet into the verdurous tunnel the placid hog came face to face with an old swamp bull, one horn broken and festered, flies covering the suppuration as well as his face. Like the wild hog, Florida wild cattle descended from domestic stock gone astray, their history of wildness predating that of the wild pigs. The cattle in the Skull Hammock area had never seen a human and were every bit as wild and leery as the deer. This bull was over the hill, used up but still mean as a snake and tough as steel wire, weighing about 700 pounds. His night had been less than perfect, his head hurt and he was not about to defer to this black pig. Big'un stopped, his small-ish eyes giving no betrayal of the meeting. The only sign of recognition was the long bristles on the boar's back rising from their resting position and the cessation of movement by his tactile snout. The bull lowered his aching head, tilted his good horn forward and began to paw at the ground, throwing clots of mucky soil to plaster the sides of the leafy passageway. Thick, ropy cords of saliva drained from the bull's nose as his agitation increased and a bovine growl starting deep in his chest eructated as a spine tingling roar with his charge. Big'un still hadn't moved and the bull's horn caught him under the right jowl and pushed him halfway around on the narrow trail but could not penetrate the tough hide. The change in the big hog's demeanor was dramatic and instant. His little eyes narrowed to bloodshot slits and the grunt extracted by the impact changed to a mouth popping "wuf... wuf... wuf..." The momentum of the attack carried the bull past his adversary by half his body length resulting in the hog's snout positioned adjacent to the bull's hind legs. The narrow trail made it difficult for the enraged bovine to maneuver and the boar quickly seized the advantage. With the frenetic side-to-side serpentine motion of a ruptured air hose the fired up boar raked the bull's hind legs as the bucking animal tried to turn and gore his tormentor. Jumping his shorter adversary the leathery bull rammed his good horn into the boar's shoulder and began to push, his lean sinewy shoulders straining like the towrope on a tugboat. Though shorter than the bull, Big'un was more compact and his front-end strength the equal of his opponent. As the horn penetrated the thick hide of the boar's shoulder, his rhythmic mouth popping changed to a high-pitched squeal and the impaled beast went crazy. In a fury of motion, Big'un hit the side of the bull's neck opening deep gashes with each stroke of his armed snout. The bull's rear legs were bleeding profusely from the grievous gashes inflicted during the first encounter; the gaskin area just above his hocks laid open to the bone. Unable to out push the enraged bull and hurting from the impaled horn, Big'un suddenly backed up, loosening the horn and allowing him to twist free of it. Still frenzied, the big hog ran under the bull and started raking the beast's belly and under parts. The sickening "Wop, wop, wo-op" of the saber like tusks hitting the bull's tensed abdominal muscles disrupted the pre-dawn stillness like a boulder hitting quiet water. Accompanied by the sound of escaping air a loop of small intestine blew out of the six inch gash in the heaving bull's flank coincidental with his rear end collapsing on the savage hog. Forced to rely on his unfailing instinct for survival, the disemboweled animal gave up and in a desperate scramble regained his feet and fled from the gory bower out to the palmetto flat. But it was too late and Big'un knew that no matter how far the old swamp bull ran his reliable pig nose would sniff him out and he would feast.

• • •

Twenty miles, as the crow flies, from where Big'un and the swamp bull were locked in their death struggle two young Miccosukee Indians sat in a pickup truck parked along Alligator Alley. The six-pack sitting between them advertised two empty slots.

"You been going back in that Skull Hammock lately?" The driver was a short, solid built kid with shoulder length hair black as a crow's wing. His name was Samchuck Tiger and he had finished high school a week ago. Like most young men of the Miccosukee, he lived for the Everglades and hunting and fishing. His truck, an old Ford 4x4, was beat up but kept in good working order by young Tiger and his friends like Jimmy Gopher sitting across from him in the truck. Jimmy was a stutterer and Sammy Tiger was tolerant of this quirk since Jimmy was four years older but many years wiser in the ways of their world. Getting no answer, Sammy continued. "My dad says that place is a place of spirits and that we should not go there." Young Tiger's speech was very proper and very deliberate.

"Fu-fu-fuck yu-yu-your dad. H-h-he jus' du-du-don't w-w-want you goin' wa-wa-with me." Once Jimmy got his tongue warmed up his speech improved. "They's hogs a-a-out yu-yu-your gazoo in that ham-hammock. N-nobody fools 'r-round back th-there 'cause th-th-they's a-a-fraid. No body g-g-got a half-track I-like me 'n I got ta-ta-three pig traps b-back in there." Jimmy was right about Sammy's father not liking him. The young Indians' fathers had been friends all their lives until they lined up on different sides in a tribal dispute—end of friendship.

Jimmy's stammer had resulted in many fights during his aborted high school career and it wasn't long before the taunted youth let his knife do the fighting. One day during his junior year, Young Jimmy Gopher carved up Sammy's older first cousin for making fun of him and came close to precipitating a shootout between his father and Sammy's uncle. School was out for Jimmy Gopher—permanently. Since then he had made his living wrestling alligators, trapping and selling wild game, especially hogs, conning tourists and pimping when his girlfriends' allowed. He had taken his friend to Skull Hammock on the two occasions his obstreperous half-track cooperated and Samchuck Tiger fell in love with the area.

Sammy sucked on the warming can of Budweiser as condensation dripped on his glabrous chest. He truly loved being a man. His voice was intense as he repeated his query. "When are you going back? I want to go with you. Think you'll ever trap that big old hog? What do you call him? Old Big'un?" The eager Miccosukee remembered the treacherous ride to Skull Hammock and the story Jimmy Gopher told about the boar he called Big'un.

Jimmy was taken to Skull Hammock while a high school freshman, by a white man who was a friend of his father as well as a former park ranger. The man, known as Doug, told the impressionable young Indian about a Miccosukee half-breed who had trailed his murderous father through the trackless marshes and hammocks to kill him in the vicinity of the big magnolia tree bearing the battered skull—supposedly that of the murderous father. The story went on about how the father had treacherously murdered his wife and her father, the avenger's mother and grandfather, in their chickee many miles to the south and on the west edge of the endless *Melaleuca* strand. Doug also said that many people believe the spirits of the murdered innocents still trod the trail from chickee to killing tree—when the moon rose at midnight on a cloudy night. The young hunter was more impressed by game sign than ghost story and from that day on his goal was to get to Skull Hammock and back with some degree of predictability.

Skull Hammock was one of the most beautiful hardwood hammocks in the glades, stretching several miles through the saw-grass marshes and saw palmetto flats. The ancient, clean limbed live oak a stark contrast to the gnarly, leather leaved water oak with its arm-like limbs and branches twisted in agonal response to some idiopathic pain. The many ferns, some tall as a man's head: leather and bracken ferns, wait-a-minute vines with needle sharp thorns demanding that the unwary trespasser wait a minute, or longer. There were moonflowers fringing the hammock, white blossoms glowing in the dark as if a curtain call for the lonely spirits destined to forever roam the endless Pay-Hay-Okee. The moist trails of rare tree snails bore testimony to the myriad life forms in these trees. Butterflies too numerous to count and too beautiful to describe flitted through the sparse undergrowth, sometimes stopping on the lacy bloom of the elderberry, lending credence to that delicate blossom's sobriquet, Queen Anne's lace. And then the banyan tree or strangler fig, a freakish combination of tree and herbaceous parasite resulting in an arboreal temple with woody columns descending from above to form rooms, passageways, dens, alcoves; a veritable dendritic condominium. The southern edge of Skull Hammock sported banyan growth of tremendous magnitude and Jimmy Gopher had not yet ventured to this part of the hammock.

Florida wild hogs were caught in pen-like traps baited with corn or garbage. Traversing the marshy, unpredictable terrain was a never-ending challenge and any pens or pen building materials had to be lightweight to be transported by the swamp buggy or half-track, the only mechanized way to negotiate the ever changing river-of-grass. Once erected, the pen had to be firmly anchored to the ground—no mean feat given the moist, quivering muck typical of the area—or the bigger hogs would lift the pen with their plow-like snouts and leave. Once trapped, the pigs would be sorted by the trapper, some taken to sell or fatten at home, some young boars castrated, ear-marked and returned to the wild with ear marked gilts to be trapped later when they had fattened or the gilts had matured and produced piglets.

Due to the tortuous route to Skull Hammock, Jimmy Gopher butchered his caught hogs on the spot, using their entrails as bait for the traps. His junker half-track had little room for carrying and the freshly butchered pork commanded a ready market.

Before taking up with young Samchuck Tiger, Jimmy had visited his traps and found total disruption; both pens overturned with gory pieces of pig scattered around both traps. The sign was unmistakable. A huge boar had taken up at Skull Hammock and would enter the trap, eat the bait—springing the trap—casually root it up and over and amble on. If the trap held pigs, the crusty old boar would lift the trap and go under, let it fall in place and dine on the smaller trapped pigs while ignoring the bigger ones who partook of this serendipitous largess with ill-concealed gusto. Once finished, out he went. Carnivorous by opportunity, wild hogs are very poorly trained in meat course manners, noisily chomping and slurping up the soft body parts, unwilling to strip meat or gnaw bone. When satiated, they amble off to rest, neither covering or worrying about the remains nor returning to consume any remnants as a true carnivore would. The result is a retching, gory scene straight out of a horror movie. A happening such as this close to home would be resolved by eager catch dogs and a .22 pistol. But Skull Hammock was too far and young Gopher didn't want to risk discovery no matter how remote the chance. He had to trap that opportunistic hunk of mean pork, quickly, or surrender skull hammock.

Jimmy soon recognized the big hog's sign and his estimation of its size seemed incredulous. It was going to take a pen of unusual size anchored firmly to the ground if he was to have any chance at success. Since his first encounter, Jimmy had referred to the unsolicitous beast as the big hog, later as big one and finally as Big'un. He knew that Big'un wouldn't tolerate another significant boar in his territory and his removal would ensure many months, even years, of routine pig trapping.

The six pack showed six empty slots as Jimmy and Sammy finished talking and the eager Sammy Tiger couldn't wait to crank the dilapidated half-track and go build a hog trap strong enough to hold a bull.

• • •

Sam looked at the speedometer and squinted into the morning sun. He had been up for 30 hours and though tired, his anxiety level was such that sleep was the last thing on his mind. His priorities, previously hazy and intermingled were now singular and focused as sunlight reflected through a magnifying lens. He was going to find Elise Jones. If Joe Billie Bloodtooth and Can Martin turned up during the search, so be it, but they were definitely low priority.

The 95 mph registered by the straining speedometer needle coupled with the hypnotic, rhythmic blinking of the radar detector were of more interest to Junk Yard than to the preoccupied driver. The dispassionate pit bull eyed the tiny blink-blink-blink like a jaded housewife watching TV. His sleek sable coat glistened, the sunlight playing off his rippling muscles as he adroitly maintained balance with the shifting seat. It was 10:00 am and Samson's dark maroon pickup was screaming along state road 82 having left Ft. Myers headed for Immokalee and State Road 29 which cut south and intersected Alligator Alley some 28 miles east of Naples. With any luck he should be at the place the Greek described in less than an hour. He hoped to God the fat man had told the truth and that the possessed Indian had gone into the Glades at that point—that Elise was still alive. His concern for her was overpowering—if only he knew she was alive—and threatened to disrupt his ingrained methodical approach to a dangerous situation. He had to find out and knew no one else could; without Samson Duff, Elise—and Can—were dead. Though more in control of his special sense, the scent of the nurse would not leave him. He would know that fragrance from a million others... instantly. His intensity deepened as he beat his hands on the steering wheel, muttering, "Damn-damn-damn..." causing JY to snap his head toward the sound, the pupils in his golden bird-of-prey eyes dilating, then returning to normal as no threat is perceived. He had sensed distress and urgency in his master's actions and responded and his bearing was now that of a fighting dog, in the pit—eyeing an antagonist.

Sam's eyes squinted as his thoughts shifted from Elise to his partner but still managed a weak smile as he mulled over their last conversation. The pair had remained silent during their retreat from Gypsy Jack's tavern, each waist deep in his own thoughts. Skeets' mood was relief and pleasure for a job well done; the caper wrapped and neatly tied. He had wanted to burn the tavern but Sam nixed that and Skeets knew when to accept the big man's advice and when to question it—Sam's current attitude definitely dictated acceptance.

Reaching the truck, Sam let JY out to stretch and relieve himself while the vehicle felt its way through the tall weeds looking for the way out. Reaching the hard road, the men remained silent for ten miles when Skeets suddenly pulled off the road and stopped behind a stand of thick scrub oak out of sight of the road.

"What're you stopping for?" Samson's question came as the truck slowed for the turn off.

"We can't just mosey on home and act like white folks. That asshole sheriff's got an APB out on us by now and I damn sure don't want a shootout with that shithead. Once he finds out about fish-lips, he'll pin that on us too. We've got to quietly collect our things and get to the cattlemen's group, make them believe our story, give them the tape, get our money and get the hell out of Dodge." Skeets' voice was monotone and Sam knew his partner was dead serious and more important, dead on target. It was unusual for Skeets' to talk to Sam in that tone and Samson began to dab absentmindedly at his face paint, wishing he could avoid saying what he knew he had to.

Wiping his face, Samson replied in a quiet voice. "You know I'm going after her. I can't just let that crazy half-breed bash her head in and I'm the only one with half a chance to get to them."

Skeets' reply was biting. "Don't be a fool, Samson Hercules, nobody will ever find those three, even if they had an army out there looking. So how're you going to do it? Smell them out like you're a big fuzzy St. Bernard sniffing through a snow slide for survivors? Man, let me tie the brandy keg around your sweet little neck... come on Sammy, grow up for Christ's..." Sam's face jerked around to face his partner and his caustic stare pinned the sarcastic man's eyes like butterfly wings to a cork board. "Back off Kirby, this is my show now and I'll dam well finish it—my way." Sam could see Skeets' face flush and his hands tighten their grip on the steering wheel when he heard Sam refer to him as "Kirby." For reasons beyond Samson's ken, his buddy had always resented being referred to as Kirby and Samson had seen many a well-intentioned man severely reminded of this quirk by an uptight Skeets Kirby. Mister Kirby was okay, but never just "Kirby." Sam went on, as much to himself as to his chastised pardner. "I don't understand why, but I feel like I can find them—if they are in this God forsaken swamp and still alive. If not, I'll at least find their bodies... look Skeeter, no big deal. You finish our contract, stay invisible and give me a week. If I'm not back or heard from by then, go do your thing."

Sam's voice was losing its edge and Skeets knew his pal was fighting with himself and though he really couldn't understand Sam's altruistic attitude he did understand his own attachment to the big guy and for that reason did not want him to embark on a hopeless chase. Skeets' reply, though soft, still had a bite. "Look, guy, let's do this right. I'll go to the sheriff and give up. Then I'll convince him to get a search party, with real dogs, to track this Indian asshole with choppers and airboats and anything else that'll crawl through that greasy swamp shit…"

"Aw, cut the bullshit Skeeter." Sam's jaw was firmly clenched but his voice was pleading as he tried to make his partner understand his mindset. "You know good as I do that this guy'll kill those two in a heartbeat if he sees or hears any commotion and you also know that once he's alone, no one, not even your army, real dogs, choppers or any other crap could ever find that Indian son of a bitch. That's his home out there, front yard, back yard and corner store. If they're alive, their only chance is for me to trail them and try my darndest to keep him from knowing it until I can get to him. And by God Skeets, I'm gonna give it my best shot…"

"Okay big guy." Sheets knew he was overruled and the only thing left was to keep the rest of their deal from washing out but he couldn't let it go. "But what if you get out in those boonies, hot on their trail and your super sniffer quits on you? What then? You're not going to just flag a saw-grass taxi and come home. You ever think about that? For Christ's sake, Samson, you don't have the foggiest notion why you can suddenly smell a fart in a whirlwind or how long it will last." This had long been on Skeets' mind but he didn't want to mention it and risk adding to his partner's confusion. But knowing Sam's determination he knew he had to touch this subject in a last effort at dissuading him or at least force him to face the fallibility of his new found sense.

Sam's voice remained calm as he addressed this concern.

"You're right and I know it but I just don't give a rip. I'm going after Joe Billie regardless…"

"Don't you mean Elise Jones?"

"Dammit, yes I do. I don't know why but I've got to find that woman." Sam's voice sounded distant, as if he were speaking far away. He was not in control of his emotions and he knew Skeets had picked up on this; he hated having this part of his inner self-exposed and emotionally he was beginning to feel like a turtle without its shell in a pond full of alligators. He knew he shouldn't attempt this rescue mission and he knew all the reasons why—he just didn't know how to stop.

Skeets conceded to the intensity of Sam's determination, turned his face to the driver's side window and with robot-like motions, started the truck's engine. He decided his pal would have to take his chances, slim to none he thought, and even though he couldn't understand why, would accept it at face value and hope for the best. He spoke slowly, still looking out the side window. "One thing, Samson. With or without your blessings I'm going to have a long talk with George the surgeon and find out what the hell went on that turned you into some kind of super bloodhound and what your chances are for losing it or not." The truck was back on the highway and with android-like precision, Skeets ran through the gears as if in a trance. "And if you're not out of there in a week I'm going to mobilize the biggest search ever held in the Florida Everglades." Even as he uttered the words, Skeets knew that if Samson didn't make it on his own he would never see him again. Search party or no.

Sam slowed abruptly to 55 mph as the radar detector lit up like a wino on sterno. JY was caught unaware and slammed into the dash panel causing the glove box to pop open. "Dam, JY, can't you handle speed?" Scrambling back onto the seat the quizzical look on the dog's face turned contrite as he figured he did something wrong causing his master to laugh out loud. "Don't worry, Junk Yard. Where we're going a spilled glove box won't amount to a hill of beans." Passing the oncoming highway patrol vehicle Sam floored the accelerator and settled back as the speedometer needle strained to catch up, the tranquilizing monotony of driving a deceitful balm to his frustrations. Chuckling about the look of surprise on JY's face caused his mind to drift to when he acquired the magnificent pit bull. The memories of that day were crystal clear in his troubled mind and he could still hear the big German, Carlos Otto, as they neared the ranch in the western part of Marion county to view Junk Yard and his littermates. These thoughts bullied their way into his mind as if some ethereal healer was prescribing them as an unguent for fraying nerves.

"Alright vise guy, slow down or you vill ram us right into the gate." Carlos' diction was letter perfect with the possible exception of sporadic lapses in syntax and Teutonic inflection. His voice was soft and expressive considering it was powered by a 57-inch chest encased in corded steel muscle; when he walked he looked like he had taken a deep breath and was holding it. Coupled with his six foot four inch height, 245 pounds body weight, arms and legs like corner posts and no neck—an impressive man. Stopping in front of the gate Sam watched as Carlos stepped down from the truck with the grace of an acrobat and opened the gate. The big man's reflexes and response times were so fast that even with the advantage of youth Sam couldn't match them—he was close! No cigar.

The ranch was large and cluttered with the rusted remains of tractors, trailers, wagons and various weird ranching implements that gave lie to the adage that form follows function; their esoteric forms gave not the slightest inkling of arcane utility. Turning to Carlos, Samson thought out loud. "Well, the directions were to go through the gate at the end of the road by the house and follow it to the left and stop by a circular board fence... whoa, thar she blows." Sam stopped and the two men got out and walked to the gate, looking around as they went. Seeing no one, the impatient German opened the gate enough to peek in. His face lit up. "Look here, asshole." Calling his protege by his pet name, Carlos motioned for Sam to look. Inside and 50 feet away was a sturdy doghouse surrounded by a baker's dozen wriggling, squirming, snarling, fighting pit bull puppies.

Sam counted to twelve before a voice caused both to straighten up in mock surprise.

"Don't go in there. Old Fanny will eat yore lunch 'n I'll hafta deal with them health people agin'." Extending his hand, the burly Bubba Overton continued. "I'm Bubba. You th' guys what wanna see the bull dog pups?"

"That's us. I'm Sam Duff and this is Carlos Otto." Samson stepped forward and returned the rancher's greeting knowing the German's reticence to southern protocol. "So old Fanny will get us, huh? I didn't see anything in there but pups. Where is the old heifer?" Sam's question was more small talk than substance since he had intuitively searched the enclosure and saw only puppies, doghouse and a few skimpy bushes with all lower branches and twigs stripped of leaves by the active, orally oriented pit bull pups.

"Ha—ha—ha, com'mere 'n look." Bubba was grinning and shaking his head as he signaled the two to be quiet and follow. Creeping around the enclosure, he stopped at a crack in the solid fence and motioned for Sam to look. Peering through the boards Sam saw a yellowish brindle bitch half buried in the sand behind the doghouse, her gaze nailed to the enclosure gate. A chain stretched in front of her, barely visible in the loose sand, one end attached to her collar. A deep, guttural chuckle from the German caused Sam and Bubba to turn and face the grinning wrestler. "Sure, she's no dummy! She vaiting for somevun to get close, then by God, she will nail their ass. Von't be me und I know she know chust how long is her chain, too." For sure old Carlos knew pit bulls!

The amused Bubba picked up from there. "Right on big man.

She knows 'zactly how long that chain is 'n she won't make a ripple 'till whatever is in range—then, zappo, it's bite city 'n you best have yore breakin' stick handy 'cause she quit school afore they got to the let goes." All three men were laughing as they started back to the gate and entered. As soon as Bubba closed the gate, he whistled twice and an obviously disappointed Fanny slunk around the corner of the doghouse, ears down, tail drooping with its wagged greeting barely discernible; piercing eyes followed the two strangers like radar. The nearer Bubba got the lower the bitch dropped until she was wallowing on her belly as her master grabbed her by the collar and tied her up short to the doghouse. Turning to the visitors, surrounded by growling, potbellied, bow-legged, snapping demons, Bubba volunteered that they had best keep their distance from the doghouse. Both men nodded.

"Look at that little shit!" Sam's exclamation was followed by some vigorous leg shaking as he tried to dislodge the tiny, reddish brown bundle of energy attached to the cuff of his trousers.

"He sure caught your ass," added a bemused Carlos. "Better get out your break toothpick for dat vun else he tear you up." The pup began to growl and shake his head like a Jack Russell with a rat. The more Sam shook his leg the deeper the growl and the more intense the shaking, culminating in a ripping sound as the be-leaguered fabric surrendered. Carlos and Bubba, examining the other pups, didn't see Sam's pup and the pant leg part company nor the older, much larger pup that left their group and stumbled towards Sam. This puppy, from a different litter, was twice as old as the seven-week old dynamo with the fabric shreds hanging from its clenched jaws. As the other pup approached, the change in the smaller pup was instant and dramatic—no more play time. He twirled around to face the larger pup, positioning himself squarely in front of the captivated Samson Duff and simultaneously emitted a deep, throaty growl that caused Bubba to look up. "Looka here, looka here." Bubba cradled the pup he was holding as he pointed towards Sam. "That little shit-eater thinks he a real man. He fixin' to whup up on that big'un." The hair on the protective pup stuck out like a halloween cat and his knobby little bowlegs were braced like baby corner posts.

"I'll be a monkey's uncle. I think this little piss-ant is trying to protect me..." The words had hardly left Sam's mouth when the big pup slammed into his smaller cousin, igniting a rage in the tiny adversary. Pushing his shoulder into the charge, he grabbed the heavier pup by its ear and with an unbelievable display of leverage and power threw the surprised puppy to the ground. In a flash, firmly attached to the ear, he straddled the downed pup and began to chew on the ear. The downed pup wanted nothing more than to disengage from this tiny bundle of toothed energy and began squalling like a banshee. The commotion attracted the other pups that were circling Carlos and Bubba like Indians around a wagon train and several headed for the two combatants, stumbling on their less than coordinated legs. Sam could see the change in the small pup's eyes as two others arrived and was not as surprised as the visitors when little JY jumped off his victim and throatily challenged them.

"That's a gutsy vun, Sammy boy, you should take him for I think he really like you." Carlos nodded at Bubba as Sam picked up the growling puppy.

"Shore has taken a shine to you." The proud rancher chimed in. "Just like his daddy. Old Solid 24 was the durndest protective son of a bitch I ever saw—and tough, man was he tough! Just about the best bulldog I ever had or seed, I guess. Got killed right after knocking old Sally up. This's his first 'n last bunch'a pups." The portly man's face screwed up and his appearance contracted to a far away glaze—a sadness. "Yep, I'll never know how good that mutt could'a been but, I'm agonna keep two 'a these pups."

"Well, I want this one for sure." Sam held the tiny animal, the smallest male in Fanny's litter, at arm's length and the pup immediately stopped squirming, became deathly still... catatonic. The only sign of life was his flashing eyes staring straight into Sam's with an unmistakable arrogance. Challenging—"I'll protect you— I'll trust you—I'll die for you—but if you drop me or mistreat me you human son of a bitch, I'll eat your lunch!" Samson read this message in the tiny dynamo's eyes as clearly as if chiseled in a marble slab. His pup. No need to look further.

On the drive back the German held the pup and the quiet look in his eye, Samson knew, was his tacit stamp of approval. "I'm going to call him Junk Yard, 'cause that place sure qualifies as one. Never seen so much junk and shit. The only halfway decent area was that dog pen. This little guy is the genuine article—a true junk yard dog." The contented pit bull owner smiled inwardly while the big Kraut, petting the dozing pup, grinned as the monotonous engine drone painted the three of them.

"Roadside stop—panther sign—roadside stop—panther sign—roadside stop—panther sign..." This repetitious phrase ran through Sam's subconscious like mice through a corn crib with his mind's eye viewing the words in concert with the synchronous throb of the diesel engine. Stretching his neck side to side to relieve the muscle tension, Sam became aware of his conscious mind flashing "roadside stop" and his eyes verified it as the speeding truck zipped by the green sign proclaiming in bold white letters, "REST STOP 1 MILE." A surge of adrenalin revived Sam's intensity and he backed the truck down a notch, searching the endless ribbon of roadside landscape before it disappeared in the vaporous mirage of speed.

"This may be it." Sam was thinking out loud but his canine passenger snapped his head around at the words and his neatly trimmed ears registered full alert. Both saw the desolate appearing shelter rapidly approaching and Samson braked sharply, pulled off the road and stopped at the west edge of the small rest stop. This one had no facilities, consisting of open concrete block shelters protecting concrete tables and benches. Nearby and anchored to a sturdy metal post was a large refuse container. Sam could hear his heart thumping as he stepped from the truck and closed the door on the eager pit bull. "Sorry JY, but I need to do this part by myself." Glancing at his watch, he clenched his lips and grimaced as he registered 12:00 noon—a little over 12 hours since the massacre-kidnapping; time was slipping away. The surrounding area was all Everglades and Samson took a deep breath as he studied the terrain south and east of the rest stop. The effect of the fresh air, full of nature's unique aromas was akin to a mouthful of cold lime sorbet after a cloying meal. Sam could smell every scent wafted by the Glades washed breezes, yet each maintained its identity, none overpowering his newfound sense of smell. He could smell the vastness of the place; its mysteries; its dangers. He couldn't get enough of this power giving breath of unspoiled nature. Samson Hercules Duff had never felt so alive. Potent!

In a semi-stooped position, Sam walked around the structures looking for tracks in the weeds that spread south into the grassy flats—any trace of a scent trail—Elise's unforgettable or Joe Billie's unmistakable. Since he had exposure to the murderous half-breed's spoor, he did not bring, or need, anything for scent reinforcement. Finding nothing Sam returned to the truck and parked alongside a shelter. Producing a pair of binoculars he scrambled from the truck cab to the structure roof and began glassing the roadside going east. This search revealed nothing until he raised the glasses to the horizon and spotted what looked to be a sign—the WATCH FOR PANTHERS sign, he thought and about a half mile away.

His heartrate went up another notch as he jumped from the roof and trotted along the road towards the sign. Learning as he went, Samson discovered he could determine most odors by stooping as he progressed, the disturbance caused by his passage enough to stir air currents of sufficient impact to lift scent enough for adequate perusal by his nascent sense of smell. There was no confusion of artificial odors to deal with, only the vibrant redolence of nature and the sweating man gloried in its presence as his mind catalogued various bouquets, some innocent, a few threatening, but all encyclopedic. Sam was in a different world. New world.

He found nothing until within 50 feet of the sign. Twin paths of bent grass in various stages of straightening caused him to stop. Simultaneously he detected the spoor of Joe Billie's pick-up truck, a smell Samson didn't know he knew. No doubt. The Indian had pulled off the road leaving a trail as plain to Sam as if paved. Containing his excitement, Samson sprinted back to his truck and the Junk Yard dog, doubts and apprehensions having evaporated. He had a start, a beginning. They were somewhere in that vast, watery wildness and only he, alone, could find them—he had to. Jamming the truck through its gears, he spun the tires as he fishtailed down the road, sliding to a stop and turning into the barely visible trail left by Bloodtooth's truck. Concentrating on the fading trail caused Sam's excitement to cool, allowing rational thoughts to ease into his consciousness. He didn't want his truck found so he would drive as far as he could—hopefully to the Indian's truck—and go from there. With any luck it would take days, or weeks, to find either vehicle. Occasionally stopping to verify the trail, Samson came to a large oak hammock and followed the spoor through the thick fringe to emerge under a huge water oak. Joe Billie Bloodtooth's 4x4 seemed quaintly out of place under the quiet canopy of the leafy cathedral; a sophisticated icon, yet naive in its unembellished but far from simple surroundings.

Chapter TWELVE

Can Martin was soaking in his own juices and it was only 8:30 in the morning. Joe Billie kept them on the move since leaving the truck before daylight and the inexorable Florida sun soon turned the dew soaked greenery into an endless, stifling steam room. Can's leg was aching like a sore tooth and his bandage was soaked from shuffling through the dew-wet grass, adding to his discomfort. The wire noose encircled his neck but his hands were free, as were Elise's. A length of knotted plastic rope dangled from the wire necklace down the beleaguered man's back and had to be kept free of leafy entanglements; a nagging frustration to the rancher. Dog on a leash. He was hatless, another source of aggravation under the broiling sun. The white circle crowning the top half of his forehead seemed out of place next to the darkly tanned lower half of his face, but the heavy wrinkles scrunched into this white skin were not any concern of the sun.

Elise's neck also displayed a wire necklace but no leash. Like the rancher, her clothes were dripping. Bloodtooth, talking to himself, led the procession, war club slung over his shoulder and a full pack riding easily on his back. He moved through the uneven terrain as casually as a stray dog crossing a deserted street. His moving lips birthed sounds but were largely unintelligible and his captives had quit trying to understand him. The big half-breed had entered a different world.

The sun dried foliage begrudged them silent passage and their progress was proclaimed by the rattling, rustling chatter of disturbed leaves and branches or accentuated by Can Martin's explosive, "Goddamn you," or, "sum bitch," when he tripped on a palmetto root or stepped into one of the myriad holes hidden by the tenacious wiregrass. Joe Billie's unimpeded progress seemed condoned by the greenery as his colorful buckskins eased along without so much as a whisper.

An occasional sigh followed by stifled, choking sobs escaped the resigned nurse but her stumbling progress was without vocal comment; she had ceded herself to the fates. The running suit was uncomfortable in the increasing heat and rips were began to appear in the cuff area; sandspurs and cockle burrs were jammed into the soft cotton from knees to toes, including shoelaces. This terrain was inhospitable and intimidating, offering no avenue of escape for intruders such as she. In every direction was only saw grass, water, thick bushes, thicker saw palmettos or dank, mucky looking bogs. Elise saw that her only chance was to go along as best she could and hope for a miracle. Another miracle, she thought, as she remembered the events just after the Indian pulled them from the truck, war club in hand.

"Time to go, turd-eater." Joe Billie's venomous words brought the stiffened captives back to the reality as he dragged them from the sanctuary of the truck and dumped their wired, hurting bodies on the leaf covered ground. This remembrance caused the pretty woman to grimace as the scenes replayed in her tortured mind; Can Martin, struggling to sit up but unable until the big half-breed grabbed him under the arms and effortlessly propped him against the rear tire. She couldn't see Joe Billie's face but his mumbling voice seemed empty, as if borrowed.

"Okay big rancher man, it's party time for you—ha-ha-ha 'n it's gonna be a baaash!" Joe Billie's voice had risen to an unnatural high pitch, almost frantic as he strung out the 'bash.' He broke into a maniacal laugh as he grabbed Elise and set her in front of Martin. She could smell his whiskey breath that combined with the musky, human-animal smell escaping the ancient buckskins threatened to gag her. Even her experiences as a nurse with diseased and dying patients did not prepare her for this primitive, uncivilized, human scent. Elise could see his eyes, sparkling and dancing in the righteous zeal of a holy quest—yet somehow empty.

His voice high-pitched, the erratic Indian continued needling his captives, doing a mock war dance as to reinforce his sanguinary resolve while tapping the club of death on the palm of his hand or thigh. Elise tried to pull her hair, now wet and stringy, from her eyes. Her bound wrists were useless but she managed to part the offending locks with her knees, saw blood on her garments and realized that she was bleeding from her wrists, ankles and nose. She felt the onrush of lightheadedness as her mind went spinning into space, stopping when she was thirteen and tied to a clothesline post in her backyard by her seventeen year old stepbrother. She was dressed in an Indian costume with Chuckie sporting a breechclout, his head resplendent in a band of grimy chicken feathers salvaged from last Sunday's home cooked chicken dinner. Free-range. Chuckie whooped and grunted as he circled the helpless girl—his version of macho Indian-ness—darting in occasionally to fondle his precociously nubile sister. These digital adventures increased, reaching such intensity that he blatantly ripped the horrified girl's costume off while displaying his sexual readiness. Chuckie's fervor driven ineptness and Elise's mother brandishing a water hose was all that saved her from being raped and the experience marked her for life. She could still see her mother screaming at the entranced boy, aiming the powerful stream of water at his throbbing groin, finally beating him with the end of the hose. In fact Elise could feel the water as she relived the terrible moments. "… wha-wha-what is it? St-st-stop." The water Joe Billie was pouring on her filled her nose and eyes and she was forced back to the present.

"Wake up pretty lady." His voice was singsong, teasing. "Want your man to see your pretty face—one last time—don't we." Elise's heart skipped a beat. What did he mean?

"What do you want… what do you want from me? I don't know you… don't have any money…" The girl's pleas had no effect on the malevolent grim etched into Bloodtooth's face. He continued to tap the club on his leg- slap-slap-slap…

"You asshole, you miserable asshole!" Can spat the words as if they were fire and could somehow consume him. His eyes were slits and the veins in his neck bulged as he struggled against the frustration of captivity. "Leave her the hell alone! I'm the one you want. Whatever it is you want just let me know, for Christ's sake. You want money, you'll get money—just tell me!" Can didn't know about the slaughter at his house and assumed the misguided renegade had kidnapped them for ransom and whatever demands he made would be met and they would be free in a matter of days.

"You right, white boy—double right. I got you, what I want and I gonna do what I want—with you." The high pitch was gone and the growly, rumbling tone sent shivers through the two captives. Joe Billie seemed rational, even the vacant stare was gone. Both sufferers noticed this, especially the trained nurse. He stopped the incessant tapping and pushed the club's gory end against the rancher's chest. "I ain't in no hurry cause I want you to know ever thing that's gonna happen, especially to this pretty girlfriend of…"

Elise screamed, "I'm not his girlfriend! I'm his private nurse! He means nothing to me!"

"Scream all you want pretty lady 'cause there's no one to hear you, just me and this here dickhead dog killer here. How's about it, dickhead…" Pushing on the club Joe Billie broke into a raucous laugh and poked at the sulking man like a demented child teasing a puppy. Martin tried to avoid the jabs but the wiring job prevented any evasive movement.

Elise's chin quivered and resignation oozed from her pores as she made one last effort to reason with the half-breed. "For God's sake, stop it! Stop it and tell us what you want! No matter what you do you owe us an explanation…" Her voice fragmented, tapering to a whimper as she tried to finish her plea.

Joe Billie seemed calm. His eyes projected a confused, empathetic glint as he set on his heels and quietly replied to the disheveled nurse. "Okay girlie, I will stop. I will tell you why we're here."

The big man's demeanor totally changed, almost as if the three were doing small talk over coffee at Tiny's cafe. Elise breathed a sigh of relief at this sign of rational behavior and she could see the rancher's stony posture soften. This was her first good look at her captor and the first chance to see or talk to him when he wasn't on the muscle. He was surprisingly handsome in spite of his disarray and filth and an unsettling pique came over her as female intuition raised its curious head. Tortured, bloodied, dirty, in fear for her life, the enigmatic woman found herself wanting to know more about this strange Miccosukee Warrior. Elise had spent two years at the university studying psychology before she went into nursing and now those long forgotten studies of psychotic behavior dropped into her mind, jarred loose from their occult roosting place in her subconscious. Always agree, she remembered, don't be argumentative. If a criminal type, offer to help—in any way you can. For some unknown reason, these anti-social types have a deep-seated need to be wanted or useful and asking for their help had defused many hairy situations—according to the literature. These tenets emerged warily from Elise's shrouded memory but offered little comfort since they represented her only weapon. What the sullen Can Martin could offer, Elise didn't know, but unless a .44 cal. magnum, the odds still favored the half-breed.

"He killed my dog." The Indian's voice resonated flat in the quiet morning stillness. The sun's rays were beginning to trouble the night-gloom and Elise could see thin spots appearing in the predawn blackness as she stared at the treetops. "Stump the only thing I ever cared for. He the only thing ever gave a good Goddam 'bout me, and that there turd-rollin' cowboy killed him!"

"I did no such thing! That frigging hound of your's like to have…" Martin cut short his outburst as he realized what he was saying. A look of disgust reflected in his face and he cursed himself. His little part in the Stump episode was a can of worms he didn't want to open… in front of Elise Jones.

Don't be argumentative; ask him for help. These thoughts burned Elise's brain and she could only buy time and pray that help was on the way. "Let me loose, please—I promise I won't try to get away." Forcing herself to appear calm, Elise lowered her voice to a seductive tone. "I want to hear about your dog, what happened to him… what kind of dog was he? How long did you have him… Oh, I hurt so bad from the wire…" Her ersatz courage took a nosedive as a choking sob aborted her plea. Joe Billie's eyes darted from the remorseful woman to the sullen rancher. His gaze portended nothing—not pity, not feeling, not understanding—just non-judgmental glances. Then, with a partially suppressed grunt, the Miccosukee stood, went to the truck and produced a pair of pliers, strode to the bound woman and cut her wire bindings save for the loop encircling her slender neck. Joe Billie didn't know why he was freeing the woman and his outward expression did reflect some degree of passivity, but his thoughts were tumbling around in his head like wet tennis shoes in a dryer. He knew he had to kill these two but bashing the woman was only to exact revenge against Can Martin—he held no personal animosity towards her. Her capitulation and genuine interest in his feelings about Stump deeply impressed him. Elise Jones was the first person to show interest in Joe Billie Bloodtooth since his mother. Besides, he thought, if she tries to run, I'll just kill her.

Can Martin's watery voice cut into the Indian's thoughts like a hacksaw. "Cut me loose." Trying to sound patronizing, the rancher's voice narrowed to a condescending whine. "I won't try anything. I promise…" Joe Billie's backhand across the man's face brought a startled "Oh my God," from Elise and a "Shut your turd-eatin' face," from the businesslike Bloodtooth. Turning his back to the simpering unfortunate he went to the front of the truck and returned with a half full bottle of Jack Daniels. Pulling on the bottle as he sat back on his heels, Joe Billie focused on the nurse and in a steady monotone told her about Stump.

Freed from the restricting wire but still stiff, Elise listened with suppressed incredulity, an occasional gasp or, "oh my God," scant evidence of her shock and dismay. Joe Billie nursed the bottle and droned on, relieved to unburden his mind, if not his soul, to an understanding human. His eyes bespoke no self-pity, only a vacantness that Elise saw as pain. This was the demented man's first emotional catharsis since reaching adulthood and it evoked a feeling that had lain dormant since the murder of his family. This was a feeling the taciturn breed would never comprehend… an umbilical cord connecting Elise to safety. As Can Martin's part unrolled, Elise could only look at her former patient's flushed face and shake her head, tears of sympathy creeping down dirt streaked cheeks to be wiped away by her grimy, bloodstained hand.

Afraid to speak, Can Martin whined and shook his head as if to say "no-no-no." But Elise knew the morose Indian spoke the truth and that Martin was not only a liar, but a cold-blooded murderer as well. At no time while telling his story did Joe Billie act irrational. Elise felt a surge of hope and for the first time since the abduction felt as if she had a chance. A scurrying sound in the thick leaves caused them to peer into the predawn stillness, straining to determine the source of the commotion. Joe Billie stiffened at the sound but settled back on his heels while his reluctant audience craned their necks in an effort to make out the two raccoons scampering around the base of their den tree. Their chattering finally gave them away and dashed any hopes of rescue that could be attendant to unknown noises. Cloaked in passivity, the pensive renegade was smiling at the little animals; wild creatures held a great fascination for the Miccosukee and he envied their insouciance.

Thinking, let me help you, Elise addressed Joe Billie as he rocked on his heels drawing lines in the thick leaves with the war club. "Help me, Joe Billie. Help me bring this murderer to justice and let the law, our law, take vengeance for you, your friend and your dog." Elise, like Can Martin, didn't know of the slaughter prior to their abduction. "Don't make yourself a murderer. I can help you… I want to help you." The big Miccosukee laid the club across his lap, folded his arms across his massive chest and directed a leaden stare at the woman. The whiskey bottle was empty and Joe Billie's countenance was vintage stoic—expressionless. Elise choked, hoping to delay the tears welling up in her eyes—a well that should be dry. She continued pleading but her bravado was thinning as it mixed with the impassiveness of the half-breed. Still not light, the nurse was close enough to Joe Billie to see his face. Focusing on his eyes, Elise felt a chill course her tired body as she noticed the man's pupils dilate and bubbles of saliva appear at the corners of his mouth; unwilling to swallow—or unable? Can Martin, not able to see the Miccosukee's face, sensed a change but was powerless to move. No one moved or spoke as the eerie silence enveloped them. Slowly, deliberately, Joe Billie got to his knees and turned his face towards the pinkish-gray eastern sky, his eyes focused on nothing of this earth. In a singsong voice he half spoke, half whispered, "yes—yes—yes, Grandfather, the journey begins, the journey begins…" Whipping his body around, the entranced man straddled the stupefied nurse and brandished the gore stained club over her head. Elise could feel the hair on the back of her neck stand as she fell back in horror.

"You die first, pretty girl friend; then the dog killing turd-eater die….slowly! Watch your pretty cunt die, dog killer… Her brains might even smell good as her pussy…" The worked up Indian was shouting as his muscles tensed, ready for the killing blow; nostrils flared, pupils dilated and fixed on Elise's ashen face. The hopelessness of the situation caved in on her as she raised an arm to protect her face, a gesture of symbolism over substance. Muttering and dispirited, Elise Jones closed her eyes and surrendered to the fates.

The seconds ticked away, pregnant, bloated to accommodate a lifetime; the stricken girl had yet to feel the killing blow. Risking a peek, Elise spread her fingers and looked into the face of her Thanatos. His tall, costumed body was bathed in the benign morning light imparting an ethereal quality to his ravening flesh. His etched face had softened and his mydriatic stare seemed now innocent and quizzical as a puppy nosing its first cricket. Joe Billie was swallowing and tension was draining from his taunt muscles like water from a broken vessel. Elise lowered her arm and pulled to a sitting position as his gaze followed her. Like a moss covered branch falling through a leafy tree, the war club came down from its killing height—ominous—unfulfilled. Elise could see the man's lips pursed as if to speak. More seconds passed.

"Mother? Mother?" Then a shout, "Mother!" Words uttered without conviction, as if Joe Billie wanted someone to refute him. Elise could see his eyes, pupils quiet with a hint of rationality reflected in his puzzled stare. It was obvious that Bloodtooth thought she was someone else—his mother? Elise had no doubt. This man had a much more serious dementia than she surmised and it couldn't be all because of a dog; a greater emotional beast was gnawing on the vitals of the perturbed Miccosukee.

The woman's reverie was interrupted as she stepped into a burrow camouflaged by the dense wiregrass and fell into the thick weeds. Her reflex gasp caused Can Martin to offer his hand, refused by the prostrated woman in a dramatic flurry of indignation. Elise wanted nothing more to do with the compromised rancher, a fact not lost on the smoldering Miccosukee. Joe Billie Bloodtooth was a confused man. He made no comment when the nurse fell but did stop as she struggled to her feet, then with a grunt continued in a southeasterly direction skirting the edge of a dank patch of saw grass interspersed with patches of dark water. The tall sedges bordering this swampy area were alive with movement as the night hunters retired and the day creatures took over. Knobby protrusions above the waterline gave silent witness to the alligators languishing beneath the mirror-like surface; no matter which direction one looked. Otters, fearless in their pursuit of food, cavorted among the gators with the impunity of a mocking bird harassing a crow. The ground under the silently moving Indian suddenly exploded in a flurry of dewdrops, leaves and grass as a covey of roosting quail tried to escape the silent danger that had snuck up on them. One luckless cock-bird flew up Joe Billie's pants leg, while another, a hen, ended up trapped in his loose fitting warrior coat. With a pleasurable grunt, the stoic half-breed plucked the birds from his garments and nonchalantly pulled their heads off, never missing a step as he deposited the warm, quivering bodies into his coat pocket.

Joe Billie Bloodtooth remembered very little of the events leading up to the aborted bashing of the nurse. These past few weeks of his life had been like a book with missing pages—one he was compelled to read. His facial features relaxed As the damp Pay-Hay-Okee morning rekindled an exhilaration he had forgotten. This feeling rekindled desires and aspirations long since pushed aside in his struggle to fit into the modern world—once a blessing, now a curse. Suddenly he was 15 years old and sitting cross-legged on the sun frizzled turf in back of the splintered bleachers with 12 Indian boys listening to the coach deliver a pep talk worthy of Vince Lombardi. The coach, a bleary eyed, overweight Miccosukee was in charge of every athletic program at the Indian School and taught civics, but baseball was the game and the coach's charged directives reeked of sincerity—a rare phenomenon for him. The reason? A strange young half-breed leaning on his wide hands, elbows locked, chewing the stem of a bahia grass seed head. His name—Joe Billie Bloodtooth.

Sammy Bearpaw had been the Indian School coach for 12 years and his only concern was that he be the coach 12 or 13 more years. After that he didn't give a rip. His record and reputation at the Indian School was perfect—he never had a winning season, or the potential, in any sport. Until now. Until Joe Billie Bloodtooth.

There were so many Joes', James', James Billies', Billies' and Joe Billies' among the aspiring Indian athletes that Sammy automatically dubbed the young newcomer, "Bloody," during the initial roll call. The track season was winding down and with baseball next the aspiring young athletes were showing symptoms of hit and run fever. Baseball was far and away coach Bearpaw's favorite sport, as it was with the student body and most of the locals and with rumors of the new super-athlete spreading through the reservation like wildfire, the interest in baseball was at fever pitch. The young Bloodtooth had been a wrecking crew on the track team his first season and the Indian School had won several meets, even qualifying for the division finals—the high point of their benign athletic history. The reason being a dark complexioned adonis that won or placed in every event Sammy Bearpaw entered him. "Bloody" Bloodtooth was all but unbeatable in the sprints and field events and with the exception of a young athlete from the Tampa area, was the finest high school athlete in the State of Florida. The Tampa boy was a year older, much better trained and promoted and was more into football, basketball and wrestling, at which he was said to be unbeatable. The Tampa boy held the top division and State record in the 100 yard dash but since Joe Billie was in a lower division the two never met in head to head competition. In his senior year, "Bloody" set a new division record in the 100 yard dash, lowering the division standard by 0.6 tenths of a second and the state record by 0.1 tenth of a second. In spite of these accomplishments, the teenager was still unknown and coach Sammy Bearpaw was determined to keep him down on the farm.

As track season raced by, Sammy took "Bloody" to show him a baseball and see if the strapping kid could hack a ball, glove and bat. It took two excursions for the elated coach to know he had a potential superstar. He also knew that as popular as baseball was, it would be impossible to keep the young Miccosukee in the Indian School after his first season unless the kid just didn't want to leave. With a little help, the potent Bloodtooth could be the nucleus for a winning season in baseball—a definite jewel for the crown of the beleaguered coach. Sammy knew it was time to have a serious talk with the more influential alumni, something he never did but now seemed imperative.

"Okay guys, let's get out there'n give it all we got.

Junior, you take the mound. Let's hit a few before fielding and wind sprints. "Bloody", you swing first up. Junior, try to throw'em by this lazy redskin—smoke'um!" Sammy's voice started in his don't-give-a-shit monotone but ended with an unmistakable sneering tone as he admonished the best hurler to "throw'um by this lazy redskin." The challenge in the coach's voice wasn't lost on Junior Otterfoot as he shuffled to the sand pile doubling as a pitcher's mound, his reddening face pulsating as much from the truth of the coach's insinuation as the frustration of it. He knew the Bloodtooth kid would hit first because coach wanted him to go against the best hurlers, especially with the three well-heeled alumni hanging by their thick fingers on the sagging chain link backstop, laughing and telling jokes as the boys trod through the stifling heat to their positions; none in the shade. Otterfoot turned and faced the catcher, absentmindedly popping the baseball in his glove. Sweat trickled down his face to drip from his nose and speed down his flushed neck. Junior Otterfoot's concentration was so intense his squinted stare could start a fire. Up went his rifle arm and his best fastball—forget his batting practice pitches— hummed toward the plate like a telegraphed message. With an overstated "craacckk," the stitched leather sphere sailed over the centerfielder's head so far he didn't try to run back. Instead, he looked up, squinted into the sun and let out a steam kettle whistle as a kind of salute to the arcing, disappearing blob of horsehide. Junior Otterfoot ground his toes in the sugary sand and angrily grabbed another ball from the ball sack. It was going to be a long half hour for the Indian School's ace.

Joe Billie remembered those baseball practices like yesterday. He remembered his prowess at bat and his teammates resentment and frustrations at his enormous talent—until the season started. Once they started winning, "Bloody" Bloodtooth was the acknowledged star and hero and any member of the team, including Junior Otterfoot, would fight at the drop of a turkey feather if anyone so much as thought about criticizing the big Indian School first baseman.

After the third practice Sammy sidled up to young Joe Billie after a grueling workout.

There were no showers so the boys hosed off from the outside spigot or walked to the tannin stained creek 200 yards from the left field line and went swimming; splashing and playing in the cool water like a herd of otters. The coach got Joe Billie by the arm as he headed for the creek and directed him behind the tiny shack that served as a refreshment stand during home games. There were four folding chairs and a large igloo filled with cracked ice and beer; cans so cold that when rescued from the frigid bath they sweated worse than the Indians. Sammy introduced two Indian School alumni to the curious youngster and handed him his first beer. He liked it. The pampered young ballplayer had cold beer waiting after every practice and game, whether home or away. It wasn't long before a clique of buddies joined him and halfway through his junior year he was introduced to the hard stuff. Joe Billie liked whiskey, especially moonshine and until his college career ended never paid for a drop.

These childhood playbacks hung around the recesses of the Miccosukee's mind like bats in a cave, waiting for darkness to set them free. Picking his way south, Joe Billie patted the whiskey bottle in his coat pocket and grinned.

He hadn't paid for this booze either—it came from Can Martin's booze locker. Glancing back, Joe Billie could barely keep his disgust from encroaching his stoic features. His feelings to-wards the slim female were conflicted—bash her head and be done with it… yet she represented a real flesh and blood link to Mary Cornflower, his beloved mother. He did, at times, see his mother's face when looking at the nurse and no matter how vengeful he felt towards Can Martin, Joe Billie Bloodtooth could never smash his mother's face, real or no. Ducking his head to hide a smirk working its way across his face, the breed toyed with the idea of raping the sexy captive in front of Martin. That would be vengeful and surely his Grandfather would approve. Joe Billie felt an adren-alin rush as he thought of struggling with the female and forcing her to submit to his maleness. The fullness in his groin caused him to stop and slowly turn to look at Elise. What if she was Mary Cornflower—what would he do then?

Skirting the eastern edge of the deeper water, the Indian plunged into knee-deep water and felt a tremendous relief as his moccasins sank into the Everglades muck. This was his land, his home and deep inside he could hear—no, feel—a yearning. Don't ever leave this home of homes. Joe Billie Bloodtooth had no inten-tion of ever leaving these Everglades. Alive.

• • •

Samson smelled no human presence as he approached the truck. JY, sensing concern walked around the vehicle with the stilted gait displayed by a fully cocked pit bulldog. His sable hackles were erect and his tail up, rigid as wire. Not knowing what to expect the protective beast was locked and loaded! Sam walked around the Indian's truck stirring up latent scents hoping not to detect signs of violence or bloodshed. He found the spot by the left rear tire where the three had sat, the scenario playing in his mind as if he were witness instead of interpreter. To his amazement he could visualize the captives; Martin propped against the tire, bound, with Elise sitting in front unbound and the big Miccosukee squatting between the two stirring the leaves with his war club and drinking whiskey. He picked up evidence of the Indian doing something to the nurse but nothing violent. Rape, maybe? But there were no sexual smells and the trail from the area revealed all were walking with Elise showing no sign of physical distress. Joe Billie owned this wilderness and had a five-hour lead on his putative nemesis but Samson knew his olfactory percipience made finding them academic and if it remained intact he would find them. Elise was alive and unharmed. Sam knew an experienced sight tracker could follow the trail since the Indian made no effort to conceal their movement. The captives stumbled through the lawn-like centipede grass patches into the mulch-like floor of the hammock—enough to confuse a sight-tracking savior. Samson Duff would not have that trouble. The introspective man inhaled deeply as he surveyed the pristine area marveling at its freshness, savoring the enormity of his gift in concert with this unparalleled beauty; that now presented a third dimension to complement sight and sound. Samson was on a high so the tiny voice echoing in his mind, "Beware the Pay-Hay-Okee! Beware the River of Grass! Beware the Everglades!" had little effect on his euphoria. Samson Duff was an intruder the mighty swamp warranted to expunge—Joe Billie Bloodtooth had a powerful ally in the ubiquitous River of Grass.

JY's interest in the area around the truck's rear tire diverted Sam's and he turned to the inquisitive pit bull. "Look it over good, old buddy, because you may have to take over if my revamped sniffer quits." Sam smiled, well aware of this dog's talent at tracking—a trait not usually found in such a breed. His comment took him back to when Junk Yard was two years old and finishing his tracking sessions. He had achieved Schuntzen II level with ease and Samson was prepping him for Schuntzen III when he and Skeets signed with a private company in the Midwest to breakup a corporate espionage ring stealing company secrets and selling them to the competition. The company headquarters was an ultra-modern building away from town surrounded by cornfields allowing employees to watch corn farming while they did high tech work. Anachronism. After several weeks undercover they pinpointed the culprit, a company vice president and set a trap.

The suspect inhaled the bait and when confronted pulled a gun and took a young blonde co-worker hostage. Not assumed to be dangerous, the "spy" caught Sam and Skeets by surprise and in the confusion exited the building and the police were called, swarming the area like ants on a dead worm. The "spy" hightailed it into the cornfields and released the hostage, hoping to escape by hiding in the morass of cornstalks until dark. Then... freedom city.

The police lieutenant in charge oozed contemptuousness for the chagrined investigators and ordered them to stand down while they (the professionals) did their job. Sam had to physically restrain Skeets, but since they had serious egg-on-face, they backed off and spectated as the police tried to corral the suspect in the corn stalk maze.

The corn was being harvested with over a hundred acres a checkerboard of battered cornstalks contrasting the proud stalks standing next, totally oblivious to their fate. Posting patrolmen on the encircling hard roads the lieutenant ordered his men to walk the fields to flush the fugitive to the perimeter guard or the searchers. It was late afternoon and darkness now threatened the police deployment making their arrogant tyro edgy. Samson's overtures were not exactly what the nail biting young officer had in mind so Skeets cautioned his buddy as he approached the young cop.

"A-hum... A-hem... Got a minute, chief?"

The lieutenant bristled. "Chief? Chief? I'm not the fucking chief of police and you goddam well know it!" The irate man's eyes flashed like lasers stabbing Sam's bemused stare, his cracking voice hinting at involuntary tone changes characteristic of prolonged adolescence. "Now what's your fucking problem...?"

"Hey, cool your jets, man. I just want to offer a little help..."

"Help hell, you're the cause of this goddamed mess..."

"Maybe so, but it's going to be dark in less than an hour and that sleezeball will just waltz across Kansas..." A look of cunning rifled across the young lieutenant's face. "Don't bet on it. I called in our chopper. Should be here anytime." His voice low, enunciation spelling bee perfect, he laid this piece of news on Samson Duff. His attitude was vintage "kiss my ass." As if to verify, the signal "whop-whop-whop" of a helicopter stirred the afternoon air like ripples on quiet water. Ignoring Sam, the young lieutenant spoke into the hand held phone, barking directives with the aplomb of a wing thumping turkey gobbler in springtime.

"Scour that field just north of the main entrance. We've got it secured. Just point that asshole out and we'll wrap this caper up. Ten-four, over and out."

Sam laughed at this tin plated display. Turning from the putative commander, Samson ambled to his truck, leashed JY and walked to the front of the main entrance near the spot where the "spy" entered the cornfield. Sam's amusement was apparent, the corners of his mouth up-turned, gray-green eyes moist with suppressed laughter. I'll give them 30 minutes, he thought, then we'll have a go. "How about them apples, Junk Yard. You ready?" The eager young dog was trembling. Ready!

The mechanical whop-whop-whop resounded like a metronome with a wet mop for a striker. The crackle of radio static and unintelligible voices gave the scene a warlike flavor raising the hair on Sam's neck.

Ten minutes more.

The sun dipped behind one of the few clouds in the endless Kansas sky injecting a sense of urgency into the searchers; an augur of failure. The fugitive was minutes away from escape; searchlights—useless.

"OK, Junkie, time to do your thing." At Sam's voice, the canine wanted to break loose and run circles as he did when a pup. His exuberance was boundless, but his training had not been in vain and this store of energy was constrained with the only outward display being erect ears, staring eyes and the quivering of his compact body.

Leading Junk Yard to the field, Sam picked a clear footprint in the loamy soil. His voice a whisper, cajoling, encouraging. "Here's where he went in. Let's get him. This is his track… go for it! JY sniffed the depression, put his tail in the air and snatched Sam so hard he almost fell down. Not wanting to lose sight of the dog, Sam held to the leash and took off with JY—eager and sure. Two security guards assigned to the area next to the building shouted a warning at the pair but it fell flat as the man and dog disappeared into the thick cornstalks. In chase mode, Junk Yard pulled Samson through the corn with unbelievable power making it impossible to keep from stumbling, much less see clearly. Though well trained, Sam knew he could not slow the beast and if he fell in on the fugitive he would risk being shot. With a whispered, "oh shit," he let go the leash, rationalizing that the dog was the lesser of two evils. Relieved, JY plowed through the meaty stalks dragging the twelve-foot leash as if a sewing thread. Samson followed the commotion and broke out of the standing stalks into a harvested section. The Pit Bull was 30 yards away, ten feet into the field—frozen. Samson stopped in his tracks trying to control his breathing so it wouldn't compromise his hearing. He could see JY clearly though the dusky light was fading. The Pit's legs were spread, giving him the aura of instant mobility. His head was down, pointing at something in the beaten down cornstalks—something Sam couldn't see. Regaining his composure, Samson eased toward the dog with every sense and muscle on red alert, envying the dog's ability. A few feet from JY, Sam could see his raised lips with clear saliva coating the porcelain teeth and hear the deep growl that would raise hackles on a stick horse. Gun in hand, the cautious operative eased to the Pit as an outline took form among the stalks—a man—his head inches from Junk Yard. A .357 magnum grew from his clenched right hand.

"OK pal... roll call." The "spy" flipped the pistol away as he saw Sam approach and slowly extricated himself from his bower, dusting his suit as he straightened up; absentmindedly adjusting his silk tie.

"Why didn't you just shoot me, pal?" Sam's voice was menacing.

"Because I knew what that dog would do. I've owned Pit Bulldogs." The man's voice was resigned, quiet. Sam asked the more obvious question:

"Why didn't you just shoot the dog, then...?"

"Because I know what you would have done. Like I said, I owned a Pit..." He never finished his statement as a covey of uniforms swept through the cornstalks and surrounded them, guns at the ready.

Convinced the captives were alive and able to walk and that Joe Billie was heading deeper into the 'Glades, Samson went to his truck to make ready—mission of mercy. Sam didn't understand his motives and Skeets' skepticism still dangled in his mind like a vaporous spider web supporting too many dead flies. He was in full camo and jungle boots. His backpack had survival gear and freeze dried food. His medicines, though Spartan, were well chosen and strapped to his waist was a knife and a 9mm semi-automatic pistol. Going to the passenger side Samson opened the glove box and retrieved a small Ziploc bag. Though tightly sealed, it caused the big man's heart to rumble as he took a deep breath and inhaled the full aroma of sensuous woman. Silently parting, the web in the aroused man's mind failed and fell unheralded into the morass of confusion—called DESIRE. Samson Duff's quest would be a pilgrimage. Classic. Damsel in distress.

Squinting into the sun, Samson Hercules Duff and the Junk Yard dog started on the trail of the fugitive Indian and his captives. Into the bowels of the Pay-Hay-Okee!

Chapter THIRTEEN

Skeets Kirby hunkered down behind the steering wheel of the small hatchback and peered through the shadows slowly enveloping the DOCTOR'S ONLY parking area at Centra County Hospital. The oaks bordering the area shrouded out the departing sun and cast darkness over the hatchback and the red Mercedes-Benz sitting across the lot with eight or ten staff cars. The past 36 hours had been hectic for the operative, beginning with Sam's departure on what Skeets considered a wild goose chase. In the interim Skeets had eased over to Orlando, left his car in a mall, rented the hatchback using faked ID and then hightailed back to Centra to see what was going on.

A lot was happening!

The daily newspaper ran a late edition that provided an overview of what was known. The Martin ranch slaughter was in the headlines with interviews and comments by all that seemed involved.

The kidnapping was a mystery. It was theorized that Can Martin and the nurse staged the gory scene and then ran off to some sun baked tropical island. Gypsy Jack Pappadoupoulis' demise was noted but no connection to the Martin slaughter was made. There was no ransom note—or leads—as to motive or reason for such atrocious acts. Skeets thought it interesting that nowhere in the news accounts could he find his or Samson's name, only a vague reference to "out of towners." The verbiage smacked of putative complicity but nothing specific so maybe no one had questioned the doctor mentioned in the accounts. Good he thought, I can get to him first.

A one-column article hidden on a back page caught his eye. A police report stating that the FBI led by special agent Robert Long was taking over the Martin ranch investigation and that Sheriff Lon McCall was on an extended leave. Hmmm, thought Skeets, so Robbing Bob's in town and Big Lon is on the carpet—good—that's why there's no APB out on us. Probably why our names aren't in the press. Interesting. Wonder what big Lon had his fingers in besides Gypsy Jack's backside?

Kirby finished reading and went to find special agent Bob Long—at least he would get a straight story—before he questioned the surgeon. One phone call and Kirby and Long were reliving old times while parked in a secluded area a few miles outside town.

"I heard you guys were in the area. What for? Vacation…?

I know better than that. What are you and Duff doing in this God forsaken place?" The senior agent's voice was a friendly monotone and Skeets knew the implications of that. Skeets also knew that Bob Long knew more than he was letting on because he had to be the one that "retired" Lon McCall. So he must have gotten him to talk but Bob owed him one and he knew the senior agent wasn't going to be cute—he just wouldn't tell him everything.

"Well, we are on a job—involving cattle rustling—nothing big enough to interest you people. Samson and I just happened to get on the wrong side of the high sheriff." Skeets wasn't about to mention Gypsy Jack, though he knew the agent would get involved sooner or later as the Martin ranch slaughter played out.

"Yea, that figures, Skeeter. I saw an APB on you two lying on McCall's desk when I visited him this morning. Tore it up. Where's Samson?" Bob Long's eyes relaxed as he mentioned Skeets' partner and the pitch of his voice changed. Skeets wished he had stopped for a six-pack.

"Sam's laying up waiting for this mess to blow over. In fact we're going to split now that I've found out that we're not wanted—get the hell out of Dodge." Skeets' mind was spinning as he tried to out think the special agent. Even though he was glad to see his old friend he knew the lean, angular man with the military bearing and pencil thin moustache was still FBI to the core. He had to remain cool and appear unaffected by whatever Bob told him and Sam knew that his questions to the agent had to be casual and seemingly meaningless.

But he had to press on. "Glad you're here Robert. Got any leads on that Martin mess? That was quite a shocker for a burg like this." Skeets really wanted to know if the agent had questioned one George Martinez, MD, but for sure couldn't just ask.

As he answered, the special agent's voice stayed low and reflective, giving no hint of suspicion or doubt. "Not really, Skeeter man. So far no one knows a thing and agent Woodham—young Ralph Woodham, you wouldn't know him—is getting a list together of possibles. Should be able to start some serious stuff by tomorrow afternoon or the next day at worst. The only ones coming forth now are the amateur detectives and kooks, you know the kind. Pester the shit out of us."

Skeets breathed a sigh of relief—so the surgeon hadn't been questioned yet. And for sure he wasn't going to come forth—he probably wouldn't even want to come fifth, or come at all! Good. He, Skeets Kirby, would have the first crack at him and hopefully find out the skinny on his partner and keep Martinez from talking about Samson to the authorities. Skeets knew that Sam's chance of finding the rampant Miccosukee and his captives were slim to none but if the FBI found out, along with the rest of the world, the Everglades would be crawling with people and nobody would make it out. Zero chance—even for the talented Samson Hercules Duff. The least the loyal operative could do was give his pal a fighting chance.

Skeets' outward calm remained as he and FBI talked about old times and how it wasn't like it use to be. Having heard enough and not wanting to push his luck, Skeets glanced at his watch and grabbed Bob by the shoulder. "Well old timer, been nice to see you again." He needed to get on with his work. "I'll tell Samson you asked about him. Sorry I don't have more to tell but knowing you, you won't need any help." Skeets voice, though flat, had a ring of sincerity and Robert Long's pencil thin moustache rearranged as his face accommodated his wide grin.

A car pulled in front of the hatchback and blocked his view bringing the Skeets back to the reality of his vigilance. It was getting dark and deepening shadows settled over the cars giving them the same dull appearance. Cursing, he cranked the hatchback and moved closer to the Mercedes-Benz hoping the Doctor would be out soon. He had no idea when the surgeon would finish but earlier inquiries had hinted that the good doctor only had rounds and no scheduled surgery. So, if no emergencies cropped up, Martinez should be out fairly soon.

The activated mercury vapor lights lining the parking area started up, looking like prehistoric sentinels roused from their slumber to slowly open their one large eye and begin their nightly vigilance. Skeets blew out his breath and relaxed, relieved that he could see better.

Two hours later Dr. George Martinez slipped out the emergency room entrance and walked towards his car. The surgeon had a load on his mind and stared at the ground as he approached the Mercedes-Benz. Martinez didn't notice the shadow that emerged from behind his car and morphed into a man....with a quiet, forceful—and yes—familiar voice.

"Evening, Dr. Martinez." Skeets words assaulted the man's ears like hail on a tin roof.

"What... what the hell...who are you?" As he spoke, Martinez backed up and started to turn but an iron grip on his shoulder kept him facing the speaker.

"Easy, easy George—Skeets Kirby—remember? Samson Duff's friend. Lighten up."

"Whaaat... Kirby? Skeets Kirby? Man, you scared the shit out of me!" Skeets felt the taut body ease and loosened his grip, dusting imaginary lint from George's shirt as he removed his hand.

"Yeah, sorry about that Doc but I need to talk to you and I don't want publicity. Know what I mean?" Skeets words had an edge but his attitude belied the sharpness of his intentions causing the surgeon to look around. His suspicions suddenly blared red alert. Skeets went on. "Let's get in your pretty red muscle car and tool over to a place where we won't be disturbed."

"Cut the bullshit, Kirby. If you want to talk, make an appointment and we'll talk in my office. Otherwise fuck off!" The surgeon's face was flushed and he was pissed off—at himself—for allowing Kirby to intimidate him. "And another thing, shove this CIA horse shit. I know you're not CIA...hell, I don't know who or what you are but you're not government!" The surgeon was worked up and the pressure of the kidnapping was beginning to show. His words reflected desperation as he berated the nerveless operative but his tone was ice water. "Screw you. I'm not going anywhere. I'm tired and I'm going home..."

The suddenness exhibited by Skeets as he grabbed the surgeon's arm surprised Martinez and the snub nosed .38 revolver jammed under his chin surprised him even more. Pushing the gun barrel up Skeets positioned the man's face until they were eyeball-to-eyeball; nose-to-nose.

With venom-laden spittle dripping from his lips, the operative hissed out his mandate. "Fuck you, Charlie butcher man and the bitch that birthed you. We're going to have a talk about Samson Hercules Duff and his super sniffer and you're going to tell me whatever the hell I want to know."

Doctor George was scared. "You can't get away with this. I don't have to tell you a Goddam thing... what right do you have...?"

The hissing Skeets interrupted the surgeon. "Listen up, Georgie." As he spoke he stopped the hissing and broke into a proper but still mocking tone. "You remember a man—a fat man—by the name of Jack Pappadoupoulis? Gypsy Jack, he was called."

"Sure, I knew of him. I autopsied him this morning. What's that got to do with us... me?" The Doctor's pitched voice mirrored his increased tension and some of his words seemed to tumble out over his teeth but George Martinez was no coward—he just didn't like trouble. "What about him?"

Skeets' eyes glinted in the light as he pulled the man closer. Lowering his voice to a harsh whisper aimed at Martinez' ear Skeets spread the cards on the table. "Fat ass Jack died of cyanide poisoning and was miss-ss-ing his left ring finger to which was applied, before amputation, a rubber band." Skeets strung out the word MISSING, spitting it into the ear of the un-amused surgeon. "Now, Doctor George, let's go have that quiet talk!"

The Mercedes-Benz eased out of the parking slot and worked its way through the lot and out into the street. The two men were silent and looked straight ahead. As the Mercedes-Benz turned into the street George eased the stick into second and cadillacked towards the stoplight with the potent car purring like a cat.

"Where to—since you're holding all the cards."

George's voice pulsated with resentment though resigned to whatever the Skeeter man had in store for him. He was becoming aware of Kirby's personality and was gradually realizing that this guy had a serious personality defect. He felt goose bumps raising on his arms. Looking ahead, Skeets' voice sounded hollow as if his mouth was birthing words instead of speaking them. Though nerveless he was definitely preoccupied.

His reply—"Your office"—was barely audible.

"My office? Why my office?" No answer.

Martinez could feel the blood swelling his neck as he glanced at his passenger. Skeets' facial expression gave no indication of an answer. He continued to stare ahead and George asked again, louder, demanding. "Why my office? Why not under a tree or somewhere? Why not…?"

The chiseled face turned and Skeets' throaty reply sent shivers down the surgeon's spine. "Just drive asshole… to your office."

George, pouting, put both hands on the steering wheel and hunkered like a little old lady driving a big car with the seat too far back. Turning at the corner he headed for his office.

George Martinez' office was clean, cool and quiet.

Skeets remained silent as they entered and he ignored the surgeon as he headed for the patient files located behind the receptionist's desk. Expertly thumbing through the manila folders, Skeets rolled his eyes and let out a sigh. "Where are they, George?

The goddam files on Samson." Each word seemed to drop from the man's clenched lips—like lead balls dropping on Martinez' skull.

But the doctor had resolved his conflicts and was not going to challenge the Skeeter man. He was going to do whatever it took to pacify this guy and live—to tell about it—in one piece. George's reply was quiet, "In my office, bottom drawer on the right. I'll get them…"

"Naw, I'll do it. Do I need a key?" Skeets' snatched the tossed keys with the precision of a duck plucking a fly from the air.

Laying the files on the desk Skeets leaned back in George's chair and put his heels on the polished desk. Motioning to Martinez to sit, Skeets opened the top folder and spread the reports on the desktop. "OK, Doctor, tell me 'bout my boy. Go from A to Z and I'll interrupt if I have a question."

Skeets' tone caused the surgeon to flush and choke back so his reply touched on the theatrical. "OK, Mr. Kirby, sir. You asked for it…" George wanted to relax but he couldn't as his mind racheted to the starting point of the saga of Samson Hercules Duff.

The harried doctor needed to unwind and put his hands on the desk leaning towards the reclining questioner. "How about a scotch, Kirby? I think I need one."

"Fine. Make mine on the rocks."

George breathed a sigh of relief as he turned to the ornate cabinet containing a small refrigerator along with various and sundry bottles of spiritus frumenti. Pouring Glenlivet neat, George stepped to the desk and handed a glass to Skeets and took a measured sip of the smooth liquid. "Ahhh—one of life's pleasures—good to the last drop! OK, Kirby, showtime1" George was feeling better. "Your pal, as you well know, showed up at Centra hospital with his head bashed in and barely alive." The surgeon leaned back and hiked his heels onto the desk opposite Kirby's; then recalled his meeting with Samson Duff. He recounted his work in experimental surgery and immunology and why he believed that cross species organ transplantation was possible. He glanced at the listener looking for signs of skepticism but found none. His listener's eyes and mein were an impartial witness—totally non-judgemental.

George got into the part preceding the surgery and noticed Kirby shuffling through the lab reports occasionally dropping his eyes to scan one. George went on. "Most of the damaged brain was anterior and not really needed to sustain life but I didn't want him end up a melon head unable to see or smell or feel emotions—ergo the transplants. I felt that the transplanted dog brain tissue would act as a matrix and allow Sam's damaged brain cells to grow replacing those of the canine. And if I stopped Sam's immune system from rejecting the dog brain cells his own cells would take over and the dog cells would be replaced returning Sam's brain to normal. It may happen. I don't know…"

Skeets took a sip of the scotch and smacked his lips as he interrupted the surgeon. "So why can he smell every musty little mouse fart within half a mile? You plan on that?"

"Hell no!" Martinez' reply smacked of self-defense. "I was as surprised as you but I have an idea about what may have happened." The surgeon shifted into his lecture mode and continued. "Since Sam's nasal passage and hard palate were shredded I had to reconstruct them before I fooled with his brain. So I used a section of ethmoturbinate from the dog including an intact vomeronasal organ with the cribriform plate, including all its nerves. Then when I filled in the brain defect I used the corresponding area of the canine brain that contained the olfactory ventricles, an extension of the cerebral ventricles found in dogs but not in man. Also, the smell apparatus of the dog is pretty much self-contained in these structures with no relays to the thalmus. Evidently my anti-transplant rejection mixture worked better than I figured and all those parts healed quickly and went back to doing what they were supposed to do. Only not in a dog's head."

George raised the glass to his lips and took a slow, thoughtful sip of the liquid. Trapping a piece of ice with his tongue the surgeon swished it around his mouth before dropping it back into the glass. "Ah – the pause that refreshes." He was ready to carry on!

"Maybe your friend's constitution had something to do with it—I really don't know—but if rejection doesn't occur in the next six to twelve months Sam Duff may be a super sniffer for life."

Skeets dropped his feet to the floor and stacked the papers, placing them in their respective folders. He spoke without looking up. "Who else knows about this? I don't see any reference to dog parts in these reports, only notations about suitable donor replacement tissues. Implying a human source, I'd say. What about it, doc?"

With a sigh of resignation Martinez dropped his feet from the desk and struggled with his reply. "Look Kirby, I told you my history. My work is significant but I can't publish anymore or let on I'm still doing this work. Don't you understand? Someday my research will be recognized as genius and ahead of its time…"

"Yea, sure, doc—maybe so. Let's get back to Sam.

How's this ability going to affect him? What about the rest of his brain? What if he gets sick? Who do I take him to—a veterinarian?"

Skeets' humor was lost on the surgeon as he handled the salvo of questions. Kirby recognized the genius in George Martinez and not capable of feeling sorry for him recognized the man's frustration in dealing with his gifts in a world devoted to mediocrity. It was truly a shame, but nonetheless true; stick your neck above the mediocre norm and your peers will do a war dance on it.

Martinez's face was flushing. "Look guy, I can try to give you answers but they're not going to be cast in bronze." Sipping the single malt George continued. "Man and apes have poorly developed sniffers and are called microsmatic while domestic animals, especially dogs and especially bloodhounds, have well developed olfactory senses and are called macrosmatic. Of course doggies don't have the brain power of a Samson Duff, so who knows what goes on when they smell something. I do know that dogs can be trained to detect anything that gives off an odor, like gas leaks, narcotics, termites…"

"Termites?" Skeets looked at the surgeon then forced a smile and let it crackle across his face. "Termites, for God's sake. Who would have ever thought?"

George warmed to the subject and his interest showed as his voice rose and fell. "…and even iron ore and flakes of skin. Hell man, a dog can smell urine at one part per million dilution and tell the other animal's gender, diet and whether or not it's friendly, submissive, dominant; if it's another dog. Trained rescue dogs regularly sniff out bodies buried under tons of rubble or even snow. Some of these canine super sniffers can identify a target scent among strong competing odors to the extent of sniffing out narcotics sealed in plastic and submerged in gasoline."

Skeets interrupted. "So how good do you think Sam will be if nothing happens?"

"Who knows?" George shrugged as he answered. "The dog brain I used was from a bloodhound—an old tracker used for years by the Centra county sheriff's department and credited with hundreds of findings—escapees, lost kids, you name it and he's found it."

Skeets face turned sour as the impact of his buddy's brain disaster and shade tree repair finally took root.

Martinez sensed this but knew there was nothing to do but push on. "A bloodhound is a big dog, up to 120 pounds for males and when a veterinarian friend of mine called asking if a surgical procedure I used on people would work on a dog, I asked why. Well, it turns out that he had this bloodhound that had been hit by a car and was hemorrhaging into his chest. I rushed over to the animal hospital but the big guy was a loser—so instead of throwing him away my friend let me process some of his organs—ergo Sam's brain!"

Skeets' face was gray, his eyes slits.

"Anyway," George went on, "the bloodhound is a remarkable breed. It's been around for thousands of years and was a favorite dog of monasteries. The monks loved them and played a part in the development of their keen scenting ability as well as in keeping the breed pure. One modern day bloodhound, if you call the early 1900's modern, was credited with picking up a scent four days old and following it to its owner—an escaped convict. Another bloodhound tracked a man for 138 miles before collaring him." The surgeon sipped his scotch, his eyes on Kirby…nothing there…

Quickly George cleared his throat, shrugged his shoulders and answered Skeets' question. "If Sam's sensory ability is as good as a bloodhound, with his intelligence and physical attributes he will be…" Here he paused and lifted his glass in a salute, "… Super Man!"

Kirby's expression changed as he drained his glass in one gulp. "And how, pray tell, will this come about?"

George never missed a beat as he answered. "Once he learns to interpret the scents, he'll be able to read a person, male or female, in a heartbeat. He won't be fooled—especially about women. He would be able to sense their desires immediately and…" He paused again and poured the Glenlivet into his glass. "… and then there are pheromones."

"Fear of what moans?" Skeets raised his eyebrows and straightened up as George threw the strange word to him.

George smiled as he replied. Obscure chemicals that are secreted by animals to be recognized by members of their own species. They play a part in the reproductive act in these animals; odors—albeit magnificent odors—that can lure some to their death or erotic bliss—or both."

George raised his glass in a salute as he continued. "Little is known about pheromones in humans and lower animals but quite a bit has been done with insects and their wind borne scents have been shown to be potent sexual attractants and stimulants." Martinez smiled as he continued. "But hell, Kirby, there are all kinds of sexual attractants—just look at the colorful boy birds that strut and show their stuff to attract some plain little ole' sexy girl bird. Gross body parts that attract females like toads that blow their throats out so madam toad will let them joy ride. Even noise! Listen to the crickets and those noisy tree frogs. If their dicks were big as their voices they'd have to get it on with a goddam mare. And you can bet your ass the crickets aren't fiddling just to test the night air. Hell, man, the beat goes on. Even light can be a sexual attractant…"the surgeon paused and broke into a wide adolescent grin. "…especially from the headlights of a red Porsche or Corvette. Man, anything goes in the game of sex!"

The scotch was beginning to get to George so he eased down in the chair as he continued. "Listen to this, Kirby. A pen of ewes not in heat can be brought into synchronous estrus by the introduction of a ram. His pheromones will cause the ewes to come into heat—powerful!" George cocked his head and let these words sink into Skeets'. "And male moths can be tolled to their deaths by the release of artificial female pheromones…

And research on these attractants is just beginning. Damn, man, think what a boon Samson would be to that kind of research…hell, think what effect women will have on the guy."

Skeets sat up, placed his elbow on the desk and put his chin in his hand. "Before you get carried away with this scientific discourse explain what you mean about the woman part."

"Well, old buddy, when your friend is around members of our weaker sex he will be bombarded by scents that will affect him sexually whether he realizes it or not.

Research suggests that response to pheromones may be automatic and not controlled by the mind. In short Samson may become an uncontrollable sexual deviate when he gets near a human female. It may be beyond his control—even with his discipline and intelligence."

Kirby's eyes narrowed and his voice lost its tone. As he spoke he was again the nerveless inquisitor. "Slow down, Martinez. You mean that Sam may be driven to rape women uncontrollably… if he sniffs these…their pheromones?"

The surgeon's voice flattened as he tried to answer. "It's possible. I've read reports where rapists have been tested and found to respond with sexual aggression when exposed to female body odors—especially those from moist undergarments and un-deodorized body areas such as the crotch and unshaved armpits. And these were done without provocative pictures or any women present…and these guys couldn't smell dog shit inside a phone booth compared to our man!"

Skeets ground his teeth like a cud-chewing cow as he blurted. "Goddam it George, what can we do? How can we find out?" I know he's more aware of every woman we've been around but I didn't notice anything different. You suppose this pheromone shit just hasn't got cranked up…or what? You suppose he's keeping it to himself? When he's around another man, I mean?"

George's eyes bespoke concern as he contemplated these questions. He wished he had spent more time in the medical library.

"Who knows? Maybe only women attracted to him will give off attractant pheromones—not just any female. We'll just have to wait and see. Sam's a smart guy and seems to have high moral character. We'll just have to wait..." His voice trailed off as he reached to refill Kirby's glass, paying attention to the silent man's contracting jaw muscles—the only sign of his intense concentration. Suddenly George was warm. More, he wanted to change the subject, "Damn, Skeets," he ran on, "it's scary as hell." Martinez' mind was thinking relax as he shifted gears and felt for any threat in Kirby's silent concern about his friend's demon—and the man who caused it.

Sipping his scotch, Martinez decided to go on with his discourse. Whatever Kirby was thinking was beyond his control so he continued. "Since the olfactory apparatus consists of sensitivity to minute electrical potential, Sam should be able to predict a change in the barometer no matter how subtle—a real-time weather man!"

Skeets' face regained its normal smile as he pondered the doctor's words. Dropping his chin the enigmatic questioner assumed the pose of a college professor questioning a tardy student. His terse statement was bathed in a deadly serious tone. "George, who else knows about this...?"

"No one." George's reply was rapid. "I..." Skeets interrupted— he was still the chiding professor.

"Where are your records? Your real records?"

Silence. George Martinez was silent, his mouth forming words not audible. His brain was churning but he needed time.

Skeets spoke. "Hey, doc, silence can be golden—or damning. I thought we understood each other." The college professor was gone and the real Skeets Kirby was talking and his half smile now portended only wickedness.

Still off balance the surgeon stammered a reply. "Uh-uh—yea... right, of course you're right. I do have other records on Duff and I guess I should have told you..."

Kirby's reply, "Be my guest, doc," sent shivers down George Martinez' spine.

George was subdued and flushed as he stepped around his desk and opened the large file drawer on the lower left side. Pulling the drawer out he reached through the opening and deftly pushed a bolt allowing the drawer to pull out another four inches. Reaching into the back compartment the surgeon retrieved several folders and dropped them in front of Kirby.

Opening the top folder by feel Skeets spoke slowly, deliberately. "Look, Georgie boy, let's put ALL the cards on the table and play." Skeets hung on to the "all" like a stutterer not able to let it loose. "I didn't realize the implication of Sam's gift and from what I'm hearing you didn't either. If word of this shit gets out my buddy will be a freak and he—we couldn't handle that; nor could you. If no one else knows then we're halfway home. If you've told anyone I mean to stop this game right now. Without you for verification no story will be credible. And, Georgie, I can eliminate any source of verification... as you know."

Skeets' tone and stare did nothing to ease the doctor's apprehension. He kept seeing the bloated, blackish, oxygen starved carcass of Gypsy Jack; not to mention his amputated finger. Kirby's voice emanated from dark places.

"You listening boy? You look sort of pale."

Martinez nodded his head and the voice continued. "You and me will handle this thing and we'll tell no one—comprende? Our secret, okay?"

"I agree..." George spoke quietly. The fires of confrontation were subsiding.

Skeets' reaction was as if nothing had happened between the men. Just drinking buddies having one for old times sake. His voice was vintage Skeeter man. "You know George, getting to think about this, old Samson could revolutionize the FBI or CIA, or hell, even the girl scouts." Skeets' eyes sparked with an unaccustomed twinkle as he went on, enjoying his banter more than the listener. "If what you say about a dog is true, then with Sam's intellect he would be able to distinguish any odor he wanted to—just sniff it and away we go! Goddam it man there wouldn't be anything he couldn't determine once he gets background info..."

"...even if a person is lying or telling the truth, just like a dog can smell fear or submission or..." the surgeon's eyes dilated as he interjected. He was looking beyond Kirby; beyond his own predicament. He was caught in the trance of self-achievement even if due to serendipity—and the impact of his surgical accomplishment was beginning to well up like a rising column of hot mercury.

The flint faced Kirby took notice of George's interest and marveled that a man stuck in the boonies could pull off such a miracle. He also knew he wouldn't believe it if he wasn't involved and he realized that it would be impossible to convince anyone, especially medical men, that Sam Duff was something special. Skeets decided that keeping Sam's gift a secret wasn't the most difficult part—explaining them would be. Yep, that would be the rub. Also, what if the gifted guy got sick? These thoughts crowded the Kirby's sculpted head like too many monkeys.

"George, what do we do if he gets sick? What effect will it have on his sniffer?" These two queries were crawling through the mass of questions in Skeets' mind.

As he answered George fixed Skeets with a vacuous stare. "We have to keep him from getting sick, especially any upper respiratory disease." Skeets noticed the look in the surgeon's eye and his lowered voice—doctor like… I have just the stuff!" Jumping from the chair Martinez walked to the refrigerator and retrieved a 10 ml vial of a white particulate suspension. "See this? This is a non specific immune system potentiator…"

"If you say so doc." Kirby's puzzled look was much more eloquent than his reply.

Ignoring the comment Martinez continued. "I developed this 8 or 9 years ago with a bacteriologist and I've been using it since to stimulate a cell-mediated immune response in patients, especially those with cancer. It's all biological—nothing artificial or chemical. The bacteriologist was able to grow this particular bacterium in a manner as to produce a potent cell mediated immune response in mammals when the culture was harvested at a certain phase of its growth and the resultant bacteria killed and fragmented a special way."

Skeets' rock face was cracking. He could barely conceal his sarcasm as he barked. "Care to put that in the Queen's simplest, Doc. I'm a mite rusty with the medical mumbo jumbo."

Martinez' instantly wilted, but his voice hardly changed. "Uh—yea, right Skeets. What I mean is that this preparation when given intravenously will nonspecifically enhance their bodies' own natural defense against any infectious or cancerous cell. Got that?"

"Uh—maybe…"

George smiled, the upward pointing wrinkles seeming out of place. "Well Skeets, look at it this way. It keeps their white blood cells at the ready so when a bad bacteria or virus or cancer cell comes on the scene the pre-stimulated cell defenders are ready to kill or eat it, or both. How's that?"

"Better."

Smiling, George continued. "In the process, some long acting immunity is produced so the preparation can act as a non-specific vaccine and cause the body to immunize itself against most of the infections they are exposed to without the need for any disease specific or conventional vaccines." With one hand George pushed his graying hair from his eyes while he gently shook the vial, watching the fine particles settle as the bamboozled listener digested this biotechnology lesson.

"In other words Kirby, see that Sam gets 0.5 ml of this stuff twice a month until I decide different. Give it S.Q.—that's subcutaneously—or just under the skin; I'll explain this to him and show him how—you just be sure he complies. If he happens to go overseas he should get an injection every week. This will keep him from getting colds, influenza and other infectious-contagious diseases that could compromise his sniffing ability. If he gets sick he should have it given intravenously at three day intervals." George broke into a grin, leaned over the desk and waved the vial under Kirby's nose as if demonstrating perfume. "It's also damn effective on *Herpes*, especially *simplex II* which you probably know best by its common name—genital Herpes… In fact Mr. Kirby, this stuff will totally knock out Shingles even when the eye is affected…"

"Shit. Now you tell me!" Skeets' feigned disgust caused the doctor to break into laughter relieving the tension in the small office. "Hell, man, I'll just take a fix along with Sam…"

Still laughing, George interrupted. "No luck Kirby. For this to be useful in genital Herpes it has to be given at the first sign of a lesion, otherwise it won't work due to the secretive nature of the old Herpes bug. Anyway, man, just see that your buddy gets it and he'll stay relatively healthy."

The lighthearted moment seemed to herald a developing bond between the two based on common cause or guilt—Sam Duff's well being for Kirby, guilt for Martinez. Kirby wasn't capable of playing the guilt card.

Both wanted to keep Samson Hercules Duff alive and healthy.

The men drained their glasses and as George poured another, Skeets spoke, this time the tone was serious. "George, now that we're through the preliminaries we need to get to the main event." He told the surgeon about the Martin ranch massacre, the kidnapping, Sam's part in sorting out what happened and Sam's quest to find Joe Billie Bloodtooth and the nurse.

George sank back into his chair as the impact of this disclosure seeped through his scotched consciousness. Kirby was right. He, they, did have a problem—BIG sumbitch problem!

• • •

The sun was merciless. Sam and JY had been on Joe Billie's trail two hours and the big man's clothes were sweat-soaked, clinging to him like tacky tape. They had no trouble following the trail even through the weed-choked water that appeared to replace what had been solid ground. Samson knew little about sight tracking but from the erratic direction of the trail he surmised that the Miccosukee was taking precautions, intentionally or not, to confuse pursuers. He knew he had to be careful.

The 'let's get'r done' Pit Bulldog passed through the dense foliage as efficiently as a wild thing, never swerving from the scent trail and ignoring the myriad small creatures disturbed by his intrusion. Occasionally he would hesitate and look towards a larger swamp creature when its acrid scent graced the occasional breeze. Not that JY wasn't interested—he would die for a chance to have a go at any of these wild things including the big reptiles basking in the sun or lying in wait barely submerged in weed choked shallows. But he knew his mission and unless given no choice or commanded by Sam he would not leave the trail—for any reason.

Again Samson wondered why he was doing this. He knew nothing of this stifling wildness; less about his new found sense of smell. He did know that Bloodtooth was a worthy adversary. He was merciless at home and his retribution would be merciless.

Feeling for the baggie confining the nurse's delicate undergarments Sam nervously kneaded it, finding its redolence overpowering—even though sealed and in his pocket. His face and neck tingled from the adrenalin rush as he fought himself over this strange emotion. There was no question about it. Samson Duff wanted to possess this woman—sexually. He couldn't control these urges but knew he had to. Ashamed of this the distraught man knew he couldn't help it even as his inner self kept whispering that he must. Bloodtooth be damned, Samson Duff had to save this woman and he was damn sure going to find her.

The hair on Sam's neck stood as he clucked to JY and quickened their pace through the green morass.

Chapter **FOURTEEN**

"Wher' be gone dat shick-un boy, you papa wanna know sure, rat now!" It was late afternoon in Russell Foucharde's back yard, nesting along with a tiny clapboard shack in the north edge of a cypress strand just south of the Tamiami Trail about 20 miles west of Miami. Russell and his only son, Jacques, moved to Florida from southwest Louisiana; Russell having been promised gainful employment on the proposed new Miami International Airport to be built in the Everglades. A few big river cypress trees, sentinel like, stood at the edge of the small clearing behind the shack casting tall shadows as the sun settled. The few bay trees interspersed among the smaller pond cypress served to cover the yard with gloomy darkness, none able to match the stately height or signature shadow of the regal river cypress.

Jacques Foucharde carried a worried look in his 13 year old eyes, nervously wiping the palms of his grimy hands on his bib coveralls while standing on one bare foot as he rubbed the other on his leg to assuage the myriad ant bites getting itchier by the minute. His bare chest covered only by the coverall shoulder straps and arms were latticed with red lines and angry, growing welts. His youthful, high-pitched voice quivered like cold jello as he answered his father. "Papa you kno' dat fightin' shick-un I lookin' for don't kno' wher' he be at but he ain't lost 'cause I gonna find him sure, 'n back inna coop he goes—bet on it!" Jacques' trembly voice rose to fever pitch as he scrambled out his reply. He was in serious trouble.

That "fightin' shick-un" he referred to was Russ Foucharde's pride and joy; a champion never defeated fighting rooster transported in style from the Atchafalaya swamp of southwest Louisiana to his new home and hopefully a full feathered harem in the Florida Everglades. Russell lived for cock fighting and his prowess with fighting birds was of legendary proportion in southeast Texas and southwest Louisiana. And Stopcock was the creme-de-la-creme of fighting cocks; fast, fearless and fucking crazy. And he was running around loose in the great Pay-Hay-Okee. And young Jacques was the reason.

"Boy, you doan catch me my shick-un you I skin rat now soon! Bet on it!" Russell's Cajun temper was up and at the sound of his voice young Jacques turned and disappeared into the unrelenting foliage surrounding the tiny yard, highlighted now by a single fragile appearing chicken coop, its only door hanging open in a mocking gesture of unconcern.

Russ was seriously pissed but as he took up the search his feelings towards his young son softened and he reasoned that the rooster could fly like a quail, was tough as a pine knot and about three quarters wild anyway. He would probably roost in a tree tonight and come looking for scratch feed at daylight. Chuckling to himself the Cajun picked up a can of mixed scratch feed and casually distributed it in front of the coop, chunking a handful into the back of the empty bird domicile. Let Jacques hunt the wayward fowl until after dark—do him good. "Dat one tough shick-un for sure." The wiry cajun was now talking to himself out loud. "He be aw rite up inna tree tonight, bet on it." still chuckling, Russell Foucharde went into the tiny house.

It was 1:00 am and moonlight cast an eerie shadow from the single river cypress standing lonesome at the edge of the dense strand, about 100 yards from the darkened shack. Though the moon had been up only an hour its austere presence seemed to mock the vaporous clouds that flitted fretfully across its globular, glowing face. Subtle as an undertow, a current of restlessness was building in the illuminated Pay-Hay-Okee. The first limbs on the big cypress sprang from the massive trunk about 65 feet above the ground, gradually shortening and becoming leafier as they neared the crown. Stopcock had flown to the lowest limb at sunset and in wild turkey fashion had jumped up two "stories" to a smaller, leafier limb and settled in for the night. Fluffing his feathers and tucking his proud head under his left wing he relaxed his body and eased forward locking his feet into their perching position. The gallant little bird was tired from being chased through the punishing saw palmettos and dense underbrush following his escape from the coop. He really liked young Jacques but Stopcock wanted some hens and he sure didn't see any around that little yard. Oh well, he would find some tomorrow after he found something to eat. He was a tough!

The game little rooster had been asleep over five hours when a feathered shadow suddenly materialized on the limb several feet from the snoozing rooster. The great horned owl arrived on muted wings and as he positioned to achieve balance, his large golden eyes turned with his head and transfixed the slumbering fowl. He quickly fluffed his gorgeous barred feathers and with the dubious grace of a drunk high wire walker eased toward the night-blind gamecock, his awkward sidesteps a model of silence and concentration. Positioning himself next to Stopcock the big bird cautiously bumped him causing the rooster to jerk upright, and still half asleep, almost fall, struggling with his wings to maintain his once peaceful perch. Regaining balance the aroused gamecock looked around but having poor night vision saw only an unrecognizable shadow. Then—bump—the owl pushed again; now with more force and Stopcock barely avoided tumbling from his lofty bedstead. He was mad! Nighttime or not!

Whatever was pushing him was in for a fight! His feathers fluffed and long neck hackles deployed making him look three times his size. The moon was bright in the cloudless sky and the fiery little rooster could barely make out the strange looking 'chicken' perched next to him. The great horned owl noted the challenge display and his large blinkless eyes fixed the rooster's weak stare and with a final push dislodged Stopcock. Before he reached ground the great-feathered predator struck the little rooster with his merciless talons and struggled into the strand before dropping to the ground with the quivering burden.

With fierce glances the great bird ate.

• • •

The steaming sun was starting its western decline when Joe Billie called a halt to his merciless trek. The trio had covered many miles, their snakelike progress always culminating in an east-southeast direction. The two unwilling participants were subdued, allowing the Miccosukee to progress at a faster pace than he thought. Even his stops to shinny up a tree to view his back-trail had barely slowed their progress. Only one such vigilance had evoked suspicion of rescuers when a flock of wood ducks had taken to the air far back but definitely near his trail. Joe Billie had to be sure. He was heading for a fishing shack not far from his old home ground and he definitely didn't want any visitors—with guns and dogs.

Putting down his backpack he sat Elise and Can Martin back to back with a small tree between them, lashed their wrists and tied the rancher's leash around the nurse's slender neck.

"Sit still. Be back in a few minutes. Anyway, do you all good to rest… ha ha."

Elise pursed her lips, but Joe Billie was gone; vanishing into the thick foliage like a wraith.

The man moved swiftly now unburdened by his captives and backpack and always downwind of his trail.

He knew that any pursuers would have dogs and no one respected their ability more than the big Miccosukee. He wanted to cut his trail behind any putative posse so he could determine how many and what kind, if any, were after him. Maybe he was wrong. Maybe no one was following but he had to be sure—and he was hungry. The appetite dulling effect of whiskey was wearing off and thoughts of the shack and food became inspiration. Passing the spot where the ducks flew up, Joe Billie worked his way into the wind always angling towards his back-trail; Grandfather's war club as well as his senses were on red alert. Step by cautious step he approached the trail until he saw the footprints of himself and the captives. Relaxing a notch the big man followed the sign with his innate sense inducing caution. Ten yards up and Joe Billie froze— a paw print visible in one of Elise's petite and distinctive footprints. The half-breed's mouth was dry as he kneeled beside a clump of reeds and studied the area into which the trail led. No suspicious sound reached his ear. Maybe it was a stray hound looking to back-track its master—but the Indian knew that print wasn't made by a hound. The track was too square with the toes tucked too tight to have been put there by a splay-footed hounddog. Bloodtooth knew dogs and sign and no hound he knew of left such a power reeking print. He followed the dog-spoor, moving silently in a half crouch, sometimes parting dense reeds and grass clumps with the war club before proceeding. Fifty yards told him he was being followed by one dog – not a hunting-tracking hound – and one man. It was not happenstance they were there—who were they?

Another fifty yards told him these followers were tight on his trail and he had better be doing something. Since the strange tracking dog was proving to have a good nose Joe Billie realized he couldn't lead them on a wild goose chase. But also, Joe Billie didn't think of one man, even though he had to be armed and one dog as a threat. He chuckled as he moved away from the trail and headed back to his 'tour group'. He would let the River of Grass do his dirty work. He would lead the two heroes further into his backyard—and death.

Laughing, the amused man turned toward the weakening western sky, his tight lips stifling the laughter. "Yes Grandfather, we will let that there man with his strange dog test his skill in this land of endless water…our land! Ha-ha-ha." These words were spoken in monotone with each word carefully pronounced so the spirits would understand. Joe Billie Bloodtooth was now guided by his Grandfather and mother—he could not lose!

• • •

Sam stopped, causing JY who was in front to stop and look back at his master as if to say, why boss man, this trail's just right! The hair on Sam's neck was standing. He sensed the presence of Bloodtooth. Dropping to a crouch, He looked in every direction aware of no specific scent but ever so faintly he smelled

The Indian. Could Bloodtooth be stalking them at this very moment? Sam knew his quarry's prowess but could anyone waylay Samson and JY given Sam's new sensory gift? The feeling persisted causing Sam to silently signal the unperturbed pit bull to his side and search the deepening shadows, his senses raw as sandpapered skin.

It was 15 sweaty minutes before the feeling left Sam.

The effort to remain motionless yet trust his intuition, knowing it could be a sign of fear or paranoia, left him exhausted. Sucking it up Samson and JY picked up the trail—this time more cautious, his fingers inches from his pistol.

• • •

Joe Billie changed direction and headed straight east, towards the old home ground and the land of endless trees, the hundreds of acres of *Melaleuca* trees south of the old family chickees and extending south and east for miles. He knew that no white man, dog or no, could survive being lost in the impenetrable maze of stinking paper-barked punk trees. Even he had to be careful but he had grown up with the leafy imported pest and he would lead his pursuers into the morass at sunset. It would be a few miles out of the way since the shack was just off the southwestern tip of the noxious growth. The trees were showing bloom and punk tree bloom was no laughing matter—to a scent hound. Joe Billie chuckled as he pictured the dog trying to follow his trail through the stinking trees. That four-legged turd-eater won't be able to smell a bucket of bird shit if it fell on him, he thought, as he turned to his bridled captives. This time the mirthful voice cracked like a drover's whip. "Come on you assholes—we got places to go—heh-heh-heh..."

Elise nor Can Martin had uttered a word since the Miccosukee appeared and rapidly untied them, dragging them to their feet with the admonition, "Get going or you dead meat."

● ● ●

It was sunset as Samson and JY searched the area where the captives had been tied. Sam stayed close to the tree trying to determine if Elise was still unharmed and became stimulated by her scent. His flushing face embarrassed him; somehow he had to gain control over this emotion. JY stopped a few yards from the tree and smelled something, causing Sam to go and look. Immediately he sensed where Bloodtooth had left the backpack, picking up the spoor he left when he went to check his backtrack. The hair on Sam's body stood and it took a few minutes to realize what had happened. So now he knows he's being followed, he thought. He also knows its one man and a dog and he's laughing this very minute. These thoughts stuck in Sam like a poison dart. What if he's killed them because of us?

"Goddam it JY, why wasn't I more careful!" Sam's outburst shook the silence so unexpectedly that JY let out a whine. "I should have known that canny son of a bitch would check his trail. Hot damn, dog, why did you let me screw up!" Samson's voice lowered to a harsh whisper as the dog licked his hand, suffering his master's frustration but not knowing how to help.

So his premonition had not been imagined. He had scented the Indian though upwind from him; he had a lot of learning to do about his extraordinary gift.

It was sunset as Samson and JY approached the edge of a shadowy wall with no end. The shadows were thick with the overpowering quietness that settles over a wilderness at sunset—the time when day sounds cease and night sounds have yet to begin—causing goose bumps on Samson. He shivered as if buffeted by a wind. Why in hell am I here, he thought, as he followed the pit bull into the tangle of tree trunks and vines. The trail was too obvious but since the trees were too close together to allow easy passage it was only logical for interlopers to keep to the animal trails crisscrossing the pithy maze. A few steps into the morass and it was dark—the moon wasn't up and the canopy denied light from the departing sun. JY had no trouble following the scent clinging to the mucky debris. Sam, more comfortable with his scenting prowess followed knowing that the pit bull was on target. His concern was studying the anointed path for sign of a trap—a posture he assumed since leaving where Joe Billie had tied the captives. However, the darkness in the grove precluded anything but smell. He could not make out JY's outline—he could only hear and smell the intent mass of dog-meat. Sam felt he and his dog were not in this mass of trees by accident. 'Intuition,' he thought, but every bit as strong as his sensing the half-breed's presence along the trail. He had to be careful—but how? His mind was racing as the bull dog struggled on passing narrow, muddy cross trails, encountering leafy debris interspersed with yellowish, saffron like bloom and becoming more abundant; settling on Sam's head and shoulders as he twisted along the trail. After fighting through the endless trees for almost an hour Sam noticed a change in JY's. He was leaving the trail, wriggling between the paper barked barriers like a hairy worm, to return after only a few yards. He stopped, causing Sam to stumble over him in the blackness. Simultaneously Samson cursed as he realized he wasn't smelling the fugitive's scent. He had been relying on the dog while his mind wandered to other details and

unconsciously blocked out the scent they were following. He knew
JY couldn't do that. Nothing short of an attack would take JY off
the track—emotion or daydreaming wouldn't; Samson envied that.
Only one thing can be wrong and if I'm right we're in deep ca-ca.

"Goddam it JY." Sam hissed, venting his frustration on the pit
bulldog. "What in hell is wrong with you?" Pulling himself to a
sitting position and chagrined after his outburst, Sam patted the
magnificent head, feeling mud and slime glued to the sleek hair
coat. Affectionately he ran his fingers between the powerful jaws
feeling the strong, white teeth while marveling at the power stored
in the compact head. Samson Duff was the only man that JY would
allow to do this and the feeling was a potent one… indeed!

Whispering, Sam spoke to his friend. "What's the matter old
man? We lose 'em?" JY's response was to silently lick Sam's hand and
sit awaiting orders. It was then that the tracker noticed the overpowering scent of the *Melaleuca* bloom—especially at ground level. He
could barely smell the dog much less the Indian scent. You fool, you
stupid fool, he thought. Of course, these are punk trees and they're
blooming and they're worse than oaks and more allergenic.

"That's why we're here, old buddy." Samson's words penetrated the like glass shards; more quizzical than declarative. JY cocked
his head. The loyal pit had never heard his master question himself or his actions. Sam continued. "That son of a bitch knew we…
uh…a dog…couldn't track him through these blooming trees.
Damn it all, JY," his voice rising, "I'll bet the asshole knows you're
not a bloodhound—or even a tracking dog. Yeah, that hombre's
a smart one!"

Risking the flashlight, Samson surveyed the grimy dog, almost
unrecognizable—but eager. A smile crossed his face, turning wicked as he thought of one thing the half-breed couldn't know—that
dog or no Samson Duff could trail him to Florida Bay and back if
he had to. Tired, grimy, eaten up by mosquitoes and no-see-ums
and lost, the man knew the fight was enjoined and the mightyPay-
Hay-Okee was sure to be more than ambiance—much more!

• • •

"Boy, you clean dem fishes rat now you hear. Doan want no spoiled up fishes you can bet on it!" Russell Foucharde's voice roiled across the shallow water to the weed lined shore like a swarm of hornets. He was poling his pirogue towards the shore and a boy, his son, Jacques and he had more fish plus two large, pissed-off soft shelled cooters for the boy to clean. The shore, about 50 yards from the shack's front door, was littered with fish heads, glistening globs of fish scales, turtle shells, various and sundry alligator parts haphazardly distributed around assorted pole racks and crude tables sheltering a variety of ice chests of unknown parentage. Empty tin cans everywhere.

Russ had come on the shack several months ago and had quickly taken to the area as it reminded him of his native Louisiana and his old stomping ground in the watery Atchafalaya swamp. Not able to keep a job, the wiry Cajun had taken to fishing, trapping, poaching—whatever—hauling fish, gator meat, frog legs, turtle meat, 'possum, 'coon and an occasional wild cow or hog carcass to Miami for quick sale in the populous Little Cuba section.

Russ didn't know to whom the cabin belonged and really didn't give a shit—as long as no one bothered him. He and the boy had been there five days and were leaving the next morning for their humble domicile just off Alligator Alley. The gator skins alone made the trip worthwhile even though going and coming was really tough. The recalcitrant little man was used to hardships. Sliding the pirogue's pointed bow into the sticky goo of the shoreline, Russell deftly stepped up through the middle of the narrow, unstable craft and with a sprightly leap from the bow landed barefoot on the thicker grass of the shore.

"Gat here'n hep me with these critters, boy—yore papa tired all rite—bet on it." Russ aimed his words at the boy and pulled the small boat onto the shore oblivious to the frenzied thrashings in the few inches of water in the pirogue's bottom. At the sound of his papa's voice, Jacques Foucharde dropped his knife on the crude slab of a table, wiped his runny nose with the back of his hand and started towards the grounded pirogue. It had taken Russ Foucharde several months to get over the loss of his champion gamecock and young Jacques for sure wanted to stay on his papa's good side. He could still see the look on Russ' face when they discovered the pitiful remains of Stopcock in the grassy clearing back of the stately river cypress. Man, was that Cajun pissed! Plus, the elder Foucharde finally had to give up the fighting chickens as it was impossible to raise them where they lived. If it wasn't the owls, it was the 'coons, the bobcats, or the occasional wild dog or coyote. So the frustrated Cajun simply gave up on his "fightin' shickuns" and started poaching.

• • •

Joe Billie was smiling and talking to himself as he eased out of the *Melaleuca* forest. His captives, like him, were plastered with dank slimy goo and covered with leaves and the saffron colored bloom of the punk tree. Can Martin was sniffling and had watery eyes but the intimidator warned him not to sneeze. The few times he couldn't comply were acknowledged by a backhand that left hand sized red marks on the subdued rancher's face. Elise remained silent, stubbornly biting her lip and vowing to see it through. Joe Billie stopped, looked up and spoke to the dark sky. "Let the man and dog rescue each other, Grandfather—ha, ha, ha…" It was still an hour until moonrise and the cabin was close by. If Elise could have seen the Indian's face she would have noticed dilated pupils and not have blamed them on darkness.

Darkness or no, Joe Billie held to course and broke out at the water's edge just down from the cabin as the moon started to show in the west. The moon's effect was dramatic, transforming the water into shimmering glass and washing over the trees and cabin like a silvery veil. Joe Billie stopped so abruptly that Elise let go with "Oh." Motioning them down and kneeling in one motion, never doubting their compliance, the wary Indian fixed his eyes on the cabin; someone was in his shack. The face of the moon was visible creating a restlessness in the young woman. Looking over

Bloodtooth's shoulder she could see wispy clouds flitting across the moon's face, some the color of dirty linen, others dark and purplish. The emergence of goose bumps caused her to shiver, the adrenalin flush abolishing her fatigue.

Joe Billie turned causing his gator tooth amulet to spin out of his open shirtfront and dangle, glowing white and ominous on his massive chest. Silently he led them from the shore to the first tree, a smallish cypress and tied them. He was glancing over his shoulder, more at the moon than the cabin and Elise thought she detected a smear of fear across his predator eyes. He's going into a trance, she thought. Something set him off—but what? The moon? The cabin? Trying not to show eye movement Elise noticed rivulets of spittle seep out his mouth as he stalked the shanty—club in hand. Martin was tied behind the tree and forced to look at the shadowy woods; Elise could see the water, the shack—everything. As if underwater the nurse strained to follow the vaporous figure as it glided to the cabin, paused to open the door and vanished. Nothing could prepare her for the thunk, thunk, thunk of the war club, its intonation emanating from the flimsy structure like beastly vomit. The moon washed stillness was defiled by these sounds and Elise broke into choking sobs. Suddenly the cabin door flew open and a small, scrawny figure sprinted to the water's edge and jumped into the grounded pirogue, gesturing and voicing unintelligible sounds. Close behind was the imposing Joe Billie Bloodtooth, in silent pursuit. The boy, Jacques, strained his 80 pounds against the pole but couldn't budge the pirogue. Dropping the pole, he jumped into the shallow water and headed out, his shadowy pursuer a few steps behind. Joe Billie caught the boy in the shallow water in front of the captives. Grasping the struggling unfortunate by the neck the massive man held him up, turning his writhing body toward Elise. The distraught nurse could hear the choking pleas,—Leave me lone, leave me lone… my papa he kill-kill you …ahh…ahh. Bet-on-it…" until the hand choked off the words.

Looking at Elise, the hard man spoke in a soft voice. "See Mother, that there dog had a pup. I fixed him good in the shack, now' I fix his pup…"

Elise screamed. "Let him go! Let him go!" As she did the Entrancer, possessed of super strength, grabbed the boy by his skinny, ant bitten ankles and bashed his head to a pulp.

Elise fainted at the first blow.

• • •

It was an hour since Samson discovered their blunder. Knowing JY would be useless in backtracking he started back the way they came but found the trail indistinct where small natural openings occurred among the tree trunks. The flashlight was no help. Thinking he could smell his own spoor on the peeling tree trunks Samson pushed his face close to every tree in the vicinity and could not pick up scent except where he had just touched. The filamentous bloom was overpowering!

"Okay, Junk Yard, let's figure this out." Sam's whisper seemed out of place—even to the dog, causing him to cock his angular head as if to reply, "Say what?" Sam managed a smile as he noted the dog's pose but continued his low-pitched voice. "Okay Injun, how's about these apples?" He produced a compass and stared at the glowing needle as it settled on the fluorescent N. "Alright pal, let's be off!" With that the grimy pair started towards the north, Samson figuring he had entered the forest from the west and that north would be the shortest way out. The going was rife with detours—bogs, quicksand, clumps of trees so thick that passage was impossible... and water. Water was everywhere, each step a sucking, stumbling, pulling effort. Mosquito city!

The moon was up several hours when they broke through the thickets bordering the northwest corner of the *Melaleuca* grove. Despite the protective coating of dried muck, insect bites too numerous to count tatooed the bodies of Samson and JY. The man's face was a raw blob. JY was better protected but his eyelids and nose were swollen and he had rubbed his face unmercifully on the trees. All in all it was a miserable pair that viewed the silvery stream just south of Joe Billie Bloodtooth's old home chickee. Sam thought they emerged at just the right place. Away from the scent stifling *Melaleuca* trees Samson inhaled a chest full of night air and was overjoyed at the return of the exotic smells to which he was becoming accustomed. Looking into the fresh southwest wind, the rejuvenated man quickly determined that they were alone. Bloodtooth and his two captives had to be south and possibly west of him as he figured to be on the west edge of the punk tree grove, most likely the northwest corner. Good, he thought, we can clean up, eat and I'll bet my bottom dollar we can skirt these shit trees and pick up bad ass' trail before daylight.

Hearing water splash, Sam spun around to see a happy pit bulldog playing in the clean, sandy-bottomed stream like a juvenile otter. Samson waded into the water—hair, teeth and eyeballs. Seeking greater depth Sam waded into the salubrious fluid, moving upstream as he felt the bottom slope away in that direction. His senses were on hold so refreshing was the water and he was scrubbing mud from his face and failed to notice the slight rippling movement of the sinuous shadow that edged toward him from the near shoreline. The huge moccasin struck with the force of a sledgehammer, sinking his fangs into Sam's left arm between wrist and elbow.

"Argghh—aahh..." Sam's cry quickly turned into a grunt of as the six-foot serpent started whip-like motions, sinking his dirty fangs deeper into Sam's flesh. Strong as Duff was, he could not get a hold on the angry moccasin or stop it. It took him a few precious seconds to realize what had happened, seconds the serpent was using as his muscular jaws pumped their deadly contents into Sam's naive flesh. This snake would show these intruders whose territory this was. Once he had finished the big one, he would give his attention to the small one still playing in the water and oblivious to his partner's distress.

Stumbling while trying to feel his way to shallow water, Samson, try as he would could not loose the writhing snake. He could feel venom pulsing into his flesh and reached for his pistol, freeing it just as he backed into a submerged snag and fell into the roiling water. The frolicking JY saw the battle and went for his master but was unable to help in the deeper water; he could only swim frantically around the participants.

Sputtering, he regained his footing and surged up for air, the snake still attached to his left arm but his right hand was empty—the pistol was gone. The water was shallower allowing him to kneel and brace his body against the powerful undulations of his mud colored adversary; still he could not loose it. The episode had lasted only seconds yet Samson was overwhelmed by a sense of urgency. He had to free his arm to stop the deadly flow of venom being pumped into his body. Suddenly the thick body stopped its punishing undulations. Sam's bleary eyes could barely make out the head of JY as he clamped down with his considerable might, having caught the moccasin just ahead of its anal vent. The bulldog's bite caused the snake to stiffen but still not loose its hold on Sam's arm. Sensing the situation, Sam forced his arm to his chest, grabbed the moccasin's body with his right hand and bit it just behind its fist-sized head, grinding his teeth into the nasty flesh with all the power in his weakening jaws. The acrid taste of the quieting serpent overpowered him as he felt his teeth against bone but his commitment was total and with the help of the powerful dog the deadly jaws loosened, ripping tortured flesh as they gave up their purchase.

JY dragged the writhing snake into shallow water and deftly changed his hold catching the creature behind its head where Sam's teeth marks had branded the noxious skin. Violently shaking his head JY killed the creature, not stopping until his grinding jaws severed its head from the thrashing body. Ears tightly pinned he belly-crawled to his stricken Master.

Samson crawled to shore hugging his throbbing arm, his body joining its violated member in rebellion against the venomous invasion caused by the bite. His vision was blurring and waves of nausea were starting deep in his gut threatening to turn him inside out. His edematous brain was trying to sort out these happenings but it just couldn't accept that Samson Hercules Duff's body was envenomated and dying. Struggling against this cerebral detachment, Sam crawled onto the grass as the first wave of nausea overpowered him, spewing watery vomitus in gushing torrents.

Reaching his pack he fumbled in it and found the vial of antivenom, cursing that it had to be reconstituted with a barely adequate syringe-needle apparatus. The paroxysms of nausea were crippling and prevented him from getting up from his knees. Finally mixing the diluent with the powdered anti venom, Sam sucked the ten ml. from the vial, cursing his ineptness as the life-saving brew slowly filled the syringe. Retching, Samson fell to a fetal position. Holding the syringe dagger-like in his shaking right he stabbed his dying arm in the purplish flesh between the gaping bite and elbow. With each frenetic stab he injected a few ml. of antivenom deep in the throbbing flesh, berating himself as a fool with each strike. Feeling the plunger stop Sam grabbed the vial of penicillin tumbled on the ground beside the pack and refilled the syringe—plunging it deep in his thigh and pushing the plunger until it stopped and fell from his weakening grasp.

Sensing JY's nearness the dying man tried to speak but his swelling tongue prevented any intelligible sound. The dog was powerless to help but in the timeless manner of dogs proceeded to lick his master—whatever part was exposed—with his warm, healing tongue. Samson passed out.

Sam awoke with JY licking his face. His benumbed brain told him he had been out 15 or 20 minutes but he really didn't know. Mental clarity suddenly returned and he quickly surveyed his bloated arm, taking particular note of the ragged wound just above his wrist. The pain was gone, replaced by a heaviness that belied reason. Whipping out his knife, Sam trimmed the jagged edges, cutting away the rotting flesh as if trimming frayed cloth; feeling no pain as the razor-like blade did its job. Seeing the exposed vital tissue, Samson wiped the blade on his pants and resheathed it. The delirium returned and Samson rolled onto his knees and started crawling—aimless movement. Reaching a thick stand of low growing silver myrtle and reeds, the feverish man tried to tunnel through the tenacious foliage. His left arm was useless and his tongue so swollen his mouth could barely contain it. A trickle of blood was starting from his left nostril and the wetness felt in his pants was the trickle of blood seeping from his anus. Collapsing into the grassy tunnel, Samson Hercules Duff passed out.

Chapter FIFTEEN

The humid mist of darkness descended over the lush, semi-tropical hammocks of south Florida, stretching from a point south of Miami to the 10,000 acres of mangrove and hammock wetlands known as the Florida Keys. Hundreds of acres of hammock were scattered throughout this Caribbean like area comprised of West Indian hardwood trees, shallow rooted in the fossilized limestone substrate formed some 110,000 years earlier. One such place, called skull hammock by the few Indians and hunters that visited it was home to a myriad of animal and plant life; unchanged over the last thousand years due to its remoteness and isolation.

This was a moonless night and the darkness went about its business in a quietly efficient way blotting out the oaks, the gumbo limbo trees, the mastic and *Lignam vitae* trees along with others. The skyline was soon gone and all was darkness save for the emergence of tiny, blinking lights darting here, darting there; the source of this display unheard and unseen.

With over 20 species of fireflies in the area the mature male firefly of the genus *Photinus* had plenty to concern himself with as he flashed his mating code with the fluorescent light built into his sleek abdomen. He was as proud of his seductive blinking ability as he was of his sexual prowess—especially when homing in on a receptive female *Photinus,* nailing her to the leaf in his vigorous display of sexual ardor—a happy bug!

Dancing around in the pitch black hammock, *Photinus* ignored the cacophony of blinks from other species of lustful lightening bug sirens, setting his sights on a vivid display of female *Photinus* blinks coming from a cabbage palm leaf about 50 yards away. He never had to travel that far for female company but this display was intriguing—the brightest he had seen. This must be quite a gal, he thought, as he darted towards the compelling signals, answering his intended with his throbbing abdomen and ignoring the blinks of other female fireflies.

The svelte female lightening bug centered herself secure-ly in one of the shallow v-shaped grooves on the palm frond as she awaited her visitor. Ms. *Photuris* had spent hours perfecting her blinking to mimic that of Ms. *Photinus* and was proud of her accomplishment.

The sun had been down a few hours and the inky blackness en-veloping skull hammock was perfect for her deception—she was excited! She could hardly wait for her amorous caller.

The charged-up, hyper-expectant Mr. *Photinus* homed in on the seductive light as if pulled by a string, landing mere inches from his intended. His arousal was amply evident as he swag-gered into his mating stance, only briefly wondering why the female wasn't in the expected—and necessary—sexual position. This puzzlement was brief as the voracious Ms. *Photuris* rushed to the male firefly and grabbed him by the throat. Her hard mouthparts efficiently severed his neck—the look of surprise forever locked in his vacant stare. Slobbering to facilitate the passage of Mr. *Photinus*' delicious flesh, Ms. *Photuris* devoured the firefly.

● ● ●

Elise awoke inside the small shack unaware of having been carried from where she had witnessed the brutal clubbing of the Cajun boy, Jacques Foucharde. Unknown to her was that her swoon had lasted several hours; due to the extreme stress of the past 24 hours coupled with the lack of food and rest. Dawn was an hour away but the full moon dispelled the predawn darkness with its preternatural glow. She raised her head slowly, taking in the crude bunk-bed on which she was lying, childlike, absorbed in the phantasmagoric clutter inside the dirty room. Can Martin was stretched on a similar bunk, wired to it neck and ankles with a shaft of moonlight highlighting his blanched features and imparting a morgue like aura. The woozy nurse noticed the lazy flow of blood, a blackish blot, from the man's nose and became aware of his stertorous breathing. Her mind quickly dismissed the harried rancher's condition as she fought through her confusion about what had happened. A roughhewn table lay on its side amid the various clutter scattered over the floor. Black, irregular shadows on the floor where shadows shouldn't be bore witness to the bloody murder of Russ Foucharde. Drag marks ending at the door were visible on the warped plywood floor. Joe Billie Bloodtooth was nowhere to be seen.

Sitting up, Elise felt her face and neck assuring herself that she was intact and unhurt. "Psst... Can? Can, you okay? You hear me...?" Her husky whisper seemed to fill the tiny room but brought no response from the rancher. Any rancor concerning her former patient had been put aside since witnessing the Miccosukee's display. The realization that their—her—escape hinged on a cooperative effort was now accepted as a given by nurse Jones. She was convinced that rescue by other persons was out of the question. Joe Billie was too formidable to be taken in this—his—wildness.

Getting no response, Elise slid her legs over the side and sat up, testing her arms and legs as she did. Her dirty clothes no longer had any impact; grimy skin and stringy hair of no concern. Elise eased over to Martin's bunk and started to bend over and was startled by the thin, watery voice. "I'm awake... I heard you whisper...didn't want to answer less he was listening... you think he's gone?"

211

"I think so."

"See if you can find something to undo me with." Can's voice was weak, but totally defiant and Elise knew that the man had answered his personal demons.

He had not quit the fight. A sense of elation swelled inside her but the reality of the situation choked it to a whispered "Thank God you're okay... we've got to get out of here—now."

Glancing around the interior she spotted a rusty toolbox and in a second was rifling through the assorted tools and junk. "Thank God!" she blurted as she displayed a pair of common pliers.

"I can't cut this wire." Elise's voice dripped desperation as she tried to cut the wire snaring the rancher.

"Bend it back and forth fast with the pliers... it'll crystallize and break." Can's nervous voice carried no hint of fear.

It'll hurt you!"

"Goddam it Elise, I'm already hurt. Do it!" The rancher's reply startled her into frenetic action with the pliers, ignoring the rivulet of fresh blood flowing from Martin's dirt caked neck. The friction-hot wire clamped between index finger and thumb Elise sighed—part pain, part relief—as it gave way, allowing Can to sit up. After repeating the procedure with the wire binding his wrists, Elise handed him the pliers and Martin's experienced hands made short work of the wire around his bootless ankles.

While Can was so engaged Elise was moving around peering out of the tattered screened windows but could see nothing in the milky gloom. Martin's hand on her shoulder caused a gasp and she turned to face him with an intent, searching stare. Can found his boots and pulled them on, ignoring the searing pain in his leg.

"What if it's a trap? What if he's out there...waiting?"

Elise's voice cracked as she looked to the opened door.

"So what. He's going to kill us anyway—me for sure. He wouldn't have to do it this way..." Can's monotone was gathering force but his rhetoric smacked of disjointed fatalism rather than action.

"He's crazy, you know," Elise persisted. "You don't know what he's liable to do..." Can cut her off. "For Christ's sake, Elise, let's get the hell out of here. I'm willing to take my chances outside—at least we'll have one." The hurt man's attitude seemed different.

A dampened spark of self-reliance seemed to have suddenly burst into flame. Maybe he sensed that this may well be his last stand. "Look around for food, anything edible—there's a bag there." Can continued, his voice stronger with each word. "...Be quick!"

Abandoning caution, the pair rummaged in the dusky early dawn light like crazed scavengers. Elise glanced up as Can shoved something into the front of his belt and turned away to continue throwing cans and assorted objects into the plastic bag, along with some matches and the pliers. Quickly he motioned her to the door and they scurried to the water's edge and headed southwest—away from the direction of their arrival. They didn't notice the missing pirogue. Dawn was breaking.

Elise's legs felt like rubber bands. Wild thoughts flashed through her mind like laser lights. What was she into now? Out of the frying pan into the fire? Could she trust the rancher? What did he hide in his belt? A screwdriver? An ice pick? A knife? He acted like he didn't want her to see whatever it was. Then again, maybe it was just the heat of battle—they were in one hell of a hurry to get out of the shack. Elise's apprehensions were put on hold; she tripped in the muddy weeds and fell headlong into the backside of Can Martin.

• • •

Joe Billie poled the narrow pirogue despite its burden. The two dead Cajuns were small and fit snugly in the bottom of the efficient craft. He was a half-mile from the shack when he slid the bodies overboard in an area he called Gator Soup Hole; a deep bay off the main waterway shot through with a pasty growth of duckweed giving it the appearance of a very weird bowl of soup. There were alligators in this hole, their duckweed headwear lending a comedic flair to beasts not renowned for their sense of humor. The bodies disturbed the greenery as they slipped beneath the surface creating a blackish defect. Five minutes later a thin blackish line

marked the passage of Joe Billie Bloodtooth from the quiet bay—
and the Cajuns from existence.

The Miccosukee was deep in thought as he guided the
pirogue towards a landing some two miles from the shack. His
thoughts were rational this particular morning as the impact
of what he had done—was doing—settled on him. For the
first time since going to Can Martin's ranch house, murdering
the help and taking the two captives, Joe Billie questioned his
actions.

"What in hell am I doin'?" The throaty, masculine voice sounded out of sync in the pristine morning stillness. He didn't realize
he was talking—not that it made a difference. It was light enough
to see and the musing Indian peered through the moisture-laden
air searching for the three sentinel palm trees overhanging the
landing place. Seeing them, he settled into a rhythmic pushing.
A great blue heron flapped over the bush fringed shore and stuck
his stilt-like legs down as if feeling for the ground, spied the silent
man in the pirogue and tried to reverse direction. Squawking loudly the reedy bird settled into the weeds and head feathers erected,
eyed the strange thing floating in its water. Sensing no danger it
retracted its partially raised wings and positioned them next to
its keel-like breast. The wings vanished as the hungry bird transformed into an iridescent, living spear. The thin smile of showing
on the man's face was as complicated as the bird's hunting stare
was simple.

The man knew he had committed a heinous act and had talked
to his dead mother and grandfather but he blamed the massacre on booze, never thinking that he may be delusional. And talking to ancestors was an accepted practice among his people. He
cursed the white man's whiskey, money, women—all complicit in
bringing him down. In his mind he downplayed his lust for revenge over Stump's death feeling that Can Martin was a no good
son of a bitch and needed killing. The other killings were due
to provocation—man thing—Joe Billie didn't think of himself as
a cold-blooded killer. Details of these escapades seemed trapped
in his hazy thoughts. He remembered taking the girl—but why?
Why didn't he just slip into the home, kill the rancher and be

gone. Mistaking the pretty nurse for his mother never entered his mind and why in God's name was he tiptoeing through the Pay-Hay-Okee with two bedraggled people, a cripple and a sobbing woman? Why did he kill two Cajuns? Joe Billie clearly remembered the shack and the bashings but had scant recollection of participating—as if he but witnessed the merciless acts.

His reverie was interrupted as he pushed the pirogue's sharp bow far onto the white sand of the landing. Departing the beached craft Joe Billie pulled it out of the water, lifted his pack and club and hastily walked to the charred remains of a fire pit; a place of many fires and meals. He was famished and in lucid moments food took precedence. This area was unique in the snow-white sugar sand that covered the ridge paralleling the water's edge and in combination with the white sand bottom of the landing area created a paradisiacal panorama. Breathtaking!

Remembering the quail, he pulled the fist-sized feather balls from his pocket. He clearly remembered catching the birds—but when? Why hadn't he eaten them? With thoughtless efficiency Joe Billie started a cook-fire and seared the quail, eating both with a can of beans from his pack and washed it down with a quenching draught of slough water. Leaning against a tree, his hunger partially satisfied, Joe Billie continued his mind search. He really wanted to be left alone. He believed that whoever was after him was the key and that they had to be killed. No one would find the Cajuns and if the would-be rescuer and dog vanished, Joe Billie would be home free. These thoughts were crystal clear—other thoughts not. How long had he been on this trek? How long had the man and dog been following? Pausing to pick up a piece of dried grass stem he picked at the remnants of the meal still clinging to his teeth, making soft sucking sounds—oblivious to his tattered clothes and smelly body. He remembered the *Melaleuca* grove and was motivated to get up and extinguished the fire. Maybe the man and dog escaped the punk trees. "Well, so what. If that there guy and his mutt find their way out, so what. I'll just kill that there dog and that there sum bitch can take his chances." Again Joe Billie spoke—again no one to hear. "Shit, I'm only a mile off my back trail—he'll have to come that there way what with his trailing dog... I'll fix his ass."

Purposed, the Indian picked up his pack and club and started over the small ridge at a fast trot.

• • •

Samson lay in the tunnel bower more than an hour before stirring. Barely able to whisper through dry, swollen lips, the stricken man called for his dog. "J... Y...? J... Y...?" He had no realization that the faithful beast was—and had been—at his side since he succumbed to the venom-induced trance. At the sound Junk Yard wiggled his grass cleaned body closer, whimpering as he sniffed Sam's lacerated arm. Reaching his face, JY licked his clotted nose and swollen face—slowly, deliberately, cleaning every inch of damaged tissue.

The dog sensed relaxation and normal breathing but the poisoned body did not move. Encouraged, the pit bulldog shifted position and licked the seeping wound on Sam's arm in the persistent manner of the canine, cleaning the stinking, necrotic snakebite. Using his gleaming incisors like surgical scissors he nipped off every piece of necrotic tissue—a wolf defleaing its pack-mate. He continued licking the glistening wound and as night wore on the seepage changed from blackish, putrid blood to a reddish, healthier discharge. The wound edges were now smooth and pink with no trace of rotten tissue. JY would suffer no distraction save to warn off errant animals that ventured too close or shift around to Sam's face when the occasional moan escaped his throat.

As the night lengthened the anti-venom injection and heroic dose of penicillin began their magic. The swellings started to subside allowing him to breathe easier and reduced the throbbing pain in his arm. JY's persistent cleaning kept the wound draining and free from bacteria buildup. The massive dose of antibiotic had prevented systemic bacterial invasion allowing Samson's natural immune defense to crank up.

Two hours after midnight the stricken man was able to move and was tossing fitfully in the grass, alternating groans with incoherent words. JY was fretting. He did not understand these actions but would not go without him. The canine allegiant never doubted that they would be on the Indian's trail soon so waiting for Samson Hercules Duff held no resentment for the Junk Yard dog.

• • •

Can Martin could hardly stand. Since Elise fell on him the pain had been unbearable. Can gritted his teeth and held his hand out to Elise but she ignored this overture preferring to crawl to a small bush to help herself up and ignored his grunted encouragement. Elise Jones was conflicted. She didn't like or trust Can Martin but he seemed her only chance to escape even if the mad-ass didn't intend to kill her. Deep down she felt a tug on her womanly instinct regarding the bewildered Indian. Pity? Maybe.

Suppose her instincts were right and Joe Billie wasn't going to bash her skull. That frightened her more than being lost in the Everglades with Can Martin. The putative conclusion of living weeks or months in this godforsaken swamp with a filthy, deranged murderer was not her vision of suburban life.

"For God's sake, Elise, don't act like that." Martin's voice was impatient. "I'm not going to bite you, just let's git the hell out of here."

"Where, Can? Where? Where can we go? You know he'll find us.

"Not if we get off our ass. Not if I can keep this sore leg working a little longer." As he spoke Elise could see the sliver of pain cross his eye. She didn't think he would get far on one leg in this place. "Here," he said, pointing to the plastic bag holding their booty. "You take the bag and I'll lead… we'll make it." Turning to face her, Can pulled a worn hunting knife from his belt and went to work on a wrist sized cypress sapling. As he hacked at the tree he referred to the weapon. "I found this in the shack. I'll be dammed if that son of a bitch is going to catch me with my pants down again. 'Sides, we'll need a knife if we're to have any chance at all."

Elise's eyes registered relief. Maybe Can Martin was changing.

Can rapidly finished the makeshift walking stick. "Let's go—we can see good now and if we stay in the water much as we can that asshole won't have any easy time following us." Can was hobbling off as he finished speaking, turning his head slightly to glimpse the grimy but alluring woman as she picked up the bag. "We'll most likely run across someone before dark—a hunter, fisherman—surely there'll be someone knocking about in these parts…" Straightening up he took off as fast as he could. He had no idea where he was.

Neither spoke as they picked their way southwest following the water's edge until coming to a cypress strand so formidable that Martin decided to skirt it. Elise noticed the painful tensing of his shoulders every time he negotiated a fallen tree or clump of reeds. She knew better what was happening to his leg in this tropic hothouse of a swamp. A cold chill coursed her body.

Lost in the Florida Everglades—alone. Biting her lip, Elise Jones lurched after the slow-motion form of Can Martin. Six hours slogging through the bogs and hammocks extracted a considerable toll from the unfortunates. The last hour was spent fighting their way through a dense hammock and as they neared the far side Can suddenly collapsed next to a gnarled old water oak—his ashen face a mask of pain. "I can't go another step, darlin."

He spoke so matter of factly that Elise wondered if he was delirious. "If bad ass is on our trail, he'll just have to come on, because I'm beat… you don't look too swift yourself."

It was difficult to fathom the change in the rancher. The meekness, even fear, that he exhibited when captured was certainly gone, replaced by a resolve and nonchalance that could be admired— under certain circumstances. But his past performance crowned his head like horn flies. Can continued, intruding in the nurse's concentration. "Hell-fire, darlin', let's see if we can get something to eat from that bag. Dam if I ain't half starved." Elise. Nonchalant.

She fumbled at the bag and sat on the carpet of leaves, cool and moist under the dried top layer. Her fear of Martin was evaporating. "Let me look at your leg." Her words were soft, almost clinical. "You can't just keep forcing yourself through this—this jungle." Can detected sympathy in these words and answered.

"Look, Elise...I know the leg's a goner but hell, what chance do I have... do we have. Fact is, I know I've been a bastard and I've not been too swift with you but these last couple days really put me to thinking. Long as we are alive we got a chance and if I can get help... in time...I can make it. I guess I'd rather die here than get my head bashed in by that crazy Miccosukee... I apologize for the way I treated you. I'm sorry..." Martin's voice tailed as he said 'I'm sorry' and started massaging his thigh above the throbbing calf trying to free his trousers plastered to the seeping tissue.

Elise opened the bag and started pulling out the contents. Coming up with a can of insect repellant she let out a long sigh and began applying the mist to her arms, hands and neck; rubbing her face with repellant moistened hands. "Here, Can, better use this on your pants leg, too. The drainage will surely attract insects." More rummaging produced several cans of beans, corn, sliced pineapple and a dozen cans of sardines.

Can watched as she sorted out the booty, commenting on their find. "Damn, they ate good, didn't they—whoever 'they' were. By the way, Elise, what did you see when we were tied to that tree by the water?" Can had wanted to ask before now but had forgotten in the haste to escape. Smoothing the plastic bag as a ground cloth Elise handed the rancher the rusty can opener and several cans, thanking God for the food and the few scungy forks and spoons found in the bag; she hated eating with her fingers.

Elise answered as Can began opening cans. "He somehow sensed that someone was in the shack—how, I don't know—then tied us and sneaked over to it and went in. I guess the door must have been open—I didn't hear any noise... anything breaking. I heard him clubbing something—somebody—and then this skinny kid ran out..."

Elise's voice broke and she choked down a sob as tears streaked her grimy face. Biting her lip she wiped her face on her sleeve and finished her telling. Martin ate as Elise talked, squinting as she graphically described the brutal killing of Jacques Foucharde but too hungry to stop eating even as a token of respect.

"Here—eat." Can's words an order. "We got to eat and git. I'll not let that maniac get to you!"

A glaze clouded Elise's eyes as the depth of Martin's words sank in. A sea change she thought. Definitely. Elise ate. Slowly.

• • •

Joe Billie's mind remained clear as he made his way through the denseness signaling the fringe of a hammock. He knew where he was, not needing to distract his thoughts for the purpose of navigation. He thought of the law and of the punishments meted out by society to criminals such as he. It was cold logic that told him he would have to accept the life of an outcast. Undesirable. Murderer. There was no need to ask grandfather or Mary Cornflower for guidance. If he were caught he knew no life sentence awaited him—in Florida—his kind got one thing, Old Sparky, waiting patiently in Starke. Joe Billie was well versed in the singular efficiency of that wooden throne. Hearsay sufficed.

For some reason, the sweating head held no thoughts of Can Martin or Elise Jones. He was recalling his life since settling in Centra County and joining up with Gypsy Jack Pappadoupoulis. A curse squeezed through his lips as the Greek's name bobbed to the surface in his churning mind. His fugitive status would prevent him from killing the Greek; he cursed him again—Joe Billie was not aware of the gristly demise of the gypsy man.

In the middle of the hammock he turned north, coming to a small stream entering the hammock at the spot he wanted to exit. He knew the stream crossed his back-trail and by wading up the rivulet he could avoid leaving spoor, so any sign left where he planned to intersect his back-trail would blend in. If anything went wrong the tracker's dog could only trail him to the shack; Joe Billie felt he could outsmart a dog.

Arriving at the place where he had crossed the creek, he had no memory of Can Martin or Elise Jones—his clogged mind rebelling. Walking backwards on the trail for 30 yards, Joe Billie stopped and surveyed the terrain with the experience gained from selection of ambush sites for the deadfalls and traps used by the wily Indian. It was easy to trap a dog but not so easy to kill one, the fact of which Joe Billie was aware. Hanging his pack from a low limb the man selected a place where the trail paralleled a blown down cedar tree. The prickly, lace-like cedar leaves still retained green color and had not shed. He tunneled under the middle making a blatant trail under its trunk so that a man would have to traverse it on hands and knees but a dog would have no trouble. Using a hand-axe Joe Billie smoothed the off side of the cedar, laying aside the branches. He worked quickly. Expertly.

Having prepared the entrance he scoured the area for a deadfall, avoiding the trail leading to the trap's entrance. It only took a few minutes to find a huge, pole-like tree trunk covered with vines but smooth. Even for one of Joe Billie's size and strength, moving the trunk into position took every ounce of strength—he didn't want to chance just hurting the dog. Kill it.

Positioning the trunk and arranging the trigger stick took more than an hour and by the time he finished the man was washed down in sweat. The trap was finished. Anything using the narrow trail under the big cedar would have to hit the delicate trigger stick and 200 plus pounds of wet tree trunk would crash down on the unfortunate's head or neck.

If the rescue hero and dog made it through the night and the *Melaleucas* and if they picked up Bloodtooth's spoor then the dog should come straight to the trap as all of the excess spoor from making the device would be ahead of the deadfall with his coming and going hidden by the small stream—also ahead of the trail.

Joe Billie was taking no chances. Kill the dog. For the first time since entering the Everglades Joe Billie took stock of his personal condition. His hair was matted and plastered to his head. The ceremonial buckskins were sweat soaked and rancid, along with his grimy body. He did not like to go filthy and after his self-appraisal a question arose—why am I like this? Oh well, I'll just hustle back to that there landing and have me a bath, clothes and all. Clean up.

He had no idea why he was dirty. Reclaiming his pack and club, the half-breed eased up the trail into the creek and headed towards three palms landing and a bath.

• • •

The east streaked with light before Sam tried to move.

He slipped into a deep sleep as the venom and sepsis crises passed. Only once had the pit bulldog left his side—after he sensed Sam's normal sleep pattern and he quietly backed out of the grassy cocoon to slip back to the stream and lap the cool water. Casually sniffing the dead moccasin JY lifted his leg and urinated on the swollen carcass, scratching a few powerful strokes in the sand before trotting back to Sam. He remained there.

Chapter SIXTEEN

Can and Elise were silent after wolfing down the victuals—a gourmet treat given the circumstances. Elise had taken several empty tins to the nearest water and finding an undisturbed spot meticulously collected the surface water. She doubted if the lamed man could walk now that he had remained recumbent. Trying to keep the insects and surface debris from entering with the water Elise happened to see her reflection in the shimmery surface. What a sight! A wry smile parted her lips causing her to remember that she hadn't brushed her teeth in quite some time, apply cold cream, much less apply make-up. The smile blossomed as she realized how quick priorities could change when the word 'desperate' was affixed to the situation—and for sure that word was affixed!

Picking her way back Elise offered Can water, setting the other two cans aside in deep shade for future use. She was beginning to take initiative—to take fate in her own hands—partially. Martin seemed to be dozing when she proffered the water and stiffly raised pain-racked eyes to her charitable gaze.

"Drink some, Can. It's the best we've got and it's wet." He drank but his eyes never let go their hold on Elise's gaze.

Again she spoke. "Can, we've got to go…" The urgency in her voice was under control and though true felt and honest was not frantic.

"Go where, gal? Go where…?" Can's reply was resolved. "I been thinking about this all morning—it's got to be at least 2 or 3 o'clock now and we—uhh… I can't just keep staggering through this swamp like we got good sense. We ain't Indians, least ways, I ain't." The mid afternoon heat pressed on them as Can went on. "That Indian, I don't think, can track us through these hammocks. He'll have to track us going in, then circle it to see if we left. If not he'll try to search the hammock. Anyway, we got a better chance if we rest up a mite before we go on." Can tried to shift his weight and barely suppressed the groans. "Unnhh…! Let's stay here until morning. Get a good night's sleep if we can and I'll feel better by then and we can find some help…give that ole bad ass a run for his money."

Elise listened, realizing that it made sense. Given this hoorah about their chances for rescue, it was easy for the nurse to rationalize the rest; that Bloodtooth couldn't find them and other people were sure to be around. Besides, Can Martin seemed to be a different man. "OK, Can, whatever."

• • •

The sun had been up an hour when the heat awakened the man. Samson Hercules Duff tried to sit up but found the grass tunnel would not allow it so he crawled—slowly, painfully—out the way he had entered, draping his sick arm over JY. He had never been as thirsty. His lips, though not swollen, were cracked giving his tongue the feeling of licking something other than its own. For a minute the man hung to the pit bull and hugged him as tight as his arm would allow. Memories of last night's encounter with the snake came trickling through his brain resulting in moistened eyes as he squeezed his dog. His thoughts were chaotic, swirling around waiting to be assigned a place and put in proper order: What time is it? How long have I been out? Where's the Indian and captives? It went on.

A wave of nausea swept over him interrupting all thoughts as a dry heave wracked his body. The second was the last and Samson fell to his side as the spasm subsided. JY licked his face.

Feeling better Sam got to his knees and in the manner of a wrestler lifting a riding opponent powered himself to an upright position. His gait unsteady, he made it to a pine sapling, holding on as a sailor in rough seas. After a few minutes his body made its adjustments and Sam was able to stand. He remembered everything—up to the antivenom and penicillin injections. After that his mind was blank.

Always organized, Samson tried to sort out his priorities but every aspect of his memory seemed of equal importance. What to do? Where to start? "Grrrhh... rrrhh." JY's warning growl ruptured Sam's concentration causing him to follow the dog's stare. He heard the noise. Wild hogs had discovered the dead moccasin and were fighting over it. Sam remembered his backpack and struggling on leaden legs reached the creek just as JY rushed a shoat trying to root the backpack. A young boar, it tried to bluff the dog with mouth popping. Didn't work. With machine like precision, JY feinted to the young pig's feet then caught him by the forehead as he lowered it to defend his feet. Death was sure and swift as the pit's spike-like canine teeth punctured its skull.

Samson chased the pigs away, stopping to stare at his vanquished foe—its remains awesome, like some serpentine monster held over from the days of kings, knights and dragons.

Sam looked at his arm. It was swollen from shoulder to hand but discoloration was minimal and fading. The wound looked large to have been done by a serpent but was smooth and clean as if attended by a surgeon. Healing was evident. A quizzical look crossed his face as he pondered the wound, remembering nothing of JY's ministrations. Shaking his head Samson glanced around for the backpack and saw that JY still held the shoat clamped in his jaws.

"Hey, guy, let go." At the sound the dog shook the 60-pound pig like a Jack Russell shaking a rat. "Hell, man, he's dead—let go!" Samson walked to the dog and stroked his neck resulting in a tail wagging and releasing of the shoat. The stoic pit rarely whimpered but did, licking Sam's hand and standing in an attempt to lick his face. His partner was back and the Junk Yard dog was over-joyed. Samson hung the pig and field dressed it.

The flurry of activity had a calming effect on Samson Duff. He realized he couldn't sort out everything and the circumstances of his condition seemed to be dictating his priorities. Joe Billie Bloodtooth wasn't the headline.

Sam became aware of an occult cloudiness in his thought processes. Something was trying to come through but wouldn't and he couldn't seem to help—to pull it out in the clear air of conscious thought. It was like staring at something in a fog, recognizable in outline but not in detail. It was a nagging frustration. Shaking, Sam went to the dew wet pack and sorted out gauze, tape and strong tincture of iodine, wincing as he applied the 7% iodine and bandaged the wound. The arm was useless even given his strength, the throbbing pain of his upper arm contrasting the numbness of his fingers.

The sun is rising fast, Sam thought, as he skinned the pig. His well-honed knife made the onerous task easy in spite of his infirmity. Sam looked at the gaunt bulldog and realized that starvation was not what they needed; first priority was food—ergo skinning the pig. This fact along with the task of feeding the dog and himself relaxed him so his poisoned mind could sort itself out. He knew Joe Billie could be nearby or even stalking them now... no, that would be next to impossible because either he or JY would smell him. Smell? It hit him like a runaway horse—he could barely smell the stinking pig and his nose was in it! Like a spent diver trying to breach the surface, the nagging thought struggled through Sam's hypoxic subconscious. It was gone. Duff couldn't smell. Shit!

Memories returned, lining up to wait their turn at torment-ing now that he was just Sam H. Duff. Ordinary. He searched his pockets until he felt the bag, took it out with unaccustomed clum-siness and tried to open it with one hand. Frustrated, he held one edge in his mouth and opened it. Exhaling he pressed the delicate contents to his face and slowly inhaled, groaning as a barely perceptible libidinous fragrance blessed his nostrils. Nothing. All lost.

"Stop eating that shit!" Sam chastised the pit bulldog for sneaking a mouthful of pig guts. The dog's eyes narrowed at the command—he dropped his tail and pinned his ears. Hungry.

"I know you're hungry… So am I. Aw shit, dog, let' s eat. We've been in such a sweat and all we do is make problems." Samson had finally come to grips with what would be his first, maybe only, priority—survival. Life.

Getting a fire going, an otherwise simple task, became more vexing due to his crippled arm. Cursing and fumbling he willed a flame, spitted the pig back-straps over the fire and sorted through the assortment of foods to complete the feast. Sam's weakness and anxiety seemed to abate and the Junk Yard dog cozied up to the fire eyeing the tenderloins with malice as saliva drooled from his wide mouth. Eat.

The food was filling and added to Sam's recuperative effort, stimulating clearer thought. Sitting against a stump and stroking JY's rippling back, Samson sorted out the events leading up to this morning. Though incapacitated, the ex FBI agent never entertained the idea of quitting. He knew that every passing minute decreased his chance to find Martin and Elise. His gun was gone, he wasn't sure where and he didn't want to waste time looking for it.

Sam didn't need a gun and he doubted if the half-breed was armed as he remembered no evidence of a firearm at the massacre. Anyway, so be it. He realized the odds favored the Miccosukee exiting the *Melaleucas* from the same side he entered since the trail had ended abruptly, meaning he headed off one way or the other—probably south and came out at the southwest edge. Samson and JY were at the northwest quadrant and Samson figured if they went south along the west side JY should be able to pick up the trail and get on with their mission.

The sun was high in the brilliant blue sky speckled with three-dimensional globs of white clouds floating about like gigantic cotton balls. Sam kicked out the fire and gathered his pack. Turning south, the once extraordinary now ordinary man, humbled by the fickle hand of fate, set out with his dog to finish what they started.

• • •

Joe Billie squeezed the wet buckskins and draped them on branches in the shade not wanting to expose the sacred garments to the searing heat since rapid drying would turn the pliable buckskin to cardboard. He was squeaky clean, having bathed in the clear water using snow-white sugar sand as an abrasive cleaner on his sweat caked body. He felt better, physically; mentally he was concentrating on his followers and the trap he set for the dog. The two captives never entered his thoughts as if, animal like, he could only think of one thing at a time. The more he thought about trapping the dog the more he smirked. It was a game—a game like the ones played in Special Forces training during his army days. Joe Billie Bloodtooth loved games. Win them!

Totally nude and relaxed Joe Billie contemplated the sun, savoring its searing radiation as he lolled, drying, on the white sand. This was as happy as he could ever be given his jackhammer existence.

Rising to a sitting position he fixed on the narrow pirogue posed, rocket like, on the sand. Remembering something, he got on his hands and knees and with practiced deliberation crawled through the deep sand. Large child.

Large sandbox. Large toy. Reaching the pirogue, Joe Billie found the narrow, battered wooden box sitting to the rear of the craft. The Cajun had used it as a seat on the rare occasion of propelling the craft from other than the standing position. The unabashed man reached in to open the box, his coal black hair falling over his ovate face like a useless curtain. His symmetrical, dark olive body rippled in the favoring sunlight like latent power waiting for instruction. Tightly wound.

Possessed of virtually no body hair the naked Indian may have been taken for a mythic figure come to life and in a languorous manner mimic the doings of humans. Magnificent man.

The contents of the box were nondescript: Knife, fish stringers, gig points, stained nylon windbreaker, fishing lures and wrapped in a filthy, stained towel—a full quart of five star Haitian rum.

Backing off, bottle in hand, Bloodtooth leaned against the shell like boat and cocked his right knee getting an erotic sensation from the feel of the friendly sand on his naked buttocks.

The smirk imperceptibly changed to mirth then laughter as he held the rum bottle over his head and looked into the blazing radiance of the sun. "Here's to you, Grandfather. Here's to you, mother. By God, we'll drink to everything, even if its just Goddam rotten rum!"

Joe Billie took a deep slug of the sweetish liquid, head high, extended, letting the sweet poison find its way down his throat like a fish sliding down the stretched gullet of a great heron.

Letting his head slump, he squeezed his eyelids together to block out the glare, relaxing his body as fluorescent ringed quail eggs danced in the back of his eyes like stars; marking time until his light seared retinas recovered from the sun shock. Eyes closed he took another swig, shorter, more deliberate, sending the alcoholic bolus towards his stomach like a cork log down a flume. The festive salute was over. Serious drinking.

• • •

Can Martin slept like a dead man. The scorching afternoon sun could not penetrate the leafy canopy sheltering the two unfortunates and dark clouds blotted the piercing rays resulting in merciful twilight. The spent leg woke him when shifting position failed to moderate its throbbing. Quietly sitting up so not to waken Elise, Can felt the cold sweat evaporating from his stern visage as a breeze wafted through the hammock fueled by the cloud cover building overhead. God, he hoped it didn't rain—it was still early for the daily thunderstorm that gave this mighty river of grass existence. Shelter, he thought, we've got to have cover if we're to get any rest at all. Can's mind was keyed. Survival.

Fever—I've got fever he thought as he turned on his good knee in an effort to get up, holding a bush as his cramped body straightened to an upright position. The effort caused more than skeletal discomfort as dizziness and nausea coursed his palsied frame. It took a few minutes of standing with head down for the feeling to abate, time spent observing the sleeping Elise Jones; alone, bedraggled, helpless—totally sensuous. Rest.

Finding his walking stick, Can hobbled to the cans of water and drank like a camel. Feeling better, he surveyed the area to find some trees, bushes, or downfalls that could be converted to shelter. Once the sun retired, Can knew that travel would be impossible and for Elise to get any rest at all would require some shelter and Can Martin would provide it. Wounded sparrow. Eagle's nest.

The west side of the *Melaleucas* proved every bit the challenge Sam had thought. Forced to make detours, his poisoned body rebelling with each step, they slowly worked south, with the pit covering the area like a remote controlled vacuum cleaner.

• • •

"Faster, you meathead!" Big Carlos' booming Teutonic voice flew at the sweating young man doing Hindu squats with the precision of a living timepiece—500, 501, 502..."I vant vun thousan in 30 minutes. I vant your tongue sticking out your ass und waving like the Johnny Reb flag." The big German had gotten caught up in the post civil war southern heritage and had embraced everything southern with an avidity to make local rednecks feel like Yankees.

Catch dogs, Winchester 30-30's, four-wheel drive, four speed stick shift pick-ups, hog hunting—the whole nine yards. No dog fighting. The lantern-jawed Otto would brook no dog fighting though he admired the American Pit Bulldog among all living creatures, knowing that their prowess, strength and fighting ability were a result of generations of proving themselves—in the pit. That pound for pound, the pit bulldog was the most efficient fighting machine in nature. Courage.

Carlos Otto was more southern than red eye gravy. Samson had been through a two-hour workout—a daily routine this summer— his second with the German and tougher than the first, something young Duff never considered possible. To say Carlos was a disciplinarian was to say Godzilla was just another lizard.

Carlos' earthy inflections were always direct with no echo as if the walls were afraid to talk back. After the thousand squats, Sam would spend fifteen minutes working the clubs, another fifteen minutes swinging the Turkish bow and then run five miles. Afterward he would sit with Carlos, sipping wine and water, his tan body glistening with earned sweat. Fierce.

Carlos outlined in basic terms how young Samson was going to do better—and better. The kicker was that everything Samson did Carlos did more. His strength and stamina were the stuff of legend. He never asked anyone to do anything he wouldn't do.

Carlos Otto had come to America with nothing save his wrestling skills.

He and wife Helena dreamed of leaving their homeland for the all-encompassing promise that was the United States of America. Neither spoke the language, learning by watching television and reading. Carlos, born big, was raised by strict disciplinarian parents, the only people he respected. He grew up on the waterfront where life's menu offered one course—street fighting. He excelled.

Young Carlos excelled in high school, being of above average intelligence but never went beyond grade school because of the circumstance of his life.

The area was replete with gyms known as workout parlors. The gangly kid that was Carlos Otto gravitated to one and established himself as a tough, no nonsense physical culturist. Wrestling, the most popular sport was next and the barrel-chested Teuton turned the full force of his physical and mental gifts toward this discipline.

By day he labored in a blacksmith's shop, going from heat and hammering to hyper-motion and sweat. It was in the forge where he lost the little finger on his left hand trying to pull a sheet of metal off a worker, saving his life; a feat, some said beyond mortal man.

By age 17 Carlos had no peer in wrestling, either Greco-Roman or catch-as-catch-can. He defeated eleven opponents to capture the European Wrestling Championship at the age of 18. He toured the countryside risking prize money to anyone who could best him in submission wrestling with only choke holds barred and the loser must give up vocally or be rendered unconscious. The unyielding German broke arms and dislocated shoulders in his career. Soon—no takers.

Migrating to the states, he entered organized American professional wrestling and turned this choreographed event upside down. He became a renegade by whipping the shit out of certain champions when it wasn't scripted and was ostracized by the promoters, touring overseas and giving demonstrations to the growing number of believers. In Japan he became a wrestling God. No Oriental martial arts expert could withstand the skill and applied force of Carlos Otto. He could make them sing.

As a gifted teacher Carlos attracted would-be disciples, none of whom met his standards until Samson Hercules Duff.

So, this was all basic training to the young wrestler Sam Duff. Carlos never let his few students think about a wrestling hold or move until their physical condition was top notch. Then you learned holds and moves so subtle and effective that at times it seemed magical. It was said of the combative German by his opponents that every time that he touched them was like an electric shock. When in combat with Otto, no opponent could deny him their hand, arm, ankle or even their head if the big guy requested it. It was never returned unopened.

So began Sam Duff's life of virtual invincibility mano y mano.

• • •

The sand covered body stirred. Slowly, painfully, it raised to its elbow and propped a sandy head on a sand covered hand. Two bloodshot eyes peered from between the squinty eyelids of Joe Billie Bloodtooth. He was cold; ominous, purplish clouds blanked out the late afternoon sun like globular designer curtains. It was raining somewhere west of him and the damp chill settled over his nakedness like the cold breath of doom.

The white sand displayed the grooves and furrows of the Indian's besotted state with the empty rum bottle leaning against the pirogue.

Inside the sand covered skull a battle was raging between rational thought and post-rum delirium. Strong impulses urged him to seek advice from his grandfather, bringing into focus the Martin ranch massacre and abduction of Can Martin and his nurse; events orphaned by his confounded mind these past 24 hours. Staggering up, Joe Billie tried to brush the sand from his body but tacky perspiration bonded the tiny grains to his skin like iron filings to a magnet. Having little patience when sober—none when drunk, the half-breed let out a string of profanities as he waded into the dark water and fell to his knees.

The refreshing liquid evoked an explosive "Goddamn!" as he splashed his face and goose bumped body.

• • •

"Joe Billie, you must do like the deer; run equally through the thick grass and the palmettos and the marsh and the hammock. Do not just practice on the firm, flat ground." Every word was given the same weight; no rise or fall in the tonal quality. The young Miccosukee's Grandfather had been training and schooling him for three years and the ten year old had developed at a pace far exceeding the old warrior's grasp. Three days a week the lad did dashes at top speed through and over the varying terrains of the omnipresent Pay-Hay-Okee. Two days of the week he ran long, slow distances, practicing his tracking skills as he loped effortlessly along following a track laid down the day before by Grandfather. The other two days he swam, mastering different strokes by age 12.

When school intervened the old warrior altered the routine, always demanding more, challenging the young natural.

Grandfather was ancient even by tribal standards, being in his ninth decade. Still revered and honored by his family, he had long sensed the casual attitude subtly projected by young tribal members. His heritage, the arduous way of the warrior was a thing of history, not of contemporary Miccosukee and Seminole Indian tribes. To Joe Billie's Grandfather peace meant only the absence of war and it was war or the threat of war that insured the peace; no compromise. Now the only battle fought by the Florida Indians was the battle of wits—Indian versus tourists. And the Indians were losing.

The ancient fighter had trained many young warriors but none had impressed him like his only daughter's son. And the young 'breed was for some deep rooted but unfathomable reason totally in awe of Grandfather's lore and heritage.

Wise beyond his years, young Bloodtooth was aware of his mentor's hatred for his daughter's husband, Joe Billie's father and his rejection of Mary's rebellious marriage.

It was years after the birth of Joe Billie that Mary Cornflower realized the values of her parents and capitulated to common sense, returning to her birthplace with her four-year-old prodigy. Humble.

Every task or challenge placed in front of the growing Miccosukee was accepted and either mastered or conquered.

"Put your head against the padded tree and try to push through it. Do as the rutting buck does to strengthen his neck in preparation for the mating season and the fighting. So strengthen your neck. Though you think the tree unmovable, close your eyes and call upon the Great Spirit to give you strength to push through this tree as you would push through your enemies. If your spirit does not honor defeat and you push your will through this tree, though it still stands, your enemy will not."

So spoke the sagacious old man and Joe Billie's resolve grew thick as his neck and though he didn't push the tree down he was convinced that given the right circumstances and stimulus—he could.

Neck, shoulders, arms chest and legs—grandfather knew how to develop and strengthen the young warrior's body. And he thrilled at the noticeable improvement as Joe Billie's frame grew and ripened week by week.

Again the old man spoke. "Do like the great cat, the panther. Stretch all of your muscles to the limit, slowly, slowly, limb by limb. Do this often, especially when you are confined and cannot properly move about. It will keep you your strength as the great cat keeps his. There can be strength in rest. These words were soaked up by the sponge-like mind of the young protégé—never to be forgotten.

The young Indian was so serious that even the somber old warrior had to smile occasionally—a process not unlike pulling one's foot out of half-hardened concrete.

Wrestling was the major contact sport of the young Miccosukee men, done informally with an elder referee. Referees were not always available so many matches ended with injury either feigned or real followed by name-calling and intimidation by the winners.

Being less than pureblood the gifted adolescent was the target of many tribal bluebloods who were older and bigger and usually threw the gauntlet when no elders were in sight. He suffered defeats, always of the body never of the spirit. No one claiming victory over the quiet youth ever had much to crow about as within a day or two the sweet cream of their conquest would turn to clabber as each bully was waylaid when alone and beaten mercilessly by an unknown wielding a stick, club, wrench or other such truncheon. No conqueror of Joe Billie Bloodtooth ever took a curtain call.

As his grandfather's training took root and his potentcy blossomed, Joe Billie's challenges came less and less and by age 14 no Miccosukee youth would stand up to him. He walked alone, a man-boy among boy-men, never a braggart or bully but never to be crossed. Not once.

Looking around for clothes, he noticed the ceremonial buckskins hanging in the branches. Painful memories sneaked from the far corners of his befuddled psyche. His eyes darted like errant strobe lights finally fixing on his Grandfather's intricately carved war club lying across his opened backpack. He felt a lump in his dried throat, his suppressed gorge rising up to taunt him.

Joe Billie's sight turned inward as he dressed and tried to choke down the drool spilling through his half opened mouth as the bile flavored cud reached his mouth.

"Grandfather!" The dazed man turned his face towards the pallid glint of the sky as he sought help from the only person he ever trusted. "Grandfather, wise old warrior, where are my enemies?" There was no question in Joe Billie's voice—only a request for guidance; he would know what to do when he found them.

As if the sagacious old man had answered, memories came leafing back like snow geese suddenly dropping from the sky into a flooded field to feed, the scattered pieces of massacre, kidnapping and trek settling in on muted wings until there were no blank spots. He knew he had to get to the shack—he had to kill the turdhead rancher, killer of Stump and kill the turd-head's girlfriend before they could get away. How long he had left them there was of no concern; Joe Billie Bloodtooth was mentally incapable of relating time to space.

Charged up and functioning like a well oiled machine the drunken man grabbed the rum bottle as he pushed the pirogue into the water and in 50 yards of the landing downed the remainder of demon rum.

It was dark; Joe Billie Bloodtooth would never be rational again. Mad!

• • •

The early part of evening was unusually dark in the hammock. Rain had fallen though the cooling thunderstorm had passed southwest of them. Martin's painful attempt at a shelter was progressing slowly when with "oh my God," Elise sat up, her expression registering the surroundings as if reflections from a TV screen. "Where... where am I?" Her pained inquiry was addressed to no one.

Elise's awakening surprised Martin and he stopped to stare at the still half asleep woman. Consciousness slowly replaced her dreamlike state and licking pouty lips she turned to the rancher. "What are you doing?" she said, averting her gaze to stare at the putative shelter.

"Aw nothing. Just thought you ought to have something to get in out of the weather so's you can get some rest tonight." As the distracted man replied, he cast his head around causing Elise to notice the darkness, at least inside the dense hammock. "We spend the night here, rest up and first light we hit out and I bet we find a road or track or somebody before noon." Can felt the flush filling his neck and cheeks as he addressed the sleepy-eyed woman. He hadn't experienced this kind of feeling since before Marti quit him; Can Martin was blushing—bashfully blushing. He was thankful for the cloaking blanket of damp blackness.

Elise's voice cut him off. "You won't be able to travel. You probably can't even walk."

"Hell I won't. I'll get some shuteye without that wire collar and I'll just walk your legs off..." Martin's voice wavered and trailed off as if suppressing a chuckle but Elise the nurse knew better. They—or she—would have to find help tomorrow if it was to do Can Martin any good.

Can spoke again as he fitted another palm leaf into the shelter's roof. "Why don't you get a fire going, nobody's gonna see it. And let's see if we can conjure up a little warm food, whatever the hell's in those cans." Seeing indecision cross Elise's barely visible face, Can continued. "We may as well behave like white folks, Elise. I'm going to do everything I possibly can to see us safely back. Whatever it takes."

Seemingly comforted the nurse got up and gathered the cans. "I'm going to clean up first, get more water and then I'll get a fire going. I-I-I'm sorry, Can, if I..." Her voice choked and the words wouldn't come as she walked away, carefully picking her way through the blackness towards the pewter colored sunset showing through the hammock.

• • •

Can Martin resumed his task. Can Martin was quivering. His fresh-ly bathed body was powdered and naked, lying on his right side with his left arm draped over Marti's silk draped flank. He could feel the rhythmic rise and fall of her chest as she feigned sleep. He knew she was pretending as this had been going on for months starting shortly after the birth of their daughter.

Can adored his wife, the way she looked and walked and talked and felt and smelled. He loved sex. For him his gorgeous wife was sex. The thought of intimate relations with other women never en-tered his mind after his marriage and the magnet pull of his bride's powerful attractant sustained him through many a temptation.

As he had many times before the ardent man slipped his hand across Marti's sleek flank and lightly cupped her left buttock with expectant fingertips, the feel of gluteal cleavage causing an un-remitting restlessness in his loins. Awakening. He was having dif-ficulty breathing. Rising anticipation coupled with urgent need caused his breath to come in tired cat pants, something he didn't want his wife aware of. No resistance.

Can slipped his hand down her Lydian body as lightly as a daddy longlegs walking on water, savoring the tingles sparking his body as his patchy body hairs erected themselves in shared antici-pation. Reaching the hem of the expensive negligee, Can Martin could hardly get his breath, the carbon dioxide buildup a further aphrodisiac. His fully tumescent organ seemed somehow a bur-den, a thing unto itself, a demon. Screaming for relief. Oh, God, he was excited!

Slowly, ever so slowly he raised the luxurious material. Martha's steady as a drum roll breathing and immobility a sign of her aware-ness. Can reasoned that a woman would have to be dead not to be aware of his fevered touch that projected prurience. Marti Martin was not dead!

Silently exposing the peach skin of her shapely bottom, Can's fingertips lightly brushed the curlyqued hair announcing her gen-italia like angels' down. Feeling no resistance he eased his pulsat-ing body closer, positioning his engorgement between her thighs just below her buttocks. A gentle, yet urgent pelvic thrust brought instant reaction—the putative coquette pushed back and jerked her breached negligee with a snap to make a bear trap proud; pulling the bedcover around her shoulders and transitioning feigned slumber to the real thing. In the blink of an eye. Not a word.

Can swallowed his bile tinged groan, rolled over and inhaled through his gaped mouth cursing his innocent organ, its ready state no longer a source of pride. Embarrassment.

Cursing, the emotionally drained man twisted to the far side and clenched his fingers trying to catch his breath, his chest pumping like a trail weary hound.

It wasn't long before Can Martin figured that if his wife wasn't going to take better care of his biological and emotional needs then he was going to forego the emotional part and gratify the biological part anyway he could. He would never trust a woman with his fragile emotions; he would only trust them with his bone. Tomcat.

•   •   •

It was cave dark in the hammock as they finished the warmed over canned dinner. The fire danced as one, then the other, absentmindedly threw a few leaves and twigs on the little blaze with non blinking eyes mesmerized by the display as the fodder was consumed by the fiery tongues.

"Time for you to turn in gal." Can spoke quietly as he focused on the crude shelter reflecting shadows from its gaping entrance like the maw of a giant fish.

Elise turned from the mesmerizing fire and replied. "Where will you sleep? It might rain or even if it doesn't there most likely will be heavy dew and you'll just get all wet and chilled. You're sick enough as it is." She truly felt sorrow for the man's predicament. He seemed not to be a bad guy—maybe just tempered by adversity. He did offer some hope of rescue—and he was a man.

"I'll be alright. I'll just keep this here little fire going and be just as cozy as if home by the old fireplace." The pain fixing his face as he mumbled belied his nonchalance.

"Not on your life, Can Martin. I feel a lot better since I've cleaned up a little and eaten and since we need each other if we're to have any chance at all, I need to take care of you. That little nest is big enough for both of us and that's the way it's going to be." Her soft tone bespoke much more than the words.

Can Martin studied the willful nurse whose interest in his welfare seemed genuine. He wasn't aware of the dropping of his head until, with a jolt, he snapped his sweating head back like a string puppet. His fever was worse. "OK, you win. I'll cozy up in there with you and I promise to behave—ha-ha-ha." Humor. Can Martin?

As he crawled to the shelter Can looked at the interior of the unique arboreal smorgasbord that was a Florida hammock. Still as death but alive with life, Can pointed his finger in different directions, a gesture visible only because of the flickering firelight. "Look at that, gal. A million little flashlights darting here, there, everywhere. I've never seen so many fireflies. What a life they must have, the little blinkers! What I wouldn't give to be one of those carefree little battery operated pixie-flies. Could forget all my problems."

The blackness obscured the relaxed look on Martin's face. It could not hide the boyish quality to his comments. "Hey, gal, look at that one...up there on that...that...what looks like a palm leaf. I've never seen one light up that bright!" Can's voice hinted at strength. Elise knew that he would need every ounce of it. Can Martin was a changed man.

Placing his fevered body inside, Can turned from the succulent presence next to him. Deep inside he felt stirrings—emotional and deep. Love.

Chapter SEVENTEEN

Samson and Junk Yard had been along the west edge of the *Melaleucas* for over three hours. Sam willed himself through the recurring dizzy spells sometimes stopping to grab a tree to keep from sitting down. Each time the pit bulldog would look back, trotting to him if the episode lasted more than a few minutes. JY never ranged out of sight, no mean feat in the denser areas.

The heat was stifling. The tropical greenery released its stored heat as if in competition with the sun to see which phenomenon was the hottest—the producer or the storer.

Samson welcomed the water interludes though his feet stayed soaked and avoided the frequently encountered groundwater, taking pleasure in the many small runoffs and streams—a pleasant, though cautious, interlude.

Sam's body was sweat soaked to the extent that he chilled with every savored breeze; not sure if the piercing chills were fever driven or normal cooling. In spite of the solar furnace, Sam Duff was feeling better and the shock of losing his paranormal sense was evaporating along with the sweat; he had faith in the single-minded bulldog.

The Junk Yard's thoughts were uniquely single minded. He knew what was wanted—to catch a man whose scent had been branded into his brain. Of this the pit bulldog had no doubts and given his ability to mark and remember he would not forget or confuse Joe Billie Bloodtooth's signal redolence if he had occasion to sniff every man in Florida.

He would make no mistake.

JY broke through a thicket and emerged on the edge of a palmetto-wiregrass meadow, its flatness accentuated by islands of cabbage palm, elderberry and blackberry strangled myrtle bushes. Suddenly he swung around to look for Sam.

JY was worried about the injured man and didn't know what to do now that Samson was moving. He had known what to do as the stricken man lay dying and would have continued his ministrations until Sam revived or died. Time had no meaning to this animal.

JY cocked his head slightly as he looked back, his body motionless as silence itself, icy eyes focused on nothing—seeing everything. Where was Samson?

A fidgety stink bird sitting on a palmetto frond next to his stilled head was snapped up, chomped and gulped down; a feathered hors d'oeuvre. JY remembered the wild pig and that it had been a godsend—at the time. But it was not enough to meet the nagging energy demands placed on him by his master's double barreled ill fortune; he ate whatever he could. Whenever.

Pawing a feather from his mouth, JY sat as a swearing Sam Duff broke through the thick fringe-growth of the flat. He noticed Sam's sodden clothes clinging to him highlighting a leanness that bordered on gauntness—face drawn, eyes hollow though still shot through with the fire of steely resolve.

The observant pit bulldog also noticed that Sam's hair now sported a silver streak through his otherwise jet black crown. JY had no way to know that the silvered hair was due to damaged scalp and was permanent. He didn't care what color Samson's hair was or if he even had hair; Duff was his guy—period. He doubted if the man was even aware that the left side of his head was growing in silver; a slightly irregular juncture running from the middle of his forehead across the top of his crown and ending a few inches before his neckline. A reminder of Joe Billie Bloodtooth's munificence with a club. George Martinez' surgical skills.

JY eyes narrowed as he watched Samson stop and look around, probably, he thought, to get his bearings while trying to understand this blend of paradise and purgatory. Ditto Junk Yard.

Glued to his every movement JY watched as Samson produced a compass and took a reading. He wanted to to lick his face and romp about like he did as a pup, but deep-rooted stoicism held this on a tight rein. Instead of this display of affection, JY sat and stared the pit bulldog stare—protective, tolerant, non judgmental—as if Duff was his ward. Child.

This protective instinct intensified as JY matured and he had no control over it as if programmed into his being. Like an ancient Samurai death held no threat, had no meaning and would have to take him from the front. Carefully.

Samson put the compass into his pocket and knelt beside the dog. "Well, old buddy, this is a break. I know you can't see from down there but stumbling onto this flat's a definite break." Sam's voice seemed alive to the canine and he reveled in its sound. "See that way? These flat woods go right to the edge of the punk-shit trees and I'll give 10 to 1 we find Bloodtooth's trail coming out and crossing this flat."

This positive tone charged up the pit, causing him to take Sam's good wrist in his potent mouth—gently—the ultimate sign of affection from the mighty animal.

Getting up, Sam started across the flat still talking to JY. "Joe Billie Badass knows this place like the inside of his pocket. He's not about to fight through this thick shit if he doesn't have to..." JY was bounding through the thick grass, nose down, as Sam's words trailed off in the unsettled air.

The sky was glaring with its unsympathetic brilliance as distant clouds inched their way towards an undetermined rendezvous, darkening with every inch of westerly progress. Strobe-like splinters of lightning cavorted along the edge of the darker clouds—too far to be heard.

The hackles suddenly raised on JY as the charged air registered the approaching thunderstorm with his conscious self. Wow, this is going to be a lulu! Wonder if Sam knows? Stopping to look back he saw that his master was following at a comfortable pace oblivious to the warning signs he sensed.

JY thought the rain a welcomed relief though he doubted Samson would share his view; nor could the irrepressible canine appreciate the maelstrom now approaching.

He did know that one of full blood was building and that its crescendo would be over their heads.

Angling toward the wall of punk trees, JY stopped as if hitting an unseen wall. Scrambling to retrace his last steps the excited dog shoved his nose into the grass and rooted around like a tongue lashed pointer looking for a crippled quail.

"What is it dog?" Sam's voice was pitched with excitement as he broke into a jog to catch. "You've found them! You found the trail! Good man." No more communication was necessary. Samson knew the Junk Yard dog had struck and JY knew that he knew.

The hair on Sam's neck raised as the red flush of adrenalin shot through his tired body signaling renewed effort; weariness shoved aside—forgotten. "Let's go, pal—find this asshole." Sam spoke loudly—brashly; to himself, quietly. "Wonder if he smells all three? Wish he could tell me." The thought of Elise Jones' danger hovered over him along with memory of her singular attractant. Well, this is the way to find out...now.

• • •

Joe Billie knew his prisoners were gone as the pirogue's sleek prow breached the mucky shoreline like an emerging gator allowing him to leap onto the short grass. Emerging from the vacated cabin, Bloodtooth went looking for sign. He had no idea of what they took from the cabin or what may have been in it—they may be armed. Sobering.

A furrow dug its way into his sweaty brow as he mulled the obvi-ous sign. The turd-head rancher was more lame as evidenced by the cutting of a small tree—a crutch—a fact that highlighted their trail as if marked by surveyor's tape. They headed south. A malevo-lent rictus covered his face when he stopped to piss in a peg-like depression left by the makeshift crutch.

South. To Skull Hammock. No way to miss as the lay of the land would shove them right to the place Joe Billie wanted them. If they tried to go east they would probably find the ruts cut by the wheezy half-track of the Indian boys hog trapping in Skull Hammock.

Thrusting his face to the darkening sky the half-breed screamed a war cry as if some ancient warrior was manipulating his body regardless of Joe Billie's tenancy. Joe Billie Bloodtooth had never heard, much less uttered, this war cry of long departed forebears.

"See Grandfather! See Mother! I have found the track of my enemies! I piss on their tracks like I will piss on their face!" The tone and diction mirrored the agitation in Joe Billie's scrambled psyche resulting in mnemonic rebirth of his dead Grandfather. "I will eat the heart of the dog killer before another day!"

In answer a bolt of lightning cracked in the distance. Looking northeast Joe Billie knew the storm was king-sized and computed it into his plans; avoid it, wait it out or use it. It was no threat to this hunter.

• • •

The sun was up in the clear sky when Elise wakened. The heat was just starting to penetrate the hammock as she slowly turned in the cramped shelter to avoid the rancher.

"You awake, gal?" Can's squeaky query caught her off quard. She hoped to attend to her toilet before the crippled man was awake. She had no way of knowing that Can Martin had slept fit-fully through the long night; Elise Jones—the sleep of the dead.

"Yes. I'm going to get water, then I'll fix whatever is left of the food and we can get going to find some help in this god-forsaken place." Her stilted voice was patronizing, causing Can to wonder if she trusted him. He was glad Elise was up as he had to piss and knew he would have trouble getting up. His leg was killing him and he didn't want the woman to see his pain or darkening trousers as his bladder sought relief.

His reply. "Yea, do that and I'll get cranked up here in a minute and we'll get this show on the road. We'll find help—we'll be fine…" Can struggled to finish, avoiding Elise's querulous inflection and hiding the expression on his pain-racked face.

Elise took the empty cans to bring water, knowing she would have to minister to the crippled man regardless of his objections. Her brow crinkled as she thought of being left alone in this wilderness.

Her thoughts were crazy. What if Can dies. Worse, what if he is so crippled he can't walk? What then? How could she leave him? What about their pursuers? Maybe they were close to rescue even as things seemed to be worsening. Tears appeared in the corners of her sleepy eyes, causing a stifled sob of hopelessness. It seemed like everything in this goddamned place was on the side of that maniacal Indian.

The rancher had a fire going when Elise returned, a few opened tins spread on the hand brushed ground. As the refreshed nurse neared, Can gestured with his opened hand toward the putative picnic set amongst the detritus of the hammock.

"Mamselle, wa-la, breakfast is served!" Another sweep of his hand indicated the unassuming spread. Elise laughed. This Can Martin was likeable.

"Can, I'm going to take a look at your leg whether you like it or not." The repast was finished and both were anxious to get going though Can could hardly get up. "We'll just have to take time now or we won't get out of this thick part." Elise's voice took on an assertive tone—not unnoticed by the rancher.

"OK, have it your way—but what the hell can you do? We aren't around the corner from the south Florida branch of the Mayo Clinic—unless you've been keeping something from me…"

"We've got hot water, that knife and I found some plants that I'm sure are Aloe plants and they have healing power. I saw them last night but I wasn't sure until this morning and it's all we have but I just can't sit back and let your leg rot off." Her voice was shrill, a sign not only of determination but a warning to Martin not to interfere. He didn't.

Elise had been married for three weeks. Her honeymoon had been a long weekend on Little Gasparilla Island, just north of Big Gasparilla Island and Boca Grande. A rancher friend of her new husband had let the newlyweds stay in a rumpled, stilt cabin facing the intercostal waterway one half mile north of Little Gasparilla pass. Elmer Jones spent his time pestering his young wife—every time he came in from snook fishing the pass on a running tide or with a tub of fat mullet from cast netting the canals and tidal creeks running into the intercostal confluence. Elise acquiesced to his amorous demands, begrudging his endurance to fish and fuck like he did—throwing a cast net was hard work!

The new wife was expected to keep hot food on the table and she complied. It was what she had prepped for.

"Hon, you got to help me'n Charlie cut them two yearlings. John-man's got the flu and we can't wait cause the sign's below the knees today and we got to get them balls out now less they bleed bad." Elmer's voice was sweet as he exhorted his bride to help with their crude veterinary surgical act. Elmer Jones wasn't about to spend his hard earned money just to get two rank young stallions gelded—unheard of in his redneck group.

Elise thought she loved the young cowboy; down to earth attitude, honesty about desires, appetites and—masculinity. She had no way of knowing that she would outgrow this simple man.

The rawboned appaloosa colt stood with neck arched, prick ears pointed like spikes, nostrils flared; 850 pounds of lightning loose in a mottled horse hide. The men on the ropes looped around the colt's neck were sweaty—more from strain and concentration than heat. Every move of the rank yearling had to be avoided by the cowboys. The sand-spurred ground was pockmarked by striking hooves, giving the appearance of a miniature moonscape, the scuffling boots adding trenches and depressions to perfect scale.

Charlie sidled up to the quieted appaloosa and tied a non- slip bowline with a soft cotton rope around the rigid neck, running the free end back around the rear pastern and returning to pass through the neck loop. Elmer held this end while Charlie repeated on the off side.

Elise watched as the two men pulled the ropes with no synchronization, causing the colt to sit as his rear legs were drawn to his belly; his thrashing put him on his side. Quickly recovering the spotted colt began slamming his head on the ground, bunching his muscles with each thrash causing his body to jump with each frantic effort. The ropes were strong and the cowboys determined. Charlie slipped in and deftly figure eighted the available hock and pastern. Turning him he repeated with the other leg, thigh muscles churning like a burlap bag overstuffed with tomcats.

The colt realized he could not free himself and in the manner of a stall-cast horse ceased to struggle. The spotted chestnut coat was coated with caked dirt and clumps of sandspurs as Charlie draped a saddle blanket over his head mercifully covering the fear drenched eyeballs.

Elmer pulled the trussed rear leg up exposing the spotted scrotum. He quickly washed the pouch with dilute bleach, its laundromat ambience causing his young wife to wrinkle her nose and squint.

Elise could not comprehend how such a proud and vigorous horse could be transformed into this vulnerable, dirt-covered creature.

"Here, gal, fetch me that bucket with the knife in it –hurry!" As Elmer spat the words, Charlie eased his 195 pounds onto the colt's neck, both hands on the rope binding the hind leg. Elise held the bucket next to her husband's shoulder allowing him to reach in and produce a razor sharp Buck folding knife, his eyes focused elsewhere.

Two testicles bulged as his left hand squeezed the base of the beast's cod-sac—a spotted balloon about to be popped.

Spellbound, Elise gasped as Elmer drew the belly of the blade across the taunt skin with no more pressure than drawing a pencil line. But no scribe could make the stretched skin sunder and spew forth a glistening glob to lie, throbbing, in the gaping wound. A second line was drawn and a second glob burst forth with blood beginning to leak from the transgressed vascular tissue. Dumbstruck. Swooning.

With little wasted motion Elmer jerked the exposed testicles free of their membranous attachments like two embryonic eyeballs pre-empted from gestation and jerked from their womb, unripe and unseeing as they dangled on stretched cords.

"The sticks, gal, the sticks…" Elmer's request broke the spell and Elise handed over an eight-inch length of native persimmon tree cut that morning, its bark carefully peeled and split from one end to within an inch of the other.

Elmer opened the split end and forced the top cord into the gap, tying the opened end with hay twine and constricting the vascular cord to render the testicle bloodless. A second persimmon branch secured the other and in one hack the proud appaloosa colt was relieved of his manhood. Elise gasped as her husband threw the now worthless jewels into the sand.

The blanketed animal could not see nor would have comprehended the final indignity as two yellow cur hounds crept from under Charlie's pickup and retrieved the two sand covered organs to retire behind the barn and savor the colt's misfortune. True Leisure.

"Now, hon, get me that hot iron—careful—get it by the handle. Use that piece of burlap… hurry!" Elmer's words caught his putative surgical nurse by surprise causing her to turn the wrong way. "Goddamit, Elise, get me that iron! This son a bitch ain't gonna lay here all fuckin' day!" The cowboy was trying his best to hold the gelding as it renewed its efforts to free itself. The explosive attempt threw Charlie off its neck resulting in a mad scramble as the men fought to maintain their advantage.

"Finish this mawther, Elmer, I can't stay on this here bronc mor'n eight seconds!" Charlie let out a bronc rider's "whoo-pee" as he settled his butt onto the appaloosa's grimy neck.

Elise was leaning over her husband's shoulder, her damp blouse clinging like skin to her unsupported breasts. She retched with every adrenalin driven heartbeat as he seared the ends of the severed cords. As the acrid smoke enveloped her face, Elise Jones, newly married, vomited on her husband's back.

• • •

Can Martin settled against a tree as the nurse put wood on the dying fire and set a tin can of water over the flame. The rancher could see the set to her lips and the faraway look in her vacant stare. Psyched!

Elise cut the pus soaked pants, thinking the worst as the stench of rotting flesh blasted forth causing her to turn away.

"That bad, huh?" Can couched his comment as a question but Elise could not mistake the tone in his statement.

"I've seen worse. You ought to see a bad gator bite, Can.

Makes yours look like a hangnail." Elise lifted a shred of dead tissue hanging over the largest wound. All this will have to come off, she thought, as she stuck the knife into the red embers. I hope he can stand this.

Placing the hot blade into the heating water, Elise secured a large fork and stuck the handle end into the hot coals. She then tore strips from Can's shirt and rolled them into bandage rolls.

"OK, Can, bite the bullet or whatever, because I have to debride this ulcerated area. The edges are undermined and it needs exposure." Her professional monotone encouraged the patient but the reality caused his hands to shake. Hide them.

"Go ahead, gal, do what you have to. I'll be fine." Can's words faded as Elise lifted the first piece of necrotic tissue and cut it off— as close to the healthy part as possible to avoid pain since dead tissue was not enervated.

She removed the offending flesh paying no attention to Can when he flinched or muttered about women's lib and equal rights.

The wound was not as extensive as Elise had anticipated but its ulcerative nature made it more onerous. Her mind was racing.

'What if's' crowded her consciousness like cave bats going to roost. What if a major blood vessel is eroded? What if he develops endo-toxic shock?

She knew the Aloe plants weren't antibiotic, but their healing powers were legendary and she was sure going to test them.

"Can... Can, I've got to cauterize this mess or you don't stand a chance." Turning, her voice flat, Elise handed him a bat sized limb. "Grip this and try not to scream—I'll do what I have to as quickly as I can."

Sweat was pouring from her face like condensation from a frosted mug. Her brow was just as cold.

Grasping the tines of the red-hot fork with a piece of wadded pant leg Elise seared the weeping lesion, letting out a terse "shit," as the cautery instrument cooled in the oozing flesh and had to be returned to the hot coals.

The smell of charring meat was overpowering and Elise was de-termined not to let Can Martin see the stringy vomitus loitering in the corners of her mouth. Stepping behind an oak tree while the fork handle reheated she let go her gorge and wiped her mouth on her sleeve. "Hell Can, breakfast wasn't that good..."

Choking the failed humor, Elise finished searing the wound and packed it with the crushed, meaty Aloes leaves. Martin was shaking as she finished.

Well, at least I tried. He—we—may have a chance.

Looking up from her surgery she noticed the darkening skies casting a crepuscular patina throughout the hammock. She hoped the shower missed them. She never considered the approaching thunderstorm as more than a summer shower.

• • •

JY followed the trail like a bloodhound but slow, occasionally having to cast in the thicker areas for the unmistakable scent of Joe Billie.

With each step Sam felt stronger, more positive about over-taking the fugitives. He steeled his mind against failure thinking only that Elise was alive; the rancher's welfare of no concern. The weather was ominous.

The tracking pit bulldog was elated over finding the trail—knowing his master was pleased. The dog had no reason to dis-like the fugitive Indian though he remembered his smell from the shack where the two hounds had challenged them. He had no opportunity to get Joe Billie's scent at the time of Sam's beating. JY grinned a wide mouthed smirk as he thought of the redneck hound—barely a workout.

Stopping, JY saw that Sam was keeping up, his stride relaxed and his breathing not forced. The big dog couldn't be happier—we'll catch this guy and his pals. That ought to make the boss man happy.

JY didn't know that the others were unwilling companions of the one who smells. He only knew he was following the same three that were at the truck where they started. The perceptive canine wished he could talk.

It would make the big man happy.

By now the pair were miles from the *Melaleuca* forest and head-ing southwest. It seemed the wily predator considered his pursuers lost or dead as the trail avoided the serious bogs and deep water. This renewed Sam's belief that Elise was alive and her captor had relaxed a notch. He knew to be careful.

Sam noted that if the oncoming storm didn't break soon it would be over them and they would have to find shelter. He whis-tled to Junk Yard and increased his pace. He wasn't sure the dog would be able to pick up the trail following the deluge promised by the malignant clouds.

JY noticed the darkening but paid no mind. His concern was the trail. He thought the restive man hurried because of wanting to find two people—he was half right.

Reaching a path through a dense hammock fringe, JY stopped. The Indian's scent was intense, fresh—not the textured smell he had been following. The other scents were the same. How was this possible? Suspicious, the schooled pit raised his head, hackles up, tail stiff. Sam came up and dropped to one knee sure that the dog was alerting him to someone's presence. Dammit, why did I have to go and lose my super sniffer—not to mention my pistol.

A glint to his steel eyes, JY continued on the hot scented trail, hackles still up. Every few yards he stopped and tested the air. Sam noticed this, understanding that something had changed about the trail but helpless to fathom it. He would have to trust the Junk Yard until something happened or he relaxed and went on trailing.

Dammit-dammit-dammit, why can't I smell? Samson's thoughts were frustrating.

"Come on, boy, we got to get it in gear or we're going to get rained on—big time." Samson's words were meant to encourage JY but it didn't work. He continued the slow pace sniffing the air every few steps but Sam didn't see anything—what was JY trying to convey?

"OK, man, let's talk about this." Sam dropped to one knee and put his arm around the thewy neck. "Look, guy, I know something's bothering you but if we don't speed things up, there may not be a second inning." Sam's words were well meant but he knew JY wasn't going to be swayed by words though the tone imparted urgency he could relate to. The pit bulldog wasn't about to lead his master into a trap—not in this life.

Sam could feel tension prowling the dog's body, hackles at attention even though Sam's words were meant to be reassuring; eyes darting in spite of Sam's confidence. A sense of helplessness filled the man's gut like hot coals causing him to stand and shake his silvered head at this recalcitrance by the loyal pit bulldog— then Samson got mad. He wasn't to be delayed by confusion, even on the part of the Junk Yard dog.

"OK, pal, if this is the way it has to be, so be it but we're going to get on regardless of what you think!" Sharp words. Sharper tone.

JY's eyes stopped their nystagmic search pattern and met Samson's glare with an openness that caused the man to bite his lip. A melding of glances and Sam was allowed to pierce the clouded window to the dog's inner self and for an instance knew the depth of the Junk Yard's loyalty. He bit his lip harder…

Sam started out ahead at a fast pace forcing the dog to trot. He knew JY wouldn't let him get ahead and by forcing the pace he could make the reluctant beast track faster. The direction they were heading seemed to follow a natural pathway and Sam guessed the renegade used it to make easier going for the captives—or so he hoped.

The pit bulldog sensed his urgency but was helpless to slow him though he wanted to please this man whose disbelief in the dog's intentions was tearing at his heart. He had no choice but to give in. JY overtook Sam and slightly altered his course, keeping his face in the hot scent that reeked of uncertainty—even disaster—for his master as he never considered danger. If he did, he would not have slowed. Danger was relevant only as it concerned Samson.

"Good man, JY, good man." Sam's voice sounded like a spoiled child as the dog trotted past him nose to the ground heading straight at the dark prickly carcass of a cedar tree.

"I knew you'd see it my way." Laughing, Sam felt a renewed confidence as the turbulent skies darkened with the hitherto seen lightning now splitting the sky like cannon shot.

Chapter **EIGHTEEN**

They smelled the hog trap before they saw it, gusts of wind from the building storm forcing the sickening smell into their faces. The putrid odor would not be ignored.

"What in the hell is that!" Can mouthed the words. "Somethin's dead, gal, somethin powerful big or powerful dead or both." The rancher had stopped and was facing the gusting wind.

Elise's shade tree surgery and aloe poultice had helped the stricken man causing his spirits to improve the past two hours. His sweating now was from heat and exertion not fever and infection. Martin thought he had a chance to get out of this mess—alive.

Elise stopped and turned. "Let's don't go any closer to whatever that is. I have a funny feeling about this…"

Can interrupted. "Hell no, let's go see. We need all the help we can get… you wait here and I'll check it out." With that he started toward the edge of the hammock, less than 50 yards, hunched shoulders testifying to the effort of walking on spongy ground.

"You're not leaving me! Not now!" Elise's pitched reply hung a smile on the somber man—an uncommon event.

Treading through the fringe of Skull Hammock the pair crossed the faded tracks of a motor vehicle. Can studied the track; one direction fading into the hammock. The track headed to the hammock seemed to point to the putrid odor causing Can to remark. "Look here, gal, an old road. Someone drives into here or at least they have on several occasions. I was hopin' we'd find something like this. Let's see where it goes and what's dead, then we can follow this sum bitch right out of here." Can never mentioned Joe Billie Bloodtooth. Never existed.

Elise was not persuaded. "No, Can, let's follow this road back. I don't want to go into that thick place… 1 don't care what's dead. Let's just get the hell out of here."

The prescient nurse started backtracking when Can whistled and started the other way. He wanted to see what was rotten and if there was a cabin or shelter nearby. Anyway, he aimed to find out.

He had gone a few yards before Elise caught up. "Can, this *is* crazy. Look at that sky—we need to get out of here right now. What if that storm decides to hit here? That track *is* our only hope." Her voice broke as she tried to reason with the man. "I don't want to be here if that storm hits and we wouldn't be able to follow an interstate if it does, much less an overgrown dirt road."

Can nodded. She could be right. He had been keeping an eye on the building storm but he figured the winds were going to carry it to the north and east of them—the worst for them would be heavy fringe rains and maybe heavenly fireworks if the gods were angry. He hoped to find shelter in the jungle of Skull Hammock.

Hunching like an overworked plow mule Can Martin pulled his stubbornness straight to Skull Hammock and the hog trap set by Samchuck Tiger and Jimmy Gopher.

The stench was overpowering. Martin walked past a magnolia tree adorned with a human skull glaring malevolently, its precarious perch insured by the single nail protruding through one eye socket.

Elise gasped but her intake of breath was not due to the skull hammock logo.

Beyond the magnolia and surrounded by cabbage palms was the most grotesque thing either had ever seen. The weathered poles of the hog trap were glistening with slime from the dew heavy mornings when the gaunt hog would suck the wet poles seeking water—adding mucus to the slimy wood.

Big'un's near 500-pound body had been reduced to bristle covered, weathered hide; large flat ribs highlighted by dehydrated skin resembled a derelict boat. The great boar-hog had been reduced to a shadow—save for the blast furnace fire that glowed in his squinty, gnat covered, weepy little pig eyes.

The ground inside the trap was a slime pit, churned by porcine feet into an ethereal compost of pig feces, urine and remains of Big'un's previous meals. Rooted areas of the foul earth attested to Big-un's efforts to escape—to no avail.

Fragments of bone, bits and pieces of hair and flesh bore evidence of the four shoats caught with Big'un. The first week in the Stygian prison had been a feast for the hog, eating the captive food; wrapping entrails around his huge snout and gulping them down like appetizers. Big'un tried to lift the trap on a few occasions but not with any sustained effort—why leave good food.

The second week was spent rooting the moist dirt and scarfing up scraps—feet, eyeballs, ears. Leftovers. Freedom.

Big'un couldn't lift this trap.

The third week took its toll. His efforts at rooting and lifting were more frenzy than purpose. His strength was waning and his flesh melting like ice in a spring thaw.

He was mad. Mad at getting trapped.

Mad just to be mad! His mouth poppings a warning to nothing, yet everything. The fire-stick of hunger was prodding him to madness. He could not be free.

The Indian boys had done a good job in Big'un proofing their trap. This behemoth would not be able to reopen the guillotine door or lift the structure and as he had on many occasions.

The hog was as surprised to see the people as they were to see him. The rancher's jaw went slack as he surveyed the macabre scene; Elise gasped, covered her mouth and started crying.

Big'un staggered towards them, his piercing eyes bloodshot with hunger—beyond fear of man. The strain made him to sit down like a begging dog, a rawboned foreleg raised to maintain his balance—it didn't work and he fell to his side, struggling like a mud wrestler to regain his feet. Shiny blowflies and coveys of gnats hovered as the slimy beast righted, head lowered, front feet planted in front of his body.

"For God's sake, Can, Let's go! I can't stand this!" Elise was screaming as the cripple tried to look away, trapped in the eerie putrescence of this beast from hell. The screams broke the spell and Can Martin turned to reassure his ragged companion and get the hell away.

As their eyes met Elise became aware of a subtle change in the rancher's visage. The resident vacant stare was now disbelief—without a flicker of change in demeanor. Can Martin's mouth screamed muted words. Unintelligible.

Elise felt the hairs on her neck tingle as she turned and gaped the vapidness that was Joe Billie Bloodtooth.

• • •

Samson glanced at the gravid clouds as JY followed the trail.

The coolness followed by patchy darkening signaled the arrival of the storm. The cedar trunk barely caught his attention as he detoured to meet JY. It was dread—disaster—that grabbed his short hairs and magnified the sound as the deadly log crashed down on the pit bulldog's muscular head. No sound escaped the trapped jaws of the Junk Yard dog; no movement coursed his body. Silence. Overwhelming.

Screaming maniacally Samson plunged into the prickly morass, fighting, oblivious to damage inflicted by this arboreal adversary. Burrowing, he reached and felt JY's hip and a rear leg, unable to get closer. Frantically he tried to find a pulse in the massive thigh forcing himself closer to the stilled dog. The sky sundered.

The sheet of water seemed laced with ice as Sam's sweating body chilled, evoking screams not to be heard over crashing water and deafening thunder. Sam's senses went on autopilot as the downpour softened the ground enough for him to burrow close to his head—what he thought should be his head. With feel Samson determined that the tremendous log was crushing the dog's head but Sam's prone position prevented the use of leverage needed to shift the sodden wood.

Unwilling to waste time trying to find a pulse Sam crawled to the dog's head and put his hand on JY's chest, pressing in behind his elbow, his rabid fingers willing to call any sensation—heartbeat. Any movement—life! Forcing his churnings and vibrations to cease, Sam achieved for the briefest moment suspended animation with all sensory receptors concentrated in his fingers.

He felt it—a vibration, a quivering, coming from deep in the chest; steadying to a heartrending drum-roll—fibrillation. Samson knew fibrillation, having felt this sinuous quivering through the chests of many dying men. He had never seen a survivor, only those fortunate enough to be taken to a facility with defibrillation capability. Without it JY was a dead dog. Sam gasped, choking back tears diluted by the torrent and the gorge of absolute catastrophe.

His pal was dying.

Sitting next to the deadfall, his screams silenced by the downpour, Sam pulled at the deadly instrument. The thudding water obscured his vision as he pulled, all the while wishing life into the stilled form.

Unable to move JY, Samson realized he would have to move the log to free the dog; he would need a lever—a pry pole. Scrambling out he felt around the perimeter of the downed cedar not wanting to leave as he couldn't see six inches in front. Throbbing arm—forgotten.

Reaching the root end he groped an arm sized, rain slicked pole, following it like a blind man to determine its utility. Satisfied, he dragged it to where JY was, grunting with the strain of maintaining balance in the deepening muck.

The lightning bolt found earth 50 feet from the struggling man, passed into a pine tree transforming its stately crown into a sunburst of lignin, continuing to the ground splitting the pine tree into kindling before fanning through the water soaked ground, Samson Hercules Duff and the Junk Yard dog.

Sam fought to maintain consciousness and an hour after the deadly strike found himself walking aimlessly, water and mud to his waist and oblivious to who or where he was. He was aware of a deep ache in his left arm and emptiness in his soul.

• • •

Elise saw the arm of Joe Billie coming at her like a slow motion baseball bat but none of her self-protective mechanisms seemed to work. Her mind was screeching at her body to duck or run but nothing was happening. The 'thunk' of hard flesh hitting soft flesh was lost and she was rendered senseless by the arm of Joe Billie Bloodtooth.

Bloodtooth vaulted the stunned woman and kicked the rancher's crutch as he fumbled for his knife. Mute, Joe Billie slipped past Martin and picked up his heavy crutch. One stroke between knee and ankle and Martin's tibia exploded like fine crystal on rock, dropping in his tracks. Excruciating. Helpless.

Turning his face to the sky, Joe Billie yodeled the ancient Miccosukee war cry—for the second time. Raising his arms he thanked the four winds for bringing his enemies to ground.

"See, Grandfather? Have I not captured my enemies? See, Mother, have I not overcome these ones who would do me harm?" Trancelike, Joe Billie didn't notice the drooling from his mouth or was not motivated to wipe his slobber.

Pigeon egg rain drops plopped around like water filled balloons, attesting to the ferocity of the storm just northeast of them.

"OK, turd-head rancher, now you see what happens to dog killers!" Joe Billie leaped past the moaning man and took the knife, shoving it into his belt as he turned to check on Elise.

Woozy, she raised to one elbow and tried to focus on the shadows in front of her, ears ringing like an unanswered telephone. Her mouth was working on words but only managed bloody bubbles. With a sigh, Elise lay back and Bloodtooth turned to the rancher, savoring his obvious pain.

The bombarding rain increased, plopping on the participants in this nightmarish drama—the darkness of the passing storm merely a dimming of the house lights.

"My Stump was eat by a goddamn croc, turd-head...'cause of you...now see who gets eat." Grabbing Martin as he babbled, the robotic Miccosukee headed to the hog trap dragging the rancher like a piece of meat. Can's only response, a grunt-like moan as the movement took him to the edge of shock.

"You animal! You goddamn animal! Stop! You can't do this..." Elise's scream was interrupted by her attack. Disregarding numbness and confusion, she flung herself onto Joe Billie's back, digging her nails into his neck and face, flailing for his eyes.

Executing a sit-down, the trained man-beast freed himself and came up with arms around her waist. His squeeze was unbearable and cries of anger morphed to squeals of distress as breath was forced from her body. Her brain exploded.

Falling was the first thing Elise felt as consciousness returned. She managed, somehow, to avoid falling but the unsteadiness was unavoidable. She felt iron fingers gripping her arm and waist. What could this be? A dream? Turning slowly from side to side, she realized her eyes were closed and willed them open. The stench of the trap blended with the grunts of its gaunt prisoner informed her that her other senses had returned.

Joe Billie stood holding her in a viselike grip, forcing her to witness the scene playing out in the hog trap. Can Martin slumped in a corner, his shattered, bloody leg protruding like a broken flagpole; eyes pain filled—distant. His right hand held the hunting knife.

"Mother, I gave him the knife...turd-head...my Stump didn't have no knife." These words seemed like the script for a silent movie—no emotion, no inflection. Words. Elise could neither speak nor turn away.

She knew the fateful rancher had accepted death and was prepared. She knew the strong heritage of Martin blood was being tested and Can Martin was passing this final exam. No pleading. No begging. No posturing. Man!

Big'un didn't know what to make of the ruckus. He knew men by their smell and had no fear since the trap was his only contact with them. What he did know was he was starving and this was food—strange—but food.

The rain had turned into a drizzle as the storm passed resulting in a clear sky as Big'un decided the thing hunched in the corner was his. His festering eyes narrowed as he lunged.

Joe Billie's maniacal laugh was the last thing Elise heard. She fainted.

•   •   •

The sun was hot as Sam finished squeezing his clothes and hung them to dry—along with his drenched body.

He was defeated—not by Joe Billie Bloodtooth but by the ill-tempered Pay-Hay-Okee. His brain was righting itself and as his fried memory fell into place, depression settled squarely onto his shoulders. JY was dead. These words were festering. JY had to be dead and Sam didn't know where his magnificent dog lay; tears flowed as he realized the finality of the Everglades. He may never find his friend. More, it was unlikely that he could extricate himself—forget the Indian and captives—minus the Pit Bulldog. Self-survival. Priority.

Wringing the cotton pants, Samson felt something in one of the roomy pockets and produced the wadded up plastic baggie containing Elise's panties. Frustration seared his gut as he stared at the sodden wad. What madness had possessed him to risk everything, including his life, to rescue some woman and a no good cowboy from the green gut of hell—for what? So that he could use up the best friend a man could have?

Guilt seeped from his pores as he remembered his insistence on forcing the cautious dog to trail faster. JY had known something was wrong—he knew he had to be careful but impatient Sam couldn't—wouldn't—trust the insightful canine. For what?

The man was weeping openly, cursing himself, Bloodtooth, the Everglades and anything that came to mind. It was going to be hard to live with what he had done and not be able to bury the great dog and say goodbye.

This was Duff's first significant defeat. His first humbling experience since his Spartan training days. First time in adult life that his knees bent by other than his own volition.

Looking at the afternoon sky, the depression of defeat metamorphosed into the rage of frustration and Sam's face pulsated, engorged veins distending as fury sought escape from the tortured soul. His primal scream echoed off the trees and into the sky, unheard by the stern forces of nature.

Samson fell to his knees and crumpled the soggy plastic bag with such venom that its bubbled sides burst like fresh blisters spraying his face with water droplets and aromatic contents.

The effect was startling. As the man sucked back his spent breath the sweetly sensual aroma of Elise Jones overpowered him causing him to reel backward and gasp like an air breathing fish. He gulped the powerful attractant and the realization settled in. Another scream—he could smell! His gift had been restored and as Samson finally accepted this fact he prostrated his naked body and gave thanks to the creator of life's force. Sam Duff's defeat was yet to be cast in stone.

• • •

Young Samson was nervous standing in the examination room with his mother. The shaggy dog on the spotless table also seemed nervous, his rolled eyes showing white like a nursing calf. The neatly groomed man wearing the blue coat with a stethoscope bridging the distance from his ears to the left side of Blackie's chest reeked of authority—and eerily, doom.

Sam was almost fourteen and couldn't remember when he didn't have Blackie. The big, rawboned mixed collie had been a fixture at the Duff household since Sam was two years old; young Duff and Blackie were inseparable these past twelve years.

"I'm afraid that Blackie has heartworms, Ms Duff." The veterinarian, Dr. Meltz, casually removed the stethoscope as he directed his diagnosis at the stately woman. "The blood test was positive and his chest sounds support a diagnosis of heartworm disease."

Sam felt his face redden as he clasped his hands behind his back and strained to hear the gospel about his dog's lack of energy and appetite—two of his most consistent traits—from this quiet spoken authority on all things canine.

What was heartworm disease, he thought. As if he had read the young man's mind, Dr. Meltz produced a jar containing a grisly object, partly cutaway showing many long, thin, whitish threads crowded into one of its chambers like so much spaghetti. Turning to give a better view, the veterinarian, still soft spoken, commented. "This is a large dog heart and these string like things are heartworms—see, son—each one can be up to 15 inches long and they occlude the right side of the infected dog's heart." As he spoke, he inadvertently shifted the heavy jar, causing a particulate cloud to rise from the bottom as to disguise the noxious creatures from curious eyes. Samson couldn't help but notice his mother avert her gaze as the veterinarian was giving his demonstration—the scummy jar wasn't very appetizing.

He continued. "Blackie may be too old to survive the treatment, but we can…"

Ms. Duff interrupted. "Dr. Meltz, I wish to talk privately with you." Turning to Samson, she continued. "Son, go wait in the car for me. I will be out in a few minutes."

His face still flushed, the obedient youngster turned slowly and reluctantly shuffled out of the exam room. He didn't understand any of this. How could big things like heartworms get inside Blackie's heart? Oh well, Samson Duff had implicit faith in the health care system in general and Dr. Meltz in particular, so it probably wouldn't be too tough to fix the loyal dog and get him back where he belonged—with Sam.

Approaching the front door, Sam realized he hadn't told Blackie goodbye—a ritual between the two. The young man never went to school or to sleep without telling the faithful dog goodbye or goodnight and Blackie never went to sleep without licking his young master's hands or face as he burrowed in next to Samson's feet for his night's rest.

Going back down the short hallway, the attentive lad stopped outside the door as he heard the muffled voices of his mother and Dr. Meltz, his strict upbringing precluding him from interrupting his elders—he would wait until there was a break or pause in the conversation before entering.

"… Ms. Duff, I really think we can help old Blackie, but it will be touch and go…"

"I understand, doctor, but what will all this cost? "Ms. Duff's query was very matter of fact.

Sam listened. He could barely make out the words over the noisy pumping of his adrenalin charged heart. He knew he shouldn't be standing there. The guilt of eavesdropping added yet another layer of blush to the young man's countenance.

"Well, Ms. Duff, these procedures are fairly expensive considering that we're talking about an animal and not a human. And there is no guarantee but without relief, old mister Blackie will probably not recover—just linger on until he passes away … Probably within a few months." The veterinarian's voice sounded as if he truly cared about the big dog sitting naively on the hard table with his labored breathing the only sign of distress, now that the good doctor was through with the blood taking and examination.

Samson winced as he listened to the vet's pronouncement.

Blackie couldn't die. Why should he die? He didn't even look sick—just a little tired, he should be okay, just let him rest. Sam wouldn't play with him as hard as usual. Sam's young mind knew all the answers.

"What are the alternatives, Doctor Meltz?" Again a matter of fact inquiry, but this time a touch of forced objectivity was detectable in the handsome woman's voice.

"…three to four hundred dollars, to answer your first question, providing there are no complications." Without pause, Dr. Meltz continued. "The alternatives are, of course, to let him terminate as his condition dictates or to possibly consider humane euthanasia. Without successful treatment his quality of life will certainly be less than desirable, especially given his relationship with your son."

Sam hung his head. He couldn't enter the room now that he had eavesdropped so long—his conscience wouldn't permit it and yet he couldn't leave. His very life was sitting on that table with two trusted, caring people in judgment, yet for some unexplainable reason Samson felt the cold wind of dread blowing against his flushed brow. More questions. What did euthanasia mean? Was that some form of medicine?

The first crack in his mother's stoic demeanor totally confused the quiet boy as her voice undulated dramatically with her reply. "I— uh—we can't afford to have the treatment…" Only the veterinarian could see the tears welling in the eyes of the distraught mother.

"I understand, Ms. Duff, I understand. Even if the treatment were successful, given the old fellow's age its unlikely he would make another year, two at the most." Dr. Meltz's tone seemed designed to bolster the woman's sagging resolve. He had been in private practice 35 years and had long since quit being his clients' conscience. True, he still rankled at the thought of putting a healthy pet to death because it's owner was moving and couldn't take the pet or because needed treatments or surgery seemed too expensive when in reality the provided services were anything but expensive given the state of the medical arts and what could be accomplished, but, oh well, if people couldn't perceive this on their own then he, now older and more practical than dedicated, wasn't going to do more arm twisting via the guilty conscience.

Sam just couldn't understand his mother saying that they couldn't afford Blackie's treatment. Of course they could. Old Blackie was one of the family and he had never even heard money or cost mentioned when he or dad or mom needed medical or dental services. To young Samson Duff, Blackie was every bit as important a family member as he or anybody else.

Sam couldn't stand anymore of this. Tears were streaming down his face and he had to choke down the spasmodic sobs, afraid they would reveal his innocent deception. Surely his own mother and Blackie's own doctor would take care of Blackie—his Blackie—surely they would!

Bloated with confused emotions, the distraught lad ran blindly from the animal clinic and buried his face in the car seat. Surely modern medicine could cure anything, even the ailing Blackie; especially his Blackie.

Regaining her composure with the welcomed assist from the veterinarian, Ms. Duff continued. "Please, Dr. Meltz, I would like for you to put Blackie to sleep and let me tell Samson that he died from the treatment. They are so close…" Even though her voice was steady, the abundant tears betrayed this calmness and the veterinarian could not deny her.

"Okay, Ms. Duff, we will take care of it for you—anyway you wish. Will you be wanting to pick up the remains to bury at home or would you prefer for us to do it?" These words from the doctor were like a tape recording and the thinly disguised cynicism might be recognized, Dr. Metz really didn't care.

A slight nod of her head signaled affirmative.

"Very well, we'll take care of it…" As he spoke he moved to a small table against the wall and picked up a box of

tissues, handing them to the tearful woman. "It will be painless."

Ms. Duff wiped at her eyes as she walked rapidly from the animal clinic.

The long drive home was one of forced silence. Sam's mind was about to explode with questions, most of which he knew he didn't want answered.

His mother's mind was also churning, hoping that her son wouldn't ask too many questions about the old black dog. She detested liars and lying and the further from the animal clinic and the devoted dog she got, the guiltier she felt. Samson Hercules Duff's mother was having an extremely difficult time.

Finally pulling into their driveway, Martha Duff felt the cool breeze of relief as she knew her energetic son would soon be engrossed in his athletic play and she could get back to housework and occupy her remorseful mind with other things.

"Mommy—uh—mother, can I ask you something?" Young Sam's voice was barely audible—a high-pitched, forced whisper, almost whining as if to signal the yearling's retreat to his earlier childhood and its less adulterated innocence.

"Yes, but be quick. I have a lot to do this afternoon."

"What does youth—youth—ah—na—youth-ah-naysha mean?"

Chapter **NINETEEN**

Samson had been moving slowly for an hour since drying his clothes. His demeanor belied his joy at regaining his paranormal gift. He savored every scent, marveled at his ability to remember previous redolent encounters and identify the myriad new ones. If only JY was here. There was no way Sam could numb out the recurring images of his Junk Yard dog. Flashbacks were blinking through his mind like a turn signal, wet cheeks attesting to this.

Only his self-discipline kept him plunging deeper into the green hell that was the Everglades. Sam Duff never questioned values, only performance and he vowed to finish this crusade—not for himself.

He wouldn't accept the dog's death yet couldn't shake the feeling that he would never see his pal again.

Lost, Sam remembered the general direction of the trail JY was following and with his grief bottled, set out in that direction, southwest. His hope was to cut the spoor or find help. The latter seemed remote as he reasoned that few people would have sufficient reason to venture into this godforsaken morass so whomever he came across would not be of much—if any—help. If only JY were here!

Squinting, he scanned the area. Sam caught himself looking for the rich coat of the Junk Yard dog moving through the scabby undergrowth—he wished!

Sam, you have to quit that. You're never going to see that dog. Looking down, Samson Duff bit his lip. He couldn't cork his emotional bottle…his tears…eternal.

His injured arm ached. Sam knew it was mending and he had feeling in his wrist and hand. The effects of the envenomation were gone and he no longer had episodes of nausea; he moved easily through the greenery.

The hum of a straining motor wafted across the silence and hit Sam just as he smelled human scent—flavored with various metallic aromas. He winced at the impact of the un-scrubbed blend. Two men, Indian, less than a half mile considering the air currents.

Color surged into his face as he broke into a run, darting through reeds and brush like one possessed. A million thoughts tumbled in his head as he corrected to follow the scent more than the sound. Maybe these Indians would help him—may-be they knew of Joe Billie or where he stayed or may-be they had a gun he could borrow or may-be they would help him backtrack and find JY … maybe, maybe. Samson thumped his head with the flat of his hand as he realized the futility of may-bes.

Regardless of his grief, his priority now was to find the captives and kill Bloodtooth. He intended to do just that.

Breaking into a marshy flat, Sam loped across the ruts made by the half track and realized he was going to have to run it down as the men would never hear his shouts over the blatter of the jury rigged motor. The mucky ground pulled at his feet like fingers as he fought across the sucking earth. Both boots were claimed by the tenacious ground as he powered on, muscles strained to the limit.

Like a rusty beetle, the half track lurched across the landscape, slipping into a muck hole, tracks churning as the machine settled into the goo, caught and slammed forward, motor groaning to settle back into its slow progression. Only the smoke spewing from under the mechanical beast bore witness to its state of health after one too many resurrections at the hands of Jimmy Gopher.

Deep into reserves beyond mortal flesh, Samson stumbled forward at an amazing speed given the terrain. Every time the half-track slipped into a hole, the open-mouthed Samson hollered hoping to be heard in the split second of silence that occurred when the transmission decided to shift or quit. He is not heard.

Gaining on the half track, Sam realized he had only a few seconds to deny the burning in his lungs, the screaming calf muscles and the numbness creeping up his injured arm. Only half aware he darted past the whining machine and collapsed as his senses told him he had passed it.

"Wh-what thu hell eh-is th-that?" Jimmy Gopher jammed the clutch to the firewall, stopping the machine as he sought to adjust the throttle and avoid the mechanical shutdown that accompanied this disciplining of the temperamental W.W.II reject.

"Goddamn, Jimmy, where'd he come from?" Samchuck Tiger was climbing down at his partner's reply. "H-h-hold it, m-m-man, wu-we don't know anyone out h-here." Jimmy had the weather-beaten .22 rifle in his left hand—in case…

Samson pushed himself up on his right hand trying to sit; he was light headed. The snakebite aftermath bounced around his mind causing him to slow his effort when the young eyes bore into him and he could smell their fear. His voice was weak. "I -I need help. I'm not going to hurt you… I'm unarmed…please!" As he finished his plea the recalcitrant machine died.

"Oh shit, Jimmy, the goddamn thing quit again!" Young Tiger's statement carried the ring of repetition as if rehearsed. Resigned, the boys climbed down and leaned against the front of the hissing relic while they sized up this strange man.

They didn't know what to say. They eyed the unkempt man in bedraggled camos, silver and black hair matted and barefoot—in the Everglades. Not the prototype of someone you would trust.

Crawling to the front of the vehicle, Samson pulled himself up and steadied with his hurt arm while he fished for his wallet. Jimmy Gopher held the .22 rifle and both boys moved to the side as the man up-righted.

"Here. I'm a private investigator—ex-CIA agent—look." He pushed the plastic I-D card towards Samchuck Tiger. "I mean you no harm."

Tiger held the card at eye level while Gopher stepped closer so he could see it. "Wh-what you doin' way out h-h-here? Na-nuthin' but sk-skeeters'n gators out here no-ways." Jimmy was nervous.

"Yea, man." Samchuck Tiger broke in. "You on some kinda job or 'signment, or somethin'? What happened to your arm?" These words brought a sigh of relief as Sam sensed the relaxation of the younger boy and knew he had a chance. "I got snakebit…" Samson started talking and the story gushed forth like an oil strike. With each spurt the boys relaxed and were soon oohing and awwing over Sam's unbelievable story.

Samson bit his tongue as he told of JY's misfortune, his heart skipping the hurtful part like a well-thrown flat rock over smooth water, dwelling on the kidnap victims and Joe Billie Bloodtooth. "You guys ever heard of him?" The abrupt query signaled the end of showtime and Jimmy Gopher returned Sam's gaze with a hooded stare.

"Yu-yea, I have. He a la-la-legend 'round these parts. Y-you tell'em, Samchuck, you n-n-know it g-g-good as me."

Samson sensed the older boy's discomfort with his stammering, especially after Sam's machine gun delivery of his story.

With perfect diction young Tiger repeated the folklore about Joe Billie Bloodtooth and the killing of his mother and Grandfather and the revenge killing of his father, James Bloodtooth at the place called Skull Hammock. The skull giving the hammock its name was that of Joe Billie's father and adorns an old magnolia tree with its carney grin and empty eye sockets beckoning all…

Neither had seen the legendary Miccosukee and were scared to death at the prospect—now—of a run-in.

"You know if he had a cabin nearby, or maybe at this Skull Hammock place?" Sam's quizzical expression was open and genuine.

Samchuck Tiger answered. "No, I don't know of any shack, 'cept maybe his old home place, but I—we—been by there and doesn't look used. No sign."

Sam cocked his brow. "Okay, where would that be, like from here?" Pointing to the northeast, Tiger continued. "That way.

Maybe five, six mile. Maybe. On the edge of punk trees—maybe northwest corner."

Sam interrupted. "Is there a stream close by, maybe with a wide part like a swimming hole or maybe a crossing?"

"Yea, just south and a little west. Good water. Bad place. Big moccasins!" The Indian boy's voice leveled as he mentioned what had to be where Sam encountered the savage snake.

Steamed blood flowed Sam's veins as he realized he had been near the renegades home-place. He had to have a camp between there and Skull Hammock. I bet the trail JY followed would have led to a cabin…the hot spear of vengeance pierced his soul. He would have his final confrontation. He wanted no weapons—it had to be that way. It would be that way. Death!

In a voice so guttural that Samchuck Tiger's mouth went slack and Jimmy Gopher's index finger tightened on the trigger of the .22, Sam asked, "How do I get to Skull Hammock?" His no nonsense tone was a little much for Samchuck who dropped his head and ran up the white flag. This brought a nervous staccato from the older boy as he realized he knew the way better than his frightened buddy. "Fa-follow this track that-a way. G-g-goes right to Sk-sk-skull Hammock, 'bout two, three m-m-mile yet. Right to old Big'un's trap."

Sam knew this would be his only chance and skull hammock must be tied to the screwy Indian in some way because Joe Billie was superstitious and the killing place of his father may be the place to bash his captives. He had to chance it—for the pit bull-dog. Samson Duff meant to avenge his dog. He meant to meet Joe Billie Bloodtooth. Hello!

Sam lowered his voice to a whisper, drawing the awed boys to him like gossipy neighbors. "I need you to get a message to a friend. Got any paper and something to write with?" Jimmy nodded and crawled back into the half-track, its cooling system gurgling like a ruminating cow, rummaging in the open dash compartment before stepping down with a crumpled book page and warped ball point pen. Removing his shirt Sam wiped the fender, smoothed the paper and wrote—thanking God the pen worked—Skeets Kirby's name, phone number and address; knowing his stoic friend would be there. Under this he wrote Samson Hercules Duff—Junk Yard dog.

"Tell this man who I am. Here, I've written it out. My full name. Tell him what happened and then do as he says. If he questions you read him that last name - Junk Yard D-d-dog." The man choked a sob as he handed the note to Jimmy Gopher. He added. "You'll be well paid, both of you. Now hurry!" Fear clung to the boys but Sam picked up the scent of excitement as they moved about like grasshoppers on a hot floor trying to start the reluctant monster— succeeding in record time and within minutes had the hammer down and were chugging back with the reclaimed bucket of bolts chewing up greenery like the eggbeater from hell.

Shoeless, Sam cut a strip from his shirt and tied it around his head pushing his silver streaked mane from his eyes as his thoughts drifted to JY. This *is* for you, big guy. for you!

Palming the knife, he sawed his pant legs off at mid thigh leaving his taunt body naked save for these cutoffs. He didn't want snag-grabbing pants slowing him. He was going to Skull Hammock—or hell. Both.

• • •

Elise's conscious awareness reclaimed her numbed body like a rising tide with the only sounds to penetrate her psyche of a primal nature. Chirping birds.

The whir of tiny wings. The chirps and clicks of grasshoppers.

The summer breezes filtered through the moisture exhaled by the leaves of the giant trees absorbing this liquid coolness before transporting it around to cool the hammock. One of which was a shocked young woman.

Elise blinked and turned her head convincing herself she could see. She was sitting at the base of a tree, comfortable in the leaves. Overhead was a roof of green, shimmering like flattened emeralds in the sunlight. The beauty of this place overwhelmed her bruises as tears blinked free of her eyes—tears she thought no longer existed.

The woman had never seen banyan trees such as these. Thick runners reaching to the ground like brown columns of some arboreal Roman ruin formed uncountable "rooms", a woody maze impossible to traverse, each columned off compartment different, yet the same, once entered. Elise was far back in this unique motel. Alone?

She felt the banshee presence before Joe Billie Bloodtooth padded to her side, squatting on his heels, offering her water from a dinged up W.W.11 canteen. There was no killing in his dark eyes—concern—she gulped the metallic liquid, letting it spill out the corners of her mouth like spittle.

Her mind reviewed her history as she studied the insane man. Was Can Martin really dead? Did she dream of Bloodtooth stuffing the groaning man into that awful hog pen? How long ago did this happen...dream or not?

"I have food, Mother. Wait here." Joe Billie's soft request confused her. I'm his goddamn mother again. How long will this last before I turn into Can's whore and he decides to bash my brains out with that tree trunk he calls a club? Elise began to weep, trying to stifle her dread. She knew she was on the razor's edge. She imagined no rescue from this nightmare in the great Florida Everglades. The vaporous madman was invincible in these environs. What happened to those rescuers?

Joe Billie must have killed them. Elise shivered and all vestige of survival abandoned her as the shroud of mortality descended.

Joe Billie returned—with food.

• • •

Samson followed the half-track trail ignoring the cuts and punctures to his feet and legs, savoring the freshening scents of nature. Glancing up, he computed one hour of light with the cloudless sky beginning to show grey. Even now he could see the outline of what would be Skull Hammock rising out of the flatwoods ahead.

His slack face sported a grin as the psyched up man dug in for this last half mile.

The sun was behind the bulge as Sam neared from the northeast, casting a pall over the landscape. He had long since smelled the putrid emanation from Big'un's trap as it carried over the flats; the unmistakable miasma of death. Who was dead? What would he find? Sam blocked all of this from his mind as the patience of vendetta trumped his concerns.

He would soon know. Joe Billie Bloodtooth would soon know.

Fifty yards from the hammock, Samson picked up Can Martin's and Elise's scent—strong—toward the hammock. The implacable man welcomed the sunset knowing the blackness of skull hammock would be no barrier to him. He managed a smile as he thought of the challenge. Crossing the rancher's spoor mixed with Elise's told him they were alive, or were. His meeting with his cunning adversary was a go—no more guesswork. The overpowering fetor clogging his nostrils couldn't be from the captives, whatever it was. Sam's smile ripened to a grin as he neared the fringe of Skull Hammock.

The darkness blotted the venerable magnolia with its signature ornament but nothing could block the mordant stench of the truculent half-breed and as he silently passed the killing tree; this smell of smells ambushed Sam's flared nostrils like ninja. He swallowed his chuckle before it escaped but he knew it was heard—in hell.

Sam stopped a few yards from the barely visible hog trap to appraise the situation. His confidence in his heightened sense was building and many olfactory discoveries were being processed by his brain—without conscious thought. By the time he stopped he sensed that the captives had been fine when they reached Skull Hammock and that Can Martin was lame – using a crutch. His enhanced sensory smell also told him that the renegade had taken them only a few hours before Sam's arrival and the devastating storm had missed this area. The pen reeked of the huge boar, interspersed with the dead rancher's spoor, and finally, scent proof that the fiendish Indian had taken Elise and headed west into the very innards of Skull Hammock.

Sam was dizzy with this, all but incomprehensible but would have traded it in a heartbeat to have a 75 pound four-legged muscle pulling him down and wagging his tail while steel trap jaws squeezed tears from his proud master's eyes. Samson Hercules Duff's heart cried—cried for this dark day when God wielded a hammer...!

Stoically, he suppressed grief as his trained eyes accommodated the darkness and he sidled up to the sulfurous pen, squinting as the satiated boar mouthed the grunts of curiosity and idled towards this newcomer. Casehardened as he was, the man had to suppress a gut wrench as he viewed the eviscerated carcass of Charles Jonathan Martin, III. What a way to die. What a goddamn way to die! God did wield a hammer this day—in each hand! Shifting to the giant hog, Sam marveled at the size of this feral monster as he surveyed the ingenious trap in the enveloping blackness. The least he could do for the man would be burial. There would be little to bury come morning and realistically, he may need an undertaker by daylight.

Forcing up the guillotine trap door, Sam braced it and slipped behind, clucking at Big'un, trying to make the wary brute move to the opening. But Big'un circled, much too chary to take his festered eyes off any adversary, or competitor, or food. He wasn't about to jeopardize his groceries, ill gotten or no. Realizing his futility, Sam decided to bait the stubborn pig—he as bait. Crouched in the entrance he put his good arm inside and waved while making a grunting sound with an occasional mouth-pop straight from animal amateur hour.

Though wary as a birddog trying to sleep on a quail feather mattress, Sam was amazed at the quickness and ferocity of the hog as he hit the edge of the opening before the man could think of moving. Instantly backing away, Sam felt the pen shudder and raise as Big'un's left tusk nailed itself to the bottom log forcing Sam onto his huge head.

Goddamn it, how in hell did I get in this shit pile? There was only time for reaction and Samson grabbed the hoary head for a purchase so to push away from the ungrateful beast. Grabbing Big'un's right ear with his healing hand allowed him to push his legs out of the way and he reached for the other ear to avoid the chisel-like tusks.

As he grabbed the left ear, the infuriated boar freed his tusk and jerked his head up with the authority of a front-loader, breaking Sam's grip. As the loose hand slid down the sloping forehead it grasped a hard object protruding from Big'un's head—his brain guessed 'knife handle.'

Unseen in the dark was the handle of a hunting knife buried to its hilt in the left eye of Big'un. As the man's grip on the handle turned to stone, the boar-hog squealed like a fresh cut shoat. Spinning violently he lurched on the slippery goo like a novice ice skater. Sam held fast.

Samson timed the hog's rear end as it spun towards the opening and pushed back on the ear and knife with all his adrenalin driven might, forcing the hurt pig to back out of the trap. One headshake and Big'un was rid of his tormentor—knife included— and vanished into the stillness to become another Pay-Hay-Okee legend.

Panting from pain as much as from exertion, Samson's gut knotted as he thought of the injured rancher's last moments. Can Martin may not have lived the exemplary life but by God he died a man. Closing the trap's door, Sam padded off into the darkness, following his nose to water. He wanted to wash off the stink and clear his mind to what lay ahead—Joe Billie Bloodtooth.

Thoughts of the sensuous nurse were no longer chewing his psyche and had cooled to whimsy since the loss of JY. For whatever reason, Sam's driving maleness seemed controllable though still much attracted by musky female presence.

Sam's problem with the Miccosukee had been the senseless slaughter and kidnapping at the Martin ranch with Sam's pursuit predicated on freeing the captives—in particular Elise Jones. If he captured or killed Bloodtooth, so be it but if not, Joe Billie could go straight to hell as far as Samson cared. Not anymore. JY changed that. Samson Duff wanted to kill the crafty half-breed— or be killed.

Calmness settled over the tightly wound man as he finished scrubbing his body, pulled on the damp cutoffs and backtracked to the big magnolia where Bloodtooth's and Elise's spoor faded into the hammock.

Squatting on his heel, he leaned against the base of the magnolia oblivious to the leering spectre hanging above his head; its charnel-like grin the implacable sneer of vengeance. Totally relaxing in the manner of raja yoga, Samson pondered. He knew that catching Joe Billie by surprise in Skull Hammock would be akin to a popcorn fart sneaking by a bloodhound. Slowly his body obeyed his mind and he settled against the tree. Meditation. Deep concentration.

His breath went in the right nostril and out the left; in the left and out the right, funneling his emotions, sorrows, plans, entire being, into one directive: The death of Joe Billie Bloodtooth. By his hand.

A calm settled over Sam as he considered his options. He could follow the stinking renegade to hell and back but there was no way he could take him by surprise—no way! Joe Billie could smell near as good as a dog with sight and hearing just a notch less; if surprised would kill the girl in a blink. The only way was to lure the deft madman away from Elise—face to face. Only way. How?

Two hours later, Samson Hercules Duff arose and vanished into the bowels of Skull Hammock.

• • •

Elise picked at the food proffered by the silent man and noticed his subdued mien, a posture she construed as the calm before the storm. The blackness enveloping the unique banyan grove was giving way to slivers of pale light heralding the moonrise.

"He comes now..." Joe Billie's mouth barely moved as the fey prediction slipped between clenched teeth.

"Who—who—comes? What did you say?" Elise's query was answered with pain as Bloodtooth jerked her up and clamped his hand over her mouth. No outcry. Her body swayed into the Indian's side causing her knee to strike something hard—eliciting another cry. Looking down, Elise saw the terrible war club hanging from Bloodtooth's neck.

"Be quiet, Mother, be quiet. He comes... Father comes at last." Elise had no fight so she stood, zombie like, as the spellbound renegade eased between the shadowy banyan runners. His father is coming? He's dead, but so is his mother and he still thinks I'm her...but who's coming? Her thoughts were confusing. No one could follow us, especially in this God-awful darkness. Not likely. Her pulse quickened at the idea that someone may be out there but reality fragmented that fragile hope. No one there—no one could find them...she heard it.

Tunka-tunka-tunka...a resonant clicking sound so gentle as to be imagined. It was real. Its muted echoes bloated the quietness with its immigrant chord. Dis-chord. Did not belong. Tunka-tunka-tunka, this tiny sound seemed lost among the giant trees and yet grew louder; closer, waxing, waning, here, there... tunka-tunka-tunka-tunka.

The effect on Joe Billie was galvanic and Elise could feel the steely fingers cranking into her flesh as his head cocked in a pose not seen before and in moonlight reminded her of a cat whiffing catnip. Tunka-tunka-tunka. What could this be?

Joe Billie's mind was colored bits and pieces of sundered memory and no matter how his disjointed brain arranged them they didn't make sense. His last vision foretold the coming of James Bloodtooth; in fact his Grandfather had told him to prepare for this visit so he could protect his mother. Grandfather had been right because Joe Billie had saved his mother when he killed his father at the hog trap or was that the turd-head rancher who had killed his Stump? As the thought of the deaf dog flitted through his memory, Joe Billie's face softened for the briefest moment before more brain fog clouded remembrance of Stump. Just who did he feed to that hog? A few of the colored bits lined up and he realized it must have been the lame rancher because Grandfather told him to go to the deepest part of Skull Hammock to save his mother. James Bloodtooth was coming. Was this his mother? Must be. Grandfather's club was ready—Joe Billie was ready...

But what was that sound? He had never heard anything such as that in the deep glades and his mind trumpeted "netherworld." He was beginning to ooze the sticky sweat of solicitude. Had Grandfather not told him everything? What was making that noise? He had to find out.

Tunka-tunka-tunka-tunka-tunka...

Elise could tell the sound was moving, shifting ever so slightly as it attracted the discomposed madman to its Circean source—like water rising up a cotton wick.

Tunka-tunka-tunka; louder, fainter, this way, that way.

The lambent moon surmounted the splotchy skyline shedding silver shafts through the leafy openings. It will be bright as day once we're out from under these trees, she thought, as they slipped through the banyan maze.

Tunka-tunka-tunka...

Joe Billie was tight as an oak tree knot. His movements choreographed. Bathed in sweat though it was cool under the shadowed shade, his implacability gone with the coming of the ethereal intonement.

It seemed to take hours to reach the edge of the banyan grove, emerging at a clearing bordered by a dark glassine stream. The moon spotlighted the grassy oval with shimmering shadows like a ghostly audience settling into their seats prior to curtain rise.

Tunka-tunka-tunka...

Joe Billie stopped, as silent memory, his meaty hand covering Elise's mouth and his fey stare blanketing the open ground to rival the moonbeams.

Tunka-tunka...

It stopped! The silence seemed fulminant and drew the man to the brink. Jellied tension encased Joe Billie Bloodtooth as his tremulous hand threatened to asphyxiate her.

The wooden chant reverberated—tunka-tunka tunka...

Bewildered or not, Joe Billie saw it. The vaporous form materializing in the center of the clearing as the resonant tunka-tunka diluted itself in the resident hammock stridulation.

Joe Billie exploded! Elise felt her body move as if she were a doll being discarded by a petulant child. Hitting the grass, she saw the Indian charge across the opening, war club held high while his bloodcurdling war cry contaminated the silken hush. Even Sam, as he threw away the bamboo cylinders and braced for the onslaught was amazed at this fulminate response. He had seen the nurse go down and her scent seemed okay, so the long awaited moment was arrived—on far less than the wings of angels.

Neither man noticed the full moon that bore witness as wispy shreds of clouds drifted across its neutral face reflecting a dark purple.

Sam ducked under Joe Billie's bull-charge and tried to take him down by shifting the momentum to his advantage. He had underestimated the man's raw strength and he felt himself floating in air like a falling leaf, his arms aching and empty. It took cat-like reaction to roll as the war-club bashed the soft grass where Sam's head had been. At the same instant Sam felt his left thigh muscle explode as the club found another target.

Goddamn it, Sam thought, as he rolled like a dervish. I can't believe anyone is that fast! Scrambling, he jumped sideways just as Joe Billie swung at his hip causing the renegade to twist off balance for a split second—enough for Sam to duck under and get a lock on his tree trunk waist. It took every ounce of strength plus leverage to drop this adversary. Slipping to an arm lock across Bloodtooth's neck, Sam looked into the foaming eyes, searching for recognition, or purpose, or vengeance—nothing. Sam was in a fight to the death with a robot and the rabid dog drool from his slack flews spewed on his face and arms. Grunting like a piney woods rooter, Bloodtooth arched up and threw Sam off, a feat of unbelievable strength.

Sam's snakebit arm and clubbed thigh were killing him, even with his locomotive adrenalin rush. The cloak of individual combat superiority was beginning to chafe. Joe Billie Bloodtooth was a man. Mad one.

Sam could only manage a partial crouch before the killing machine had steely fingers clawing for his eyes and throat, his war club lost after Sam's attack. Samson's honed reflexes kept him from total disaster as he spun and kicked the grunting Indian solidly on his lower ribcage, reaping a surprised "Aahhh..." as his heel recoiled from the rock-hard chest and pain shot to his hip.

The force of the battle carried the combatants to the edge of the creek and Samson knew if the raging breed got him in the water it would be over as his stricken arm was useless and he could barely stand. He had underestimated this foe.

Scrambling on all fours through the tenacious grass, Sam headed away from the water. Confused. Beaten. What to do? He knew he had to get this guy in a crooked head scissors hold—how? The distempered Indian wasn't tiring. Sam was dumb-founded as Bloodtooth overtook him in the grass and kneed him in the ribs with the authority of an army mule, driving him to his back; mouth open—gasping—unable to think...

"Ah, Grandfather, I am defeating my enemies. Now my mother will be safe." Joe Billie faced the moon as he ranted and a tingle coursed his charged body. The face of Sam Duff appeared in his mind causing his expression to drain away. This fallen foe was not his father. Who is this man? I know his face...

All transpired in the blink of an eye as Bloodtooth leaped to retrieve his weapon while Samson lay gasping on the killing ground. Joe Billie raised the war club.

Neither victor nor vanquished noticed the ripple that disturbed the hushed grass on the far side of the clearing, the whisper of ruffled greenery the only mark of passage. A resolute zephyr was blowing through the grass towards the combatants to blend with the breath of death.

Had Bloodtooth noticed the wraithlike movement of the grass, he would not have comprehended its determined source.

The gasping Duff, his glazed eyes fixed on the slobbering Miccosukee as his totem of death heralded its mortal descent, would not believe the compact apparition churning toward them. Even as his face bulged with familiar scent his tangled brain rejected recognition...Said—no. Said—couldn't be!

Samson's mind could not process the gaunt, mud-caked specter powering through the grass on three resolute legs, its broken left shoulder jerked along like the tail of a kite. Bone grated bone with each agonized step as the abrasive grasses rubbed more skin from the useless leg. The left side of its head was caved in and the throb of pain was visible in the pulsating bruised flesh pushed by edema into the right eyelid making vision a conscious effort. The needle-sharp thorns of wild blackberry coated its face like blackish peach fuzz, clumped in the clotting blood oozing from the gashes...

Soundless came the Junk Yard dog.

He broke from the taller grass in front of Bloodtooth as the club of death began its deadly journey to his beloved master's head. The rapt Indian barely glimpsed the movement before the obsessed animal was launched at his throat and only by his beast-like reflexes did Joe Billie avoid mordant jaws.

Arms extended, throat exposed, the death dealing Indian twisted his shoulder to ward off whatever had jumped at him, aborting the war-club's deadly journey but in the manner of the pit bulldog, JY touched the man's turning shoulder with his good forefoot and in a flash went for another hold, latching on to the unprotected right biceps muscle with vice-grip jaws.

Sam could only watch in disbelief as the dog-caught man let out a sharp grunt and started beating the pendulous animal with the war-club; unable to generate punishing force due to the closeness of JY's head to his own.

Each futile stroke of the club cranked the pitiless jaws down another notch as the massive neck and back muscles began their rhythmic contractions, pulling the dire maw ever tighter—ever tighter—until even the stoicism of lunacy was breached and Joe Billie Bloodtooth's exertional grunts swiveled to cries of pain. These piteous outcries catalyzed the Junk Yard dog and with the grisly feel of fang on bone, further fueled the fires of retribution.

JY didn't hear the lightning bolt that hit just before he came to in the churning water by the downed cedar tree. He vaguely remembered gagging up water as he tried to lift his unwilling body to avoid drowning, barely reaching the tree and pushing himself into its branches as the torrent shot beneath. But he did remember the trenchant stink of Joe Billie Bloodtooth and as the jumble of events gestating in the half dead animal's mind slowly came to term, a blood feud was birthed—with the owner of the signal spoor. Everything else vanished from his mind, Samson Hercules Duff included and remembrances of him would not crack his amnesiac shell until just before the fateful, final confrontation.

The rain stopped and the Junk Yard dog pulled himself from the tree and began his singular quest understandable only to those who have fathomed the workings of the laser focused, scary pit bulldog mind—a privileged few.

There would be no licking of wounds. No whimpering. No distractions. No quarter given—or taken—or quitted. So long as he had breath.

The sight and realization of JY sent a jolt through Sam, restoring his confidence, giving him incentive and he kipped to his feet as the struggling pair neared the mirrored stream.

The besieged Indian had no idea what caught him and only recognized it as a dog when the pain became unbearable. His mind was jumping in and out of reality like heated popcorn kernels. Visions flashed through his bedeviled brain—Stump, his hounds, the dog at the fish camp where he beat Samson—but none settled in to quiet his bafflement.

Then he knew! It was the dog he set the trap for. It had to be. A dog that should be dead. Devil dog!

JY and Joe Billie were face to face and in a desperate attempt to fix the reality of this beast growing from his arm, the madman looked deep into the squinted eye of the Junk Yard dog—through the dilated pupil to his empty soul—and began screaming as if a wild man; he had looked through the fire of hell and saw ice—the frigid reflection of his mortality. Terminus.

Spinning with the force of demons, Bloodtooth mustered every ounce of his maniacal strength and threw the pit bull into the stream, the mouthful of quivering biceps muscle firmly gripped in adamant jaws. Insulted arteries spewed bright red from the useless arm like busy fire hoses.

Samson was on the dumbstruck man before JY hit the water, putting the babbling Miccosukee down like a sledged steer. A quick glance saw the shadowy figure of Elise almost to the water's edge as Samson expertly flipped Bloodtooth to his stomach, pulled his arms forward and locked his combat hardened knees on either side of the tousled head. The spurting blood from Joe Billie's useless arm turned the scuffled sand into a gory mess as Sam tightened and twisted his powerful thighs with all the might left in his agonized body.

Joe Billie didn't know what was happening. He could no longer swallow his copious drool and his face was being pressed into the ground by a relentless force so potent that movement was impossible. His mind began flashing moldy pictures of his murdered father and himself, stopping at the mental image of James Bloodtooth on his knees and a young Joe Billie holding his Grandfather's war club high overhead, trying desperately to bring it down on the hated man's skull. But it wouldn't move. The pressure on his neck was unbearable. He had to free the club, to kill his father...he had to...the pressure...the club was stuck overhead—free it...his neck...

'CRAACCKK!'

Joe Billie Bloodtooth heard the sickening sound and violently exhaled as the envisioned war club was freed and came crashing down. But the sound he heard—his last—was not the club bashing his father's head—but his own neck breaking!

Overhead, the glowing moon frowned at the dark wispy clouds drifting by, halfheartedly trying to confuse its all-seeing vision.

Samson Hercules Duff began to shiver...

27776515R10172

Made in the USA
Lexington, KY
22 November 2013